the

FRENCH
HOUSE

HELEN FRIPP

the

FRENCH HOUSE

bookouture

Published by Bookouture in 2021

An imprint of Storyfire Ltd.
Carmelite House
50 Victoria Embankment
London EC4Y 0DZ

www.bookouture.com

ISBN: 978-1-80019-306-2
eBook ISBN: 978-1-80019-305-5

This book is a work of fiction. Names, characters, businesses,
organizations, places and events other than those clearly in the
public domain, are either the product of the author's imagination
or are used fictitiously. Any resemblance to actual persons, living or
dead, events or locales is entirely coincidental.

For Tara and Charlie
Hold fast to your dreams

'Why should we build our happiness on the opinions of others, when we can find it in our own hearts?'

Jean-Jacques Rousseau

CHAPTER 1

Reims, 21 July 1789

Revolution

Nicole stopped at the crossroads on this glorious morning and considered her choices. Should she take the rue des Filles Dieu, a shaded, godly alleyway for obedient girls leading straight to her convent school, or a forbidden detour across the open square, where the sunlight quivered in a haze above the cobbles?

She flipped a coin, caught it on the back of her hand and shut her eyes. *Pile ou face*, heads or tails. It didn't matter – the forbidden square was always going to win, especially on market day. It was the only real choice, brimming with promise, and she ran towards the sunlit square.

At King Louis XVI's statue, she stopped to pat the stone horse's weathered muzzle for luck, dipped a mock-curtsey to the king and froze… A noose was slung around the king's neck. And someone had daubed droplets of red paint under his regal eyes. The king was crying blood! Surely this wasn't Xavier's work? He sometimes gave the king a charcoal moustache or stuck a geranium under the horse's saddle to protrude from his arse, but never anything this macabre.

So it must be true then, about the news from Paris. The whole town was simmering with it. *Quatorze Juillet*, the day France turned upside down. The king discredited. The people's republic, the revolution. Loud arguments on street corners and endless gossip, all about something miles away. The noose and blood was the kind of thing that happened in Paris, not here in safe, sleepy Reims.

Defacing an image of the king was a serious offence – one the Comte's soldiers would be sure to punish. They were an undisciplined gaggle of bored thugs who regularly patrolled the streets for someone to beat, including truants, even rich ones like her.

Nicole walked as fast as suspicion allowed to the safety of the square. On market days, the place was usually teeming with *champenois* farmers setting out their bright stalls like sacrifices to the tall cathedral that guarded the square. But not today. The old widow from Aÿ stood disconsolately by a couple of fraying baskets. Her straggly parsley had bolted and the meagre handful of mouldy onions should have been pickled long ago.

The haggard jam lady from Allers-Villerand was there, as always. Nicole might only be eleven, but she prided herself on *noticing* and that jam hadn't sold for the last three markets. She knew because the lady had spelt strawberry wrong on this batch and anyone who could read was too polite to say.

She didn't recognise the man from the butcher's stall selling skinned rabbits on the other side of the square. Their raw bodies were topped and tailed, with furry heads and paws, bloated flies drooping over them like drunks.

'Xavier!' Nicole had spotted her friend standing next to the rabbit stall chatting with a gaggle of mates. She'd know him a mile off, with his compact frame and wiry black hair and she had hoped she would see him here. He would love the treasure she had in her pocket, a shiny green beetle, iridescent like a jewel.

He pretended not to hear her and arced a gob of glistening spit onto the cobbles. She was impressed.

He had been her playmate until her body made her different from him. She missed him now she was at school and he had to work. So why wasn't he at her papa's wool mills today?

'Xavier, look what I found!'

He ignored her, so she marched closer, hand outstretched to show him the beetle.

'It was on the rose bush in Monsieur Moët's vineyard.'

Xavier smiled, but then remembered he was with a crowd of mates.

'So what?' he sneered. 'What the hell is it anyway?'

'Everyone knows it's a rose beetle, you stupid grape-eater,' she countered, smarting at his betrayal.

Xavier pretended not to care, but Nicole could tell he did by the way he sniffed and tossed his head. Grape-eater was the worst insult anyone could give in a wine-grower's town, what they called workers from the Marne Vallée who didn't know anything about vines, and ate the profits.

'*Aristocrate*,' shouted one of his friends, like it was a dirty word.

'Leave her. She's just a kid.' Xavier jerked his head at Nicole. 'Get lost, *laide*.'

Xavier had always been kind and he probably meant to be now. But the *ugly* – *laide* – stung. He constantly teased her that she was so petite she'd snap, and that her grey eyes were like a wolf's rather than a girl's and her reddish blonde hair looked like it was going rusty.

'You don't own this square,' she snapped.

'We do now. *Va te faire foutre, aristocrate*,' the mate shouted. Fuck off, aristocrat.

'I am the same as you,' she protested, holding up her fists, flashing her pale eyes in fury. She might be small, but she was fast and strong and equal to any shouty boy. Damn that her mother had twisted her hair into stupid girly ringlets for school, today of all days.

Xavier pushed her. 'Are you stupid? He'd crush you like a bloody ant.'

'Fighting little girls, young man?'

It was the Comte d'Etoges looming over them, all the way from the château! His red silk coat blazed in the sun in stark contrast to the drab workers in the square, who glowered menacingly at him.

The Comte twisted Xavier's arm behind his back. It looked like agony, but Xavier didn't wince and Nicole was glad.

'Apologise to Mademoiselle Ponsardin, you stinking little ruffian.'

The Comte pulled Xavier's arm higher until Xavier turned ashen with pain. Nicole was scared he'd wrench his shoulder right out.

'Sorry,' he said, grimacing.

'And you. Act like a lady, not a street urchin.'

Street urchins beat ladies any day. 'Let him go. He was helping me,' she said.

'Know your place and assert your natural authority, young lady, or this rabble will imagine they are the deserving poor and demand justice. How old are you?'

'Eleven.' She refused to add 'sir'.

'You'll learn. Give an inch and they'll take a mile.'

He stomped off and Nicole pulled a face behind his back to impress Xavier, but he was already returning to the stall to stuff a rabbit in his sack. The butcher didn't ask for any money and Xavier looked ashamed. Then she understood – the rabbits were alms for the poor. She wished she hadn't called her friend a grape-eater.

Around the square, the red geraniums in the urns were neglected and withered, the houses were crumbling and the paintwork was peeling. Crops were dying in the fields again this year. Nicole couldn't remember a year when there'd been a celebration at harvest time, nor a big creamy moon lighting a magical evening of dancing, like she had heard about in the old days. Every week, the whole town prayed for a good harvest, but God wasn't listening. This was why they were rioting in Paris, her father had told her. The aristocrats were stuffing themselves while the workers starved. Queen Marie Antoinette was so stupid, she'd offered cake to the poor instead of bread.

But Papa hadn't told her the most gruesome part. Xavier had told her about *that* in graphic detail. The workers in Paris were going to rise up and round up all the aristocrats, take them to the Place de la Revolution and chop their heads off with a gruesome new thing they'd invented called the guillotine. It could efficiently kill ten aristocrats an hour, Xavier had told her, a big blade that slid down a frame and did the dirty deed, with aristocrats lining up one after the other, witnessing the death of their fellows and family before getting the chop themselves. Nicole had shivered, wishing he hadn't told her, and hoping it wasn't true.

She looked down at her dress, almost the same red as the Comte's jacket, coloured with the kind of rich dye that the people in the square could never afford. Would she herself be counted as an aristocrat? But it was a fact that the king and queen weren't in charge any more. The world was different and she felt frightened, even here, in her square.

She wished she'd gone to school after all, but the cathedral bell began striking. She would be too late and the nuns would tell Papa, so she might as well make the most of the trouble to come.

On the ninth toll of the bell, crowds of people filed into the square to queue at the rabbit stall. Most were country people, too poor to be regulars in this part of town. The butcher doled out one rabbit each. Some had sacks, others wrapped them in their aprons, a few didn't have enough fabric to spare and held the meat by the ears. She watched for a while, then ran to the bakery.

'Nicole! No school today?' said Daniel, the baker.

'The coin landed on tails,' she lied.

'Again? Tut tut. The nuns will cane the skin off your knuckles. Let me see?'

She held out her hand and showed him the welts from the last market day she had played truant.

He handed her a *religieuse*, a big, round choux pastry with a smaller one on top, filled with cream and topped with chocolate to resemble a nun. 'Here, you can pretend you're biting their heads off.'

She bit hard.

Daniel's wife, Natasha, gave her a snowglobe to shake, a world of glittering frost and gilt ballrooms. Natasha was willowy and dark, with sallow skin and knowing brown eyes. She wore dirndl skirts edged with stitched patterns and symbols, like a Romani, and best of all she was from Russia, a world away from the little town of Reims. Nicole loved her stories of far-away icy wastelands and golden domes.

'Delicious.' Nicole grinned with her mouth full, when something splintered the *boulangerie* window and shattered it to the ground.

'Ach,' screamed Natasha, tracing figures of eight in the air as the patisseries were pierced with shards.

Daniel scooped a rock from the bakery floor and stormed out, waving it in the air. 'Who the hell threw this?' It was the stone hat from the king's statue.

Outside, the old widow was on her hands and knees scraping spilt onions back into her baskets and the jam lady screamed vengeance for her smashed jars.

Three men straddled Nicole's lucky statue of the king and the horse, bashing at it with hammers. They knocked off the easy bits first – the horse's ears, the king's foot, a length of his sword, egged on by a gang of men who were using the spoils as missiles.

'Not the horse!' Nicole yelled.

'Hush! Get back here, you'll get hit!' Natasha urged, ushering her behind the counter and wrapping her in her skirts.

Amidst the chaos, the queue at the rabbit stall was still going. Muddy workers from the field, widows in black headscarves, barefoot, skinny children with grown-up, scabbed faces. The square was so busy now that she'd lost track of where Xavier and his friends had got to.

A gunshot ricocheted around the square. The queue froze, a child howled and the butcher dropped the rabbit he was holding. The three men slid down off the statue and slinked behind its broken flanks.

'Nobody move!'

The Comte d'Etoges was back in his flashy silk jacket, this time at the head of a battalion from his private army, who fanned out into the square, blocking all the exits. A group of soldiers wrestled the three statue destroyers to the ground and handcuffed them. A roar of protest tore through the crowd.

The Comte's powdered wig and white face made him look like a menacing ghost and his cool, fixed expression was more disturbing than the crowd's anger. His voice boomed over them, but he wasn't shouting.

'These vandals have committed a crime and will rot in jail for the remainder of their days,' he said calmly to the desperate bystanders who'd been innocently queuing at the rabbit stall. 'The rest of you are charged with poaching and will be severely punished.'

'They're hungry, you can spare them,' Daniel shouted back.

'Hush, *milaya*,' Natasha beseeched her husband, hugging Nicole to her.

'Name, scum?' said the Comte, pointing the gun at him.

'Daniel. From the *boulangerie*.' He pointed to the smashed window.

Behind him, the priest creaked open the big cathedral doors and raised his hand.

'Calm, in the name of Jesus!' he bellowed.

Someone threw the horse's ear at the priest and ran before a soldier could react.

Nicole screwed her eyes tight and waited for lightning to strike. The gargoyles would come to life and scream hellfire and they'd all burn for eternity for throwing stones at the priest. But God did nothing. The priest staggered back inside and slammed the church door. He was supposed to be in charge. Coward!

The Comte waved his gun at Daniel. 'You, tell your *comrades* to disperse. Those rabbits are stolen goods.'

Daniel folded his arms. 'These people are starving. The rabbits are already dead and decaying. They're no use to you.'

'Daniel, look out!' shrieked Nicole as the Comte cocked his gun and shot.

The baker slumped, clutching his chest. Natasha flew to him, black hair streaming. She tore open his shirt and screamed, her hands slippery with blood.

Don't die, don't die, prayed Nicole, cowering behind the counter.

Natasha cradled him, ripped her skirt and pressed wads on the wound, but blood leached over her fingers. The old widow from Aÿ untied her scarf to make a bandage and limped stiffly towards them.

'Don't move!' the Comte bellowed.

She halted, face tight. Everybody stopped dead.

Natasha was alone, keening like a madwoman in the sudden silence. Nicole sneaked out from behind the counter and ran to them.

'*Bordel de merde*, stop I said!' the Comte yelled at her.

A bullet shot past her ear and the crowd roared again. She flung her arms around Natasha's neck. The air was so thick and hot, it hurt to breathe. Daniel's eyes were open, but unseeing.

'Is he dead?' she whispered.

Natasha didn't answer.

'Take aim!' ordered the Comte.

The soldiers shouldered their guns and pointed them at the horrified crowd. Surely God would intervene now? The cathedral door stayed locked.

Natasha cradled her husband in her lap, appalled, a pietà in the square. Nicole huddled behind her back.

'Go home and don't look back, little one,' said Natasha steadily.

Nicole got up, straightened her skirt and walked slowly towards the Comte. He kept his gun on her, adjusting the sights as she came closer.

'You killed him,' she spat.

'These people are thieves and that, little girl, is called justice.'

'I will never forget,' she said quietly, 'and neither will they.'

She kept her eyes on him and walked on. She belonged here, with Natasha and her dead husband, with the workers and their scraps of stolen meat. She ducked behind the pump in the rue de la Vache and turned to watch. She would be their witness.

'Let this be a warning,' shouted the Comte. 'Go back to your work. Anyone who defies the rule of law will die like your friend. Men, let's go!'

The statue defacers were bundled into a cart and beaten with rifle butts as they were driven off, defenceless and handcuffed. The soldiers melted away and the Comte followed in his carriage, wheels crunching gravel.

The widow from Aÿ was the first to reach Natasha. She crossed herself for Daniel and whispered in her ear. Natasha nodded and allowed two men to carry Daniel back to the bakery, holding his hand to her cheek. He looked heavy, like his soul was gone, vulnerable, bloody and raw as the dead rabbits.

Men slid off their caps, women bowed their heads and the crowd stayed rooted in respectful, stunned silence until Daniel and his makeshift cortège disappeared inside. Then the rabbit queue erupted, hurling the table of meat in a swarm of flies and heaving over the urns of withered geraniums.

Peeking from behind the relative safety of the pump, Nicole saw Xavier rip a torch from the blacksmith's, igniting a hay bale that sprung wild flames in the stifling heat. The crowd smashed the windows of Moët's wine merchant, poured stolen brandy on the flames and chucked in the bottles, glass popping and exploding in the fire. A new gang set upon the king's statue, more organised this time, a foreman yelling instructions, until it toppled to the ground and crumbled into pieces.

'Goodbye, *mon grand*,' Nicole whispered to herself, a farewell to the broken horse, but she was glad about the smashed-up king. The Comte deserved to be smashed up, too – *vive la révolution*!

She jumped up to run home through the chaos.

'Watching the poor suffer for fun, rich girl?' One of Xavier's friends blocked her way.

'No! The baker was my friend.'

'The Comte spared his own though, didn't he? No bullet in the belly for you. You're one of them, a rich, spoilt little *aristocrate* who'd kill us for a rabbit.' He slapped her face.

She spat in his eye and ran, cut down the snicket, his footsteps close behind. She darted sideways down allée Libergier, then swerved along rue du Cloître towards the convent. A spooked horse reared, towering over her. She detoured left, past the silversmith's broken windows, dodging a mother dragging her wailing toddlers and then – bang! A body encircled her. A greasy waistcoat and grubby britches. She kicked hard.

'Ai! *Putain*, you can pack a punch for a squirt!' He dragged her through a doorway. She struggled and scratched like a cat. The door slammed shut. 'It's me for fuck's sake!'

'Xavier!'

Nicole fell to the ground and sobbed.

'Daniel's dead.'

'I saw everything. I hope that fucker the Comte burns in hell. Follow me before you get yourself into more trouble – the whole town has gone mad, including you. You could've been killed,' he said proudly. 'I know a place to hide you away.'

They ran down a back alley and slipped through a hole in the fence into a yard full of wine barrels. Xavier heaved aside a stack of hay bales and lifted a cellar door.

'*Vas-y.*' Xavier gestured to dark steps. 'Get in, and stay there. I'll find your papa and tell him where you are.' He thrust a lantern into her hands. 'Don't light this 'til you've bolted the door behind you. And don't look like such a sissy, I thought you told me you weren't afraid of anything. Go right down inside, we'll come back and find you when it's safe.'

Xavier winked, but he looked afraid, too.

She hesitated. 'What about you?'

'I'm not a little rich girl, I'm one of them, which works in my favour for once. Go on then, close the fucking door so I can get the hell out of here,' he said.

Nicole plunged into the darkness and bolted the trapdoor behind her. Her hands were slick with sweat and her stomach pitched as she fumbled to light the lamp. The flame jumped and lit the steep cellar steps, but she couldn't see to the bottom and it was dark and silent as a tomb. She held her breath. Xavier had never let her down. There was the time she got stuck in the apple tree trying to prove she could climb higher than any boy and he helped her down. And the incident with the farmer where she had to hide for hours when she got caught driving his horse cart round the orchard. Xavier had returned, as promised, to tell her when the coast was clear.

She held the lantern higher and struck out down the stone steps. At the bottom was a long corridor. She waited, alert for footsteps. Nothing but muffled silence. She pressed on down another corridor, and turned again, further into the labyrinth, feeling safer with each turn. It was surprisingly warm and the walls were chalk white. She touched them. Damp, like sponge. Lamps lined the walls and she tore her dress to make a spill to light two of them.

The space filled with light and she saw that she was in a wine cellar. It was beautiful here, with rows and rows of neatly stacked bottles, straight passageways and lofty vaulted ceilings. Light funnelled underground through tall chimneys and the wine bottles gleamed, green as the River Vesle. This was a fairy grotto after the horror of the streets, a place of safety, order and alchemy.

Nicole sat on a barrel and closed her eyes, suddenly exhausted. It was only now she thought of the terror and injustice she had witnessed. Daniel was dead, murdered like an animal. She belonged to the workers in the square now, and shared their rage, grief and desperation. She spat on her palm, like she'd seen Xavier do to seal a bet, and made a pact with herself, there and then, for Daniel. She would work to build her own wealth, her own power, and she would use it for good, for her own revolution.

CHAPTER 2

Eight years later, September 1797

Republican date: Fructidor, year V

The Crimson Grape

Everything changed, and nothing had changed. Europe was at war and all the talk was of a brilliant young general, Napoléon Bonaparte, who was advancing his battalions against Italy with great success. It was hard to imagine marauding armies in the Reims countryside, and apart from Monsieur Moët boasting about his schooldays with the great general, and heated exchanges of news in the bakery, it all seemed far away to Nicole. The Comte d'Etoges, who had shot Daniel dead almost in the spot she was standing, was dead himself, slaughtered at the guillotine. Nicole crossed herself at the thought. Xavier had been right about that gruesome invention. Many lives had been lost and turned upside down since the day, eight years ago, that the revolution had begun, and she had taken refuge in the cellars.

The days and years had different and incomprehensible names now. The republican state had restarted the calendar to the beginning of the republic, and renamed everything so no royalist or religious references were made. There was no more October or

November, but instead Latin or made-up names that reflected the weather of that particular month – Brumaire, 'mist', or Frimaire, 'frost'. Everyone was in a muddle with it, never mind the illiterate workers who'd always learnt everything from previous generations. The old cathedral with its gargoyles and filigree stone was now the people's Temple of Reason, but people still worshipped their old Christian God in secret.

Nicole crossed the square, past the boys who were crowded around the new statue of the Goddess of Reason to smoke and make owl calls. The Goddess of Reason was really Saint Joan of Arc on her horse, but no one dared say it out loud. The boys stubbed out their cigarettes on the horse's hooves and sauntered off to the waiting carts to join the rest of the town for the grape harvest and, in that, life in Reims continued as it always had.

Not for her, though. Until recently, everyone had just accepted her as an anomaly, a rebellious child who loved being outdoors and doing everything at a million miles an hour, whether she was galloping a horse at breakneck speed, or pitting her wits with the boys in their games in the square. She wished she could join them now and ride out on the cart to the vineyards, but Nicole's presence was required at home. Life at nineteen was a tedious parade of potential husbands, expectations of womanly submission and hand-wringing parents. Worse, her straight, slippery hair was pinned against its will into curls every day which took hours, and Maman insisted on a wardrobe of tight-fitting, stifling dresses. For someone who was always in a hurry, the dresses were like vices.

Thankfully, Josette took pity on her and tied her corsets loose. And today, even Maman had to agree that her new empire-style dress made from light, loose cotton and silk suited her petite figure, so at least she could *move.* That was today's victory, and no one could stop her stealing Papa's wine manuals and reading them on the nights the moon was in her favour to teach herself, if no one else was going to. Every day, she found a way to contravene a rule without anyone noticing – it was the only thing that kept her sane until she could somehow escape the womanly constraints that had settled around her as she grew.

When she reached the crossroads and was out of sight of anyone who might tell, she undid her bonnet where the ribbon chafed under her chin, shook her hair loose from its pins and faced the sun to just *breathe.*

The cathedral clock struck the hour. She'd be missed if she didn't hurry, but before turning the corner towards home, she paused at the crossroads to touch the horse's nose, her talisman now that King Louis XVI's statue was torn down. A champagne cork topped Joan of Arc's sword and an empty bottle balanced in the crook of her arm. That much hadn't changed.

'A saint drunk in charge of a horse, tut-tut. Who would do that?'

She spun round and there was Xavier, short, stocky and suntanned, secateurs hanging from his belt for the harvest. He used the secateurs to sweep his thick black hair from his brow and stubbed his cigarette to join the others.

Nicole jerked her chin at the statue. 'What's this?'

'Art.'

'You mean Etienne chucked you out early from his bar and you took the opportunity to taunt your boss?'

'Talking of which, there he is, sliding your way as fast as shit off a shovel.'

An imposing man advanced towards them, grey hair tamed into a wave from a strict side parting, strides oiled with the ease of the rich. Xavier made himself scarce, but it was too late for her to escape.

Monsieur Moët bowed. 'Your parents advised this horse was a favourite of yours.'

'He brings me luck,' Nicole replied.

'You'll need it, mixing with those peasant boys, and you know you shouldn't be out without a chaperone. It's a good thing I'm here, *n'est-ce pas*? Our little secret.'

'I don't need to keep any secrets with you, Monsieur Moët. My parents are happy to let me walk to the square on my own,' Nicole lied. She gave him a tight, unfriendly smile and turned to leave, but he wouldn't go away.

'Your eyes are better than mine, Mademoiselle Ponsardin. Is that one of my corks?' asked Monsieur Moët, straining to see the top of the sword.

'I'm afraid it does say Moët,' replied Nicole, just able to make out the capital 'M' from where she stood.

'I'll see they are punished. Was that Xavier Jumel I saw you talking to? People like him are not our kind and shouldn't be encouraged, Mademoiselle. I'm sure you mean well, but it's just not the *order* of things. They can get the wrong idea and then where would we be? Come,' he commanded, 'I happen to know, contrary to your suggestion, that your parents would rather you *weren't* wandering around alone. It was them who sent me to get you.'

He tugged his shirtsleeve free of his jacket, twisted his crested cufflink and held his arm out for her to take.

She politely refused. This was his third visit in a week and an afternoon of endless stories about his esteemed friend and associate Napoléon stretched out ahead like a dusty journey on a featureless road.

For a man usually in a hurry, he walked painfully slowly back to the house, pointing out the property and businesses he owned along the way, as if she ought to be interested. She tore a bunch of lavender from a hedge. Bees scattered lazily.

Monsieur Moët stiffly picked a rose and gave it to her, most of the petals dropping from the plucking. She reluctantly added it to her lavender bunch, hoping no one would see.

'You shouldn't be fraternising with servants. What will people think? Especially now you're of marriageable age…'

A trap she couldn't quite name closed around her.

'You want that, don't you?' he pressed.

'I'd rather be fraternising, quite frankly, Monsieur Moët.'

'You will change your mind.' He fixed her with his uneven gaze, one eye assessing, the other issuing a warning. 'You can't stay single forever and I would hate to see you in a match that wasn't worthy, or worse, ruin your reputation by talking to street boys. I would protect you, fund any dresses you desire, as long as they're properly feminine. Your papa has let you run wild; however, even he agrees it's time you joined society. I could teach you, help smooth some of those harsh edges, charming as they are. I must say, you do have some advantages. Your eyes are wide and strangely pale and so full of life. And the way the sun catches that red tinge in your fair hair makes it shine like a… a…' He was clearly struggling, so she jammed her hat back on and tucked her hair up to save him the effort, mortified by his botched compliments. How to be kind but unencouraging?

'I'm determined to *keep* my sharp edges, Monsieur Moët. I like this dress, it's light and easy and I can run in it. And I should tell you, I really am unteachable – the nuns at the convent tried valiantly, but to no avail, I'm afraid.'

From his smug look, she was clearly meant to be grateful for his veiled proposal. Maman and Papa must have given him permission, without a word to her.

'Of course, you need time to think, as tradition dictates,' Monsieur Moët said confidently.

They walked in awkward silence to the house. Thank God Xavier hadn't witnessed her humiliation; she'd never live it down.

'I won't marry him. He just wants your vineyards.'

Her mother huffed. 'You're too much like your father. Too much like a *man*, with all your talk of independence. So brutal in your assessment of what most young girls would leap at.'

'He's twenty years older than me. He wants to lock me up in that big house of his and keep me there to order his servants around and dress up to entertain his military friends and try to impress *Napoléon*.'

'Too many *opinions!* People get killed for them, shouting them in the street, murdering, denouncing the church. My advice to you, Barbe-Nicole, which I know you won't take, is to keep your opinions to yourself.'

Nicole rolled her eyes. Nobody ever used her full name, Barbe-Nicole, other than her mother, and even then only when she was truly angry. Her older sister Clémentine giggled.

'I think he's handsome, even if he does have grey hair,' said Clémentine shyly.

Maman's eyes lit up at her elder daughter's attractive acquiescence. 'Exactly the kind of opinion it is suitable for a girl to express. Nicolas, will you talk some sense into the girl?'

Her father took the cue (which Nicole was sure had been pre-arranged) and cleared his throat. 'Babouchette, you can't stay here forever and you crave freedom. You're nineteen years old. A woman must marry to gain her freedom. His money would provide anything your heart desired.'

'And a gilded cage to enjoy it in? I just can't throw my life away on a man who wants a *poupée*, a doll, for his drawing room,' said Nicole.

Her father suppressed a smile.

'Nicolas! You're encouraging her.'

Nicolas Ponsardin was a big, gruff bear, a self-made captain of industry who'd built a fortune for his family through his woollen mills and vineyards. He took his daughter's hands. 'You owe it to him to consider his offer, seriously and with clarity, as only you can. You would lead a comfortable life with him. He's a good man and it's a good match. You might not believe it, but he is also very fond of you. In fact, you might even call it love. Be practical. But in the end, your choice…'

'She'll always take the contrary position. She takes pleasure in it,' Maman protested.

'She's a thinker, that's all. She needs to assess the options for herself. Let her,' said Papa.

Nicole took the opportunity to escape. What a mess. What if this was the only serious proposal of marriage she ever received? In all the books she'd read, the beauty accepts the beast or kisses the frog and is rewarded. What nonsense.

The Ponsardin family home was one of the grandest in town, with rooms no one ever went into and light pooling through a wall of French windows which spilled onto the vast gardens, but Nicole felt stifled in here. She paced across the polished chequered hall until she reached the heavy front door. Josette opened it for her, winking conspiratorially.

Out, out, out into the morning air, down the rue de la Vache back to the square. She respected her papa, but it wasn't right. Was it possible to marry and still follow your dreams, make your own money? She'd never seen it. Husbands owned their spouses and wives had to beg or scheme for what they wanted. A visit to Antoine and Claudine, faithful old friends of the family – her mother's dressmaker, and her father's cellarman – would help her get her head straight. It always did.

She stopped at the *boulangerie*. Natasha ran it alone now. She had aged more than she deserved to since that horrible day eight years ago. Her mouth was pinched, her dark skin sallow at the cheeks, grey strands peppered her black hair and her kindness had dissolved into a weary determination.

Nevertheless, Nicole regarded Natasha with envy, mistress of all she surveyed – the highly polished counter showing off her neat trays of shiny fruit *tartes*, glossy *religieuses*, pastel-coloured macaroons, a wholesome wall of *ficelles*, baguettes and *pains de campagne* stacked in baskets, lined up smart as soldiers, ready to sell. To be *doing* something. Something with purpose and satisfaction.

'*Bonjour.*'

'Nicole.' Natasha's tired face creased into a smile. 'You have that fire in your eyes today. Planning your own revolution?'

'Just visiting Claudine and Antoine.'

'Ah, *bon.*'

Natasha immediately picked out three plump *religieuses*. She knew their favourites.

'I make these for him,' said Natasha. Nicole knew who she meant without asking. 'The first thing my husband taught me when I arrived from St Petersburg.' She scattered a pinch of salt on the floor, muttered a Russian oath and looked up to the heavens.

Nicole nodded in sympathy. No need for words, but Natasha picked up on what she had hoped was her supportive, empathetic expression.

'I take pleasure in small things. Don't you worry about me.'

Natasha wasn't the only one. The revolution had made widows of too many women in this town, both rich and poor. Even now, Napoléon was at war with Austria and had an insatiable appetite for despatching the souls of young men from the battlefield to heaven – or hell. Without a husband, you were a second-class citizen if you were lucky enough not to be on the streets. Not Natasha, though. She had her bakery, and hardly a day went by when Nicole didn't drop by for a patisserie, or to pass the time of day.

She took the string handle of the neat waxed paper package: a small piece of perfection repeated a hundred times a day.

'*Merci, Natasha, bonne journée.*' She hesitated.

'*Qu'est-ce qui va pas, ma petite?*'

Yes, something was very wrong. She wished she could ask Natasha's advice about Monsieur Moët, but if she was going to refuse him, it wouldn't be fair if others knew, even if he *was* arrogant enough to think he could mould her into his imaginary perfect wife.

'*Non, tout va bien. A demain!*'

'Tell me when you're ready!' Natasha called after her. Sometimes Nicole thought Natasha really could see right into people's minds.

Down rue de l'Etape, along rue de Cordelliers, left at the rusty tap that had dripped as long as she could remember, along the alley and through the fence to the barrel yard where Xavier had hidden her the day of the revolution. The entrance to the other world of wine and cellars, of *industry*. She felt the same excitement when she went to her father's wool mills. The looms clicking, the clerks with their piles of parchment, the women whose fingers threaded the machines so confidently. The fine cloth that emerged at the other end, giving a shape to the day, a useful outcome.

She knocked on the door to the house that overlooked the yard.

'*Claudine, Antoine, c'est moi!*'

'*Ah, la petite sauvage. Monte*, come up!'

She took the steps two at a time, her boots clattering on the old stairs. No need to be ladylike here.

'I claim sanctuary from matrimony and slow death!' she shouted, then stopped short.

Antoine and Claudine were in their usual spots by the fire, but there was a third person sitting in *her* chair. A man with a violin in his lap, looking very much at home. He waved his bow at her in greeting.

'Granted, but it's a terrible waste,' he said, leaning back and crossing his long legs. He didn't look like he belonged in Reims, neither like a hunting country squire type, nor a farmer. His dark hair was shoulder-length and his angular face was unusually expressive when he smiled. His embroidered jacket gave him a bohemian air, like a Hungarian poet.

'*Approches-toi au feu, il fait froid aujourd'hui.* Sit by the fire.' Antoine beckoned to Nicole. 'And hush, marriage isn't *so* bad, even for a determined tomboy.'

There was nowhere left to sit, and the man didn't get up.

Claudine bustled over and took the *religieuses*. '*Merci*, I'll make coffee and bring plates.'

Claudine gave Antoine a wink and he disappeared into the kitchen with her to help, leaving the two of them alone, with no introductions.

'There are only three... I'm sorry,' Nicole said, shooting a glance at the man.

'François Clicquot. *Enchanté.*' He jumped up and kissed her on each cheek, holding onto his violin. 'Have you ever considered how such a chastely named pastry could be so evil and delicious?'

'A nun needs evil to fight, or what would be the point? Though all the *religieuses* I've known made a religion of whacking my knuckles with a ruler.'

He smiled. 'An unwilling scholar?'

His dark, blue-green eyes were a startling contrast to his pale skin and dark eyebrows.

'I was always escaping.'

'You prefer liberty with danger rather than peace with slavery?'

In quoting her favourite author, he had summed up her feelings about pretty much everything, including Monsieur Moët. She blushed.

He rummaged around in his violin case and brought out a battered copy of Rousseau's *The Social Contract.* 'I never leave it behind.'

'Come and sit down, *sauvage*,' said Antoine, bringing in the tray of coffee.

The corners of the man's mouth twitched into a grin and she cursed them for using her nickname in front of him. She remembered François Clicquot now. Her father was friendly with his family. In fact, they lived close by, but he had been away at boarding school.

Claudine served the *religieuses*. François took one, tore it in half and offered a piece to Nicole, which she refused.

Claudine and Antoine didn't ever feel the need to fill a silence, so no one spoke. Compared to home, this was a plain place, bare floorboards scrubbed clean, worn wooden chairs and a rag rug by the hearth that Nicole had helped Claudine make as a child. No servants, no fuss. This simple easiness was what she came here for and François seemed to sense that, so he kept the silence, too. She stared into the fire, felt him looking at her. The coffee was warm and nutty, but his curiosity unnerved her. She drained the cup.

'I should be getting back,' said Nicole.

'Are you sure?' Antoine looked at her with an unreadable expression. 'We're going to Verzenay with François to oversee the harvest. Join us? Our picnic can easily stretch to four. Please come, see what happens before the grapes get to the cellars. It will take your mind off your demise-by-matrimony,' he smiled.

'Have my share of the picnic. Come on, it's a glorious day!' said François.

'My parents will worry,' she said.

It would be the second time she'd slipped out alone today and they would miss her and fret. But watching Xavier and the others leave for the vineyards a few hours ago from the square, she had longed to be with them. Now here was an offer to do exactly that. Antoine was one of the most respected cellarmen in Reims and knew everything there was to know about wine production. She would be able to actually join the harvest instead of just read about it. Papa never allowed her to go with him to the vineyards. It was a man's world unless you were working, and not for ladies, he told her. She hated that word, lady. It just meant being shut away in a gilded cage with invisible boundaries you couldn't cross or question.

'I can send a boy,' said François. 'I owe you now that I have eaten your evil nun cake.'

'The Réseau Matu authorised the harvest just this morning. Everyone will be in the fields,' Claudine encouraged.

'It won't be the usual carriage ride to observe from afar that you're used to. You have to get in amongst the vines, join the pickers and feel the sweetness on your fingers – the smell is intoxicating,' said François.

'But the pickers hate owners getting in the way, don't they? I've heard them scoffing at the "gentleman farmers" and muttering about hobbies.'

François laughed an easy, warm glow her way. 'You're observant for an untutored truant! We're going to my father's vineyards, and I work hard, have done since I can remember. It's not a hobby for me, it's my life. When I was sent away to boarding school, I even missed the stripped black vines in winter. And summer in a classroom was torture when I knew the vines were flowering, followed by budburst, then working into the night by a bright June moon. If you're happy to put in a bit of hard graft, you'll be hooked, I promise.'

Back to the house for embroidery and marriage wrangles, or bouncing down the baked roads to the vineyards to be amongst the workers with this intriguing man? It was impossible to resist.

The clock struck twelve in the old church when they arrived at Verzenay. The vineyards stretched away in every direction, blue shadows pooled under the vines in the bright sun. Families and farm workers gossiped along the vines, muzzled donkeys stamped, ready to take their wooden cartloads of grapes to the press. Children cut bunches of grapes next to their mothers. Grandmothers picked out bad grapes, everyone working to bring in the harvest before the heat of the afternoon. These were the families of the revolution and they were better fed than they had once been under the old regime, but this was still back-breaking work: the men bent under the weight of the heavy baskets, and women pulled their headscarves across their faces against the sun.

François offered her a hand down from the barouche and he spun her to the ground in a carousel of sky and vines.

'Grey and blue,' he said. 'Like the sea at Calais. The colour of clouds.'

She blinked, not understanding.

'Your eyes,' he said.

'See you back here in an hour,' Antoine said, jumping down and linking arms with Claudine. 'We need to check in at the press.' They were off before she could reply.

'Come with me, there's something in the vineyard up on the Montagne you should see,' François said to Nicole. 'It's quite a walk though.'

She lifted her skirt and scuffed the dirt with her sturdy boot. 'Napoléon's army could march to Austria in these.'

'I remember you as a child, you could outrun most of the boys. Come on then.'

They climbed a hill towards the forest, throwing up clouds of chalk as they walked, dusty butterflies skimming the poppies and cornflowers, larks buzzing.

When they reached a remote patch of vines, François pointed.

'There, see the yellow rose? Exactly there.'

At the rose, François counted three vines along and peered at the foliage. Lifting up the dark leaves, he revealed a bunch of crimson grapes. Not purple, or white, or anything in between, but ripe grapes the colour of holly berries. She'd never seen any like it.

'I thought you'd be impressed,' he smiled.

'You hardly know me.'

'But I remember you.' He picked two grapes.

'Don't! They're the only ones!'

'They'll die and wither and no one will ever have tasted them. Isn't that sadder?' He popped one in his mouth. 'Aniseed, almond...' He savoured it. 'Then clover. Try it.'

He handed her the second grape. Nicole hesitated. It was a lurid red.

'Go on, we will be the only two people ever to taste them. They're delicious.'

She took it and popped it into her mouth.

'Sour!' she spluttered, spitting it out.

'You might have pretended!' he laughed.

'I can't pretend, I have to say what I think.'

'You've passed the first test of wine tasting,' said François, 'Be honest, don't humour the grower, act for the buyer and you'll never go far wrong. Come on, I'll find you some sweet ones.'

They walked back to the busy vineyards and François gave her a flat basket for collecting.

'Pick the best first, along the entire row. This is a grand cru vineyard, so be careful. These beauties have worked the entire summer, quietly growing sweeter.'

'Like my perfect sister. Personally, I'd rather be the picker than the picked. What happens after this?'

She saw how ripe fruit hung heavy on the vines, felt the stickiness on her hands, breathed in the pungent scent. Actually being there was nothing like the dry manuals she'd squinted at by moonlight.

'It's a beautiful process, *sauvage*,' François replied. 'The whole thing, from picking to pressing and tending the vines. The blend, the bottles in the cellars, slowly turned. It's what I love. The *terroir* here in Verzenay produces the best grapes for champagne. You are picking the finest Pinot Noir. They will be blended with the Pinot Meunier over there. The black grapes grow best here on the Montagne. And the third grape for my champagne is the Chardonnay. We have another vineyard on the other side, on the Côte des Blancs. That's where we grow our Morillon Blanc. This is my place, where I'm happiest.'

Nicole nodded, remembering the first time she'd arrived in the cellar on the day of the revolution, the deep green bottles so neat, so safe and enchanting in the candlelight. This was where those bottles began their journey, with picking in the maturing sunlight.

'Mademoiselle Ponsardin!'

It was Monsieur Moët striding towards her in a big hurry, smoothing down his sideswept grey locks in eager anticipation of reaching her. She wished him a million miles away.

'You'll wake up sunburnt tomorrow without a parasol, and vineyards are for workers! And I had thought you might want to be at home with your parents, *in discussion*. My carriage is nearby. Come.'

'I think you've met Monsieur Clicquot?' Nicole replied coolly, determined not to respond to his comments.

The men shook hands frostily.

'Are you accompanied?'

'Yes, Monsieur Moët. With Claudine the *couturière*, so don't fret. I'm not a wilting flower you need to protect.'

'Where is she now? It would be remiss of me to leave you alone…'

She could barely breathe for the sense of claustrophobia he brought with him, like a windowless room closing in around her.

François interjected with a smile. 'Monsieur Moët, she is well looked after with me. I know her family well. Our fathers are good friends.'

Monsieur Moët appraised François and clearly didn't like what he saw.

'Your poor mother would be frantic if she thought Claudine had been so neglectful. I'll find her for you.' Monsieur Moët buttoned his jacket and took the path to the press, careful to ignore the workers who greeted him along the way.

'*In discussion*,' François mocked behind his back. 'About what? One of those men who thinks he owns the whole of France, including you.' He picked a grape. 'This one is perfect.'

She bit through the skin, immediately forgetting about Moët as a burst of sweetness was released – a kaleidoscope of soft rain, mellow sun, a year's worth of dusks and dawns, frosts and summer breezes, the taste of the *terroir*, right there on her tongue.

CHAPTER 3

Late October 1797

Republican date: Brumaire, year VI

Truth and Dare

Antoine and Claudine had saved her from death-by-marriage. François had been their doing, a carefully planned campaign, given an early start the day that Nicole clattered up their stairs unexpectedly after Monsieur Moët's proposal.

But of course they'd noticed how unhappy she was, Antoine and Claudine told her. They'd known her all her life and they could see she was fighting a losing battle against the growing pressure to marry. Any day her papa could agree to an unsuitable match, with her best interests at heart of course, but she'd be trapped forever against her will. When François had visited Antoine to consult him on the acquisition of his latest grand cru vineyards, he was like a breath of fresh air compared to the small-town rigid traditionalists who would be deemed a match for Nicole. François was well-travelled, open-minded, cultured and a dreamer. The way he spoke so poetically about the vines beguiled everyone he met, and his quick wit and intelligence would be more than a match for their restless, rebellious Nicole.

A firefly, he called her. Quick and sharp and charged.

'*Chérie*, the carriage!'

Nicole checked herself in the mirror before running down to take it. Why had she asked for a whole month to consider Moët's proposal? Because she didn't know how to say no, and it seemed a decent amount of time to give him as her father had advised, unfair to dismiss his proposal in a shorter time span. Still a week to go before she could get it over with, but it was an eternity now there was François.

Every minute without him was dull. She found an excuse to bump into him every day, touring the Ponsardin family vineyards. If she was to consider Monsieur Moët's proposal, she argued, she should spend time in his milieu of winemaking. François was always working at the Clicquot vineyards nearby, with a new thing to show her every day, he promised – a blend to taste, a delicious pinot to try, an undiscovered place where the poppies edged the cornfields, catching the sun in flames.

Sometimes at dusk, the time of day when the sky turned translucent blue like Chinese lacquer, they watched the clouds turn with the sunset, making out shapes.

'A bottle of champagne,' said Nicole.

'Wrong shape, it's clearly a bottle of Gamay.' François concentrated hard, eyeing her sideways. In the dying rays of the sun, his skin glowed in the rosy light.

'How on earth do you know?'

'I don't,' he laughed, hugging her close.

The shapes didn't matter, but staying a little bit longer was everything and they would linger until the last fine thread of light on the horizon would send her parents searching for her in the dark.

As the month had mellowed and the days grew shorter, they'd fed each other blackberries from the hedgerows, and they had never tasted so dark or sweet to Nicole. When they could escape for long enough, François laid his jacket under the twisted beech trees in the forest of Verzy and they read together, from Rousseau, or Voltaire. Neither of them could concentrate long enough to read anything of note. It was a game of chicken to see who could last the longest before meeting eyes and stealing blackberry-streaked kisses.

On the day the ripe October sun had shone through swollen raindrops and lit them in a thousand spheres of warm rain, they were caught at the walled vineyard at Villers-Allerand. They polkaed up and down the rows at the sheer joy of it all, soaked and laughing, François singing to the sky at the top of his voice, whirling her skilfully through the vines.

Now, with a week to go before she could release herself from Monsieur Moët's proposal, she stood in the vast hallway of her family home and saluted herself in Maman's prized Venetian mirror for her good fortune.

'*Vite, chérie, Claudine est arrivée!*' shouted Maman.

Her mother kissed her on both cheeks, delighted to see her in her new silk dress, hair brushed into a chignon.

'You're growing up, Babouchette. About time.' She winked.

Whatever guilt Nicole felt was swept away by the thought of François, the daily poems and letters he slipped into her pocket, and today's invitation to meet him at the lake. Nothing else mattered.

The lake was green, like the Vesle River, translucent and made pale by the chalk banks. François threw a stone and the October sun picked out ripples in silver.

'Not bad,' said Nicole.

'What does it take to impress you?' laughed François.

'I don't know. A dragon? Wine from water?'

'We're going for a swim. I promised you, something new every time we meet. Turn around.'

He undid the laces at the back of her dress, loose enough to take off.

'You do it,' he said.

Nicole hesitated, but his 'something news' were always irresistible. She took off her dress and turned to face him, her body a shadow under her muslin slip. He touched her shoulder. A breeze shuffled the oaks. A new hunger engulfed her and he kissed her. When he let her go, she felt as dizzy as she had when he had spun her down from the barouche.

'Now!' he yelled and pushed her in, stripping his shirt off and jumping in after her. The water screamed cold, her blood rushed and tingled and when she came up, he kissed her again, the water muddy and sweet and slippery between them. They laughed at the shock and kissed more deeply this time, hands in places they shouldn't be, couldn't stop until she broke away, afraid of the intensity.

He took her hand and they floated on their backs, aching, watching the swallows turn pale green as they darted over the water. Iridescent dragonflies clouded amongst the lilies.

The hour was over too soon. The sun dried her before she dressed, but she was still cool from the water and they held hands as far along the path as they dared. As they passed the derelict house, Nicole spotted a well. She delved into her pocket for a coin.

'Make a wish,' she said and closed her eyes, ready to throw. *Freedom*, she thought as she threw the coin. She found another in her pocket and handed it to François. 'Your turn.'

He recoiled. 'You shouldn't have done that.'

She laughed. 'Then I'll throw it for you.'

She closed her eyes and smiled. *Happiness for François*, she thought, and the coin plunked into the water, far below.

When she opened her eyes, François was gone. If this was a joke, she wasn't going to laugh. She stood for a while, waiting for him to return, scanned the woods while pretending not to in case he was watching her. He didn't come back. She had forgotten her pocket watch, but at least half an hour must have passed as she waited, and the sun lost a little of its brightness.

Antoine and Claudine arrived, and still no François. Anger and hurt mixed in a confusion of feelings. How dare he? And at the same time she longed for his warm arms around her. She wanted to cry and she wanted to rail at him for his thoughtlessness, if only he'd appear.

'Where is your young poet-vintner?' Claudine smiled.

'I-I don't know. I closed my eyes to make a wish in that well and he disappeared.'

They waited as long as they could. Antoine scoured the woods and came back shrugging his shoulders. Nothing.

She kept half expecting him to appear, laughing on the side of the road. It was something to do with the coin that she threw. He had the look of a wild animal, oscillating between fight or flight, and he had clearly chosen to fly. She could cry and shout and blast him for his selfishness, while wishing she could throw her arms around him and understand.

Claudine put her arm around her and said nothing, leaving her to her pain.

Nicole ran through the moment over and over again that night. He hadn't even said goodbye.

A slow week dragged by. She went obsessively every day to the place in the stables where they swapped hidden letters, and each day the empty space was like a kick in the stomach. She had only known him four weeks, but François filled her life with new vitality and, until now, not a day went by when he hadn't left her a hidden message or poem. Had she just imagined everything that passed between them? Was she just another stupid girl who'd been bowled over by a handsome liar? Was he hurt somewhere, crying out for her help, or was he with another girl, taking her to his vineyards and waxing lyrical about the vines? Still, she was too proud to ask Antoine and Claudine where he was.

After seven days, three hours and thirty minutes, she knew what she had to do. The shop would be closed now, but Natasha would give her an answer. She rushed to the *boulangerie* and banged on the door.

Nicole told her everything, and Natasha gave her a little bag of salt.

'You're sure you want to do this? It doesn't always tell you what you want to hear, *milaya*.'

'I'm sure.' Nothing could be worse than the torment of not knowing.

Natasha clicked her amber beads, whispering oaths Nicole didn't understand. 'Throw!'

Nicole threw the salt. It scattered over the tiles of the *boulangerie*.

Natasha scrutinised the shapes.

'Caution.'

'Anything else?'

Natasha swept the salt into a pile in front of her. 'That's it. Caution, my little whirlwind. Take time to measure, to think. You are disappointed?'

'A little. I thought…'

'It would tell you that the course of true love never did run smooth, but all would be right in the end?'

Nicole flushed.

'Caution is all it says. I saw what was going to happen to Daniel using the old ways. It's never wrong, even when it tells you what you don't want to hear.'

There were times when Natasha could be so *pessimistic*.

'Yes, I'm a dour old woman, but I'm wiser than you. Only you know the answer.' She opened the door and hugged Nicole tight. 'Go now, take the night to think. You know your own head.'

Too much time had passed for forgiveness. The moment she got home, Nicole picked up a quill.

Cher Jean-Rémy Moët,
I am delighted to accept…

She sealed the letter and, as an afterthought, sprayed it with a careless squirt of lavender water. She gave the note to Josette to deliver post-haste, made her swear not to tell her parents.

This small town loved nothing more than to gossip, and François would hear of her betrothal to Moët and be sorry and be insanely jealous, understand how it felt to be abandoned without warning. She couldn't just passively wait, she had to *do* something.

Five minutes after the letter had left her hands, she knew it was a mistake.

It was already dark outside, but she flew out of the door to try to stop the letter. Josette was nowhere to be seen. At the rue de Vergeur, the blue lantern of the *poste* was already out and the door bolted. So this is what Natasha had read from the scattered salt, she realised with a horrible foreboding – but too late and goodness knew what she had set in motion with her rash behaviour. *Please God, just let François come back.*

At the stables, her new foal, Pinot, stamped at her arrival. She nuzzled him.

'Why did I write to Jean-Rémy?' she whispered.

Pinot had no answer, but her heart jumped. A letter was poking out in the secret hiding place by his feed. She brushed away the straw with trembling hands.

> *Forgive me, Babouchette. I only wanted to release you to know your own mind, but I didn't know how to do it and I was cruel and I am deeply sorry.*
>
> *Moët's offer on the face of it is a better one than mine. He is solid and stable. I am prone to mood swings and excess and you should know this. The last week has shown you what I am. Sometimes I am deeply afraid of my own happiness. But I also have the capacity to love so deeply and I have never loved anyone like I love you. I love your wit, the way your boots are too big for your tiny body, the way you flit around in them like there's never enough time, the way you taste the land and all its colours, the way your hair is highlighted red in the sun, the shadow of you in your muslin slip. So marry me. We'll run a vineyard, taste the land together.*

And then she understood. All she wanted to do was forgive him completely and just love him. She knew instinctively that life with François would be full of bumps and twists, but between them a taste so sweet, so intense, she could never forgive herself for going through life without experiencing it.

She wrote back, *Yes, yes, yes!* and put it in the place beneath the straw.

*

The *yes* was the easy part, but now everything was a mess. She had accepted Monsieur Moët out of spite. She went to Papa's dark, panelled office and sat in the high-backed chair, sitting up as tall as she could. On the other side of his ordered leathered desk, he looked forbidding and official, seeming to represent everything she wanted to fight. Nevertheless, she begged him to help her, told him she *would* marry François and he knew her well enough to know she would not be persuaded otherwise.

Papa was severely vexed that she had played such a girlish game with her eminent suitor and she berated herself for her bad judgement in the matter, but only in the moments she could stop thinking about François.

The next day, exactly one month after Moët's proposal, and a glorious lifetime with François, Papa took her to his own vineyard at Rilly to meet old Philippe Clicquot, François' father, to make final arrangements for her marriage.

The day was glorious, and the vine leaves were autumn russet and gold. As they strolled to the vines, Nicole made the assessments which were almost second nature to her now after spending so much time with François in the vineyards – orientation, incline, the surrounding vineyards, the shape of the leaves to indicate the varietal, *tick, tick, tick*.

Papa bent to check the last roses of the season, planted at the end of each row to indicate infestations and counted on his fingers. 'The roses are clean... my prediction is, harvest on the fifteenth of September next year and it'll be a bumper crop.' He held out his hand. 'Bet on it?'

'It's not fair to make bets I know I'll win. It's obviously going to be the first of October and it will be the best ever. This crop will belong to François and me, and it will be our first Clicquot vintage.'

'I hope that's not the only thing you'll make. I want to see my grandchildren enjoying these vines before I die. You've made a mess of everything with Monsieur Moët, but I do believe François will make you happy.'

'Stop it!' She blushed. 'But we do want children. A bohemian boy like François who'll play gypsy violin and a little girl we'll teach to blend the best vintages on the Montagne. I wish Maman would understand.'

'Your mother does want you to be happy, Babouchette. She just thinks Monsieur Moët is a better prospect for you. We'll bring her round. If François can charm my little girl into marrying him, he shouldn't have any problem with your mother. Monsieur Moët is Mayor of Reims, though, and she's got stars in her eyes.'

'She's not the one marrying him and I'd make a terrible mayor's wife.'

Papa looked at his watch. 'Maman will be here soon. I told her to meet us here to discuss your marriage. Why on earth did you send that letter to Moët in the first place? You're supposed to be the canny one of my girls and now he's told your mother it constitutes an official agreement. I've always helped you out of your scrapes, but I'm not sure how I'm going to extricate you from this one honourably.'

Why was Natasha always right? *Caution*, she'd said.

'Who *cares* about Monsieur Moët's version of honour when all he thinks about is money? He just wants his imagined version of me, not the real one.'

'I can't imagine why anyone would want to take on the *real* Nicole,' he teased. 'Especially the one that's made such a hash of things. But it won't be as easy as you think. Monsieur Moët is creative in revenge, and he's a great politician. Cross him and his retaliation will be subtle and untraceable.'

'He's just used to everyone saying yes. He's not *that* clever and I refuse to be afraid.'

'You've never been scared of anyone and that is why you are *always* in trouble,' he said proudly. 'But this is a small town, *ma petite*, we all need to live together, and like it or not, he *is* a powerful opponent.' He handed her an old enamel tape measure. 'On with you, and make sure you keep it taut.'

Nicole unwound the slippery silk tape and paced along a row of vines to the edge of the vineyard until her father was out of sight.

'Ready!' she called.

'Hold it there, keep it nice and tight and make sure you check the figure twice!'

She trapped the tape under her thumb and committed the measurement to memory – 204 *pieds du Roi*, king's feet. Since the revolution, they were supposed to use metres and kilometres, but all the country people still measured *à l'ancienne*, the old way.

'Hold it there a second!' shouted Papa.

Nicole waved an acknowledgement, felt in her pocket for François' note and ran her fingers over the embossed letters, *François-Marie Clicquot.* She whispered the words 'Nicole Clicquot'.

Three sharp tugs were her signal to start winding in the tape. She turned the little crank, careful to keep it smooth, but the tape stuck and she dropped it. When she stood up, the figure holding the other end was close enough to make her heart leap.

'Keep winding,' said François.

The last time she'd seen him, he'd left her alone by the well and she'd imagined their reunion in a million different colours, he contrite, she gracious. But he was here now, and that was all that mattered.

'I shouldn't have left you, *ma sauvage,*' he said.

'I didn't understand.'

'It hurts to love you so much,' said François quietly. 'I have moments where I need time for myself. I know you will understand.'

'Just kiss me,' she said.

François trembled as he held her, resonating with the breeze. The warm autumn air smelt of woodsmoke and the heady perfume of grape harvest still lingered.

'Grow vines with me,' he whispered.

'I already said yes.' She smiled.

'I'll love you more than anyone else could, but you have to be brave. You know that?'

'I'm marrying the cleverest, most handsome man in Champagne, that's all I need to know.'

He swung her round until she was dizzy. 'Here we are, being bought and sold like a couple of prize heifers,' he laughed. 'I wouldn't have accepted you if this vineyard wasn't part of the deal.'

'I want wild strawberries every day, even in the winter.' She pushed him away. 'And no touching the goods until it's all signed and sealed.'

She ran to her father, who was bent over a trestle table at the vineyard entrance with Philippe, François' father. Both were noting down vineyard measurements like generals strategising for battle. Just a few papers signed, money and lands exchanged between the families to secure their children's future, and no one could stop her marrying, not even Maman.

It had to be a *fait accompli* well before Maman's planned arrival at midday and Papa had chosen the location carefully, here in her parents' favourite vineyard, on the very spot he proposed twenty years ago. Perhaps here, remembering that day, her mother would relent.

She hugged her papa. 'Thank you!'

'Slow down, Babouchette, you'll smudge the ink! Philippe, you remember my daughter?'

'So this is the little thing that's captivated my François, eh?' said Philippe. Grey curls framed a kind, anxious face. 'Bright and quick as a firefly, I see, as he described you. There's a fire in those pale grey eyes that is more than a match for him. And hair the colour of a pale sunset, just before it turns red, I think were his words. Well, well, such is the poetry of young love, but I see in this case there is no exaggeration.' He smiled at the pair.

'Flattery will get you everywhere, Monsieur Clicquot,' Nicole replied, glowing.

He kissed her on both cheeks.

When the church bell struck the first chime of midday, Maman's barouche turned the corner, scattering chalky white dust. As it settled, the driver jumped out, helped her down, and paced towards them so fast she had to run to keep up with him.

Nicole stopped short. Maman had brought Monsieur Moët with her! He was dressed even more formally than usual, in a high collar and dark suit which looked far too hot for the weather. He walked stiffly across to the two men bent over the table between the vines, and nodded an aloof greeting, manoeuvring himself to get a good view of the papers.

'*Mon Dieu*, what's this? Signing over your vineyards to the Clicquots? I trust you intended to pass this in front of the town council? All transfer of vineyards is null and void unless approved by the committee. Our Champagne region has a reputation to maintain, gentlemen, so I'm afraid this won't be binding.'

'Marriage makes it binding,' said François.

'Ah, then it all makes sense. But that is another contract that cannot be fulfilled, as she's not yours to take,' said Monsieur Moët.

'I am not anyone's to buy and sell. He is *my* choice,' said Nicole.

'Nonsense, Nicole. Girls don't *choose*,' interrupted Maman, flicking her fan in annoyance, the feathers wilting in the late-autumn sun. 'We are very fortunate that Monsieur Moët has agreed to overlook any indiscretions and take you anyway. Just think, Babouchette, you could be married here next week, on your parents' wedding anniversary. Everyone says the weather's going to be fine, it always is on that day, *n'est-ce pas*, Nicolas?'

Papa was outmanoeuvred.

Monsieur Moët jumped in. 'Your mother has persuaded me that the stress of our upcoming nuptials has perhaps caused you to behave out of character and so we agreed, out of respect to our joint arrangement, to bring the date forward.'

'*Chéri*, isn't that testament to Monsieur Moët's generosity and affection, which deserves our utmost respect?' Maman said to Papa.

'As does Nicole,' said François. 'I left her alone and this misunderstanding is my fault.'

'I have no doubt this mess is your fault,' Moët replied, flushing with anger. 'Unfortunately, Mademoiselle Ponsardin and her family cannot have the full picture of what it means to marry a Clicquot. In addition to all this money, and the prized grand cru vineyards they're signing over, there's a less palatable inheritance. Philippe, tell them. The bad blood that's run through the Clicquot family ever since anyone can remember. And in the countryside, we remember a long way back.'

Philippe blanched visibly and Nicole could have struck Moët for his casual slanders.

'We'd still be ducking witches if we took notice of old vineyard gossip. The only truth in all this is that I have more feeling in my little finger than you do in your whole bitter, greedy old corpse,' snapped François.

'You, François Clicquot, are a known dilettante, a dangerous radical and a *melancholic*.' Moët swept the papers off the table. 'These are *worthless*.'

Even Maman looked shocked.

'How dare you, Monsieur! Enough!' Papa exclaimed, colouring with anger as Philippe scrabbled to gather the papers up. He squared up to him, ready for a fight.

'What's her favourite colour?' François interrupted.

Moët regarded him with contempt. 'Don't be ridiculous, man. I don't know. She's a woman, she likes *gold*, and diamonds.'

'The colour of a slice of cucumber when it's held up to the sun. Her favourite grape is Pinot Noir, she named her new foal after the fruit she tasted on my land. She loves Rousseau and prefers lace-up boots to shoes that pinch.'

'All very touching, until you need to put food on the table. It seems my fiancée's parents have allowed Nicole to get to know you a little *too* well.'

'She is never out of my sight, or without a chaperone, Monsieur Moët…' Maman pleaded.

'Apart from when I swam with him in the lake,' said Nicole. 'Or the day we stole the boat for a picnic on the Vesle, or the full moon when we listened for budburst in the vines at midnight.'

Papa raised his hand, in possession of himself again. He gave Moët the conciliatory smile Nicole had seen him use when his clerks came to him with a dispute at his mills. 'Monsieur Moët, I can only apologise. My eldest girl is good like her mother, but my youngest is a little too wilful, like me. Please apologise, Nicole, and let's find a way to settle this amicably.'

Nicole steeled herself, trusting her father. 'Monsieur Moët, I am sorry. I should never have sent the letter to you.'

'No you should not. You should be careful, leading men on.'

Papa held up a settlement paper. 'You are angry, Monsieur Moët, and rightly so. In business, there would be a financial penalty for reneging on a contract. My dowry to the Clicquot family was to be thirty thousand livres. If ten thousand of that was redirected to your business at Epernay, would that redress the broken contract?'

Monsieur Moët quickened. 'It's not just about the money. I'm sure in time that my affection would have been reciprocated…'

'There are vineyards, too,' her father said, tapping the paper.

'Which ones?' interrupted Monsieur Moët, putting on his spectacles.

Papa pointed to the figures they'd noted down. 'We just finished measuring today, so it's all up to date.'

'Is this one really 204 *pieds du Roi*? That is more sizeable than I thought.' Moët scooped up some soil and ran it through his fingers, tasted a little on his tongue. 'Grand cru. These vineyards, especially Tois-Puits, would be wasted on these two novices. They'd kill the lot within a year.'

Papa smiled. 'It would certainly put my mind at rest to see them pass on to good hands. The vineyards would have been amusing, a hobby, but they will be well provided for without them. And I would feel, along with the money, that I had bought myself out of a contract honourably, should you accept.'

'You'll send the papers directly and agree on all three vineyards?'

'It's the least we could do.'

Nicole felt she was going to explode. He didn't deserve this, despite her transgression. She wouldn't be the first girl to break off an engagement, nor the last. But François squeezed her hand to steady her.

Moët sniffed and raised his chin to make himself taller, refusing to look at Nicole. 'I see the young couple are hell-bent on their course and I have no choice but to wish them every happiness they can hope for. Due to their *meetings*, it would be impossible for me to take the girl now. I can only withdraw and accept reasonable compensation.'

'Graciously said, Monsieur Moët. Please, take the horse. We can get another for the barouche later,' said Papa, shaking his hand.

'Send the papers directly to my office,' he instructed, kissing Nicole's hand. 'You have a lifetime's lessons to learn, my dear. Allow me to demonstrate the first, that even *you* can be bought and sold.'

'Don't threaten us,' François confronted him. 'There are things we have that you will never buy. You know she's special, and one day I'll make her Queen of Reims.'

'My dear François, you'll ruin her,' said Monsieur Moët, walking away.

Papa caught François' arm. 'Let him go. You have Nicole and he has nothing. Those vineyards are worthless, too, apart from Rilly. The Clicquots still own the best vineyards in Champagne, everyone knows that, and they will be yours. Use them to make the finest vintage – the sweetest revenge needs time to mature.'

François scowled. 'I know you're right, but I still hope the bastard gets fruit rot; he doesn't deserve a sou from you.'

'Come on,' said Papa, kissing Maman on the cheek. 'Remember twenty years ago, just here, when I begged you to marry me and your parents, quite rightly, disapproved of me?'

'You were a rogue then and it's no different now,' said Maman with the ghost of a smile. Then to François, 'It's done, so make sure you prove me wrong and make her happy.'

It wasn't quite the triumph Nicole had imagined. The way Monsieur Moët looked when she apologised to him for the letter betrayed something unexpected. He was hurt, and Natasha had always told her that was more dangerous than anger. She tucked the uncomfortable feeling away in a corner of her heart and promised herself she'd make up for it sometime in the future. Natasha would say 'what goes around comes around'.

Antoine worked through the night to make the cellar beautiful for the wedding. Candles lit the place where Nicole had first taken refuge on the day of the revolution. She'd since learned that the cellar was actually owned by the Clicquots, just another piece of the journey that had led her to this point in her life, which felt so unaccountably lucky. It was Thermidor, sixth year of the republic, though everyone knew it was really August, in the year 1798.

She peeped into the cellar from behind the curtain and saw Jean-Rémy Moët sitting straight-backed next to Monsieur Olivier from the tasting committee. Only she knew what it cost him to be there. He was just one of the many dignitaries invited by the Ponsardin and Clicquot families. Nicole had her own way with her choice of husband, but the wedding was her mother's.

Such a *fuss*, hidden away in the cellar so that her mother could bring in Priest Lescelles from the cathedral. He was hiding like a criminal now that the cathedral was the Temple of Reason. He no longer spat fire and brimstone at his congregation, but there was plenty of opportunity to glower about heathens heading for eternal damnation after the revolution. The heart had been ripped out of the church, but the hidden priest was her mother's coup. Not just anyone could sneak him out of hiding for a wedding. It took time and resources – and the Clicquots and the Ponsardins had both – she and François would never have to worry about money. This was the coming together of two great families of Reims and her mother wasn't going to let anyone forget it.

None of it mattered today. Nicole was glad they were getting married in a cellar rather than the cathedral. They had met and courted in the vineyards amongst the skylarks. Spent months watching the leaves turn from acid green to yellow and red, the grapes grow mellow, the poppies in the cornfields turn from crimson to drooping purple. They had helped turn the presses, overseen the blend, watched the fermentation once, then twice. Despaired at blown corks, spoiled champagne and late-spring hailstorms, rejoiced at carts of green bottles heading for the ports, danced to the accordion at the harvest feast of St Rémi.

Who would have thought that she, the smallest and plainest of her cohort, would marry for love?

Love or otherwise, it didn't matter to her mother. The Clicquots were a prominent family, worthy of the Ponsardins, according to Maman's measures, which were harsh.

François' father was obsessed with his vast, lucrative textile business, as was Papa. They spent many happy evenings comparing notes, and everything was just right.

That Papa was delighted was the icing on the cake. Nicole would have married François whatever anyone thought, but she and Papa had a special bond and everyone told her they were alike. She hoped so. Papa was shrewd, dynamic and a leader of men.

Priest Lescelles arranged the gleaming offertory vessels and opened his Bible on the makeshift altar. He had anointed the kings of France in Reims Cathedral with the sacred Sainte Ampoule. Now he was hidden in a cellar. Fortunes rise and fall in a heartbeat. Nothing could ever stay the same. Traditions of hundreds, maybe thousands, of years had been overturned the day of the revolution. Life was uncertain. Natasha had always warned her of that. But today was her day and she was marrying François and it was perfect.

She walked steadily up the aisle, thanking herself for the sturdy boots hidden under her dress, grateful Maman hadn't noticed she'd swapped them for her silk slippers. If she did now, then *tant pis*, too late. Claudine had made her dress from layers of sheer ivory muslin in the empire style she loved, fitted low across her shoulders, and she felt as light and seductive as a glass of champagne. François was waiting for her at the altar, and he would take it off her tonight. She felt that everything she had done in her life so far was propelling her to this moment, like a sunlit current in the river that would always have found its way to the sea.

Trestle tables with white tablecloths were laid out in the vineyard at Verzenay for the wedding breakfast. The vines were in full flower and the air was filled with the scent of lemon and vanilla and summer. Bunting fluttered in the vines, wine bottles glinted in the sun, silver salvers were piled high with delicacies, and conversation brimmed above the lark song.

'Look,' said François.

Natasha had insisted the cake should be a secret until now, and he took her to see it. There were five tiers, and around each cake were crimson grapes hanging from icing vines.

'Did you tell her about the bright red grapes you showed me?' she asked, surprised.

'No, and you destroyed the last of the evidence when you spat them out! Just a coincidence?'

'It never is with Natasha.'

If it was one of Natasha's signs or spells, it made Nicole feel uncomfortable. She picked up François' violin to distract herself. 'Play for us?'

An extra row of tables was set out for the vineyard workers. Xavier was already drunk, whirling Natasha, protesting, to the strains of the violin.

Afternoon turned to evening, a big yellow moon rose, moths flung themselves at the candelabras and the accordion had everyone jumping to its bellows. When the night dew clung to the black shawls of the seated widows, making them shiver, the crowd began to disperse.

François wrapped a warm cloak around her bare shoulders. 'Time to go, Madame Clicquot.'

He handed her up into the barouche and put a black velvet blanket over her knees. She felt like a diamond in a box.

'Where are we going?'

'You'll see.'

They waved goodbye to the wedding crowd and old Widow Joubert caught her bouquet and cackled, much to the disappointment of Nicole's unmarried school friends. Her sister Clémentine beamed her beautiful smile, Xavier gave them a lurid thumbs up, Natasha traced a figure of eight around them with an amulet, Maman dabbed her tears, and Papa waved enthusiastically, blowing kisses. Monsieur Moët had already left.

Alone at last. Nicole tucked herself into François' arm and watched the moon blur as the carriage jolted.

He turned off the main track, and Nicole counted ten vineyards before they came to a shepherd's hut.

'Is this it?' she laughed as he spun her down.

'Close your eyes,' he whispered.

He led her forward and she opened her eyes. Lanterns dotted the walls, throwing prisms of light all around. The floor was covered in Russian rugs and in the corner was a big silver urn, etched with patterns that looked like Natasha's salt bag. In the middle, a low bed, piled high with furs and a window in the roof revealing an expanse of sky above it. A fire cracked and spat in the chimney.

'It's beautiful,' she said, giddy with the romance of the place.

'Come.'

He led her to the big urn, bubbling and warm. He turned a little tap and gave her a patterned glass.

The warm brandy made her woozy and as she sipped, he silently took the hairpins out of her chignon, caressed the place on her shoulder where her hair fell, then kissed her brandy lips. Putting his arm around her, he led her to the furs, tenderly laid her down and stood back to regard his sultry wife with yearning, blue-green eyes.

'Come here,' she whispered above the fire's roar.

He took her, there and then, with her dress still on, the stars astonished above them. He took her dress off and did it again, more slowly this time, and she was dewy and slippery and the stars shattered into a thousand pieces just for them.

They talked under the furs until the sun came up, together, sticky and warm. Nicole had never thought it was possible to be as happy as this.

He brushed her hair away from her eyes. 'It will be a good harvest this year.'

'How do you know?'

'There are more shooting stars than usual. I've watched all my life from here. The more there are in June, the better the harvest.'

'How long has this hut been like this?'

'It's my little piece of Russia. The rugs and furs are collected from my travels. They appreciate champagne even more than the French. And certainly more than the English. The urn over there, that's a samovar. Every Russian house has one and it's always bubbling. It's an extraordinary place, Babouchette. Like the east and the west have collided and they've taken the best of both. We'll go one day, together, sell them our best champagne. I'll take you on sleigh rides and show you minarets and we'll drink in underground bars, side by side with peasants, and tell them about Rousseau.'

'Russia...' She dreamed. She tangled herself around him and the sun began a new day in vermilion rays.

CHAPTER 4

October 1799

Republican date: Brumaire, year VIII

The Tasting Committee

'My wife, Madame Clicquot.' François introduced Nicole to the assembled tasters.

They nodded, tight-lipped, not bothering to disguise their annoyance at the presence of a woman. After over a year of marriage, people still found it difficult to accept that she was just as much the boss as her husband. In the wine calendar, the wine tasting committee was the most important moment of the year. Only the most highly respected 'noses' in the region were invited to arbitrate on which wines would make the finest vintages and which would be relegated to become a common *vin de table*. That such an upstart, never mind a female one, should be admitted to the sacred circle was, in their opinion, an outrage.

Nicole brazened out the raised eyebrows, harumphs and turned backs with smiles and greetings, François shooting her admiring glances for her boldness.

Never mind the revolution, that Napoléon was waging war in Egypt and that uprisings and lawlessness were constantly bubbling up across France. The tasting committee must endure, tradition must be upheld and young women most certainly should *not* be admitted. Jean-Rémy Moët, their *de facto* leader, encouraged this viewpoint whenever he had the opportunity and, more, was constantly petitioning her and François to sell him their best vineyards, always wanting to 'help' in any way he could. That was how she knew their business was becoming increasingly respected. She had Monsieur Moët good and worried.

The base wine was decanted with a slow gurgle, the bottleneck wiped reverently between each pour, solemn as a church.

Nicole sniffed the first glass, rolled it around her tongue.

'Pinot Meunier,' she said quietly, afraid to be proved wrong.

François nodded in encouragement.

The committee spat and pronounced their verdict. 'Silky, blackberries. Single wine, grand cru, but not for this champagne.'

The next wine was poured. Nicole sniffed, rolled and spat.

'A complex Pinot Blanc. Clover and cornflowers shared the soil with the vines. It will make an interesting top-note to the champagne. I recommend we include it.'

The venerable Monsieur Olivier, the head taster, took another noisy slurp, pressing the glass to his quivering nose, then spitting.

'I agree, this will be good for the blend. I know the vineyard, she's right about the flowers too.' He grinned at the committee. 'Your husband has given you a kind head-start, *chère* Madame Clicquot.'

'He doesn't need to. I can taste it, right here in the grapes.'

The next wine was poured, then the next. She called each one correctly, more confident as time went by.

'If nothing else, she's got a good memory,' said Monsieur Olivier. 'We have tasted ten wines, and each one has been on the nose.'

François laughed as they came out into the sun and looked out over the Clicquot vineyards. 'It was more like they were sucking lemons than tasting wine.' He kissed her. 'They'll just have to get used to my wife being more talented than them.'

She was triumphant. It was the result of two years of hard work, of shadowing his every move in the vineyards and at the press to learn. She learned about the *terroir*, the conditions and 'magic' that made a grand cru vineyard, the press and the blend, and the qualities of each varietal, nuanced by the soil that nourished them. It was magic, alchemy, science and chance in myriad colours.

Their fledgling wine business was growing, and it was their shared joy. They rode out every day side by side, kicking up dust on chalky paths to check every detail. They railed at spring hailstorms, delighted at budburst, watched the tendrils as they wound themselves around the posts and created a solid foundation for the plants to grow. They joked with the workers, understood their trials and tribulations, prayed with them to the harvest saints at church on Sundays and talked into the night about the finer points of viticulture. François made it sound like poetry. Sometimes, too tired to go to bed after their long days, they made love by the firelight and woke in the morning, still in each other's arms, with the embers glowing white and hot.

His delight in her knowledge of the wine business still made her feel like the sun had come out after over a year of marriage. This was the perfect moment to tell him her news.

'I have a surprise.' She took him to sit on the millstone, away from the workers and prying ears. 'Another blend, more important than anything in that room.'

François pulled her close. 'More important than our first vintage?'

'I'm pregnant,' said Nicole.

François buried his head in his hands. Was he hiding tears?

'I could taste everything so clearly and I just *knew*. I've known for a week, but I wanted to be sure. You have given me two gifts. A palate that can discern any grape, even its position on the Montagne, just by tasting. But best of all – a baby, François. We're going to be a family.'

François jumped up to face her, his jaw set. He had that wild animal look in his eye again, like the time at the well, as though she wasn't there. Her heart lurched.

'Jesus Christ, Nicole, why do you think I'd want to bring an innocent baby into this world? The poor child will be half me. There's a war on, no end of evil. How can you sit there smiling like you've turned lead to gold?'

He disappeared into the vines. It was the same as before. She waited, but he didn't return.

She couldn't breathe and nausea overcame her as the carriage sped her home in a blur, bumping through the vineyards, jolting her fragile bones. She ached for his arms around her and her baby, but he didn't come home.

Evening came, then night. Still no François. She fantasised about the knock on the door, the *sorry, it was such a shock, please forgive me, Babouchette.* At dawn, the bed was freezing and she was sick. She heaved herself up to clean the bowl. Josette would suspect and she couldn't tell anyone without him there. A knock at the door, a horse passing, sent her flying to the window for his return, only to be disappointed over and over again. Everything tasted false and she could barely eat without wanting to retch.

She and François had chosen to live mainly at their simple house at Bouzy, in the middle of the vineyards outside Reims, instead of their fashionable house in town. It was a mellow stone house, like a child's drawing, with a path leading to the front door, four symmetrical windows and an inviting glow at the hearth. A rough kitchen table where Josette prepared the food, wooden chairs and threadbare cushions in front of the fire, bookshelves overflowing with their favourite authors and wine manuals, always flooded with light, and until now, happiness. It was their hideaway, a far cry from the grand mansion she had grown up in at the rue de la Vache and it was easy to hide her grief here amongst the vines.

After a week passed, she told Josette that François had been called away unexpectedly on a sales trip. Her secret pregnancy created a wall between her and the people she loved. How could she talk to her mother without telling her? How could she face Natasha's piercing eyes without her just *knowing*? She buried her head in her wine manuals to distract herself from thinking about him every second. Between these pages, life was straightforward, one simple action of planting leading to an inevitable flowering, fruiting and yield, as long as you followed the rules.

November brought gloom and driving rain and misery, and finally François. He appeared, bedraggled from the storm, looking like a ghost, almost hidden by the biggest bunch of purple irises she had ever seen.

She tore them off him and flung them at the wind and they scattered over the garden like confetti.

'You abandoned me when I needed you,' she raged. 'Coward!'

'I'm worse than that, Babouchette. I'm that and everything that could be bad about a human being.' He looked haunted and gaunt.

'I'm sick, I'm weak and tired and pregnant and you just walked away. You're not the man I thought I married.' Everything was so mixed up. She was angry and hurt, yet so relieved to see him.

'Let me come in, Babouchette. It's still me, but there's a part of me I need to tell you about. The part who disappears when you need me most.'

She drew him inside, afraid.

'I need you here, all of you.' She moved the piled-up wine manuals off his chair and stoked the fire. 'Don't leave anything out. I'll try to understand.'

He held his hands to the flames.

'The well was so deep, you couldn't see the bottom of it the day you threw the coin. When the black descends, that's how I feel, like it's so deep it will never end and I have to get away before it overwhelms me. It comes when I'm happiest.'

'Happiness makes you unhappy?' she asked, trying to understand.

'You remember when we visited Calais? The beach glittered and the sea was flinty grey, like your eyes. The waves rolled in with such force, it was exhilarating and frightening to watch. The undertow, the very thing that creates the energy and excitement, could drag you under and drown you. That's how it is.'

'You're scaring me, François.'

'It *is* frightening. A winter sunrise is so beautiful and intense it hurts. A summer's evening in the vineyards turns a thousand different colours and the birdsong at dusk is deafening and I want to dance and sing and shout. Then I know I'll have to pay and it will turn to dust.'

'All those times we danced?' Something inside her turned cold with dread.

'I go to the river, you know the part where it's so wide you can't see to the other side?'

She nodded, turned away so he couldn't see the tears.

'Sometimes something bigger and more powerful like the river sweeps the despair away.'

How could she not have known this about the man she had married?

'I'm not strong enough for three. I need you here, with me,' she said.

'You have the whole of me, the dark and the light. You think I'm weak, I can see it in your eyes, but I *can* fight this. You just need to let me be alone sometimes. I promise I'll never leave again without telling you.'

'Give me some time to think, I need to try to understand. I *will* try, I promise.'

He put his hand on her stomach. 'How's our baby?'

'Missing his papa,' said Nicole. But she couldn't forgive him. It was her turn to leave.

Natasha narrowed her eyes.

'There is more than one thing,' she guessed. She was making dough, ready for the next day. She slapped it on the block and flour flew up in a cloud, waiting for Nicole to answer, kneading rhythmically.

'I'm pregnant,' she blurted and promptly burst into tears.

'*Milaya*, don't cry, it's a happy thing, no?'

Natasha gave her a floury hug, handed her a big napkin and held her tight until the tears subsided. She sat her down gently. There was flour everywhere – on her face, her dress, on Natasha's apron and hands. They both looked at each other and laughed.

'That's better,' said Natasha. 'Now, tell me everything.'

Natasha listened without interrupting. It was such a relief to tell her.

Natasha thought for a while. 'The Tsar's second cousin suffered in the same way. We heard about it in the palace kitchens when I was the pastry cook there. He was the most charming man I have ever met, apart from François.'

'Not so charming now.'

'*Yes*, charming. *Yes*, the right man for you. No one is perfect, my young friend, including you.'

How could she be on François' side?

'You want me to rail and shout and roll my eyes with you at how men are? Well I won't,' said Natasha. 'Look at yourself. You have a child inside you, something I was never blessed with, and God knows I have lain awake at night filled with regret and longing. Your husband is the most charming, intelligent man in Reims and he is yours. There is a saying in Russia. With the brighter light comes the darker shadow. I've seen the way he looks at you. No one else could make you so happy. When he's fragile, cherish him. Enjoy each other when he's well. Things can never stay the same. You knew in your heart how he was, and you married him anyway.'

Yes, she had seen it and buried it inside her. The fizzing, heightened gaiety, the days of deep despair she had mistaken for worry about the wine. She forged a straight path. Sharp-eyed, efficient, fair, astute, like her father. She got things done. François dreamed.

'How do you see so clearly, Natasha?'

'I've lived longer than you, that's all.'

'I've been meaning to ask you something since my wedding day.'

'Yes?'

'How did you know to decorate our wedding cake with crimson grapes? Did you know that François and I found a bunch the first day we met?'

A shadow flew across Natasha's face. 'You found bright red grapes? What was the first thing you thought of?'

'Blood. Fresh blood. The colour when you cut your knee and it's really red.'

'A strange coincidence, that's all, I suppose. I thought of them in a dream, with the red to symbolise love and of course to represent both of your love of the vines.' She opened the door for Nicole to leave. 'It's late. I need to finish my bread, *milaya*. Go back to him and be happy.'

When Nicole went into the night, back to their house in town, relieved, happy and scared all at once, she could see Natasha silhouetted, spinning her salt bag in furious figures of eight.

At their grand Reims house, the hall was filled with irises. Extravagant, fluffy, purple-scented bunches stood on the hall tables and in the vases next to the sweeping stairs, covered the marble mantelpiece, reflected a million times in the mirror-lined drawing room, lined up in jugs on the long dining room table.

'I got more than you could destroy,' said François. 'Where have you been? I was worried about you both.'

The *both* was the best part. She threw her arms around him. It was impossible to stay angry with him now he was back home, standing in front of her. She adored the way his dark eyebrows arched upwards in the middle when he smiled, opening up his angular, intelligent face into such an expression of delight at seeing her. He held her tight.

A man came marching into the hallway. He fished one of the irises out of a vase and put it in his buttonhole.

'Widow Joubert can surely take the rest of the year off, my friend. You must have bought the entire greenhouse.'

François shook his hand, beaming at Nicole. 'Let me introduce my oldest friend, Louis Bohne.'

A shock of russet hair, a ridiculously large wolfskin coat and a smile as warm as brandy. He bowed and kissed her hand. 'At last, François has done something sensible.'

'He's just back from Russia. You don't mind if he stays a few nights?' asked François.

'I have tales from ballrooms lined with amber, descriptions of fashions beyond your wildest dreams and dark deeds from bearded Cossacks to pay you with.'

'Just the dark deeds will do,' said Nicole, disappointed not to have François to herself, but charmed by this new friend.

Louis was the Clicquots' star travelling salesman and no sale, no village or town was too far. He would travel a hundred miles into the wilds of Norway for the prospect of selling a ten-year-old vintage for a week's wages, or brave the furthest-flung Russian steppe to reach a rich landowner's summer *dacha* to lay out a Clicquot champagne, blended by Monsieur Olivier himself at the most sophisticated, sun-kissed grand cru vineyards of Reims. Indeed, he was indispensable, and was a shareholder in François' fledgling business.

François poured a glass of their sweetest champagne.

Louis took an exaggerated slurp. 'A triumph of *terroir* and skills passed down for hundreds of years, from Dom Perignon and beyond.'

'Is this the puff you give your clients? It's more like going to the circus than buying a fine wine,' laughed Nicole.

It got so late that Josette made the fire twice, but still the tales flowed. Louis could barely sit still and told his stories pacing the room. He loved the open road, he said, the parties and the kitchen gossip.

François was on sparkling form and she took Natasha's advice to heart. Enjoy today.

The next morning, she woke before dawn. François was gone again. Her heart somersaulted at the note on the pillow.

Vine roots never die. They turn black in winter, but spring brings tender leaves to risk icy winds and thunderstorms and soak up the May sun. They see the sun rise, draw the mist to themselves in the early morning, take their food from the pale land, listen to the lark rise and fall in the summer. They catch the moon on their leaves, see stars leap, leaving

trails of shattered light. I can taste each vineyard and so
can you. We were meant to be together, but happiness has
turned to dust for now.

I don't ask forgiveness, but trust I will be back.

François

Slipping the note under her pillow with shaking hands, Nicole choked back the tears, and her fear. *Stay strong for him, and for our baby*, she told herself. *He always comes back.* But she couldn't just do nothing. The dawn turned vermilion, the same as their wedding morning, and with it a familiar determination. She dressed quickly, slipped out while the house was still asleep, and jumped on Pinot, her favourite colt, tying cloth on his hooves so no one would hear.

When she reached the Montagne, the vines were suspended in a cloud, above them a minted, clear sky. Further on, cold wind disturbed the surface of the pale lake where they had swum countless times. She pulled her cloak around her. Another mile downstream was where she prayed she'd find him.

Owls hooted and the hairs on the back of her neck bristled. Royalist rebels were known to terrorise the French countryside with their uprisings, and they communicated using owl calls. Innocent people, even women, were mistaken for republicans and were beaten in revenge. France was not a safe place to bring a child into. François was right about that.

She spurred on through the dawn light. The further she galloped, the wider the river, until she heard its roar. As she rounded the bend, there he was, boots in the furious torrent, the river so wide and fast here that its roar was shattering.

She edged closer, soothed her horse to be still so as not to startle him.

'François, I'm here,' she whispered.

He bellowed at the river, arms outstretched, shirt flying open in the wind.

'François!' she yelled.

He roared to the river and it roared back. One step forward and it would sweep him whirling down the raging tide.

Pinot understood. He didn't make a sound when she lashed him to a tree and rushed to François at the edge of the torrent. She barely felt the shock of cold as she waded in to reach him. The river pulled at her as she grabbed his shoulders and fell back with him, away from the current, using all her strength. She had him flat on dry ground before he could resist, snaring him with legs and arms outstretched. He rolled onto his back and pulled her to him.

'I'm here,' she whispered.

An eternity passed. He opened his eyes and focused on her, bewildered as a drunk.

'I knew where to find you, it's me, and I understand.'

He blinked. 'Talk to me.'

She counted to ten, then back down again.

'Louder.'

She named the grapes she knew, listed her school friends, the sums she could remember, anything, clinging to him, too afraid to move, the wet grass freezing them both as she screwed up her eyes and willed her François back to himself.

Heavy footsteps snapped her eyes open. Louis had come.

'How did you know?'

'This is how it is with him, I've known him all my life, it's best to let him be,' he said quietly. 'Take my hand.'

He helped her up and put his jacket round her shoulders. François was soaked and shivering and Louis showed them both into the waiting carriage, promising to walk back later for Pinot.

*

Louis knew what to do. The three of them spent long days around François' bed, playing cards, telling stories, staring into the fire. They took turns to keep watch and, after a week, François began to join in with the stories. When it was Nicole's turn and Louis was busy, François and she made plans for their baby. Their child would learn to ride as naturally as walking, memorise a poem every week and if they had a girl, she would be everything and anything she wanted to be, with curls like François' and grey eyes like Nicole's.

When it was time for Louis to leave for his next sales trip, Nicole kissed him.

'I'll never forget everything you've done for us. Ever,' she smiled.

'It's the worst I've seen him,' he said as he loaded the cart with crates of wine to travel to Paris. 'He must love you very much.'

CHAPTER 5

August 1805

Republican date: Thermidor, year XIII

Firefly

Clémentine ran, skirting the sunlit roses, sousing the air with sharp lavender as she skimmed the silver bushes. Jelly-legged with giggles, she staggered and collapsed in a heap of muslin and curls. Nicole caught her, scooped her up and spun her around, laughing at the sky.

She buried her face in her daughter's hair, breathing in the childish smell. Her blonde curls were so like her sister's. Two Clémentines in her life, sister and daughter, carbon copies of each other. Her little daughter was a delight, and she never imagined she could love anyone as completely and fiercely as she did her darling Mentine. François looked on from the terrace, waving a letter. She picked a piece of lavender, remembered the day Moët had proposed, and luxuriated in her choices.

'Let's go and see what Papa is doing.' They set off, holding hands. 'You can ask him all about our trip to Russia.'

'Are we going now?'

'Not now, but soon, Mentine. Can you remember how old you are?'

'Five.'

'That makes it seven years since he promised me, on our wedding night. In Russia we'll tuck you up in furs and take you on sleigh rides, show you the palaces and towers topped with blue and gold onions.'

'You can't get blue and gold onions, silly!'

'You can in Russia.'

François put Mentine on his knee, ruffling her strawberry curls and passed the letter to Nicole, with a trembling hand.

> *Moscow is a disaster. It's rotten to the core, and bad faith is the order of the day. There are at least three people to bribe for every sale and no profits to be made whatsoever in this glittering hellhole. No wonder the palaces are made of gold and amber; all the money is kept for a privileged few. The excess of luxury means that brokers like me, after all costs are deducted, gain nothing. Foreign companies are seen as nanny goats ready for milking. Even if I do secure orders, it is unlikely we will ever get paid. I am sorry, my friend, to write such bad news, especially in a year where the harvest promises no hope for the coming years.*

> *Louis*

Nicole slumped on the chair next to François. Sending Louis to Russia had been a mistake. Napoléon's advance across Europe was voracious. Britain and Russia were now allies against the French, and Louis would be caught up in it all. Their sunlit garden was a long way away, but the endless war wouldn't leave them alone.

'He must stay and keep trying. If anyone can do it, he can. He's defied the odds a million times and the only alternative is to sell everything up to Moët. You know he'd pay over the odds for anything we'd sell him, he's so desperate to push us out of the business,' said François, his angular face pale and delicate as glass, even in the hot sun.

She would recall Louis immediately, without telling François. Their friend, the man who could charm his way out of any sticky situation, was clearly in danger and she refused to risk his life. England and Russia, their biggest markets, would do anything to thwart France and in particular the trade of one of its proudest exports: champagne. The very thing that was their lifeblood was becoming a casualty of war. She worried François was becoming one, too.

They had packed Louis off with such hope, riding a wave of stellar sales in Prussia and Austria.

'Forget London,' François had urged, his blue-green eyes glittering, 'and those pasty-faced English. There's a fortune for us in Russia. The palaces are dripping with gold.'

Louis had ridden off wearing his wolfskin coat and a rogue's grin, with seventy-five thousand bottles of their finest vintages, pretty much all the stock they had.

'Papa. Are there really blue and gold onions in Russia?' Clémentine asked excitedly.

'Of course! And orange potatoes and pink peas. Go and find Josette for your lunch. I need to talk to Maman.' He waved. 'I love you, *je t'aime*!'

'*Moi aussi, Papa.*'

'Never forget it!'

But Mentine was already skipping to the door.

'We're not going to Russia, I'm sorry,' said François.

'What for?'

'I promised to take you. I promised to look after you. You should have taken Moët's offer. Those English are eating out of the palm of his hand and Napoléon will be guzzling Moët's champagne at his ball tonight.'

Nicole shook her head. 'Would Moët have made me laugh? Would he have taken me swimming in the lake, or let me have a hand in his precious vineyards? Don't consign me to hell with him. I wanted you then, and I want you now.'

He looked at her in despair. 'The vineyards are hell now, Babouchette. There's nothing we can do. The grapes are withered like raisins before we've even had a chance to pick them. Louis took all we had with him and half the champagne stock was cloudy when it arrived. It was a gamble and you can't gamble with nature. It's beaten us. I should never have sent everything.'

Cloudy champagne. Every producer's curse, caused by sediment. It took months of labour to turn bottles in the sand in an attempt to coax out the sediment caused by the yeast, which was essential to the taste and second fermentation, but which left their beautiful creations *bleu*, cloudy. Thousands of bottles and thousands of hours of labour. They'd tried everything, including releasing the sediment by *transversage*, pouring the clear wine from one bottle to the other once the sediment was released, but at the expense of the all-important fizz. She shuddered at the memory of the time she'd bought a 'clarifier' product from the barrel-supplier, and almost killed one of her top tasters with the poisonous stuff. In that, their business was no different to anyone else's, but the person who could solve the sediment conundrum with no loss of fizz would be rich, that much was certain.

His spine protruded through his thin jacket. François' moods swung with the highs and lows of the business and now, he was dangerously low.

It was then that Nicole made a pact with herself, just as binding as the one she made the day of the revolution when she promised to build her own wealth and to use her power for good. This second one was for François. She didn't know how, or when, but *she* would solve the sediment conundrum. It would make them rich and successful, but most of all, the advantage over their competitors would be such that François would never need to worry about their business again.

'We'll weather one bad harvest,' she said cheerfully. 'Of course we will. It's happened before. Look at me.' She pressed her palm to his cheek. It was slick with sweat. 'The black well again? Despair? You can't see the bottom?'

'I feel terrible.' He tried to muster a smile for her. 'But I don't want you to worry. Not tonight.'

'Go to bed, *chéri*, you'll feel better in the morning.'

'No! We're going to Moët's ball or he'll think it's sour grapes if we don't. I've promised to play the violin and, anyway, I love showing the world you're mine.'

Her heart leapt, still, after seven years of marriage. Louis' letter didn't mean ruin, just a bad year, like the others.

Nicole went to her study. She'd prove to François how a bad year was quickly followed by a good one, maybe two, then back the other way again. She unlocked the drawer and pulled out the ledger. He couldn't argue with the black and red ink. Here, neatly in the thick pages of profit and loss was the cycle of hope and ruin they had faced since the day they had married. She preferred to contemplate it like this. Dispassionate, neatly added up and taken away. No pain, no dashed hopes, just ink on paper.

She looked back to five years ago. Bottles ruined in the heat: twenty thousand. Losses: thirty thousand francs. Bottles shipped: thirty-five thousand two hundred. Labourers paid: two thousand francs.

The figures didn't show the months spent tending the vines, digging the earth, tying the shoots to poles, the blending, nothing of the workers looking for portents in the stars, praying to the harvest saint.

She turned a couple of pages: 1802. The Treaty of Amiens. Peace with Britain and an opening up of the trade routes again. She, Louis and François had leapt to the violin, loaded their best samples of 1800 vintage champagne into a trunk for Louis and sent him off to London. It was another disaster. Moët had a stranglehold on the market, strutting around all the grand houses, hiding his support for the overthrow of the French aristocracy, playing cards, dancing their mannered dances, shooting a hundred-weight of unsuspecting pheasants out of the sky, handing out phials of his wines.

'It's a closed world,' Louis had complained. 'They're terrified of the revolution and they look at me like I'm a criminal.'

That summer, like this one, the sun would not leave them alone. While her sister idled in the sultry heat, boating on the Vesle River with her friends, she and François watched the grapes shrivel on the vines. She had cursed the sun and closed the shutters in the house, dreaming of foggy mornings and dewy grapes.

She ran her finger down the ledger. Last April was the beginning of their current disaster: seventy-five thousand bottles had set off, bound for Russia. More than their entire sales for 1804. She left the next entry clear to see how things turned out. It could easily come right yet.

François peered round the door. 'Mugging up in your study again, Babouchette?' He kissed her head and she leant back into his arms, hastily putting her hand over the numbers in the red deficit column.

'Come and get ready,' said François. 'We can't change anything, however hard you stare at the figures. I have something for you.

And don't worry about Mentine, she's already tucked up in bed. She fell asleep while I told her a story about a young girl with strawberry curls who defied a man with a gun, right here in the cathedral square during the revolution.' He kissed her. 'Mentine always look so sublimely peaceful asleep.'

His about-turn of mood filled her with optimism. Why not start right now?

'Give me ten minutes, I'll be up!' she breathed through his kisses.

She hurried outside and across to the press, filled a box with sand and picked four bottles of champagne that were in second fermentation.

'Don't touch those ones, they're nearly ready and you'll dislodge the sediment!' scolded Antoine.

'We can spare them, and I'll bet two of them will be cloudy however careful you've been,' she countered, feeling giddy as a schoolgirl.

Antoine tutted and returned to his work, shaking the bottles one by one and replacing them in the sand.

Nicole spirited her bottles away to a dark corner in the basement of the house and carefully placed them upside down in the sandbox, stood back and brushed the sand off her hands. This would be her secret – she had no idea how, but she would do it. No matter that a resolution had eluded champagne producers down the ages; she planned to observe, learn, experiment and start again, for François. If she could solve the sediment problem, shorten the time it took to slowly turn and shake the bottles to coax the sediment to the neck of the bottle – riddling, Antoine called it – and make sure every bottle was reliably clear in a shorter time, François would never need to worry again. She imagined his delight at her clever idea, locked the door behind her and ran upstairs to join him.

François was waiting for her, smiling. 'Your cheeks are flushed, you've been running. Is this one of your schemes? Sit down for a minute and close your eyes, Babouchette.'

She sat on the bed, closed her eyes tight and felt a heavy package and the rustle of wrapping drop onto her hands.

'Now open them.'

François was himself again, ready for the ball, unruly hair tamed for the occasion, a striking, long-limbed figure in his embroidered coat and slim trousers. More handsome than ever, she thought proudly.

Thick paper printed in gold and blue hid the contents of the parcel from her. She tore it open to reveal a red velvet dress, and a box. She picked up the dress first and held it up against her.

'As beautiful as the day I met you. I bought it for you to wear in Russia, but you might as well wear it tonight. Put it on, then open the box.'

She slipped it on. The red velvet was the same colour as the crimson grapes they found on the day they met. She knew he would think the same.

'Open the box.'

Inside was a Russian doll that looked remarkably like François. She looked up in surprise.

'Keep opening.'

The next doll was her. Grey eyes, straight strawberry blonde hair and a red velvet dress, the same as the new one she was wearing. Next was a little Clémentine, with the same colour hair, but curly, and her father's blue-green eyes.

'It's us. I love it!'

'Open the little one. There's more.'

Inside the smallest doll was a gold chain hung with a filigree insect. She held it up to the light. It was a firefly, intricately enamelled and underneath a yellow gem body, cut so it shattered the candle flame.

'A yellow diamond. A firefly and champagne all mixed up in one rare combination, like you. If I go first, remember me by it. Now get ready, we'll be late for the ball and it can't start until the most glamorous couple in Reims arrive.'

He kissed her and left.

Josette helped pile her hair up. The necklace glowed like a honey moon on her skin. François made the darkest days into the loveliest.

At Moët's mansion in Épernay, torches lit the way, through the grounds to a Petit Trianon, Louis XV's fashionable classical Greek-style mansion at Versailles, which Moët had built a faithful replica of in honour of his friend Napoléon. And, of course, to honour himself.

'A replica monument for a replica king,' pronounced François to Jean-Rémy.

Moët clicked his heels and nodded in reply, François' sarcasm lost on him. Nicole giggled.

The first three dances were theirs. The waltz was her favourite. He whispered into her hair and spun her so fast her feet lifted off the ground and she was flying, oblivious to the rest of the world. After that, he was no longer hers. He never was at a ball or party. It was on these vast, glittering stages that François came into his own and she left him to his stories to join the tasting committee for vineyard gossip.

Since the day of her first tasting committee meeting, she had forged herself a place as something of a novelty, an honorary man, so nobody batted an eyelid when she joined the circle of men, pulling on fat cigars. She lit a thin cigar for herself, crinkling her nose at the unaccustomed smoke.

'Oat is definitely superior to flax to tie the vines,' pronounced Monsieur Olivier, rolling his burgundy around the glass, checking the legs.

'Oat. No question,' she agreed. 'Flax is far too rough on new shoots.'

'Quite right, Madame Clicquot. And what, may I ask, is your opinion on the best rose to indicate greenfly?'

He passed her the decanter of burgundy. Ten years old at least, deliciously earthy with notes of leather, cherry and mushrooms.

As she sipped, a man in a blue coat edged with gold braid appeared and bowed to the group. His dark fringe was cut high above his forehead and hung square below his ears in *tresses oreille de chien*, dog's-ear style, with a pigtail at the back. His skin was a sallow yellow and his deep-set eyes had a penetrating, feverish gaze.

'May I join you, gentlemen?' The man turned to Nicole and bowed again. 'And lady?'

'*Oui, bien sûr.*' Monsieur Olivier stubbed his cigar and scrambled for a suitable chair for the leader of all of France, General Napoléon. It had been rumoured he would be in attendance.

Everyone shuffled down one place.

Napoléon sucked on a fat cherry, his favourite fruit, apparently.

'I hear you *messieurs* are the best producers in these parts,' he addressed them with a winning, radiant smile.

They rushed to introduce themselves. Nicole kept quiet. Being a woman and going unnoticed occasionally served her well – it was his bloody wars that were at the heart of her troubles today.

The committee, *her* committee, were rapt. Not content with meddling in the whole of Europe, there was apparently nothing Napoléon didn't know about winemaking. What he didn't know could be answered in the pamphlet *he* had commissioned, Chaptal's *L'art de faire, gouverner et perfectionner le vin*. A copy was handed to her, as if it was the Holy Bible itself. Chemistry had been elevated over centuries of knowledge handed down from family to family and the *feel* of the *terroir*, watching the sky for the weather. She flicked through. Some of it *did* make sense. To control some of the processes, mitigate some of the elements of chance would certainly change things for her and François, especially if she succeeded with her riddling experiment. However much she disliked the man, he had done his homework.

Polished buttons and a sash interrupted her thoughts. Napoléon was standing right over her. 'You are absorbed in Chaptal instead of dancing, Madame…?'

She held out her hand for him to kiss.

'Madame Clicquot. I don't agree with all of it, but some of it isn't bad for a chemist.'

'And how would you know so much, may I ask, Madame Clicquot?' he asked, amused.

'I have a hand in winemaking with my husband. Method and chemistry might help the uninitiated, but there is no substitute for an instinct for the *terroir*, the grape on your tongue, the soil between your fingers.'

'Are you suggesting that I am uninitiated?'

The committee looked on in horror.

'You must be very busy with your wars. Leave the wine to the experts.'

Monsieur Olivier let out an involuntary harumph at her audacity. Some of the others turned away to disassociate themselves.

'Of which you are the leader?' continued Napoléon provocatively.

'One of them.'

He laughed. 'You would have loved my old aunt Geltruda. She tended the vines with her own hands and taught me to love them.' He took her hands. 'Tsk-tsk, as rough as hers, and so young.'

'Working hands. Stupid to be trapped in drawing rooms full of painted dolls.'

He winked at the committee. 'Gives you boys a run for your money? These are tiny hands and that's good in a woman. My aunt *had* to work the land. I take it you don't?'

'I choose to.'

'A good revolutionary woman's place is to produce strong sons and beautiful daughters for our great republic. You're too delicate for field work, Madame Clicquot. Leave it to your husband. *Enchanté.*'

He sauntered off, surrounded by the committee, who were now his enthusiastic acolytes.

If you ever return, you will be drinking my *champagne and thanking me for it*, Nicole projected to his back.

'Don't mind him,' a dark-haired woman who had been listening from behind the committee whispered in her ear. 'A general has to be a complete arse if he's going to win. It goes with the territory. Believe me, I know men better than anyone. I'm trying to avoid that one over there.' She pointed to a red-faced soldier. 'Mind if I join you? Just keep talking.' She slumped into a chair and fanned herself. She was barefoot, a ring on every toe, with very short hair and a thin red ribbon around her neck. She held out her hand. 'Thérésa Tallien.'

Nicole took it and introduced herself, captivated.

Thérésa Tallien – the legend! Her short hair and red ribbon was called *coiffure à la victime*. A close shave with the guillotine indicated good breeding in Paris and the fashion was to flaunt it. Everyone knew about Napoléon's wife, Joséphine Bonaparte, and her friend Thérésa. Queens of the Paris salons. Thérésa had scandalously divorced her second husband, and had at least eight children by about three different men. In 1794, Thérésa and Joséphine had been jailed in a filthy cell at *La Petite Force* for seventeen days, waiting for the guillotine. The story went that her lover, Jean-Lambert Tallien, stabbed Robespierre to death with a Spanish dagger, a gift from Thérésa. Jean-Lambert was now a national hero for the overthrow of the guillotine's biggest advocate. Since then, Thérésa was known as 'Notre Dame de Thermidor', but even murder was not enough to snare this exotic butterfly. She bored of Tallien and divorced him, setting herself free to roam around with Joséphine and Napoléon in outrageous fashions, with rings on her toes. Nicole stayed put, fascinated.

'Do you, darling?' Thérésa asked.

'Do I what?'

'Deal in men, of course. What else? Don't think I didn't spot you, holding those poor men in your spell.'

Nicole laughed. 'Wine's my trade. These men are from the tasting committee. They begrudgingly allow me to talk to them about business.'

'Nonsense, you have them all enthralled.'

Her Spanish accent rolled the words like hot coals and she had the straightest, whitest row of teeth. She pointed to Napoléon with a long fingernail. 'He favours Moët's champagne. Never stops talking about the fine bubbles, the taste of France. Joséphine and I must have polished off crates of it just between the two of us. It really is the only drink a lady should consider. Which is why I drink whisky.'

Nicole spat her wine out laughing.

François appeared at her side. 'Spitting!' he said proudly. 'Not content with instructing the wine committee, I hear you have pressed your superior knowledge on our illustrious leader. I hope your harsh words won't ruin us.'

Thérésa gave him an intense stare. 'Who's this you've been hiding all evening? Do you know each other, because if not, I suggest you make sure you do.'

'My husband, François.' She introduced her new friend to him.

'Oh, you've bagged him already. Well done, my dear, your impeccable taste clearly stretches beyond the vineyards. In that case, I'll leave him to you.'

'If I didn't have to spend so much time cleaning up after my wife's loose tongue, I'm sure I'd find the time to get to know you better, Madame Tallien.'

'Next time I need someone to put Joséphine's husband in his place, I'll know where to send him. Nicole seems very keen on this wine business of yours, but I fear Napoléon has been a bit of an irritation to her plans.'

'And mine,' said François. 'All our most lucrative markets abroad are closed to us.'

'Then I will have to make up for my friend's bad manners. I'll introduce you, *mes amours*. There are crates of champagne sloshing around at every salon I go to in Paris. A vivacious country girl and a handsome husband, making their own champagne. They'll adore you. I'll send for you as soon as I can arrange it. That's a promise.'

'The Paris markets are the dream for us. We do have some contacts, but an introduction from you would be wonderful,' smiled Nicole, slightly mesmerised by this beguiling woman. With a recommendation from the notorious, glittering Madame Tallien, their troubles could be over.

'I break my marriage vows every now and then, any sensible girl should, but I never break a promise to friends. Now, I suggest you take your wife to the dance floor before she's stolen away from under your nose.'

The room whirled as they danced. The prospect of introductions from the queen of Paris society would be a godsend, if they could find anything in the cellars to sell. The new hope buoyed up François, who was in wild spirits.

When Nicole was too dizzy to dance any more, they stepped outside for some air. A big orange harvest moon hung in the sky and the stars were bright and clear.

'Let's spend the night in the hut, my firefly. We can share my horse and Josette can watch Clémentine.'

Yes, thought Nicole. With Paris secured, why not forget their cares for a while with a night at their secret hideaway?

The horse galloped through the dusky vineyards, the moon lighting their way until they arrived at the shepherd's hut. The room was prepared as it had been on their wedding night. All the lanterns were lit and the bed piled up with furs, the samovar bubbling and a fire in the grate.

'You planned this!'

'Our anniversary. Did you forget again, Babouchette? Too busy with your head in those ledgers.'

The gifts he'd given her before the ball made sense now – how could she have forgotten?

'Shut up and kiss me.' She closed her eyes.

'It's cold.' He turned away. 'I'll make us a hot toddy.'

She took the glasses, disappointed. 'What's the matter? Your hands are shaking so much the glasses are clinking. Here, let me help you. Get under the covers.'

She got in next to him, put her head on his chest and gazed up at the stars. He was ice cold, even under a pile of furs. A fixed roof would help on this derelict old place. What were they thinking, dashing here on an unseasonably cold night?

'See that one, straight above? Orion, the hunter. The three vertical stars are his sword. I used to think while he was in the sky that I was protected, but I'm not so sure now.'

'What do you mean?'

His voice was distant; something wasn't right.

She turned to kiss him, but he was already asleep, his breathing shallow and fitful. Clouds covered the moon and the sky turned damp grey. François shuddered in his sleep. She pulled the covers up to his chin and wished they were at home with a fire burning.

Sleep eluded her. Nicole got up, walked out into the night air so she could think, stumbling while her eyes got used to the dark.

They'd ploughed everything they had into the business. Regret was useless, but it caught in her throat, weighed her shoulders. Things hadn't ever been this bad.

She kept walking. Owls called unspoken regrets into the night. Dawn was a watery streak in a grey sky, revealing shrivelled vine leaves and dried-out grapes.

She trudged back to the hut and touched his cheek to gently wake him. Brushing a fly from his eye, she gasped. It was wet. She bent closer. Blood! She grabbed a lantern and held it close to his face. He was crying blood! She pulled him upright. He slumped to the side. She shook him. He grunted, but didn't wake. She dabbed the blood with her dress.

'François! François, for God's sake, wake up,' she whispered. Then screamed. 'Help! Someone. Help us!'

A flock of starlings screeched overhead.

She ran to the door. Thank God, workers were moving amongst the vines. 'Help!'

A figure came running, brandishing a stick. Xavier. She dragged him to François.

'Christ.' He felt for a pulse and crossed himself. 'Jesus Christ. Holy mother of God. Stay with him. I'll get the doctor.'

'Hurry!' she croaked.

She warmed him with her body. Covered his hands with hers, entwined her legs with his. He didn't move. She prayed. She cried. The embers hissed and spat. The starlings shifted direction in the sky. She knew then his soul was leaving. She pressed her body tighter against his.

'Don't go, François. Stay with me.'

Then she saw it, on the ground next to the bed. An empty phial of rat poison.

'Sweet Jesus, François.'

She checked herself. Just a coincidence. Everyone kept rat poison somewhere on their property.

Horses' hooves threw up dust at the door. She shoved the phial under the bed.

The doctor rushed in. Warm hands helped her up.

'Let me look at him, Madame.'

He tried to rouse François, listened for his heart, felt his pulse, on one wrist, then the other. He turned to face Nicole and shook his head gravely.

'I'm sorry.'

Her knees gave way as she tried to push past the doctor to reach his lifeless body.

Xavier helped her up and led her gently to the fire. 'Let him do his work.' He kept his hand on her shoulder, bowing his head.

The doctor pulled away the bedclothes, unbuttoned François' waistcoat and shirt. She gasped. Black spots covered his skin.

'Typhoid, Madame. A classic case.'

She hid her face in Xavier's jacket. He hadn't taken the poison, she couldn't have prevented it and he didn't want to leave her, but what difference did it make now?

The doctor continued, 'The black spots, the bleeding. It's very contagious. It's taken half the camp of soldiers out on the plain. It's the close quarters that spreads it. I'm so sorry, Madame Clicquot. It comes quickly. Xavier will take you home. Leave the rest to me. I will prescribe something to help you sleep.'

'You're not the usual doctor.' Why did she care about that now when her world had just fallen apart?

'Doctor Moreau. Xavier knows me and you can leave everything with me. Your family doctor is away, I'm afraid. Now sleep.'

The sleeping powder drained her strength, but Nicole couldn't sleep and the tears wouldn't stop. Clémentine's hand turned cold in hers as she muttered about heaven and a deathly reunion.

'Will he come back?' she asked, her voice quavering.

'No, sweetheart. He won't come back.'

'Why do you look sad? I'm scared. I want Papa!'

'Come here, Mentine. Just give me a cuddle.'

Mentine was rigid in her arms.

Sleep came, then went. Every time she woke, she remembered, and it broke her anew. When her parents arrived, they prised Mentine's fingers off her, took her away and sent her to bed, tucking the sheets in tight as a grave.

Nicole woke at dawn. François was there in the half-light. She reached out but he was gone. Shadows breathed loneliness. Among it all, a question like an alarm bell clanging inside her head.

Rain battered down all day, lashed the windows all night. Nicole flung the sleeping powder in the bin. Useless. No powder could smudge reality. A lit candle chased away the shadows. She blew it out, in case he was there, in the darkness, needing her. The night of Moët's ball turned to nightmares. She hadn't noticed enough, too busy showing off to Napoléon, not seeing his suffering. God didn't care about her prayers for sleep, and the night stretched into longing.

The next day dawned, dragging up a weak, reluctant sun, the rain still falling in rods. She was in their grand town house – she couldn't bear to visit their little sunlit house in Bouzy where they had been so happy – so she could slip straight into town unnoticed, and find out the answers to her burning questions. If she left now, the household would still be asleep.

She scrabbled in her drawer for her black veil and slipped out of the back door. The rain froze her dress to her skin; her heartbeat churned in her ears. She laboured through the familiar streets, now unfamiliar, as on the day of the revolution. A new, dangerous place.

She hurried to the side of town, where human waste ran in the gutters, and hunted down the sign, a skull and crossbones. Inside, a pockmarked girl with scarred hands emerged from behind the counter.

'A bottle of rat poison, for an infestation in my daughter's room.'

The girl clucked in sympathy and reached to the top shelf. 'This should do it, Madame. A few drops where they're entering the room and a few near the droppings.' She flicked a clean sheet of paper over on the pad and licked her pencil. 'Address so we can clean up when they're dead? Two francs extra. Well worth it.'

'No need. My stable boy knows what to do. There is something that worries me, though: my daughter's very young. What would happen if she ate some by mistake?'

'Make sure she doesn't, Madame, it's horrible. I've seen it myself. Blood out of your eyes, the flesh on the body bruised as a plum with black marks. We advise moving out of the room during the treatment, Madame.'

Nicole pressed a coin on the counter, took the poison and fled. Outside, she retched, poured the poison over her vomit and watched it snake into the open sewer. She fumbled for a lavender bag, choked back more bile and tears and stumbled on. Somehow she got back to the square. The stalls were out, the cathedral still there, just a normal day.

The same symptoms. Would things have been different if she hadn't left him in the night?

CHAPTER 6

December 1805

Revolutionary date: Frimaire, year XIV

Wax Tears

The marble entrance hall of their house in town was filled with irises. He was waiting for her, with armfuls more of them, rain lashing the windows. Her heart filled, but then he was crying, tears of blood sliding down his gaunt cheeks.

Nicole woke with a start, rolled onto his side of the bed. Dead four months. Today was his thirty-first birthday.

Mentine was humming in the bedroom next door. When was the last time she had held her daughter? She couldn't remember. Dragging herself out of bed, she peeped through the crack. Mentine was having a tea party in the nursery with the Russian dolls François had given her, a little cake in front of the father.

'Happy birthday, Papa,' her little daughter voiced.

'You remembered! Blue and gold onions. Yum, my favourite. How did you know they tasted of sugar?' said the papa doll.

'You told me yesterday, silly, so I flew to Russia and got them in a purple field.'

Mentine lifted the mother and child dolls and huddled them together against the father, then poured them each a cup of tea.

When Nicole went in, Mentine slid the papa under the table and carried a cup to Nicole, face scrunched in concentration, slopping water.

'We're having a party. Tea, Madame?'

Nicole sipped the tea. 'Delicious. Good job I'm so little. I can fit into the Mummy's chair.'

'Would you care for cake, Madame?'

'*Merci, ma petite,*' said Nicole. 'Is it someone's birthday?'

'No. Me and Josette made it for fun. It's chocolate.'

'Doesn't Papa want some?'

'He's not at this party.'

'Why not?'

'He's in Russia. He'll be back next year,' she said firmly.

Nicole picked up the doll from under the table and put him back in his chair.

'Oh, look. He's back now.'

'No!' Mentine flung it across the room. The doll broke in half and she stamped her foot. 'You'll be sad and go away and I want you to stay and play.'

'I'll stay and I won't be sad, I promise.' But Nicole felt that her heart would snap.

'Don't talk about Papa!'

'Why?'

'It makes you sad. I'm not allowed.'

'Of course you are.'

'Do you want strawberries or tomatoes and jam on your bread?'

'Hmm, tomatoes and jam, I think. Sit on my knee and we'll eat them together. I'm not sad now, am I? *You* make me happy.'

Mentine cuddled in. Her warm little body felt so sweet, and Nicole stiffened against a threatening tear.

'Now you're sad. Everyone always lies to me!'

'I'm sad that Papa isn't here and so are you, but that's all right. You can be happy *and* sad at the same time. The good thing is, we have all the special memories of Papa between us. Let's make a new rule, *ma petite.* From now on, we start and finish each day by talking about Papa. You go first.'

'He crossed his eyes and fell over and made me laugh,' began Mentine, entering into the spirit of this new game.

'He told us what all the stars in the sky were called.'

'He kissed you and it was disgusting!' Mentine giggled.

'He took you riding on his fastest horse.'

'He made up stories about cats.'

'It's his birthday today,' said Nicole.

'I made him a cake.'

'His favourite is sweet blue and gold onions, isn't it?'

'How did you know?' Mentine's eyes were round with astonishment, and Nicole's heart melted.

'Of course we both know. He was your papa and my husband and he belonged to us both. Between us we can remember everything and never forget him.'

Nicole picked up the doll, pieced it back together and replaced it at the table, swallowing a lump of grief.

'See? I'm not crying. You can talk about your papa whenever you like. Sometimes we will be happy and sometimes we'll be sad, but I'll never go away from you again, Mentine. Now, I've got a good idea. Let's go to Natasha's and buy a real cake. We can celebrate together, just you and me, and talk about the things we remember.'

'Yes please, Maman! Can I choose? Can I hold your hand all the way there? Can we skip?'

'All of those things.'

*

How could everything be the same? She hadn't been to the *boulangerie* since François had died, but here it was, the long swirl of the brass handle polished to within an inch of its life, the big wooden door and brass step scrubbed, and a brazen display of patisseries in the window.

'*Bonjour*, Nicole,' Natasha said stiffly.

'*Bonjour.*'

She hadn't seen her friend since the funeral. Natasha hadn't visited once, and on one rare occasion when she had ventured out, to breathe the outside air and escape the ghosts in the house, Natasha had crossed the road to avoid her. Nicole didn't have the strength to question Natasha on her unaccountable behaviour.

'We need that one,' said Mentine, pointing to a luscious *millefeuille*, the biggest cake in the shop. 'We're having a party.'

'Oh? What's the occasion, *ma petite?*' Her demeanour completely changed and softened speaking to her daughter.

'Me and Maman are having a tea party for Papa.'

Natasha whisked away the cake, expressionless, out to the back and shut the door to wrap it, then called Mentine to collect it. Nicole longed for a sign of affection from her friend. Perhaps she thought everything was her fault. After all, Natasha had been the one to warn her about caution before everything had fallen apart and she had ignored her.

Mentine came out with one of Natasha's special packages, neatly wrapped with gold ribbon. 'She said as it was for Papa and I was such a good girl that it's a gift from her.'

'*Merci*, Natasha!' Nicole shouted to the back, but there was no reply and she felt lonelier than ever.

That evening, Nicole put Mentine to bed and, the minute she was asleep, she ran downstairs to the empty drawing-room and sobbed. The evenings were the worst. People were kind, but she missed him just being there, no effort, no ceremony, just the two of them chatting about the day. She hadn't visited her secret riddling room since he died, either. Hard to imagine that a time had existed where she was so full of optimism about the future that she thought she was capable of anything. The corner of the basement where she hid the riddling sandbox and upturned bottles seemed utterly pointless and stupid now.

The battered leather chair he loved still described his shape, but it was fading. Next to the chair, a spindly table held a pile of books he read to her from: Diderot, Rousseau, and the manual that was just an endless list of grape varietals – but it was their favourite. They both loved the sounds of the grapes they'd never heard of. Whole evenings were spent guessing where they came from – Clairette, Muscat d'Alexandrie, Aramon, Auxerrois blanc (easy!), Jacquère.

She opened his violin case. It was gloomy and dark, but she knew it so well that she didn't need to see. Yellow velvet, turned mustard with age. A box of resin falling apart, warm wood and scrolled f-holes, brought to life in his hands, filling the room. She held it up to her chin to feel him against her. Nothing.

When Josette came to announce a caller, she waved her away. The well-meaning scrutiny, sympathy and subsequent forced reassurances from her were worse than anything.

'Sorry, Madame, it's just Xavier and he says it's urgent.'

'In that case, send him in, thank you, Josette.'

His Sunday best was stretched incongruously over his broad chest and his cap was pulled down stoutly on his forehead.

'What are you doing sitting here in the dark all on your own?'

'Sit anywhere, apart from that leather chair.'

Xavier perched awkwardly, legs apart. Dear Xavier, always her stalwart through the years, and her most trusted overseer at the vineyards.

'I'm no good at pussyfooting around, so I'm coming straight to the point,' he said.

'It must be important if you've chosen me instead of Etienne's opening time.'

'It *is* important. I can't think of another way to put it, but Clicquot Ponsardin and Company has gone to hell.'

'*What?*' This was not what Nicole had been expecting to hear.

'The harvest wasn't brought in, the grapes are still hanging there shrivelled like an old man's bollocks, Monsieur Olivier and his tasting gang are off sniffing for Moët and the press yard is covered in milkweed. I know this is a delicate time for you, and I've left it as long as I can. The weeds and the grapes don't matter so much, it's just it's Christmas and none of us have been paid since the end of September.'

'September! I only know the date because it's his birthday today, but that's nearly three months. I've left you all to cope without me. You know you could have come to me earlier. I've just been so...'

'You don't need to apologise to *me*. I knew you wouldn't mind my saying, though. But... his birthday, today? I'm so sorry. Terrible timing on my part.'

'And you, Xavier, you don't have to be kind! It will only make me worse. Look, I'm writing you a cheque now. I know what courage it must have taken for you to come and talk to me, and I'm grateful. You must always feel that you can. People are scared to talk to me about anything meaningful, and it feels like living in cotton wool.'

'Just write the bloody cheque and let me get to Etienne's. I'll raise a toast to him, don't you worry, he was a good man. I wish I could do more for you. I'll cash the cheque tomorrow and if it's all right with you I can dole it out. I know where the wage slips are down at the press. You look like you could do with a good night's sleep.'

She scrawled out the cheque, noticing the ledger, open at the place she had last left it, blank for good news, the day François died. Her beautiful, clever husband had loved this business and her, in equal measures. He had made them both into poetry. And now all was turned to ashes. She'd been in such a fog that everything but her sharp grief had been a blur, just a meaningless background to the searing vision of François lifeless in their secret hideaway. Any good memories of him just made it worse. She'd neglected the business and refused all visitors. The only person she'd have liked to have seen was Natasha, but her friend had inexplicably abandoned her in her hour of need, which just completed her overwhelming sense of loss.

She slammed the ledger shut and handed over the cheque.

'I've got something else to say…' began Xavier.

'Oh really – how long have we known each other?' said Nicole. 'Just come right out and say it.'

'Still got the scar where you hit me with that bloody stick. We were four.'

'Then tell me what it is, Xavier.'

'They're saying he should have been buried at the crossroads.'

'What?'

'Monsieur Clicquot. The whole town's oozing with it, like pus in a sore. They're all saying he did it to himself because he had a few bad years at the vineyards. I don't like talk behind people's back so I'm giving it to you straight.'

Nicole's sadness bloomed to fury. 'My François died of typhoid – *and* he was better than this whole town of small-minded insects put together. If I ever hear one of them even *think* any different, I'll personally throttle them with my own hands.'

'I had a few fights about it myself. Leave it with me. There's nothing else for them to talk about, that's all there is to it, but I didn't want it going on behind your back. Sorry for any upset.'

He gave her a rough handshake. He nudged his cap up and it was then she noticed bruising around his left eye as he was leaving.

For the first time in months, she was angry. To be buried at a crossroads was the country people's way of saying that François had taken his own life and left his little family to take their chances. Small-minded, superstitious, mean gossips that they were, whispering at the bakery, crossing themselves as they passed her. They should keep to their business, and she to hers. She couldn't stand this dreary place a minute longer and she flew to the drawer to find the letter.

> *My darling, dark days. You have an open invitation to Paris. I promised and I never forget a promise. Come and forget and bring your little daughter – my brood will adore her. This is not a formal sympathy card, so you'll forgive me, but even this cloud has a silver lining and I intend to be it. Come soon.*
>
> *With love, Thérésa*

What had Nicole been doing for the last four months? She couldn't face Christmas without François and the town was too small and full of hurtful gossip. She dipped her quill in the ink and wrote two letters – one to Thérésa to gratefully accept, and another to Moët to say she was open to discussions about selling.

He'd been angling for the Clicquot vineyards ever since she married François and she just couldn't face the memories any more, least of all run a business, as was clear from Xavier's necessary approach to her about the wages. She and Clémentine had a small allowance from her parents, which covered all their living expenses, so they could survive. If Moët was running the vineyards, at least the workers would get paid on time. He could afford it, even though the markets were dead and everyone was talking about an impending war with Russia.

She hesitated over the letter to Moët. François would have been devastated. But she had to accept that he wasn't here any more, and every part of the poetry of the vineyards, the cycle of growth, harvest and blend, hurt too much. If she stayed here, it would destroy her – she was living a half-life in the shadows of her marriage.

And what about Louis? She wasn't capable of being responsible for him, or anyone else apart from Mentine, she told herself. She'd write and tell him from Paris, or in person when he returned.

She took care to write her Paris return address on the back of the letter to Moët for further negotiations and left the two letters on the hall table for Josette to post in the morning. Exhausted, she headed upstairs to curl up next to Mentine, warm with sleep, in her bed.

In Paris, it was Mentine's turn to abandon her. From the moment she encountered Thérésa's eight raucous children, she was absorbed into a cycle of teatimes, horse riding, impromptu plays, fights and reconciliations. After only one week, Mentine was as rowdy as the rest, running as fast as any of the boys, and falling asleep most nights in her arms, heavy and still and sweet as a plum.

After another of these busy days, Mentine immediately fell asleep in her soft feather bed. Tonight, Nicole kissed Mentine's forehead and left her to prepare for Thérésa's ball, standing in front of the mirror to tidy herself up. Thérésa had begged her to attend, and she had agreed to please her, but she was a disaster. A skeletal face, dull eyes, dark shadows, lank hair. A ball was the last thing she wanted tonight.

Thérésa appeared in the reflection. 'Look at you! For goodness' sake, you're not in Reims now. Come with me.'

She swept her to a flower-filled boudoir, gilt mirrors lining every available space, a dressing table scattered with a jumble of hairbrushes, combs, jewellery, powders and perfumes. Invitations and notes from admirers filled the mantelpiece and spilled carelessly onto the floor.

'Let me, please, darling.'

Thérésa unhooked her dowdy black dress in front of the mirror and slid it off her shoulders. Her slip was next, and then she was naked. Nicole felt a kind of pride to be bared to her friend, and found herself smiling at Thérésa as she spun her round to face her.

'There's a butterfly inside that chrysalis,' Thérésa murmured as she leaned in, cupping Nicole's breasts and drawing her close. An electric charge ran across her skin where Thérésa touched her. She smelt of cotton and tasted of salt as her tongue explored her mouth, until a knock on the door sent them reeling apart.

What just happened? Is this how women behave in Paris? She wasn't sure, but it made anything seem possible. It was the first moment in four months she hadn't thought of François.

The maid came in and bobbed a curtsey and discreetly averted her eyes as Nicole slipped behind the screen to cover herself.

'What is it?' asked Thérésa, cool as a cucumber.

'General Roussillon is here to see you, Madame. He made a special request…'

'Get him a glass of brandy and put him in a corner. I'll see to him later.'

'Yes, Madame.'

Nicole's lips felt bruised.

Thérésa bustled over to the armoire, pulled out a blue-grey dress and held it up to her, their moment forgotten. 'Perfect. The colour of your eyes, like a soft winter morning. Put it on, but don't look yet.'

Nicole closed her eyes and submitted to her powders and rouges. Thérésa slicked on the lipstick with her finger, tenderly pressing her lips, then used the same for her own.

'Red suits you.' She twisted her hair, pinned it, stood back and clapped. 'Now look.'

A beautiful, luscious woman with glittering eyes was reflected back at her. Her lips looked like she'd eaten a punnet of blackberries and the dress was a winter sky. She swung her hips and the silk rippled. They giggled.

'Thank you,' Nicole whispered.

Thérésa kissed her shoulder. 'You're a businesswoman. Use *all* of your assets.'

'I'm not a businesswoman any more, just a widow, no longer Madame, but *Veuve* Clicquot. François is dead and my duty is to withdraw into grateful silence, or marry again splendidly,' she said bitterly.

'*Finally* you're beginning to see sense. A nice man to take your mind off things, instead of moping about like a tired old washerwoman. I have the perfect person!'

'I won't marry again. I'll endure the party, but only for your sake.'

'Darling, I know you'll change your mind. Lonely women always do. But let me tell you something. I know you genuinely loved your husband. Very quaint, by the way. But you'll recover, and when you do start to look elsewhere, you mustn't hook yourself to someone who can dictate your every move. You have produced a child, you have married. Society will happily accept you as a woman of means in your own right now. Just think how lucky you are. You think I am calculating, a manipulator? I see it in you, too. I saw it that day in Reims, at the party, the way you held court with those men.'

Nicole shook her head.

'I know that old reprobate Moët is desperate to get his grubby hands on your prize vineyards. Don't let him. We all survived the revolution. For what? For men to be free and women to be shut in their houses? I know that isn't what you want.'

'I don't know what I want any more.' She thought of the pile of correspondence with Moët. He would sign tomorrow and take the whole wine business and land off her hands for triple what it was worth if she agreed. But she kept stalling, not quite able to make the final cut.

'I saved my neck from the guillotine by being an observer of people. It makes people eminently malleable if you know all about them. But let's have no more being serious tonight! You can think tomorrow – you can be anything here. No one will judge. These people are survivors, and they have been through a bloody revolution to be here, each in their own way.'

Thérésa steered Nicole out of the boudoir. Footmen bowed as she passed, following her with their eyes.

Entering the ballroom, they strolled through the gathering, Thérésa making a stir as she fluttered past clusters of guests, strutting men in uniform, sneering women in empire-line dresses, the braver ones sporting Thérésa's *coiffure à la victime.* A quartet played in the corner and the chandeliers threw prisms in the candlelight. Nicole's sharp eyes picked out the quality of the crystal, caught the 'M' for Moët on the champagne corks before they were popped.

'General Roussillon, my favourite soldier!' Thérésa pecked him on the cheek.

'Meet my dear friend Nicole Clicquot. She's just up from the country, so you make sure not to tease her.'

And she was gone, leaving the General following her smooth back and raven hair until she disappeared into the crowd. Nicole flew daggers into that perfect back. How dare Thérésa burden her with the title of *paysanne*, country peasant?

'From the country? Whereabouts?' the General muttered, still more interested in Thérésa.

'Reims. Where the cathedral of kings is.' She gulped her champagne, doubting everything about the evening.

'Don't drink that muck, it'll make you ill,' she heard a voice with a German lilt behind her say.

Nicole swung round. Long boots, damask waistcoat and a fat cigar.

'Louis!'

'*La sauvage.*'

The General melted back into the crowd as Nicole hugged her friend tight.

'You're safe! I heard about the dangerous situation in Russia and wrote several times to call you home, but we... I never heard a word back from you.'

'I never got it, communications are terrible and the situation is dire. The talk is of a French invasion now that Napoléon's made it as far as Moravia, so all French in Russia are seen as spies. Four months on horseback across the forests and steppes, then ship and barge. I would have come straight to Reims, but Thérésa told me she had lured you here.'

'Louis... did you hear about...?'

'I wrote straight away. You didn't receive my letter either?'

She shook her head, aware of curious eyes on them. 'I knew you would contact me if you could, but it wouldn't be the first time one of your Russian letters went astray. Everything's been such a blur. I still have letters I can't bear to open.'

'He loved you more than most men could in a hundred lifetimes. Are you managing?'

'I keep busy.'

'You are always busy, Madame Clicquot.'

'*Veuve* Clicquot now,' she replied, getting used to her new title of *widow*.

He kissed her cheek; both blinked back tears. 'Dance with me.'

They wove through the crowds, and stepped onto the dance floor, her widow's dress forgotten in a heap in Thérésa's boudoir. No one cared who they were as the chandeliers glittered and the candles cried slow wax tears. The revolution had taken indiscriminately, and everyone in this room had suffered.

The room spun and silk dresses blurred, Louis' arms tight around her. He whirled her through the tall doors into a freezing garden. *François.* The last night they had spent together they had danced like this.

Louis touched her hair. 'I've never seen it like this.'

She held his gaze, and wished that things were different… but she had to tell him about her negotiations with Moët. She owed him that much.

'I'm thinking of giving up the vineyards. I've offered them to Jean-Rémy and we're discussing terms.'

'You can't! Not yet! You just need time. You haven't concluded the deal?'

'Not yet, but the vineyards were François' dream, not mine. I just don't have the heart any more, Mentine is suffering and I don't need to do it for the money.'

'François would never have allowed it. It would break his heart! *I* won't allow it,' he said sternly.

'I've already begun the negotiations, Louis.'

'François would haunt me if I didn't stop you. I know the last letter I wrote was full of doom and gloom, but I had only just arrived and it's true, things aren't what they were. The country is suffering from the war, just as we are. But after introductions from my network of contacts, it's clear there is still a vast echelon of rich with the means to buy, and they are crazy for French champagne. The fact that it's in short supply just makes it even more sought after. This ball is nothing compared to the luxuries of Moscow and St Petersburg. Don't forget that they still have an aristocracy there and their wealth is beyond imagining – there is no other representative who knows them like I do. Things will change, the war won't last forever. We can't give up. If you work your magic at the vineyards with your beautiful blends, you can leave the rest to me.'

'But your letter? We lost everything.'

'And grapes stop growing on the vines? Come on, it was just a setback. You of all people surely thought that?'

'I have thought nothing since he died.'

'He put everything he had into those vineyards. He put his *life* into them and into you. And you're thinking of signing them over to Moët? We can't let this happen.'

'There is no we. And no one would listen to a woman running a vineyard. Who would do business with me?'

'You're not just any woman. You are Nicole Clicquot. There is a tradition in Champagne of entrepreneurial widows. Family business is in the region's blood. Remember Widow Blanc who ran the depository in Paris? No one argued with her. And Widow Robert who supplies your barrel wines? Fierce! If I was in trouble on a battlefield, I'd choose her to hide behind.'

'They don't have independent means. They've been success-ful because they *had* to do it. I don't. Mentine and I are well provided for by my parents. But it's work or the workhouse for those women.'

'It's work or slow death for you. Are you really going to retire quietly into black dresses and veils, or give yourself to a pompous arse who wants you for your name? If they have never worked with you, they can never appreciate you.'

'I'm too tired to do it on my own, Louis. And scared,' she confessed for the first time.

'Then do it for François. You owe it to him.'

'I paid my debt in tears.'

'Tears are no use to anyone, Babouchette. François *lived* for those vineyards, and for you and Mentine. Do you think he'd be happy to see you locked up in a big house? His daughter pushed aside in a new marriage, a new man in charge of his lands, or worse, Moët? There's gold in that ballroom, waiting to buy your champagne.' He picked a flaming torch from its stand and drew letters in the night sky. 'Veuve Clicquot et Compagnie. Pretend, just for tonight.'

'I'm getting too used to being called a *veuve*, a widow. But it does give the company name a certain cachet, at least.'

She looked at Louis, passion burning in his eyes. She realised he loved their business as much as François had. The glittering ballroom was ablaze, filled with life and possibilities. What was she going to do when Thérésa tired of her and found another plaything, as she surely would? Go back to her lonely study, stare at the old ledgers she had left behind and wait for inspiration? She hadn't yet concluded her negotiations with Moët. In fact, she'd dragged her feet, despite his many communications with her on the subject since she'd reached Paris.

'Just tonight, to see how it feels,' she agreed. 'No promises, but there is still some stock which would go for nothing if I did sell to Moët, and I'd much rather see it appreciated in crystal goblets at a soirée in Paris than rotting in a Moët warehouse.'

Louis clapped his hands and beamed. 'That's the spirit! We can make it work, I promise. Your name will be the talk of the ballrooms of Russia!'

'No promises, I said, but let's go in then and talk to these painted dolls. Which one do we start with?'

'See the lady with the chestnut hair and the diamond barrette? She is Madame Champs-Ricard, the richest widow in Paris. We'll start with her. I am sure she'll be sympathetic to your cause, and everyone here is on the lookout for new blood. Watch me and learn.'

Nicole linked arms with him and went back in. Veuve Clicquot, a woman in command of this ballroom, herself, and a burgeoning wine empire, with her trusty and charming salesman at her side. François would delight at the sheer fun and daring of it all.

CHAPTER 7

December 1805

Republican date: Nivôse, year XIV

The Parisienne

New Year's Eve morning. Only one more day until this horrible year was over. Nicole propped herself up on her pillows, fluffy as marshmallows. She pulled the tangle of linen sheets and cashmere blankets to her chin, pushed her feet to a cool part of the bed and swooshed them around on the cold smoothness. The sheets smelt of Thérésa's perfume and the sun slid through the heavy drapes, dust motes dancing to her mood. Shouts, door slams and pounding little feet at full pelt permeated the house at Thérésa's vast home at rue de Babylone.

A million miles away from Reims and their talk of burying François at a crossroads. The dust hung heavy in its suspension of light, then disappeared in the gloom. She shook herself. Today was a good day. François was the second thought she had had on waking, not the first. She had got through Christmas in a riotous, pungent bouquet of Thérésa's parties, soirées, card evenings and theatricals. The vanilla taste of waxy candlelight, the tang of cheated suitors, a top note of scandal and debauchery. A heady elixir to treat her grief. She was Thérésa's doll. Hers to dress up, take around, show off and play with whenever she felt like it. No decisions, no responsibility. All she had to do was effervesce to Thérésa's bidding and everyone was delighted.

She didn't love Thérésa like she loved François, nor how she loved her sister or friends. She knew that her friendship with her was unique, that the way they kissed and kept each other warm at night transgressed what society would call right or normal, but somehow with her, it didn't matter. In fact, it made her see how anything was possible, how the narrow confines of society *could* be smashed, in any way she wished. To Nicole, that was captivating.

These were her conclusions in her rational moments, but whatever she thought was, in reality, useless. Thérésa was irresistible, heady, intoxicating. If Thérésa chose to seduce you, it was impossible to resist her, soul *and* beautiful body. Their nights together had a dreamlike, illicit quality that suited her grief and allowed her to abnegate all responsibility.

'*Maman!*' Mentine burst through the door, trailing a brood of little ones diminishing in height, and in varying states of dishevelment. 'Can I go riding? Monsieur Bohne is here and he said he'd take me with him to the Tuileries. I'm going to wear my new muff and blue dress and all the ladies will see me and think how fashionable I am and the officers will turn their heads and I'll be grown up and the talk of the town and the belle of the ball like Thérésa and the whole of Paris will remember the name of Clémentine Clicquot.'

Nicole was not the only one in love with Thérésa.

'Stop. You're going so fast you're making me dizzy! Come and kiss your *maman*. Of course you can go.'

Mentine jumped onto her bed, followed by two more of Thérésa's girls. Their silky hair and perfect foreheads were exquisite, and her stomach lurched. All her happiest moments were tinged with sadness, wishing François could be there to feel it with her.

'Right, now shoo. All of you. Go and get ready and tell Louis I'll be down before he goes.'

She was dreading the meeting. He was not going to like what she had to say, but she owed it to him to tell him straight.

Louis' smile warmed the room.

'You've been difficult to get hold of, Veuve Clicquot.'

'I'm sorry, Louis, it's just I've been so caught up in Thérésa's social life. There never seems to be a moment for anything else.'

'So I gather. I'm starting to hear your name in some of the most elevated company,' he said darkly.

'Don't tease me. I'm just Thérésa's escort for a while. I like it. It helps me forget.'

'Don't forget too much, *sauvage.*'

'Let me be, Louis, just for a while.'

'I'm not sure I like what I hear, the way people talk about you, in connection with her. She's a one-off, a curiosity, a beautiful, walking scandal from another world, immune to society. But that's not you, it's not what you are. The vineyards are crying out for you. When are you going back to real life?'

'Don't be such an old prude, Louis. You're as bad as all those small-town gossips I left behind.'

His hurt look made her angry for the guilt, gave her the steel she needed.

'I'm not going back – ever. I know we had fun at the ball, selling up my champagne to those old widows. But I have a new life now.' The last whirling weeks had convinced her that she could make a new life here.

'But that's what I came to tell you. You remember Madame Champs-Ricard, the night of Thérésa's ball? She's buying! She thought you were charming – you're quite a curiosity in wine sales. She's cancelled her order with Moët and placed it with us. Ten thousand bottles! It's the best start to a new year we could wish for. How can you run the press from here, Nicole?'

The mention of Moët's name gave her a stab of conscience. She still hadn't finally concluded with him, but she had promised him a trip to Reims to sign as soon as she could face going back.

'That's just it, I can't stomach it. I'm happy here, Mentine's happy. Why would I want to go back to that little town?

'That's not you talking, it's *her*.'

'*You* can work with Moët. He'll be delighted with the order. It will make the business easier to sell as a going concern, and you with it, my top salesman.'

Louis flushed. 'That's how you see me. Something to sell as part of your business?'

'No! It's just I have nothing left to give. I just want to forget, Louis…'

Thérésa swept into the room. 'Darling, what have you done to him? He looks like he's seen a ghost.'

Thérésa held out her hand to Louis. He kissed it, reluctantly.

'You can't hog her forever, I'm afraid. She's very much in demand. Nicole, darling, you must get yourself ready for our little gathering. What *is* that hairstyle? I'll have my hairdresser come to your room in half an hour, then you'll be ready to scintillate Paris, my little country firefly. Louis, isn't it wonderful to see a spark in those grey eyes?'

'Quite the Parisienne,' said Louis.

Nicole allowed herself to be ushered away by Thérésa, ignoring Louis' glowering. No need for any more discussion. She was decided. Moët's offer was good. She would sell to him and live here in Paris with Mentine, and put all the memories of her and François' life well and truly behind her.

When evening came, she was too weary for another soirée, but Thérésa begged and they arrived fashionably late to find a roaring party in full swing.

Shouts and laughter drew Nicole through the house into the gardens, where a commotion was fizzing through the crowd like champagne bubbles. She joined them, looking, followed their eyes to the balcony.

'Jump. We can catch you!' shouted a young soldier.

A young man was holding court, two floors up, eyes wild with liquor and the party. He staggered. 'Alright I'll do it. Promise to catch?'

'Stop being a mummy's boy and trust to fate. Step into the void. Death or glory!' the soldier shouted back.

'Make the net! And tell my mother I love her if I don't make it!'

The crowd sighed and giggled at the filial sentiment.

The soldier issued orders to his fellows, who lined up to face each other, linking hands.

The man leapt, arms spread like a bird. 'I can fly!'

The crowd drew a collective breath as he fell. Nicole screwed her eyes tight shut, waiting for the nauseating thud. Applause erupted and she opened her eyes to see him caught in the human cradle and neatly deposited on his feet.

'Bravo!'

Thérésa was next to her, shouting and clapping, perfume clinging to her transparent dress. 'Encore! Encore!'

The man bowed.

Nicole was elated and angry at them all at the same time. How could they play so fast and loose with life?

Another man appeared on the balcony, auburn hair in a careless shock, silvered by the moonlight.

'For the Clicquot vineyards!' someone shouted. Nicole froze.

'Darling, it's your little business partner, Laurent… Léo… no, Louis, that's it. For you. Blow him a kiss. Delightful!' squealed Thérésa. 'You've got them all in the palm of your hand.'

'Yes, or no?' Louis' eyes fixed on her as he cried out. The crowd's eyes followed his gaze. Gradually, they found her, with Thérésa's help, pointing coquettishly at her friend.

Nicole shook her head, horrified.

'Say you'll keep them and I take the stairs to the ground and devote my services to you forever,' Louis shouted.

A woman next to her sighed. Others fluttered their fans at the sheer romance.

'Save him. Keep the vineyards,' lisped a beautiful young thing in a white dress.

'Let him jump. Take his chances,' roared a soldier from the line-up. 'I'll make sure we miss. Give your vineyards to me and we'll make beautiful wine together.'

This brought a barrage of laughter.

Her eyes locked with Louis'. His arms were stretched out, like Jesus on the cross, and he took a step nearer to the edge.

'I'd give my own life for you and the vines. If I jump, you're on your own forever,' Louis declared. He was drunk as a lord.

'Stop it, please, you'll break your neck!' shouted Nicole.

'I'm in your hands,' he said, staggering closer to the edge.

'I can't promise, Louis, Come down!'

He launched himself. The line-up wasn't ready and they scrambled to catch him. Someone screamed in horror. She held her breath, rigid with fear.

Louis landed, safe. She didn't wait for his look of triumph. How dare he make a fool of her?

She ran, through the gaudy crowd, swiping at angry tears. They were laughing at her. Someone put out a foot and tripped her and she bruised her knees on the floor. She tottered up again and stumbled on. A man caught her arm and drew her too close. She slapped his face to screams of laughter. 'Take a joke, country girl!'

Outside, she stopped to catch her breath. The sky was full of stars and she longed for the silence of the Reims night, the smell of dew on the soil at first light.

'I immediately saw my error on the way down, but it was too late. It certainly sobered me up.' Louis fell into step with her, struggling to keep up.

'Go to hell.'

'Those are not your people, Nicole.'

'You can't hold me to ransom. Just leave me to live my life.'

'I've decided. The moment they put me on my feet. I'm hitting the road again. You can reach me if you need me, but you won't sell me along with your barrels and vines.'

'You do what you need to and I'll look after myself.'

'They see you as a rich widow, ripe for the taking. Nothing else. Be careful.'

Louis turned on his heel and was gone. The loneliness was crushing.

Nicole kept walking, all the way back to Thérésa's mansion on rue de Babylone, Thérésa's choice of tight satin slippers slicing her feet.

A large glass of bourbon helped her sleep, a habit she'd got into here. Blissful unconsciousness descended. All night, she dreamt of falling. She woke with a pounding head to a knock on her door.

'Messenger for you, Madame.'

'Tell him to leave a note.'

'He says it's urgent. He has to tell you in person.'

Nicole threw on a robe.

A young boy was cowering in the hallway, eyes wide at the opulence of the gilded mansion.

'I've memorised it, Madame Clicquot.' He cleared his throat and looked at the ceiling to recall the words, which were delivered in an expressionless monotone. 'What the bloody hell are you doing up there poncing around with a lot of aristos? You are needed here. The guild has voted you to lead the St Vincent day parade for the village of Bouzy on the twenty-second of January – the first woman ever to have the honour, not that you deserve it. You have abandoned us, but we want to honour your husband and he thought so highly of you, we hope you accept and return as fast as a Parisian nag can manage it. Give young Emile here a gold coin for his trouble. He can't read and neither can I, so say what you need to him. He has a good memory for words, which is why I sent him.'

The boy doubled over in relief when he finished.

'You forgot to tell me who the message is from,' laughed Nicole. 'Let me guess. Xavier?'

The boy beamed. 'How did you know?'

Nicole tapped her nose. 'You must be hungry. I'll show you to the kitchens and you can eat something.'

'No time, begging your pardon, my mother packed me bread and cheese. My cart is waiting outside, it's on a delivery and I have to go on the rounds, then travel back with him today. Ten thousand bottles on it, all to one address – Madame Champs-Ricard, the richest widow in Paris! They're yours, Madame. Clicquot on every cork. Louis organised the order with Xavier. He said that you sold it together at a ball. Nice work, Madame. Never seen that much go to one place.'

'Who's your mother?'

'Marie Jumel, Madame.'

Marie, a prostitute Nicole had seen a lifetime ago, hawking her emaciated self round the square on the day of the revolution. Marie was now one of her most loyal employees, thanks to Nicole's trust in a 'fallen' woman who was simply trying to feed her children.

'You send my best regards to your mother. And take this for your trouble.' She handed him two gold coins, which he bit, sucked his breath at the authentic yield to his teeth, then shoved deep into his pocket.

'I am not to leave without an answer,' he said importantly.

'You can tell Xavier of course I will come. I wouldn't miss it for the world. Can you remember that?'

The boy hissed in derision. 'Easy.'

Perfect. She could escape Paris for a while, honour François at the parade, then put it all behind her in a deal with Moët.

The day of the St Vincent Fête des Vignerons was bright and cold. The patron saint of vintners was smiling on them, people said. Last year, there was hail and it was a terrible year. The bright January sunshine was a good omen and people crossed themselves as they stepped in time to the tambours and cornets, past the *mairie* with its *tricolore* snapping smartly in the breeze.

Nicole's bonnet and scarlet Bouzy robe gave her a kind of anonymity and importance. The town was in festive mood, all whispers about François forgotten, at least for today. The vintners had actually given her this position in the parade to honour his memory, so perhaps she'd been a little hasty in condemning the whole of Reims as her enemy. The first woman ever to lead the parade – François would have been so proud. He would have delighted, too, at their triumph over tradition.

Girls held ribbons sewn to floats piled with barrels, wine bottles, winter flowers and vines. The tasting committee smiled in greeting, wearing robes coloured according to their villages, or leather aprons and caps depending on their status. She pictured Thérésa laughing at their earnest country ways, but Nicole was surprised to realise that she felt at home, even without François at her side.

When the swirl of Natasha's brass shop handle glinted at her in the sun, she strained to see her face at the counter. To her delight, Natasha ran out of the shop, bolted the door hastily and fell into step with her.

'The prodigal returns. Reims is glad to have you back, Babouchette.'

Nicole looked at her friend. So different from Thérésa, and with so much unsaid between them.

'Those are the first words you've spoken to me since François.'

'I'm so sorry. My heartbreak was so deep that I didn't have the strength for a friend, and I can't forgive myself. I hope that you can. It was like Daniel died all over again. The memories of cradling his head, blood on the street.'

Natasha fingered her horseshoe necklace with trembling hands and made a quick movement, like a figure of eight, in front of both of them. Nicole noticed a few tiny grains of salt form the shape.

'We have both suffered,' said Nicole. 'What should have brought us together set us apart, it seems. But let's not talk about it, I'm just glad you're here now.'

Natasha linked arms with her and squeezed her close. 'I'm glad, too. I've missed your rebellious ways. The town has been a little too *ordered* without you and your wild schemes. You are submitting to Moët, I hear.'

Nicole gasped. 'Not *submitting*. How did you know?' she whispered, not wanting her Bouzy guild to hear before the deal was done.

'I have a way of seeing, even when you are far away.'

'Giving away patisseries in return for gossip?' laughed Nicole.

'Let's just say that sugar loosens the tongue.'

'Nothing is settled. But you're right, of course. You always are! I'm meeting him in a couple of weeks to discuss terms. I don't have the heart any more.'

By now the parade was almost coming to a halt in the cathedral square and the band was deafening.

'Your business *is* your heart. Meet me later, at this address.' Natasha pressed a note into her hand and melted away into the crowd.

How wonderful to have her old friend back! But why this mystery?

As soon as the ceremony was over and she was safely at home, Nicole opened the note and grabbed her cloak. She was glad to escape the townhouse in Reims, where François' ghost still lived.

She'd recognised the address immediately – Antoine and Claudine. There was rarely a time when she entered that house and something momentous didn't happen... François standing by the fireplace with his violin, eyes full of mischief. She smiled to herself, then quickened her step. A good memory! A picture of him, so vivid, that she could smile at it without wiping away a tear.

She clattered up the stairs, two at a time. Claudine was waiting.

'Hush, what a racket! You're not ten years old any more!'

'I was so looking forward to seeing you. Plus, two stairs at a time is tradition.' She smiled at her old friend.

'Paris has done you the world of good, I see. Now, I've got a pot boiling on the stove, come and get warm. I've got your chair ready.'

'Where's Antoine?'

'You won't see him, he's in the cellars. He's got thousands of the things to shake and turn for riddling, and you know how fastidious he is.'

'It's why he's my foreman.' Nicole choked on her words. She thought of the cellars, full of magic, Antoine slowly turning, faithful and knowledgeable, as much a part of her life as eating or drinking. Then there was her riddling experiment, untouched since the day she'd hidden it in the basement, so full of hope, thinking she could save François. Was she really going to give it all up?

Natasha was waiting by the fire for her, dark eyes reading the flames, sitting in François' chair. 'This is where he used to sit, isn't it?'

'How did you know? He was sitting right there the day I met him.'

Natasha snorted. 'It's not magic. If that's *your* chair, where else was he going to sit? Now. I have a proposal for you.'

'I'm intrigued.'

'I'm getting old.'

'No…'

Natasha waved her hand. 'I'm getting old. It's a simple fact. Happens to everyone, even me. I want to go back to Russia and you will help me.'

'You sound sure about that.'

Natasha threw something invisible into the fire and it leapt. 'I am. What I have to say will be irresistible to you.'

'François is in Russia?'

'A joke at his expense?'

'A relief to be able to.'

'You are healing, slowly. He will never leave you, but one day you will walk with him at your side without grieving.'

Nicole took her friend's hand and pressed it to her cheek. 'Thank you for your wise words. I know you are right, but I can't imagine it. I almost don't want to imagine it, because then a little part of him will be gone.'

Natasha stroked her hair. 'Patience. You will let him go when the time is right.'

Nicole gave her a watery smile and changed the subject to save her tears. 'How can I help you get to Russia?'

'I want to go and see my mother, one more time. She's ill, possibly dying. We talk across the stars to each other. You can do that if your bond is close, but I want to touch her one more time before she leaves this world.'

'I will help however I can.' She knew better than to question Natasha on exactly how she intended to travel to Russia alone through pitched battles at every border along the way.

'Good, then you are coming with me. And you're bringing fifty thousand bottles of champagne and wine with you. Louis sent me this to show you – he said you were being your usual troublesome self and wouldn't look at it if he sent it direct.'

Natasha placed a pink order slip, signed by Louis, on the table. Nicole picked it up – fifty thousand bottles, for the Great Palace in Tsarskoye Selo, St Petersburg. Louis had told her that there were possible markets in Russia, but not that he was actually in the process of securing an order of this magnitude.

'What! That's almost my entire stock. In fact, it might not *be* my stock any more if Jean-Rémy gets his way. It's only two weeks until we meet to discuss a deal. I've been holding off all the time I was in Paris, and in truth, it was me who proposed selling in the first place. Even if I was still in the business, the rumours are that all the ports are closing and trade is closed to all French exports now that the British and Russians are talking of allying.'

'Exactly. We have to move quickly.'

'But Louis had to come home because it was too dangerous for the French. And now he's secured a big order?'

'He told you there is still a massive market for your wines, even though the official line is no French exports. But when he heard you were thinking of selling, he didn't want you to act rashly and throw in a big order as a sweetener to Moët, or let slip that Russia was even a possibility. Moët would be all over it like a dog on heat and any advantage for you would be lost. He waited 'til you were safely back here amongst your friends. And he is a very good friend to you, my dear Nicole. The order's right here in black and white in front of you. If you take me, I can get us safe passage. I still have my contacts there.'

'Natasha, there are other ways you can get to Russia. It doesn't have to involve me, or a massive shipment. Perhaps I could accompany you, but I'd have to leave Mentine and…'

'And nothing. You're wasting time.'

'Everyone seems to think they can push me into returning when I just want to go.'

Natasha shook her head in frustration. 'Do you want to go when you hear that Moët is intending to sack Marie for running what he calls a "house of tolerance"? She depends on you. Or that he intends to build a house over your finest vineyards in Bouzy, the one where yours and François' shepherd's hut is. The one with the vine that grows the sour crimson grapes? Or that any workers who transfer with the deal will work longer hours for less pay and that many will be without work? Even if you don't care about yourself – and you obviously don't – you are not free. Many of the town depend on you.'

'My life is in Paris now.'

'You're tiring of it already. I know you. I can see.'

A journey to Russia with Natasha, accompanying fifty thousand bottles of her finest? Running the trade blockades? Nicole thought hard, back to her final week in Paris, the swirl and glitter. Really, it was all a veneer. Natasha was right – she knew her, more than anyone in Paris did. Deep down, they all saw her as a curiosity from the country, a peasant girl in Paris, only as good as the fashions she chose. Thérésa had hardly noticed when she said goodbye. And Mentine was happily installed with the other children at rue de Babylone for now.

'For you. For your mother. Let's try it.'

Natasha narrowed her eyes. 'For you, too, Babouchette. For us both. And I have found a less demanding partner for you than Monsieur Moët. It seems the whole town think I have your ear. Dear Philippe Clicquot has asked me to petition you on his behalf. I know you've always refused his money, but you should let him help. Your father-in-law is desperate to have a stake in the future of the business on behalf of his son and it's wrong of you to refuse him. You see, the decision is out of your hands.'

'It seems it is and rather than *submitting* to Moët, it seems I must submit to you.'

She could blame Natasha, or convince herself she was doing the right thing for Philippe Clicquot and his son's legacy, or the temptation of the fifty-thousand-bottle sale, but she knew this feeling had begun at the Fête des Vignerons when she had taken her place amongst Champagne's finest producers. New shoots of hope and ambition, whatever the odds. The excitement of the sale, a chance to beat the competition, new customers to taste the subtleties of her finest creations.

She picked up the sale bill again and studied it for the buyer's name on the order slip, mentally sifting through her ledgers to make sure they were good payers and would be worth the effort.

Natasha met her hungry gaze. 'Finally you're seeing sense.'

Claudine bustled in with a tray of coffee. 'All settled?'

It was a conspiracy of kindness.

CHAPTER 8

February 1806

Republican date: Revolutionary calendar abolished

Contraband

Nicole took the same route to Moët's as she had the day she first met François. It was good to be back amongst the vines, even on this bleak February morning. As the carriage sped through the landscape, she saw in her mind François, a stranger then, pointing out the larks hovering over the poppies. It had been difficult to concentrate on what he was saying with those blue-green eyes smiling into hers, a mellow harvest sun melting the air. He'd explained about the *terroir* and the different grape varietals, ripe and heavy. Today the vines were dormant and black, the larks were long gone and the meeting with Moët filled her with dread and loneliness. She breathed in the musty smell of damp soil. No matter, the black vines would sprout fresh shoots again soon.

The meeting was at Moët's own Petit Trianon, the replica Versailles summer house built especially for Napoléon's visits, an incongruous wedding-cake of a place. Her watery reflection in the mirror pool looked much more sure-footed than she felt as she strode along, gulping in cool air fresh as Vinho Verde.

Moët was waiting, beckoning impatiently at the doorway.

'Follow me, *ma chère*, it's all arranged. You have made a very good decision, one that will benefit your whole family.'

Moët shepherded her like a demented sheepdog, ushering her along with his hand on her elbow. He found time to admire a gallery wall.

'Just a few miniatures by Isabey,' he prompted.

Isabey was the darling of the fashionable Paris set. He painted miniature portraits for disproportionately large amounts of money and Moët had a whole wall of them. They were of himself, his family, Joséphine, Napoléon – the most influential man in Champagne and in the business. A word from Napoléon meant thousands of francs' worth of sales. Monsieur Moët meant to demonstrate that his pockets were deep enough to ruin her, but she wasn't about to add her vineyards to his riches.

Nicole gave him what he clearly wanted from her by way of response. 'Very impressive,' she conceded. 'Before we go any further, I—'

'You have been through enough, *chère* Nicole. I have taken care of every detail for you,' Jean-Rémy said, handing her a package. 'Not another word until you've opened it.'

Out of politeness, she untied the ribbon. It was a wrapper of fat bulbs.

'Grapevines are such a bore, and require an awful lot of skill, but these are irises, the highly scented ones. You adore them, I hear. Indulge your growing hobby and plant them yourself, appreciate the soil under your fingernails if you must, but you'll find these so much more *feminine* than vines.'

She scrunched them up in their wrapper and handed them back. He had always got her so wrong. How could he think that she would be satisfied with such things? What was she thinking when she even considered marriage, or selling up to him?

'So thoughtful, Jean-Rémy, but I came to tell you I'm not selling after all.'

'I don't expect anything in return. Your feelings have already been made clear to me on that score, but I insist on helping a bright young widow in need. One last thing, and you are free. Please open it and I think you'll be persuaded.'

He handed her an envelope and she tore it open. It was a cheque for the business and the vineyards, double what they were worth.

'I'm not selling,' she repeated, unsure whether he had genuinely not heard her, or was merely pretending.

'The vineyards will go to rack and ruin, and it will be such a waste – and for what? To play at business when you have no head for it? You'll find other distractions after the terrible tragedy of losing your husband. This amount will make you an independent woman of means. I present you… your freedom,' he said with a flourish.

'Jean-Rémy, I don't think you can have heard me…' This man really was a self-regarding pompous arse who was incapable of *listening*.

'Take it. Not another word.'

'I don't want it. I'm not selling the vineyards. I came back to Reims to run them myself.'

His eyes hardened. 'Of course you're selling. You have already agreed and you must understand that a gentleman never reneges. This isn't a drawing-room game, Madame, you can't just change your mind on a whim. A woman has never run a vineyard in Reims. It's just not how things are done. I shouldn't have offered you extra, you're proud of course and you don't need it. I'll write it out for the amount we agreed so there is never a question of obligation to me, if that is so odious to you.' He went to his desk and hastily scratched out a new cheque. 'Take it. I'm only thinking of you. I won't be so generous when the vineyards fail and you can't pay your workers. You'll be living with debts you can never repay. Your poor parents will be wrapped up in your downfall.'

'There will be no dramatic downfall, much as you might wish it. And I'm not reneging, I merely told you I was open to talks. My mind is made up. I'm not selling. And my parents fully support my decisions.'

'That's true, they have not adhered to the proper conventions in your upbringing, I have observed *that* in the past – no wonder you are so *determined*. It's a trait unbecoming to a woman! I'll give you more time. I've been protecting you from the rumours about your husband, but you should know they say the Clicquots are bad blood. I may have alluded to it before, in anger, but people talk. Stupid superstitions, but you know this town as well as I do. No one will do business with you.'

'They have nothing else to think about,' she snapped, incensed. 'Don't wait. It's vines that are in my blood, nothing else. I'll prove them all wrong.'

Jean-Rémy narrowed his eyes and looked at her for several long seconds. Then he spoke again, more coldly than before.

'This is a wine town and it's mine. When you've failed, come to me and I'll buy your vineyards for the small sum they'll be worth by that time. Until then, I'll be watching your every foolish move. Good luck.'

Jean-Rémy lit the cheque over the candle and thrust it, flaming, at her face. It hung in the air, caught up by the heat, then dropped in ashes between them.

Thank God she'd asked the carriage to wait. She'd made an enemy of the most powerful vintner in Champagne and there was no time to lose.

*

It took less than a week to organise everything. Tonight was magic: inky, star-pricked, velvet, with an icy bite that kept them on the move. The stable was in darkness, the horses blinkered, even in the gloom, to stop them from being frightened as Emile fixed the carts to the fastest steeds Nicole could muster. Their hooves were shod in sackcloth as instructed. *Good. All in order here.*

She slipped out of the stable side-door. She didn't need a lantern; she knew every step of the way back to the Bouzy press and cellars.

In the vineyards, the pale paths stood out against the dark vines. It would be easy to see anyone approach that way. Out in front was the hamlet, a few houses strung along the road. Plenty of places to hide, but the villagers were unlikely to wake. These people were as predictable as the sunset and sunrise, their lives tethered to nature's rhythms.

In the cellars, the bottles calmed her nerves. She knew every one of them – had counted and noted them against the bailiff's reckonings. She had forgotten how much each one of these quiet green chrysalises meant to her, the golden liquid inside as delicate and short-lived as a butterfly when released, but bringing pure delight while it lived. Where would each one end up? The amber ballroom in Moscow? A secret rendezvous between lovers? A wedding party under the trees by the sea, the whip of salt heightening the senses?

She ran her hands over the smooth glass wall of bottles. Some, like François, would never reach maturity. Some already had a cancer growing inside them, the sediment waiting to spoil the wine.

Fifty thousand bottles, all to be loaded tonight, under cover of darkness. Antoine, Claudine, Xavier and Natasha were packing trunks as fast and quietly as they could.

The clock struck one and she hurried over to Xavier.

'We'll never have it done.'

'Takes as long as it takes,' he said stubbornly. 'It's got to be right. They'll have the lot off us if it's not. Those Dutch customs officers are looking for any excuse to take it to the nearest whorehouse to loosen up their fancy women. They'll pour it down their throats like piss. Go and fuss around someone else before I lose count and fuck the whole lot up for you.'

He heaved the sacks over the bottles, the nutty smell of coffee filled the air and he slammed the trunk shut.

She picked up a candle stub to inspect the inscription: *Café. Pays d'origine, Reunion.*

Customs would allow coffee through the blockades, even if it was closed to French wines.

'Excuse me, Madame.'

Nicole stepped aside as a field hand hefted the trunk onto a trolley ready for loading. He looked half-starved, but handled the heavy chest as if it were empty.

Xavier held up the lantern to help him see. 'Drop that and I'll string you up by the balls.'

The man smiled good-naturedly. 'I'd rather hold onto them, *camarade*,' he said as he carefully lowered the trunk down.

Nicole turned to Xavier, concerned to see a stranger in their midst. 'You haven't introduced your friend?'

'We needed some extra muscle and Monsieur Châtelet might *look* like a runt, but he's got more strength in those arms than a bull,' he said, grinning. 'You don't need to worry, I've worked the fields with him for years. Talks like a toff, works like a bastard. He'll have this lot packed and loaded in the time it takes anyone else to take a piss. You asked me to get you a driver you could trust?' Xavier slapped him on the back. 'Solid gold.'

Monsieur Châtelet bowed. 'At your service. Xavier's in charge of strategy, I'm merely an operative and if I don't get this lot done, he's already informed me of the consequences, so if you'll excuse me…' he said with a wry smile.

She studied him for a moment while he worked to satisfy herself. There was something about Monsieur Châtelet, the way he held himself straight and assured, his fair hair and uncalloused hands. The *camarade* sounded clipped, not at all like the Rémois accent. His clothes were different, too. They were patched, but the trousers were fine wool. Many fortunes had changed places since the revolution and this man had seen better times, but there was no question that he was a good worker.

Natasha had stopped packing and was in the corner, studying a parchment, spread out in front of her.

'Only three hours until we leave,' said Nicole, irritated that Natasha was not packing bottles. She needed everyone, even Natasha, to help or they'd never have it done.

Natasha didn't look up. 'You want me to pack with the rest? Not now, I'm checking the stars for our journey. We should wait a day,' she said emphatically.

'Impossible. There's only one Dutch sea captain in the whole of Amsterdam prepared to take us, and the corsair sails in three weeks. Not accounting for the two days overland to Charleville-Meziéres, the barge trip alone would usually take three and a half weeks. We'll have to sail day and night as it is.'

'Always in a rush, Babouchette. You will ignore my advice, as always, but there will be trouble.'

Natasha took out a bag of red powder and made a circle around the chart in the mud.

'That should help, but no promises,' said Natasha.

'If it makes you feel safer – but I have planned it to the last detail.'

'We think we have control over our fates; it is easier like that,' said Natasha.

The clock struck the half-hour. Time could seem interminable in the early hours of the morning, but not this night. The hours shrank, sucked all the time they needed. Nicole stepped outside again to check for Moët's spies. This shipment could make her reputation, fly in the face of all the detractors in this town. If it failed, she would be a laughing stock, Philippe Clicquot would lose his investment and Moët would be forcing her to sell again – this time for the pittance he had threatened.

She dared herself down towards the vineyards, the darkness thickening as she left the comfort of the building. The stars were gone now, obscured by clouds. A figure loomed, or was it an animal? She picked up a shovel and carried on. She tightened her grip.

'You weren't really thinking of using that thing, were you?' Soft lips brushed her cheek, a quick tongue entangled hers.

'Thérésa!' Everything about her was unexpected and Nicole was confused, delighted and angry all at once.

'Put that thing down, you're making me nervous.'

Nicole ushered her back to the press, watching out for prying eyes.

'For goodness' sake, we're not in the Bastille. I made sure no one saw me.'

'When I wrote to you, I never expected you to come all the way here,' whispered Nicole.

Thérésa kissed her again. 'You're fizzing with your secret mission.'

'It's nerves,' Nicole laughed. 'I'm leaving tonight, I can't delay, even though you've come all this way.'

'Paris has been a bore without you around, but there may be a teensy bit of self-interest at play. You remember the general with the killer's eyes?'

'General Roussillon?'

'What a good memory you have. There are so many, they meld into one for me. He's a powerful man and I might have allowed him to assume too much. Love turned bitter is a dangerous thing.'

Nicole nodded, thinking of Moët.

'Darling, I've come all this way from Paris to see you and I asked the carriage not to change horses so that I got here in time. I'm here to join your little adventure. Won't that be fun? Just the two of us.'

A male voice protested, 'Nicole, who is this? We agreed. No one else.'

'Thérésa, meet Philippe Clicquot, François' father, and my new business partner.'

Thank God a distraction had arrived. Thérésa would never endure life on the road with its hardships and privations. Nicole couldn't allow anything or anyone to stand in her way and she needed time to think.

Thérésa scorched him with her brightest smile and held out her hand. '*Enchantée*. I see now where Nicole's handsome husband inherited his looks.'

Philippe didn't take the hand. He was already nervous about the scheme, and he found it hard to cope with unexpected developments in any circumstances, never mind these.

'Could I have a word with you in private, my dear,' said Philippe, glancing apologetically at Thérésa. He hated to cause offence.

Pulling Nicole to one side, he unfolded a letter, grim-faced. It was from Moët.

Monsieur Clicquot,

The necessity for this letter greatly saddens me. We have been business associates for many years and I have always respected your integrity. Our ancient tradition of winemaking has until now been an honourable business between gentlemen and I consider your recent collaboration with Nicole Clicquot a gross transgression of our ancient codes and, as her father-in-law, entirely contrary to her best interests.

Her business and lands were mine in all but the final signature on the contract. Should you refuse to support my claim, I fully intend to do everything in my power to put a stop to your venture and save Madame Clicquot – a new widow, not in her right mind – from further public embarrassment.

Cordially,
Jean-Rémy Moët

'What is your position?' said Nicole, furious at Moët for upsetting Philippe.

'Let's not waste any more time on it now, and don't you dare worry about me in all this. You have my complete faith.'

The letter shook in Philippe's hands. His nerves were not his greatest asset, but she had enough for them both.

'Thank you for your confidence, Philippe. Once this shipment is delivered and paid for, we won't need Moët. And we both know who we're doing this for,' she added softly.

'Of course I trust you implicitly, but surely the more people who know, the more chance we will be discovered, my dear? I do worry about you,' he fussed.

Thérésa, who was adept at eavesdropping from the most unlikely distances, glided over to Philippe before Nicole could reply. She flashed him one of her winning smiles.

'Don't forget that I escaped the Bastille without a hair being harmed on my head. Paris society is a viper's nest and I know very well how to deal with a man like Moët. Please don't give it one second moment of concern, Monsieur Clicquot. I will be an asset,' she purred.

As the clock struck three, the cart was ready and loaded, exactly on schedule, and Thérésa was now somehow part of the travelling crew, despite everyone's misgivings. Nicole, Thérésa and Natasha loaded their own possessions into the cab and jumped up behind Monsieur Châtelet, who whispered in the ears of the excited horses to calm them.

Two hours later, as the sun rose over the sleepy village of Isles-sur-Suippe, Nicole breathed again. They wouldn't be recognised this far away from the Montagne de Reims and the open road stretched, flat and straight, as far as her eyes could see.

CHAPTER 9

February 1806

Changing Places

'Only three different kinds of *tartes*,' Natasha tutted as they pulled past the *boulangerie* in Rethel.

Thérésa and Valentin Châtelet smirked. Monsieur Châtelet had refused to get involved in directions, laugh at the escape they'd just made, marvel at the sunrise or generally be a part of their adventure. He just waited impassively for instruction, or spent his time with the horses. Except every time Thérésa spoke, when his indifferent expression softened.

Bloody fool, thought Nicole, steeling herself against a jealous stab in her stomach. The melting glare of her attention never lasted long.

At Saulces-Monclin, Natasha nearly wept at the beautiful creations in the patisserie window and Nicole conceded to a short stop for her. She bought a delicate *macaron à la fleur d'oranger* and a pert Saint-Honoré and took apart the flavours, remembering the creations she and Daniel had made in their youth.

'If my mother stays alive long enough for me to reach her, this is what I'll make her,' sighed Natasha.

The landscape was flat as a Russian honey-cake and they passed farm workers, field hands and squires who stopped and waved as they rushed by. After their midnight flit, the day was uneventful. Her band of travellers turned heads as they passed through the towns and villages, though they did their best to look inconspicuous. A milk-skinned beauty with a Spanish accent, a dramatic Russian woman with a penchant for macaroons searching for portents in the sky, a young widow in an ungodly hurry with a cargo of coffee, and a field hand who didn't look like a field hand.

They thrashed the exhausted horses, not stopping until they were safely in Francheville. The horses were blowing and sweating when Monsieur Châtelet pulled up the wagon at the hotel a few kilometres outside of Charleville-Mezieres, where the barge would be waiting for them the next morning. Stiff and dusty, Nicole gave the hotelier a gold coin to have the wagon locked into the barn and Valentin Châtelet agreed to sleep there to keep guard.

Even leaving the wagon for a couple of hours as Valentin joined them for dinner made Nicole uneasy. Her whole future depended on what was in that barn. She ordered a bottle of heavy Francheville burgundy to soothe her nerves.

Places have their own character, their own feel and smell, and she could taste it now in this wine, a top note of the vanilla sun on the Meuse Canal, a reminder of the next leg of their journey.

Valentin drank most of the bottle himself, so she ordered another. She didn't mind. Perhaps the wine would loosen his tongue.

'Do you have family?' she asked.

He didn't look up from his dinner. 'No.'

Thérésa flashed her eyes at him. 'Come now, a good-looking man like you with those melting brown eyes? I find that hard to believe. No golden-haired wife watching the gate for your return? No poor deceived girls in a string of dull villages hoping you're gazing at the same moon? You can't tease us any longer. We have *weeks* together ahead of us and you have kept yourself an absolute mystery. It's not fair!'

'*Life* isn't fair, Madame Tallien.' He glowered.

'Leave him to his secrets if he won't share,' said Nicole. 'We'll make our own entertainment.'

She ordered him a cognac. He rolled it around in the glass and savoured it, closed his eyes and breathed it in.

'This is good,' he said, raising his glass.

She rolled the brandy in her own glass. 'Grande Champagne cognac from Bordeaux. Not the kind of thing a field hand would ordinarily drink.'

'Bringing secrets into the light helps the shadows fade,' said Natasha.

Valentin poured himself another glass.

'I *had* a wife. And children. But now I don't. Is that enough information for your little *soirée*?'

'If that's all you wish to give,' said Natasha.

'It is.'

'I had a husband, once, but no children,' Natasha offered. 'I caught his blood in my skirt.'

Valentin drained his glass. 'I'm sorry for your loss.'

'The revolution?' Thérésa enquired.

He nodded.

'Many dear friends died on the scaffold. Their only crime was their birth,' Thérésa sympathised.

'You survived pretty well,' he said bitterly. 'Everyone knows *your* story.'

'They know the story I wish to portray,' replied Thérésa. 'We all survive as best we can.'

'I'm sorry, the revolution has made actors of us. We have swapped places with our former selves, taken on new personas to protect us,' he said guardedly.

'I'm afraid yours isn't very convincing, Monsieur Châtelet. As a field hand you stand out like a sore thumb,' said Nicole with a warm smile. 'If it helps, your story will never go further than this table.'

He swallowed, and seemed to prepare himself to speak. 'My daughter was blonde, with green eyes. She kept spiders, loved horses, and me. They sliced off her head.'

Nicole thought of her sweet, perfect Mentine and her heart grieved for this suffering soul.

'I was in the Bastille,' said Thérésa gently. 'The people who no longer exist are still in my heart. They filled it to the top. I won't love again.'

'My wife, daughter and son all died on the scaffold in front of my eyes. My life is over, but I don't have the courage to die. There's nothing more to tell.' He stood and bowed to Nicole. 'Your cargo's safe with me. My story will have at least assured you that I'll guard it with my life, which matters nothing to me. Good night.'

Thérésa followed him.

By the time she crept back to the room, the church clock had already struck four in the morning. Exactly five hours, thought Nicole.

Thérésa smelt of hay and night air. Her hand followed her body's contours under the thin sheet and set Nicole on fire, then just as quickly abandoned her for her own bed.

The thought of her and Châtelet together tortured her. But no one owned Thérésa, least of all her. Like a blazing sunset, or a shooting star, you just had to be glad that you were there to witness it occasionally.

She slowed her breathing and forced herself to focus on the arrangements for the next leg of the journey, going over in her mind every detail of the planned mission until she drifted off into a fitful sleep, haunted by visions of Châtelet's family at the guillotine.

Early the next morning, Nicole was relieved to see Monsieur Châtelet ready and waiting, the wagon secured, horses calm. She estimated another hour to Charleville, where the barge was arranged for 6 a.m. An hour to load, and they'd be safely sailing along the Meuse, the waterway that would carry them all the way to Amsterdam. A journey of two and a half weeks, *please God*.

The sun was shining, the horses were speeding along at a fine clip, last night's cloud had lifted and for the moment they were all intent on their mission. Grief came in waves and Valentin Châtelet's story brought everything back too vividly. The receding of the wave might give even more power to the next, but while it receded, you had to make the most of it. Today at least brought calm waters for all of them.

A couple of hours into their journey, a battalion of soldiers could be seen marching towards them. Châtelet pulled over to let them go by, but the officer called for them to halt. Nicole eyed them in their scarlet coats and tricorn hats, bored young swaggerers with swords.

The officer stepped forward and bowed to Châtelet. 'Papers, Monsieur?'

Nicole produced them from her bag. 'You'll find they're all in order. This is my cargo, and the driver here is working for me.'

The soldier shook the papers open, taking his time to scrutinise the documents.

Natasha drew a secret figure of eight on her skirt. 'Trouble. I warned you,' she whispered.

'That's one hell of a big load for a lone peasant and a few female accomplices to handle, is it not?'

'It's the widow's coffee, bound for Russia,' said Châtelet.

Thérésa jumped down off the wagon. 'A cargo of mercy. An old woman's life savings invested in coffee to take to her dying mother and relatives in Russia. She has a long way to go and is weary from the road. Indeed, we are in a hurry to reach Charleville-Mezieres to meet our cargo barge.'

His expression hardened. 'Heart-rending. You realise all the trade routes are closed to Russia?'

'We'll take our chances. Let us pass,' said Châtelet. 'On what authority do you stop fellow citizens on the road?'

The soldier marched up to him, sword drawn. 'On *mine*. You *are* high-handed for a peasant, aren't you? Hiding something, are we, citizen – or should I say, *Seigneur*?'

Châtelet said nothing. The slightest whiff of 'aristocrat' would give these bored young thugs a good excuse for mayhem.

'Get off your high horse and kneel.'

The officer's men sniggered.

Châtelet stayed where he was. 'You do not have the authority.'

The soldier stroked Châtelet's throat with his sword. '*This* gives me the authority. Get down, scum, and kneel.'

Châtelet jumped down, taking his time, and spat in the officer's eye.

The officer kicked him down, sword pinning him to the dirt. 'Filthy, inbred aristo. Think you're better than me? Lick my boots.'

Châtelet spat again. The soldier thrust and Nicole looked away as Châtelet cried out in shock. Thérésa's eyes set in determination and Natasha crossed herself.

'How dare you!' shouted Thérésa, her voice piercing as a gunshot. 'Step away this *moment*, or General Tallien will hear of this outrage! Your rank and name. Now!'

The officer withdrew his sword from Châtelet's bleeding chest, but stood his ground.

'We are workers, like you, loyal citizens. Let us pass,' Natasha pleaded. 'A good soldier shows his men he is merciful, or the world is lost.'

'He stays where he is, keep back!' commanded the soldier as Thérésa rushed towards Châtelet. 'Men, inspect the wagons. They're hiding something.'

Châtelet's blood pooled on the dusty road. Two infantrymen prised open a coffee chest to dig through the coffee beans. Nicole held her breath.

'Satisfied?' called Thérésa. 'It seems you don't believe me. I am Thérésa Tallien. If I say the code word *white goose*, does that mean anything to you, fool?'

The officer's eyes widened and he stepped aside, saluting. 'Madame Tallien. My sincere apologies. You can't be too careful…'

'You use your rank to cause trouble, soldier. You may continue this time, but keep a cool head. You are here to protect, not throw your power around like a crazed schoolboy. Instruct your men to leave the medical bag with us, and be on your way.'

'Yes, Madame.'

He waved over a young soldier with rosy cheeks who was surely no more than fifteen years old. The boy dropped the leather medical bag at Thérésa's feet and shuffled backwards, then scuttled back to join the battalion who were already marching away.

Natasha set to work stemming the blood, prising the wound open to inspect it. Nicole couldn't watch.

'In future, don't involve *us* in your death wish,' admonished Thérésa as Natasha tore the bandage with her teeth.

'Press hard, here,' Natasha instructed Nicole.

Châtelet was barely conscious as they heaved him onto the wagon and made him as comfortable as they could.

'We need to get him to Charleville,' said Thérésa, 'as quickly as possible.'

'I'll take the reins,' said Nicole.

'I would expect nothing less of my country girl. You can really drive four horses?'

'I've never done it before, but I'm sure it's not that different from two.'

They started slowly. Natasha held Châtelet in her arms, sang him Russian lullabies. After an hour, Nicole's hands were blistered from holding the reins and relief flooded her when the roofs of Charleville welcomed her, a sunlit canal at its centre.

'He's hiding something,' whispered Natasha whilst he slept. 'Something more. What if he's related to the family that killed Daniel? Life is full of dead ends, but there are times when things come full circle. Maybe that's why he's here, bleeding into my skirt.'

'You have melancholy thoughts,' tutted Thérésa. 'Life needn't be so dull. We faced down danger and here we are.'

'For now,' said Natasha, squinting at the horizon.

They reached the canal, where a brightly painted barge was waiting, as arranged, but Nicole scrutinised the scene carefully before going closer.

People were going about their business, loading and unloading, shouting and swearing as crates bumped up against each other. Great loads were winched backwards and forwards over the canal and lowered onto barges, destined for the port or further inland. It all seemed normal, but did any of these men belong to Moët? Who among them was sent to spy on her, or worse, stop her? There was no way of knowing and all she could do was press on.

'This man can't travel any further, he desperately needs to rest,' said Natasha, carefully peeling Châtelet's soaked bandages to replace them with more. 'We have to stay the night here.'

'She's right,' said Thérésa. 'There's nothing *to* him, apart from bone, muscle and grief. I'll stay here with him and you go on. Two is less conspicuous than four and the barge pilot knows where he's going. I'll sign us into the inn as husband and wife and no one will suspect a thing.'

'But you've come this far. And how will I know the code word if we get into any more trouble?'

'Oh *that*. There has to be *some* advantage to humouring powerful men, apart from jewels and a roof over your head. Politics is a little hobby of mine and I make sure I keep my hand in. My ex-husband loved code words and it can't hurt to have more than you need of anything.'

'But…'

'I saw you when Châtelet helped me onto the carriage.' Thérésa gave her a knowing look. 'Jealousy is such a useless emotion. Your place is there, with the cargo. Besides, someone needs to deal with this.' Thérésa handed Nicole a letter, smeared in Châtelet's blood. 'I found it tucked in his shirt. I thought it might be a clue to what happened to his family, so I read it.'

Route: Rethel, Charleville-Mezieres. Destination: Russia.
Barge at Canal de la Meuse 23 May. Fifty thousand bottles
of champagne. Route onward so far unclear.

Thérésa handed her an addressed envelope. Smudged by blood, it was clearly marked.

Jean-Rémy Moët
Hôtel Moët
Épernay
Champagne

'What have you *done* to upset poor Monsieur Moët that he would go to such lengths to stop you? Have you been a little too successful? Get your champagne onto that barge and fly. Leave the rest to me.'

CHAPTER 10

February 1806

Loyalties

The shire horse paced along the hot, turgid canal, dragging the barge at a lethargic plod, oblivious to the urgency of his task. Nicole could only submit to the motion of the boat whilst the sun beat down and distract herself by watching the sparkles on the brown-green water. Natasha spent the morning clicking her beads and making salt shapes on the deck.

'Everything's so *slow*,' Nicole grumbled, already missing Thérésa.

Natasha looked at her sideways. 'You find me dull compared to her. She is dazzling, but be on your guard.'

'I'm sorry. I just can't stand this slow barge when there's so much at stake. You've known me all my life, through thick and thin. Sometimes I wish I could hide from your scrutiny!'

'It's a curse,' Natasha replied. 'I would rather *not* know. I know my mother is dying and that my journey is the only thing that's keeping her alive. It's thirty years since I last saw her and I've missed her every single day.'

'Yet you've never spoken of her. Tell me about her.'

'Ach. Broken memories. My two brothers stayed in the village with her. I was the only one to leave. They were wild. Dmitri used to make me ride with him on his horse. No saddle or reins. I cried at first, but then I felt like a tiny seed, flying across the tundra on the wind. I could have landed anywhere and grown. I remember her cold pink cheeks after a day out in the fields, the smell of lentils and herbs. We were always cold; there was never enough wood for a proper fire, but she made up for it with her love.'

Natasha paused and took the snowglobe she'd always given to Nicole to play with as a child out of her pocket. She shook it and watched the snowflakes float and settle on the little figures in the tableau, wrapped in capes and fur muffs. The miniature world seemed to take Natasha off into a reverie.

'She was beautiful when she was young. Her one extravagance was to decorate our bread. Girls with plaits, bouquets of flowers, sprays of holly, a tablecloth spread with plates and cups and piled with jellies, bread fit for a queen. She was only fifteen when she had me. Her hair was straight and black like mine, and her eyes were black, too. She can't have been much more than thirty, not much older than you, when I left, but she already looked old. Hers was the grinding life that peasants have lived for hundreds of years. Your revolution has changed all of that here. Daniel's blood was not wasted, that is my comfort.'

'He believed in the revolution,' said Nicole, realising that one of the reasons she was on this barge, hauling a cargo she hoped to smuggle against all the odds to Russia, was to give François' life meaning, too. 'You've borne it all with dignity and spirit, dear Natasha.'

'I don't want pity. My life has been one of relative prosperity. I love the *boulangerie* and I have my independence and dignity. My mother had neither. It's allowed me to be an observer of life.

I don't *know*, I *see*. I am invisible behind my counter and people unwittingly let me into their lives. I knead dough, feel the gritty flour on my fingertips, decorate it as my mother taught me and listen. Things happen in full sight if you just open your eyes and keep quiet. I see charged glances between lovers pointing to their morning croissants with no appetite, their eyes glazed with a kind of madness.' Natasha tutted, eyeing Nicole. 'Do they really think nobody notices? I've seen what the world tolerates when they look the other way, too. The bright-eyed children who come to beg stale bread, orphaned by poverty, turning from rosy-cheeked innocents to angular, dead-eyed thieves. It drove Daniel to challenge the Comte in the square that day. I've seen good things too. Girls with flowers in their hair blushing over cream meringues with their beaux, returning over the years to show off their babies, plump and creamy as the meringues. You were one of them.' She smiled.

'A million years ago,' said Nicole.

'If I've learned anything, it's that anything is possible. Impossible dreams happen – but not if you stick to the rules, Babouchette.'

The Canal de la Meuse meandered through the Belgian border and became the Maas. Days and weeks slipped by. Villages and towns lined the water, in places sleepy, elsewhere alive with commerce: cargo winched back and forth, barrels rolled noisily into warehouses; cows cooled in the shallows, women washed clothes and screeches of laughter echoed off the water. With so much traffic, it was a world of waiting at locks, mêlées of shouts, instructions and tall stories. Over the border, the same flat horizons met them, but the fields were full of precious tulips. Windmills creaked like big, ticking clocks, marking lost time.

The night before they were due to sail from Amsterdam, they arrived at a flight of thirteen locks. It was already past dark, and the night was moonless. The barge pilot refused to negotiate so many in the dark, so Nicole agreed that an early start would give them plenty of time to meet the 3 p.m. deadline she had agreed with the ship's captain.

'Thirteen is too unlucky to leave it until tomorrow,' Natasha warned.

'Let's not push our luck tonight, in the dark,' said Nicole.

The water roared as it rushed through the lock gate, swallowing the dark space above it. François might have been drawn to this in one of his black moods and she wouldn't be there to save him. She shivered at the ghost.

The clock struck three, then four. Sleep wouldn't come. She ached for François, for Thérésa, for Louis. Better to rise, even if just to freeze on deck. Pulling a shawl tight around her shoulders, she stepped out, the horizon a dirty smudge of dim light. Thirteen locks stepped steeply down, but at least they were the first barge in the queue and the minute the sun was high enough to light the fields, they'd be off.

Careful not to wake Natasha, Nicole crept up onto the towpath to get a better look at the locks. She peered into the first; the black was water way below, with most of the ladder visible above water, so deep it would surely take a good half an hour to fill.

As she looked closer, water began to trickle in, though she hadn't seen anyone open the gate. There was something about the depth that gave her that edge-of-a-cliff sensation, drawing her into its depths. Absorbed in her thoughts, she heard someone behind her too late, moving very fast. They grabbed her waist from behind, gripping so tight it took her breath away. She opened her mouth to scream, but a hand clamped it shut. It tasted of salt and grime.

'Don't start what you can't finish.' His hiss was hot and rancid at her ear. 'Give up the shipment, go home like a good little girl.'

He held her over the edge of the lock. The water began to roar as it spewed in, the level rising.

The man's grip tightened, his stinking body pressed against her. 'Advice from Monsieur Jean-Rémy Moët.'

'Please,' she choked, terrified.

He let go, but the force of the release made her stumble and she fell forward into the icy water which rushed in at her. She clawed at the surface, fighting to keep her head above the foam, her dress dragging her under. Gasping, she tugged off her underskirt and it was sucked out of her hands by the undertow. She shot up out of the water, fighting for air. The water swallowed her scream and gagged her, the level churning upwards. Thrusting for the black sky, she surfaced again and took another shuddering breath. She could just make out Natasha craning over the side.

'Help me!' she shrieked.

'Spread your arms and legs and *breathe*. Save your energy!'

Back under again, water booming in her ears. A figure scrambled down the ladder and stretched out his hand. She fixed on the lifeline, but the drag pulled her back. Hope heightened her choking panic. Her lungs burned and her legs ached with cold and effort.

'You can do it! Kick for your life, this is not your time!' screamed Natasha.

Nicole thrust with all her strength and gripped the hand, felt herself pulled forward.

'Keep your head up, I'll do the rest.'

The man yanked her to the ladder and she gripped it, afraid to move. He put his arm around her and his face came into focus. She froze in terror – Châtelet, Moët's man!

'Hold on to both sides of the ladder. Find the bottom rung and climb before you freeze to death and the water catches up with us,' he urged.

Natasha stretched her arms out above her. 'Look at me, don't look back. Just climb.'

She heaved herself up. The rungs were slick with green slime, the ladder was vertical and every muscle cramped, but she wasn't going back in that water. At the top, she collapsed on dry ground and shook uncontrollably in Natasha's arms.

Luckily, Natasha had been woken by the movement of the barge as the water level began to change and she realised Nicole was missing. As she'd searched for her on the deck, she saw Valentin grappling with a man, and heard Nicole's screams.

'It was Jean-Rémy...' Nicole gasped urgently. Then, in case they hadn't understood her meaning, added, 'We have to leave – now!'

'Shh, hush. Let's get you dry and warm. I thought I'd countered all the bad omens, I must have missed one,' said Natasha.

'Never mind omens. *Immediately*, I said! We *cannot* miss the boat in Amsterdam.'

'I know, we'll go. It's all settled, Valentin is going to help us.'

'Valentin is Moët's man! That turncoat is not coming near my shipment. He betrayed us! He's not here is he?'

Natasha held up a hand. 'Hush. Thérésa sent him on as soon as he was well enough to travel, and we can trust him now. He's explained everything to me. We'll get you fixed up, and just promise me you'll hear him out. We need all the help we can get.'

In dry clothes, she stared into the wood burner in shock while Châtelet stoked it.

'Let me help,' he murmured.

'Like you did before?'

'Moët doesn't know I'm here. I know the low-life fool who did this; it was one of his paid henchmen. He wanted to scare you,' said

Châtelet simply. 'But even Moët wouldn't have wanted to nearly kill you. His man is an ignorant blunderer – he's known for it. Thank God I was here to deal with him – he won't be bothering you any more. I knew Moët would try something desperate. I'm sure he's convinced himself he's doing you a favour by forcing you to give up your wine business.'

'Favour! He's a madman. Jean-Rémy never does anyone a favour, without taking something for himself! I'm not afraid, even now. And why should I believe you? Thanks to *you* he knew all my plans. To think that I actually felt sorry for you!'

'Moët found me on his land, almost dead, running with lice and sores,' said Châtelet. 'He fed me, listened to my stories and took pity. I would have done anything for him, even stop a determined woman like you. He asked me to find a way to gain the confidence of your man, Xavier. When he asked me to drive for you, Moët couldn't believe his luck. Intelligence right from the inner circle…' He eyed her apologetically. 'Moët convinced me it was for your own good – that is, until I met you. You have a fire in you that I don't want to be responsible for extinguishing and your daughter is the same age as mine was. Thérésa helped me get stronger and I came to find you – at a distance, because I knew Moët would try something.'

'If he thinks I'm stupid enough, or weak enough…' stuttered Nicole.

'He thinks everyone is, compared to him,' said Valentin. 'Which is *his* weakness when it comes to you. You are a business-woman. Use me, I can help.'

What the hell else was Jean-Rémy capable of? Of course she was afraid, all alone with an old Russian woman and a turncoat for company, but what other choice did she have?

Natasha narrowed her eyes at Châtelet. 'I'll be watching you. When you're in sight *and* when you're not.'

'I expect nothing less of you, Madame. Judge my actions and you'll see. I will make you three promises to help Nicole beat him. This much I can do, but it's going to take a lot of her courage, too.'

'She's got plenty of that,' said Natasha proudly. 'Tell us your plan.'

First, Châtelet brought Nicole a shorn-off winch as proof of his fidelity. The sun was still not quite risen, so she and Natasha were able to creep unseen along the queue of barges to confirm his next piece of information. Holding the lamp closer to the barge inscription, it was as he told her: *Moët et Compagnie*, no doubt a cargo of champagne headed for Russia, covered by a tarpaulin.

Natasha tutted, 'Love turned to hate is an ugly thing.'

Back on the barge, Nicole hastily emptied her purse, made ten neat, equal piles of coins, and waited.

Châtelet kept his third promise and returned with ten strong men from the local village. Their eyes widened at the coin stacks.

'Not now. Afterwards, when every single crate is loaded. Get to work and if you are finished in an hour, this is yours.'

Her pocket watch always kept good time and Nicole checked it now. Eight hours before the ship sailed. If this went well, they'd make it easily. The men started work.

'You've secured a boat at the bottom of the lock flight?'

'As promised. It's there.'

The shorn-off winch caught her thumb and the jagged edge drew blood. She dropped it next to the coins.

'You've seen his barge isn't going anywhere. No one can pass this point without a winch for the lock gates. It will take them all day to fix it. Do you trust me now?' asked Châtelet.

She ignored him. 'Guard the money,' she said to Natasha as she scooped it up and placed it in the safe. Tucking the key in her secret pocket, she set off for the port authority cabin, the next part of Châtelet's plan. It was a risk, but she took satisfaction in seeing Châtelet's men heaving her crates down the towpath past the locks. With a barge secured below the locks, hers would be the only cargo leaving this place for Amsterdam today. Thanks to the shorn-off lock-gate winch and the boat at the bottom of the lock flight that Châtelet had secured for her, Moët had absolutely no chance of doing the same.

She was glad she'd taken the precaution of packing so well that the bottles wouldn't clang, and also writing 'coffee' on the crates. No matter how much money she offered, the men would know they'd be risking their liberty handling illicit champagne – better they knew nothing about it.

Straightening her back, she knocked on the port-authority door next to Moët's barge.

The customs officer stubbed out his cigarette and straightened his cap.

'It's a bit early for a visit from a lady,' he said, stepping out and closing the door behind him. 'We open in an hour, come back then.'

'I have information relating to that cargo,' said Nicole, pointing to Moët's barge.

'Do you now?' replied the man.

'May I come in?'

'Say what you've got to say,' he said, staying where he was.

'It's a criminal matter.'

'Is it really?'

He gestured for her to continue.

'There's forbidden cargo on that barge,' she said. Through a window, she saw someone move inside the office.

'And what would that be?'

'Champagne,' said Nicole. 'Bound for Russia. You'd lose your job if it was found out, so I thought you should know.'

The man's expression changed. 'I see. Why don't you step inside after all?'

Pleased, she followed him in, but he slammed the door behind her. Jean-Rémy Moët sat behind the customs desk.

'It's not at all safe here, my dear,' he said, raising an eyebrow as her nostrils flared in fury. 'I promised your father I'd bring you home safely. It seems Valentin has switched sides. And who can blame him rushing to aid such a charming damsel in distress? He's a complicated man, but whatever heart he had was taken in the revolution, so do take care with your new friend. However, as you see, I have friends everywhere and I never rely on one single point of failure. It pays to always have a back-up plan.'

Moët and the customs man bowed to each other in satisfaction.

She turned to escape, but the customs man blocked the exit and turned the key in the lock.

'What the hell are you doing?' she demanded.

'I'm sorry. My boat needs to be on its way before you are,' said Moët. 'It's better just to calm down and let it happen. How bad can it be? You must see, this is no business for a woman. The first rule of business is that it's for men – it's money and power and dog-eat-dog and you're in deep.'

'You overbearing, deceptive, dishonest, thieving…'

'And you expect to sell me down the river while exporting your own champagne to the promised land? The second rule of business is that you must see things from more than one viewpoint,' said Moët, infuriatingly smug.

'If you don't care about me, there's Natasha. Her mother is dying, she needs to get to her before it's too late. Jean-Rémy, why can't we *both* sell in Russia?'

'It seems you have been doubly fooled. I helped Natasha file papers for her mother's death years ago. She asked for my assistance in the matter when I was Mayor.'

He looked out of the window and drummed his fingers while the revelation sank in. Dear, clever Natasha had more than made up for abandoning her after François' death now, by giving her a reason to carry on.

'An hour or so will do it,' Moët continued. 'I'm sure you won't want to come back to Reims with me, but you would be welcome. After an hour, you are free to go, but in the meantime, I must keep you safe here. One day I hope that you will see that I only act in your interests.'

'I would rather drown here than die a death in drawing rooms.'

'I'm afraid you have no choice. It's the natural way of things,' Jean-Rémy said, pressing a large gold coin into the customs officer's palm as he left.

Nicole's pocket watch chimed the half-hour, then the hour, as she paced the little room. There was no more money, no more chances.

Outside, harsh morning dawned – time was rushing by and each minute that passed made her burst with frustration and fury. She banged on the window, but the customs officer pulled her back and shoved her onto a chair.

'You're a little vixen, aren't you? Just sit nicely, or I'll need to tie you up.'

Men were busily hauling cargo, scrubbing boats, preparing for the day. A knot of sailors clustered round the Moët barge, unloading, no doubt, to use her barge beyond the locks. She watched in a rage of despair, but something wasn't right. Instead of heading down the towpath past the locks, the men were running with armfuls of bottles into the fields. A man was raging at them and someone restraining him. She squinted to see more clearly and gasped. Jean-Rémy was handcuffed, held hostage by a man in a customs uniform.

'*Putain, bordel de merde.* Thieving peasants! I'll remember each and every one of your criminal faces!'

'He's got a worse temper than you,' laughed the customs officer. He stood up, unlocked the door and opened it with a sweeping gesture. 'You're free to go,' he said. 'Monsieur Moët's champagne is being distributed. We might as well – if it got to the port, it would be poured away as an illegal export.' He handed her a white feather tied with a narrow red ribbon. 'She said you'd understand. It seems you have friends in high places.'

How could she ever have doubted her beautiful, clever friend! Thérésa loved a riddle, but these clues were obvious. At least there was someone she could trust to get things done properly, apart from herself.

He bowed. 'My apologies for the charade, but you were the honey for our trap. Madame Tallien arranged everything, and we've been waiting for you all week. Safe journey with your coffee, Madame.'

The sun blazed ready for the next leg of her journey as Nicole rushed along the towpath back to her boat. Sweet freedom and cool revenge were a heady mix and, as she passed him, Moët was issuing threats to a frightened-looking *gendarme* about his great patron, Napoléon.

'The third rule of business,' she said to him as she headed back to her cargo. 'It's not what you know, it's who you know.'

Châtelet kissed her on both cheeks and helped her onto the barge below the locks.

'Where will you go?' she called to him as the barge pilot buckled up the shires for the final leg of the journey.

'Home,' said Châtelet. 'Back to my hometown, to face the past and maybe start a future, or at least to grieve and remember them as they were. Don't give up, and make it all work for that little girl of yours, and in memory of mine.'

CHAPTER 11

March 1806

The Most Audacious Vintner in France

Amsterdam was the loveliest sight Nicole had ever seen. The barge sailed through the outskirts where the houses squashed together, tall, painted and slim like a box of artist's pastels. Cloistered girls watched from the big windows with canal-dappled faces, waiting for a husband. She, however, had the sun on her face and a cargo of liquid gold in the hold. Natasha smiled and waved at the children who ran alongside the barges, sticking out their tongues. Merchants bustled onto the towpath straight out of the front doors. Flower stalls splashed colour, fish flashed as maids stuffed them into their baskets and old men saluted her barge as it cut the water.

The mariners' church clock read 11.30 a.m. precisely as they took the feeder canal into the port. With no time to lose, the barge pilot went off to find men to help unload, while Nicole shook out Captain Johannes' instructions.

Having memorised the route, she hurried along the harbour, feeling like the most audacious, canniest vintner in the whole of France. The boats looked glorious, their hulking prows rising up like castles out of the water. Women mended nets, silvery fish scales made the cobbles slippery underfoot and the choppy breeze promised adventure.

She scanned the boats for the name, *De Dolfijn*. Nowhere to be seen. They only had three hours before the ship sailed and she was anxious to find her captain so the men could load the cargo as soon as possible. The place was infested with thieves and if they didn't hurry, a good knife through the ropes would mean the end of her champagne.

With so many big boats in the water, the place was surprisingly deserted. Nothing was as the captain had described when he'd sent her joining instructions for the ship. There wasn't a soul to ask about the next stage of the cargo's journey, and even if there was, she didn't want to draw attention to herself. She fished in her pocket for another glance at the instructions, trying not to look like a stranger as she scanned it for the landmark of the customs house.

With the sun on her right, she was definitely heading east. Thank God, exactly as instructed, the *Douane* sign appeared in big gold letters on the side of the warehouse. Next, a right turn down the alleyway, eyes ahead, ignoring a cluster of dockers leaning on the corner eyeing her and there it was, an unassuming low black doorway, flanked by grimy windows. She squinted at the plaque, which read *Kapitein Johannes de Vries*, and gave a sharp, optimistic tap to match her mood. No reply. She tried again, and was rewarded with a slow shuffle towards the door. It opened a crack and an old lady's face peered through.

'Nicole Clicquot,' announced the most daring wine merchant within a thousand miles. 'Captain Johannes is expecting me.'

The door swung open. 'Hello, my dear,' said the old lady. 'There you are. He *was* expecting you, but he sailed yesterday. I'm so sorry, he couldn't wait. He heard about today's port blockade and sailed straight away. The whole place has ground to a halt and there was no way of getting word to you.'

Nicole stood in shock. 'But he must have left instructions – a replacement ship?'

'I'm sorry, Madame, he was in a mad rush. It was leave yesterday or never and he took his chances.'

'I can't possibly take my shipment home again, and without proper storage, it will spoil. I've already paid him a large deposit. I'll wait for him to come back.'

'You'll be waiting a long time. He's back in three months.'

'*What?*'

'I'm so sorry, Madame. The brown cafés are full of men who lost their fortune today. The warehouses are piled with goods waiting to sail and no one knows when the blockades will be lifted. Nothing leaves by sea. That's the instruction, or Napoléon will kill us all. Did you hear he crowned himself King of Italy today? I am French, but I speak convincing Dutch. If I were you, I'd keep your mouth shut and hurry back to France. It's not safe here.'

The door slammed in her face. Nicole pulled her cloak tight and hurried back across the deserted docks, mind racing. Fifty thousand bottles languishing. Nothing in or out of the port. She was ruined and she was taking her investor, dear old Philippe Clicquot, with her.

By the time she arrived back at the boat, she was shaking in shock and she scrambled down the steps to board. Her heel caught and she slipped, grabbed for the handrail and missed. A body caught her and helped her gently onto the deck. Louis Bohne.

'You're in a rush,' he said quietly.

'What are you doing here?' she gasped.

'Natasha told me you'd agreed to my sale and were going to Russia. I was on the road and only just got her message in time, so I came as soon as I could, despite your last words to me in Paris. Go to hell, I think they were. You certainly got here earlier than I thought possible, even for you! I arrived last night and expected to be here for days waiting for you to arrive. You must have been travelling day and night.'

'We have. I'm sorry I was angry, but it's no use anyway. The whole venture is a massive failure. Have you heard? All ports closed to trade.'

'I've known since I arrived yesterday.'

'It's a disaster, I should never have tried it. I've made enemies, dragged poor François' father into the whole mess. Moët was right.'

'What's he got to do with this?'

'It doesn't matter any more. He wanted to destroy me, but I've done it myself, without any help from him. I've got to get my champagne out of here. The place is crawling with overenthusiastic *gendarmes* and customs officials, looking for French transgressors and I'd be no use to anyone in a Dutch prison.'

'You're right. My German accent will save me, but you're a liability. I can arrange for someone to escort you home and I have a contact with a warehouse a few miles from here. I'll get your bottles there safely and it will buy us time to make a plan.'

'But the bottles need to be in a cool cellar, not a warehouse. Any big change in temperature will be a disaster.'

'Do you have any other ideas?'

She gritted her teeth. 'No. But I can't leave you here; come back with me.'

Louis shook his head. 'No, I need to get these bottles stored and then I'm taking my chances on the road. You need the business and I'm not giving up.'

'*We* need the business, Louis, and I'm past all that. I'm *never* giving up, not until the last bottle has left the warehouse and the last grape has dried on the vine and even then I'll plant more and start again.'

'That's more like my Babouchette. The one who charmed the most handsome man in Reims into marrying her, then made his vineyards the best in Champagne.'

Their eyes met at the mention of François and she knew what she had to do.

'What if you take some of my bottles overland with you? There's still a chance if we're quick. You know the routes like the back of your hand and, as you say, they'll never know you're French, or that you're carrying French champagne – it's all still packed and disguised as coffee. I just can't leave it all to ruin in the warehouse.'

Louis saluted her and broke her a warm-hearted smile. 'Genius, Veuve Clicquot. So, finally, you see what's good for you and you'll let me help you? Just as well I didn't die in my balcony dive. Those Ruskies have an insatiable taste for champagne, war or not.'

She rolled up her sleeves. 'Right, let's get this lot unloaded.'

Louis stopped her gently. 'I know you don't like taking orders, but please, leave it with me. You're better off getting out of here with Natasha and not drawing attention to yourself. Plus, the vineyards need you. If I get some of your orders fulfilled, they'll be desperate for more,' said Louis.

'I wish I could come with you.' It was almost hopeless, but they had to try.

'Keep your head high. Your ambitions are too big for that little town and they'll savour your defeat.'

'I'll watch her,' said Natasha fiercely, emerging from below deck. 'I have been a stranger there all my life. I can teach her to be immune.'

It was a treacherous trip, but if anyone could get at least some of her shipment to Russia, it was Louis. And she could see that look in his eye. Where she saw danger, he saw the open road, new fellows to hail, adventure, prospects to charm. Whoever married him would have a hard time pinning him down.

The journey back to Reims was a nightmare of torturous nights full of regret, staring at the starless sky. What was she thinking? Louis could die helping her. The captain's housekeeper's words came back to her. Anyone French was in danger, even in Amsterdam, never mind on the trade routes through Prussia and into Russia.

By the time she arrived back, she was exhausted. She avoided her town residence and went straight to her house in Bouzy, where her maid Josette was waiting with a bowl of onion soup and a sympathetic smile. She couldn't face the town, not yet. They would see the failure in her eyes and there was no way she was giving them that. She fell into her bed, Josette fussing around her, stoking up the fire, begging her to rest. A few nights among the vines would restore her, give her enough time to gather courage to face down the gossips until she could make another plan.

Outside her window, the vines lit up against the night sky, stretching as far as she could see. Despite her absence, the vineyards were as they should be. Xavier and her loyal workers always made sure of that, but it was never quite as neat or ordered as when she was supervising everything. Still no buds – they wouldn't appear until May – but the first full moon in March was the time to bottle new champagne, when they transferred the wine blends from barrels to their bottles and the warmer weather would help with the second fermentation to produce, they hoped, the liveliest bubbles. Her first priority must be to gather the committee to assess the next blend.

Three days later, the tasting committee gathered in her press. She was grateful that Monsieur Olivier had agreed to an urgent meeting. It was a busy time for them and her business wasn't exactly a priority.

'When are the others arriving?' asked Nicole.

Monsieur Olivier was reluctant to meet her eye. 'It will just be myself, Monsieur Var and Monsieur Faubert today. The others aren't available.'

The committee *always* came as one. This was a rebuff, but she had to press on. She could make the blends alone if she had to, but it was bad politics not to involve them.

'No good. Reject,' pronounced Monsieur Olivier when he tasted her best Pinot Noir.

The scaled-down committee nodded in agreement.

'Are you sure?' protested Nicole. 'Last year was just right for these. They're from my prime spot on the Côtes des Bar. It would make a wonderful blend.'

'You're losing your touch, Madame Clicquot, I cannot agree,' said Monsieur Olivier. 'Gentlemen?'

'Just a little too acid,' said Monsieur Var, spitting.

'A couple more weeks on the vine and it would have been perfect, but sadly…' added Monsieur Faubert with a delicate cough.

Nicole took another sip. They were wrong, but she moved on to the next. And the next. Each one was rejected.

Monsieur Olivier patted her hand. 'Standards must be maintained. My humble advice is to wait until next year. Patience is the greatest virtue in the wine business. Undue haste and risk-taking just don't pay off, I'm sure you understand that now. We must all stand together to maintain the reputation of the Champagne region, put aside individual profit for the greater good. I sincerely hope you have better luck with this year's crop, Madame Clicquot.'

The men shook her hand and left so quickly she didn't even have time to ask after their wives. When they passed Xavier on the way out, he spat at their feet.

'Xavier, what was that for?' asked Nicole.

'I suppose they rejected all your blends?' he asked, glowering.

'How did you know?'

'That running sore, Moët, put them up to it. The whole town's buzzing with it, like wasps round jam. You're a disaster. You've lost everything. Pissed Philippe Clicquot's investment against a wall, consorted with a high-class prostitute from Paris whilst making a mad dash for the coast with a fortune in champagne. He says it's no surprise, with madness in the family.'

'What's that supposed to mean?'

'The rumours are back again, fertilised by Moët's own brand of stinking manure. They mean François. They say you're like him. You take too many risks and when the going gets tough you fold. There's not a man within a hundred miles of you who'll do business with you. He's made sure of that.'

CHAPTER 12

July 1806

The Arrogance of Women

Another stifling day, with the water troughs as dry as Nicole's heart and the grapes withering on the vines. The news of the failed shipment spread like wildfire. What better way to pass the long summer evenings than discussing the failure of the arrogant Veuve Clicquot? At least her beautiful little Mentine was home from Paris and she was her world, but even that was difficult, trying to protect her from the gossip in this little town.

She scraped her fingers across the rough trough to *feel* something. Her world was getting smaller. The window of opportunity had been narrow and she had failed spectacularly. The blockades could last for months, years even. French exports, particularly anything as wonderfully French as champagne, were vilified and blocked. Her best trading countries – the Holy Roman Empire, along with Britain and Russia – had formed the Third Coalition, cutting her off, and she was trapped in the tiny world of Reims, in a sea of hostility and humiliation. And she hadn't heard a word from Louis since the day they'd said goodbye on the docks. What had she been thinking, sending him back to Russia?

She steeled herself as she crossed the square in front of the cathedral. The gargoyles shimmered in the heat, mocking her. Maybe she *was* going mad.

The wholesome smell of baking caught in her throat as she hastily smudged away a tear. Madame Olivier was gossiping at the counter with Natasha and her heart sank. She needed to speak to Natasha alone.

'Still stuck at Amsterdam?' Madame Olivier asked Natasha.

Natasha acknowledged Nicole with a glance and gave Madame Oliver a purse-lipped nod in reply.

Madame Olivier pressed on, oblivious to Nicole's presence. 'She'll ruin poor Philippe Clicquot with her wild schemes, that one, as if he hasn't suffered enough. I can't believe she dragged *you* into it too, when you've worked so hard to build your reputation alone in this town…'

The wine taster's wife was an enthusiastic gossip, with far too much time on her hands. How dare she! Nicole opened her mouth to protest, but Natasha stayed her discreetly with a raise of her hand, and let Madame Olivier continue.

'And Monsieur Bohne, left in poverty, consorting with an aristocrat on the run from the authorities. It's all right for her. She won't starve, her parents will make sure of that. She'll have to learn. Leave it to the men. Monsieur Moët tried his best to help, I believe? How could she have possibly refused his kind offers, a woman in her position?'

'Perhaps you could ask her yourself.' Natasha nodded in Nicole's direction.

Madame Olivier swung round. 'My dear. Here's me gossiping as always and you're right *there*.'

'Indeed I am. Monsieur Moët is not the saint you imagine, you know.'

'Oh?'

Nicole could see that the chance of some unique knowledge of the Veuve Clicquot situation clearly grabbed Madame Olivier's attention. She forced herself to suppress the need to tear her down a strip or two for her unkindness.

Despite the town gossip's pinched lips and gimlet eyes, there was something needy and vulnerable about her, and Nicole had heard the rumours about her controlling husband. A germ of an idea began to form.

'The truth is, he tried to stop me in the most underhand way,' said Nicole, mustering up as much of a tone of friendliness as she could. 'And me, a widow, just trying to continue my late husband's legacy. François *lived* for those vines. He almost loved them into life. Unfortunately, Monsieur Moët respects my business enough to want to try to stop me. I can't believe this town doesn't see right through him. I understand he had the temerity to override some of your husband's blending decisions recently, *n'est-ce pas*? He's powerful enough already, isn't he?'

'Really? What happened?' Madame Olivier was completely hooked.

'You think a woman isn't capable? That only her husband should meddle in wine? I bet you know just as much as he does. You grew up in this town, we all did. It's in our blood. You must have tasted hundreds of wines, discussed the ins and outs with your husband over the years? He doesn't have the inclination this year to attend my tastings. Perhaps you and some of the other wives would lend a hand?'

'I'm sure my husband would *never* condone such a—'

'The husbands need never know. English tea parties are very fashionable at the moment and you can tell them that's what you are attending. We'd have more leisure to talk about what *really* happened on my trip to Amsterdam. There were some frantic moments, I can tell you!'

'Marvellous idea,' said Natasha. 'Let the men *pretend* they're in charge!'

There was a glimmer of admiration in Madame Olivier's stare. 'Yes, it's always better to let them think that. It makes them so much easier to manage. In that case, I will accept, my dear.'

'I will send an invitation with Emile. If you could prepare the ground with some of the others…'

'You can count on me, Madame Clicquot.' She paused. 'I'm sorry for your loss. And I'm sorry that you heard me gossiping. My mouth just opens and out it comes, with no thought. Please don't take it to heart.'

'I understand. *A bientôt.*'

Madame Olivier left.

'How could you have let her continue?' said Nicole, but she didn't mind. Maybe bumping into Madame Olivier was what she had needed.

Natasha squeezed out from behind the counter and hugged her. 'It worked out for the best, didn't it? Hearing her gave you a little spirit. It's been a while since I saw that spark in your eye. Don't cry. Things will get better, I promise. I've *seen* it.' Natasha delved into her pocket and sketched a figure of eight around her head, salt skittering on the floor. 'Now, let me guess, two *religieuses*? I hear Mentine is back from Paris for the holidays. You'll accept a gift to help you celebrate?'

Nicole hurried home clutching the cakes. Her first foray out to face the town and a minor triumph. Her heart was still beating when she shut the door of the house on rue de la Vache, a letter from Louis she had collected from the post office trembling in her hand. She opened it, tucked her hair back and smoothed it out, smiling at the careless splodges of candle wax.

My dear Nicole,

I made it and so did your champagne! I am safely in St Petersburg, but I found much to worry about as I crossed Saxony and Prussia. All the talk is war, spreading as far as the grand square I see out of my window. It's a beautiful morning and the idea seems unbelievable. We'll see.

Despite the beauty of my view, it's you I see as I write. You're smoothing the paper and tutting at the spilt candle wax. Don't frown! I won't go short of candles, so don't fret about the waste, or about me. I have friends here, including one that will surprise you. Thérésa! Or La Tallien, as she is affectionately called here.

She's my ticket to every fashionable happening in this town. And this is a very fashionable town. Acres of tulle, a mine's worth of diamonds and gold. Even the men swathe themselves in chinoiserie. I'm very dull in my wolfskin coat and boots, which I like to think makes me exotic in Reims. Thérésa has persuaded me on a shopping trip tomorrow…

What? Was there no one she couldn't bewitch? Louis, on a *shopping* trip, such cosy domesticity?

…but don't worry, her superficial charms don't penetrate my thick skin. It's you I'm here for. The Empress Elizabeth is pregnant with her first child and I predict a tide of champagne to celebrate the birth.

That's the good news. There is bad, too. The place is buzzing with Napoléon, his next move, his unstoppable desires on the world and on Russia. That makes being French here tricky. My German origins help me, and Thérésa is strangely immune to any danger.

Now business. Thanks to your charming friend's connections, we were invited to a state banquet at the Great Palace in Tsarskoye Selo, a paradise away from St Petersburg. Thérésa was of course thoroughly bored by the whole thing. She only had her eye on the prize and, within half an hour, we were introduced to the Tsar and Tsarina.

She explained how Napoléon preferred Moët, but anyone of real taste in France preferred a glass of the Veuve. Created by a petite young woman, blonde ardente with shrewd grey eyes who talks to her bottles as if they were her children. The finest champagne on earth. The Queen of Champagne.

My advice to you is to save every single bottle you can from those I left stored in Amsterdam – do not compromise on quality...

As if I ever would, Louis Bohne!

...and ship them immediately to St Petersburg. Leave the rest to your faithful servant.

Nicole imagined him taking another sip of burgundy, warmed by his success, pulling his wolfskin coat around him, with that grin that charmed society hosts across Europe.

She picked up a bottle of Bouzy from the mantelpiece and hugged it. The cool glass against her hot cheek felt wonderful. Enough.

This news leaves me only to say, I make progress with the Don Quixote *book you gave me and think of my patronne every time I pick it up.*

Your Louis

'*Maman!*'

Mentine burst into her office, and careered towards her. She stopped short.

'You're not sad again?'

'Come here, *ma petite.* Did you know that you can cry with sadness *and* happiness? These tears are happiness. I have good news from Russia. Papa would have been proud.'

'You mean they'll buy all your golden champagne and drink it in their onion buildings?' she exclaimed, bright with excitement.

'Who told you about golden champagne?'

'Thérésa. When she wasn't all dressed up and going out to a ball, she came to the nursery and told us stories. Our favourite was about a handsome man and a beautiful woman who could taste the land and the sky and make it into magic champagne. It made me think of you and Papa. Now you *are* sad!'

'No, I'm happy again now. That's a lovely story. Look here, I bought us a treat from Natasha.'

Nicole unwrapped Natasha's *religieuses* and Mentine ate quietly.

'I much prefer Thérésa's stories to Mireille's.'

'Who's Mireille?'

'Mireille Olivier. I play with her in the square. Her grandpa is Monsieur Olivier, the wine taster.'

'What stories does Mireille tell?'

'Oh, boring ones. It's better when she shuts up and I beat her at hopscotch.' Mentine looked away.

'That runs in the family. The Clicquots have always been good at hopscotch. People tell all sorts of stories that aren't true. Tell me what Mireille says, and we can play a game. True or false.'

'Papa was weak-minded.'

Her heart careened with grief and anger, but she was careful not to show it.

'False. He was the most poetic, kindest, cleverest man in Reims. Next.'

'You should stay inside and wear pretty dresses and stop meddling.'

'False. Just because you're a girl doesn't mean you should stop doing anything you want to. Some girls like to stay in and wear pretty dresses. I don't. I want to do lots more things. Sometimes you have to be brave. Sometimes people don't like other people doing things that are unusual. But that should never, ever stop you. Next.'

'You dig the soil with your own hands, like a peasant.'

'She got one right! True. There's nothing like the feel of the soil in your hands, knowing it will grow the grapes that make the golden champagne. It's magic. You can't make champagne without knowing every single thing you need to do to make it good. You can tell her that. Her grandpa would agree.'

'I will,' said Mentine in a small voice.

'Let's not talk about Mireille any more. She *does* sound a bit boring. You have a bit of cream on your forehead. How could such a tiny amount of cream end up in so many places?'

They giggled.

Conniving, small-minded, pious, gossiping, two-faced snakes the lot of them. Nicole was going to Amsterdam to save whatever Louis couldn't take the first time round and send it overland to him and his Tsar and Tsarina. She'd scrap the rest and start again.

CHAPTER 13

August 1806

Praying for a Miracle

The moon was in her favour, bright and crisp. The stables smelt of hay and sweat. Nicole took off her riding glove to feel the bay's soft muzzle, then slipped on the harness, buckles jangling in the darkness, the horse stamping at the imposition.

'I'm not doing it,' said Xavier, folding his arms tight.

Nicole led the horse out and thrust the reins at him. 'Then I'll have to do it myself. Hold these.'

She lifted the carriage shafts, her arms barely reaching between the two, and heaved. The cart didn't budge.

'I'm going, so you might as well help me.'

'You look like an ant trying to shift a rock. Here.'

He gave her back the reins and she dropped the shafts. Xavier had it fixed up in seconds. She jumped up.

'Lift up my trunk and tie it down. I'm not going to be stopping much.'

'You're stubborn, but I never thought you were stupid.'

'It will only take about a week to get to Amsterdam if I'm fast. Don't worry, I'll change horses on the way. Listen, Louis won't leave Russia until the new consignment arrives. Things are desperate there since Napoléon's advance – anyone French is under suspicion. I'm so worried about him; he's already been robbed once. He says if I get everything to him in the next month, he promises to leave.

'You know how it is. If I don't go to Amsterdam alone to rescue my bottles, the whole town will write my business off, and I can't afford another race to the border. Not with Moët – or any of the other vintners for that matter. Just tie up my trunk and wish me luck. Mentine is safe with my parents, and don't forget to tell Madame Olivier I'm visiting Thérésa in Paris for the end of the season. That way, the whole town will know within hours. They'd much rather I was sifting through potential husbands in Paris than sorting my bottles in Amsterdam and earning an honest living.'

'You'll need a bloody miracle if you think you can do this alone,' said Xavier, securing the ropes on the trunk.

'Miracles happen every year, right here in my vineyards, and I'm not letting any of it go to waste.'

'Do what you bloody well like then. Just don't come crying to me when you get robbed or raped on the road, or break a wheel in a rut, or get kidnapped by one of those cheese-breathed, foul-mouthed Dutch sailors.'

'I can't come crying to you if I've been kidnapped,' she retorted.

Xavier tutted, but with a glint of pride he grumbled, 'Go, while it's still dark. And don't worry, I'll pick up the pieces here while you're off on your wild goose chase.'

She cracked the whip. The cool night air stung her cheeks; the road ahead was bright and moonlit. She flew as fast as the bay was willing until the vineyards turned to farmland and the sun introduced the new day with a blazing show of mackerel clouds.

*

Amsterdam was sultry; the docks were deserted again, the air so thick it was like breathing cotton wool. Her black widow's dress clung to her and a bloated sun lolled on the horizon. Sailors and dock workers sprawled outside the taverns, still up from the night before, too much time on their hands with no ships sailing in or out, drunkenly catcalling clusters of prostitutes. Some of the girls were very young, emaciated and sallow, collarbones protruding above pushed-up breasts. Someone's baby, now a dead-eyed skeleton. Fortunes rose and fell fast in war. At least she was keeping her own employees in work.

Nicole hurried past, grateful that the prostitutes rendered her invisible. When she reached the warehouse where Louis had sent the majority of her stock, she unhooked the keys from her belt, wiggled the lock open and turned the handle, dreading what she would find. The warehouse smelt musty. Pallet upon pallet was stacked high to the ceiling. Her heart sank. It would take weeks to get through them all. She unbuttoned her sleeves and focused on the pallet in front of her, pulled out a bottle and held it up to the light. A fungal finger gloated at her from inside the wine. Ruined. She started a reject pile, ready for the cart to take them to the merchant who would pour her precious wine down the drain and reuse the bottles.

She worked through ten pallets, each one the same story. Ruined, ruined, ruined. Nearly fifty thousand bottles, the result of battling the elements, back-breaking harvest, press, fermenting and careful blending, to end up going nowhere, crammed into this grim shed next to a dull grey sea. Such bad luck was just unfair. A day earlier and these bottles would have made the ship to Russia. It would be so much easier to leave the whole bloody lot to its fate.

After another ten pallets, the sun was already high outside the window. Time was elastic in this place and hunger pangs reminded

Nicole to unwrap the neatly folded greased-paper package her hotel had provided. The baguette was as good as Natasha's, still fresh, and it smelt like home.

She remembered Natasha's parting words, *You make your own luck, and you are a lucky person.*

She devoured the rest of the baguette and set back to work.

It took three weeks of working day and night, acting as judge and jury for every one of her precious bottles. Each night, she huddled back along the canals to her small hotel, then rose at the first light of dawn to resume her task, the kindly owner of the hotel pressing a food package into her hands as she left in case she forgot to eat.

She was determined that she would save every good bottle. If she could get even five thousand bottles to Louis, it would be something. At least he'd come home and be safe from the escalating situation in Russia.

Chatting to the wine helped with the loneliness. Each bottle had its own personality, its own life to live. 'You,' she told a salvageable red, 'will wind up a track in the sunshine where the larks hover above the poppies, crimson against yellow grass, to a mellow country house. There'll be a simple wedding, with wild flowers and fiddles. And you,' (the bottle of Chardonnay felt dangerously warm to the touch), 'may lie for years in a cellar, waiting for a longed-for baby to be born. I hope for their sake you are opened.' She picked up a bottle of champagne. 'And you, my beautiful friend, are for starlit lovers.'

At last a good batch! She kissed the pristine bottle. Crystal clear, a smart cordon of fizz, corks intact. She remembered her abandoned riddling experiment in the basement and resolved to try again. And keep trying. She'd be rich if she could guarantee this quality every time and François' name, the name he had given her, would be famous down the generations. She'd be laughed out of town if anyone knew the extent of her ambition, but barely a day passed when she didn't turn the problem over in her mind and try to find a solution.

Each good bottle received a kiss as she lined them up: enough to supply a whole palace! She remembered Louis' news that the Tsarina Elizabeth was five months pregnant. It would be these bottles that would help celebrate the royal birth in December. It *was* possible to get it all overland to Louis by then. Surely Natasha could conjure up just a little bit of extra luck for the journey!

At last, when the task was nearly complete, she summoned Xavier's driver from Reims. When he arrived, she was relieved to see that he had a kind, open face and she recognised him as one of the boys who was always in the square, now grown up, who she'd known forever, even if she didn't know his name. Good, Xavier had chosen well. She needed all the friends she could get. She nodded a bright *hello*.

'Pack these carefully. The roads will be rough. Make a nest of hay for each bottle and don't spare it.'

She supervised until she was satisfied, then continued sorting, giving the driver the map Louis had sent her with the best and safest routes into Russia. She tucked a note on the final champagne bottle in the batch for Louis.

The minute this is sold, you are to come back immediately…

She pictured Louis touching the bottles she had kissed.

Come straight back, you are needed here. Your Nicole.

She thought better of the kiss and smudged it out.

Finally she was standing on the docks next to a glowering sea, surveying her work, the wind knifing at her hair. Most bottles were condemned to death and piled on wagons, ready to be poured away. The cheque in her hand was pathetic. The scrapped bottles yielded one hundredth of what they would have been worth had they survived.

But four thousand were piled up on her wagon bound for Louis, enough to prove once more the worth of her vineyards and blends. Enough to establish the name of Veuve Clicquot in the valuable Russian markets. Enough to get Louis out of there the moment his business was done.

'Go!' She dismissed the driver. 'Make sure every single one of these bottles gets there. You will be rewarded for speed.'

As the wagon jolted away, she allowed herself to think of it. A year ago today, François died. She checked the position of the sun. François' champagne was finally going to Russia. The wind was blowing in from the east, the direction her bottles were headed in. Natasha would say that was a good omen, and why not believe it?

When the wagon disappeared, the weariness came over her like lead. She could go to sleep now, right here on the docks. A coil of rope would be a featherbed, but there was no time. Back home it was harvest and she belonged there.

The journey home was exhausting, but at the final leg before Reims, her faithful Pinot was waiting for her, fresh and watered. Xavier's dire predictions about her travelling alone had come to nothing and, as she jolted into the vineyards, the morning mist clinging to the vines, the sky was soft with sunrise and the field hands were already out picking, small dark figures moving purposefully. Thank God again for Xavier.

She jumped down and bit into a grape. The hot summer was in the sweetness, mixed with the taste of the chalky earth that had nurtured it. A good harvest. Borrowing a knife from a picker, she sliced off a bunch and placed it with the others in the basket.

'*For you,*' she whispered to François. He had planted these vines with his own hands.

CHAPTER 14

November 1806

The Women's Tasting Committee

September and October were seared with lack of news from either Louis or her bottles. Every time a letter was delivered, or a post horse churned up the dust, Nicole's stomach lurched, and every time disappointment burned. What a relief to find hope in the arrival of the women's tasting committee, who she would teach to help with the blends, and even replace the men who refused to help her. She also congratulated herself, developing allies at the epicentre of her detractors. When the horses kicked up the gravel in the press yard, she ran out to greet the carriage.

'You're early, but please come in. Xavier's setting everything up for the tasting. Just the two of you?' asked Nicole.

'Just us. Quality, not quantity, my dear,' said Madame Olivier.

Nicole stooped and picked a piece of milkweed from the gravel to hide her disappointment and took them to the tasting rooms. They'd been set up for at least five more people, with tall stools and tables, neatly laid-out spittoons, starched white napkins and polished wine glasses, all beautifully arranged in the simple brick room attached to the press for the purpose. She directed Xavier to take away some of the tables and chairs and his face darkened in sympathy.

'May I introduce Mademoiselle Var,' said Madame Olivier.

'Please, call me Joelle,' she said shyly. 'How exciting, to be mistress of all you survey!'

'It's my life,' said Nicole. 'We're waiting for Natasha, then we'll be four. Still enough to make up a little tasting committee. Please, sit.'

'Before Natasha arrives, is there time for advice from an old lady?' said Madame Olivier.

'And a sympathetic old maid?' said Joelle.

'Oh?'

'They should just come out and say it, or it's not fair,' said Madame Olivier.

'Who?'

'Pretty much every woman of standing in this town.'

'I'm not sure I want to hear this.'

'You have a right to know. And a right to reply,' said Madame Olivier. 'They're saying that you bring shame on your father.'

'How? My father is more than capable of fighting his own battles, and I can definitely fight mine.'

'Why fight battles? I am saying what you don't want to hear, but your little daughter – Mentine, I think?'

Nicole nodded.

'Mentine didn't ask for her mother to bring shame on her little head. Rumour has it that your salesman is in Russia – a dangerous place for him to be in these times. Philippe Clicquot partly bankrolls your endeavours and all this risk – for what? For you to indulge yourself in this hobby, acting like a *man*?'

'Mentine's reputation is in danger because of people like you! I am running a business nearly every family in this town has a hand in. You blindly follow old rules and traditions, what for?'

'Rules are made for a reason. Men do business, women look after the home, unless they have no choice, like your friend Natasha, for instance.'

'Has the revolution changed nothing?'

'Not for women.'

'If you believe that, then why are you here?' said Nicole, exasperated. 'Did you just come for more fuel for your idle gossip?'

'Come, come, my dear,' said Madame Olivier. 'I'm sure it's escaped no one's notice that I *do* like to know everyone's business. But the way you spoke to me in the bakery did alter my opinion of you, and I must admit, we were intrigued. We came here to find out more about you, but also, who else in this town could teach us about what has always been a man's domain? No one has ever singled me out for anything as interesting as this.' Madame Olivier gestured to the wine-tasting accoutrements.

So she was a mere curiosity to be stared at. Nicole began to regret her invitation to these ladies.

'I'm late, my apologies.' Natasha stood in the doorway. 'This is the first time I've closed the bakery in thirty years and it was difficult to leave.'

Xavier appeared carrying bottles. 'Welcome to the coven,' he growled.

Natasha sat up at the tasting tables with the others.

'Now. You all look like you've seen a ghost!' Natasha fished out some parcels from her bag and put them on the table. 'Recognise these?' Natasha said to Madame Olivier, revealing a key wrapped in velvet and an icon of Saint Rémi.

Madame Oliver didn't reply.

'You gave them to me when Daniel died. No one was kinder than you.'

'The key to the bakery,' said Madame Olivier quietly.

'And Saint Rémi. You gave me the key to my new bakery and the rent has been far below the market value ever since, thanks to you. You said that the Saint Rémi meant I belonged to the town, when everyone else thought I should go back to Russia. You told me your husband was cruel and you wish he had died instead and that you had my freedom.'

Madame Olivier went pale. Natasha clasped her hand and pushed up her sleeve. The outline of a purple hand-shaped bruise revealed her story. Madame Olivier yanked down her sleeve, ashamed.

'Still, after all these years?' said Natasha. 'Let Nicole be. I am an outsider. I see situations differently to you and I can see it's in her blood. It makes her alive. Your influence in the town could set her free, my kind friend. And, Mademoiselle Var, I have something for you, too.'

Natasha pushed a linen pouch in her direction.

'Open it.'

Mademoiselle Var spilled the contents onto the table. 'Pips?'

'Lemon pips. You've visited the bakery nearly every day since the revolution and made me tell you again and again how I travelled here from Russia, what I saw on the way, how things are at home. You tell me how much you'd like to see the sparkle of the Mediterranean, visit your relatives in the south, but you can never go, as your father refuses to take you and a woman can't travel alone. What's stopping you?'

'It's impossible for a woman to travel alone, obviously,' said Mademoiselle Var, surprised that she even needed to explain.

'Not for Nicole. She's brave enough to flout the rules, but we punish her for it. Search your hearts, ask yourselves why? Because she's doing what you feel you can't. I don't judge. We all create our own cages, but don't create them for others too.'

'We've said our piece,' said Madame Olivier. 'I've already gone on too much. I always do. Perhaps we should just press on with the tasting. At least if my mouth is full, I can't put my foot in it again,' said Madame Olivier apologetically.

Nicole poured out some glasses. 'You haven't told me anything I didn't already know, Madame Olivier, and I appreciate your honesty. Sometimes the truth is hard to say, and to hear. Shall we just leave it at that?'

Natasha carefully wrapped the icon and the key back into their velvet pouch.

'We'll start with the white,' said Nicole. 'Madame Olivier, I'm sure you know how it goes, but Natasha and Joelle, just breathe in the aroma deeply, take a big mouthful with some air, then spit. Don't think about it too much. Just try to identify the taste – the first thing that comes into your head.'

'Anything? I thought there were certain words you needed to use,' said Joelle.

'There are no rules, and everyone tastes differently, that's part of the fun,' said Nicole. 'Just imagine you're describing it to a child. Tell a story.'

Joelle took a sip, and spat. 'The south, sunshine on water. Umm, lemon trees, almond blossom, the sea.'

'The almond blossom is spot on!' said Nicole. 'A good wine transports us.'

'Strawberries, hay, new riding gloves. The long summers before I married,' said Madame Olivier, breathing deeply from the glass.

'The perfect rosé, in that case. Xavier, this blend can be laid down.'

They moved on to the next wine.

'Toasted flour, lemon custard, Black Sea salt – it has a very particular taste,' mused Natasha.

'You're right, although I have no idea about the salt,' said Nicole. 'Nevertheless, a good set of notes for champagne.'

'Of course it is. The fruits of my own labour, that one,' said Xavier. 'Louis'll sell it for a fortune in Russia.' He grinned, wiping out the glasses and pouring out her best red blend.

'So your salesman *is* in Russia? You should get him out of there,' said Madame Olivier.

'He only made it as far as Saxony. There is a reasonable trade there, so that's where he is. He's German, so his contacts in the region are good…' lied Nicole.

'Not as good as Russia though. Especially for champagne. I'm probably saying too much again, and I know you take more risks than most, but if you value him, bring him back. Everyone has recalled their salespeople from London and St Petersburg. They're arresting anyone French, I hear.'

Nicole sent a prayer to her precious cargo making its way overland to Louis.

'Sadly, he wouldn't listen to me even if I did,' said Nicole.

'I'll say one thing, you certainly inspire loyalty,' said Madame Olivier. 'Xavier here won't hear a word of criticism against you, so my husband tells me. He's like a bull in a china shop on your behalf. I'm yabbering again, but here's another offer of loyalty from me. You're determined to continue, I see that now, and I'm sorry if my mouth speaks before my head has checked it for offence. What I really wanted to say is that I'd like to help you. I can bring you intelligence from the other vintners. The men can't wait to impart their superior knowledge to each other and they're always in my house, discussing all the latest details and happenings.'

'Why would you do that for me?' said Nicole.

'You're a free spirit. I wish I could be, but this will be my little bit of freedom, a secret.' She pulled up her sleeve to reveal the extent of the bruise, right up to the elbow. It was vicious. 'And my revenge.' She held up a hand to bar Nicole's embrace. 'No sympathy! I don't want that.'

Nicole stepped back. 'Then I gladly accept, Madame Olivier. Thank you.'

When they left, Nicole went to her study. A new friendship. From such an unexpected place! She hadn't realised until now how lonely she was, in grief and battle for the last year.

She put down her quill and stared across the vineyards. Emile was dashing through the press courtyard towards her, waving a letter. Her heart galloped.

'Emile?'

'It's very important.'

'Were you asked to say anything?'

'It's from Thérésa and you are to contact her the minute you've read it. Shall I wait?'

'Yes. Go and ask Josette for some lunch. Tell her I said so.'

She tore open the letter. It was dated St Petersburg, 23 September 1806. *Almost two months ago*, thought Nicole. Slow, even by Russian standards.

My darling little vintner,

Your companion lights up every time he speaks of you. He substitutes his love for you with his love for your wines, my wild country merchant. I will leave this knowledge for you to do with what you will. I know you country girls remain loyal even to the dead.

That is my good news, but there is also bad. Louis has been arrested as a spy. The jails in St Petersburg are no more salubrious than the ones in Paris and, as you know, I am very familiar with their filth and cold. I bribed my way in with the handsome young jailer in the only way I know how (a little light relief in the darkness. You are welcome). Louis told me to ask you to forgive him. How foolishly romantic! He said he would escape to make your name. Don't cry. You give him hope and that is what he needs in dark days.

I will do what I can when I have escaped this precarious situation where all French citizens, even me, are accused as spies.

Your Thérésa

Nicole let the letter fall. Louis could be dead by now. And all because of her relentless obsession with Veuve Clicquot et Compagnie.

CHAPTER 15

March 1810

Camouflage

Louis didn't come home. That year, or the next. Four years limped by. Nicole anxiously kept track of Napoléon's advance across Europe, and prayed to God that Louis was still alive. When the news came that Napoléon had taken Berlin, then large parts of Prussia in the autumn of 1806, Nicole was laying down the blends and planning her next shipment for Louis, still optimistic she would have news of him. In 1808, a late frost ruined that year's harvest and Napoléon crowned his brother King of Spain. Rumblings of discontent abounded amongst even the most fervent of Napoléon's supporters and the grip of poverty closed tighter around France, thanks to endless wars and lack of European trade. As Nicole saved what she could of her blighted vines, she looked for Louis, half expecting him to appear with miraculous orders secured for better years, but there was no news.

Even Thérésa was unable to work her magic; incarcerated French weren't considered important enough to keep proper records of. There were times when news of his death would have been better than the dull ache of hope. Now, in 1810, Napoléon had divorced Thérésa's oldest friend, Joséphine, formed an alliance with Austria through his new wife, Marie-Louise, and continued his warmongering unabated.

Not a day passed when she didn't imagine Louis appearing on the horizon, a skeleton in a wolfskin coat and a warm brandy smile, with a million stories to tell. Perhaps what the town said was right, that she was bad luck, that her arrogance had killed two men.

She snapped awake. Still dark, the cathedral clock tolling 5 a.m. Lighting a candle, she pulled on her morning gown, crept into the basement and checked on her experiment. Useless. A quarter of the bottles ruined and cloudy, no better than the quota in any cellar across Reims. Why did she think she could find a solution that no one in the entire history of winemaking had ever managed?

In her study, she creaked open the account ledger. The figures looked no different from 5 a.m. yesterday, or the day before, or in fact every early morning for the last four years. There had been some sales – she took the time to ensure the highest quality in every bottle that left the cellars, and a few buyers still had enough money to pay for luxuries, but in general, sales were down for everything. She'd just about managed to keep the vineyards and press going over these hard times, through economies and favours. But her business didn't have the cash reserves of some of the longer-standing operations, and now there was barely enough to pay the wages.

Two of the few black entries in the ledger were from selling her sapphire ring, and the other from the sale of François' gold-plated cutlery canteen. No need for fancy dinner parties any more. Thank goodness for her parents – at least she and Mentine wouldn't starve, but that money wouldn't help the business.

She fingered the yellow diamond firefly François gave her the night he died. That alone was sacrosanct. Every last cushion and chair would be sacrificed to the business if she needed it, but not the firefly. The stark figures in black and red were unyielding. *Can't they lie, just this once?* She made minute adjustments until her eyes stung, trying to do something useful until the sky turned a shade paler and she could race to the vineyards.

On her way out, she stared at herself in the hall mirror. A pinched face stared back. *You'll ruin your looks with all this work*, Thérésa had warned. Nicole pulled on her riding gloves. *I'm living for two, for me and François, and I'll live twice as hard.*

The spring sun was warm on her shoulders as she rode out into the vineyards. The land didn't judge and it yielded to her touch. Her field hands were already out digging trenches and they stopped and waved as she passed. A band of renegades, like her. None of the regular field workers would agree to work for a woman, even in these hard times. Her workers were dropouts, outcasts and rejects. Emile's mother, Marie, had been a notorious whore, but her digging was quicker and more efficient than any man's. She smiled a gap-toothed salute as she passed. Christophe-Baptiste's one leg had left him begging on the streets when he came back from Napoléon's war. No longer. He still had two hands, and they were proficient at banging in the stakes needed to tie the vines.

The orphanage kids were Xavier's idea. A ragbag of undernourished, foul-mouthed, twitching, snivelling lads. At fourteen they were big enough to be useful and if he taught them well, they would always have a job in Champagne.

'You're not shovelling cow shit, you're digging *trenches*.' He held up a stick. 'This wide, even, all the way along or I'll send you back to the holes you crawled out of.'

'The only hole round here is yours and it smells like shit!'

Xavier gave the boy a good clip, grinning with pride, crow's feet radiating. They were all getting older. The soil didn't age though; every year it looked the same, the pale crust turned over to reveal a moist underbelly full of worms as birds hovered, bagging a breakfast of wriggling meat.

'Morning, Xavier, how's the planting going?'

'Forty centimetres apart. And I've been over that soil so many times I could wash my arse in it. You know it makes no difference whether it's forty-five or thirty-five centimetres?'

'*Bon*,' she said, shaking out her ruler and working the length of a row, measuring for herself. '*On est presque là.* Move this a little to the left...' She secured a stick at the exact point. 'This one needs to move here.'

She carefully planted the vine, sprinkled it with sand and tramped it down with a little of the *fumure* – the ashes from the quarry. All being right, these grapes would taste clean, bright and creamy, a perfect accompaniment to oysters. She already had the right Paris buyer in mind.

'Give me that,' said Xavier, grabbing the ruler. 'You have company.'

Moët, advancing towards her from the place where his vineyard abutted her own. It seemed wherever she looked he was always there.

'Nothing is to be left to chance,' she addressed the men, tugging a root out of the soil and sniffing it. 'Horseweed. Give the new vines a chance! Each one of you is responsible for making sure they are in pristine soil. I will keep you all in jobs and pay every person here a bonus if we have a good harvest. War or no war, we will keep selling and that will keep us all in jobs. But it all depends on the vines. What you are doing now will lay the ground for Chardonnay, for our best *vins mousseux*. *I* am giving my best territory to it. Centre of the slope, facing south. I expect the best labour *you* can give in return. Between us all, our wine will be the best.'

'I admire your confidence,' said Moët as he arrived at her side. 'But you know you're wasting your time.'

'It's the best waste of time I can think of, *n'est-ce pas?*'

He pointed to a withered shoot down the line of vines. 'Keep an eye on that one, you can't afford to waste a single plant in this operation.'

'Your advice is invaluable, Jean-Rémy. I imagine the day it's not so forthcoming and dream of what might happen.'

'A man sees the detail and the bigger picture simultaneously. I won't disturb you further – there's clearly a lot of work to do here.'

She saluted. Let him think what he liked. Thanks to her continued failures, she and Moët had reached an uncomfortable understanding. He'd even shared a few trade secrets and introduced her to a decent bottle supplier when hers went bust. An introduction from him smoothed any worries they might have had about opening a credit account with a woman, and it was easier to keep him sweet where she could. He enjoyed bestowing his superior wisdom and having it accepted, so for now things were stable and she even had some standing amongst the vintners as a tolerated curiosity.

He saluted back, spurred his horse and rode on by. Every small victory built towards a bigger one, Natasha said, but Madame Olivier had delivered bad news the day before. She had it on good authority that a banker's cheque written by François' father, Philippe Clicquot, had not been honoured. He still had his personal wealth, but the business account was running dry. Nicole resolved not to take another sou from him, and to pay him back everything with interest when things came right.

She joined the band of orphanage boys, grabbed a spade and helped with the digging. The responsibility of all these dependants pushed her shovel deeper. Louis disappeared, François… and poor Philippe. What would she do if it all fell apart?

She turned over another shovelful of earth. The only way was to push forward, create the finest wines, keep her team together.

François had taught her that a vintner was only as good as his workers, and respect grew from working alongside them. After all these years, François' face had faded, but every now and then her memory clarified, like ripples dissipating in a well, settling to a clear reflection. The reflection smiled and her stomach flipped.

Fragmented dust hanging in the sunlit, silent cloisters of her childhood school, the crimson of her woollen dress on the day of the revolution, the taste of the mellow harvest sun in a Muscat, François leading her on a wild polka in their walled vineyard at Villers-Allerand. Like a year in the fields, her life had come full circle and yet here she was, still completely alone.

When the trenches were dug, she headed for Natasha's bakery. It felt like home on days like this, each patisserie a little celebration.

'You are melancholy, my dear. Come,' Natasha said, leading her by the arm to the kitchen and sitting her down. 'No time for brooding. I'll cast a spell that will make you happy.'

Natasha sprinkled salt at her feet and knocked the table three times.

'Knocking and a bit of salt? Life's pretty simple if that's all it takes.' Nicole took a sip of Natasha's hot coffee and sighed.

'You *want* to believe. And I know you can't stay unhappy for long. It's not in your nature. You just need a friend to tell you to stop.'

As she kissed Natasha goodbye, a bird smacked into the bakery window and fell, stunned, to the ground, its speeding heart pounding visibly. Natasha's face darkened and she hurried inside, crossing herself.

Nicole shivered and paced across the square past the cathedral, where a tall figure standing by a loaded barrel cart beckoned. Moët again. It was one thing bumping into him out in the fields, surrounded by her workers, quite another to be trapped alone with him.

She held out her hand in place of a curtsey and he gripped it tight.

'I'm afraid all the ups and downs of your little hobby business is the talk of the town. And even you can't believe that your rogue salesman Louis is ever coming back. It's been several years now since he disappeared with most of your stock, I believe?'

'I'm a habitual provider of entertainment for this town, why stop now? I have enough planned to get the gossips through the whole winter.'

He let go of the handshake. 'That's where you and I part company. I hate to add to your worries, but a person's reputation is all, and yours is seriously in question. I'm telling you as a friend.'

'Everyone has had their ups and downs these past difficult years, it's part of the business. Why is *my* reputation particularly at stake? I hope you're not going to bore me with your "man's world" argument again?'

'There's a delicate matter that perhaps isn't right for a busy square, so I encourage you to step into my office.'

'Not now, Jean-Rémy, I'm meeting Xavier at the press in half an hour.'

'You'll understand the urgency if I mention a certain Doctor Moreau?'

Her legs buckled and her heart slammed in her ears. Monsieur Moët ushered her into his office in a blur.

'Sit there, my dear. I hate to bring up difficult memories, but you must face up to it.'

'What do you want from me?' Nicole asked quietly.

'Unwanted pregnancies, sexual diseases… suicide, nothing is beneath our learned Doctor Moreau. If there's enough money involved, he'll cover anything up, isn't that so?'

'All doctors work for money,' she stalled, afraid of where this was going.

'But this one has a reputation he can't shake off, a bit like you.'

'Just come out and say what you want from me.'

'Nothing at all. It's more about what I can do for you. I'm sorry to tell you that Doctor Moreau is in jail for falsifying death certificates. The investigative bodies are doing a very good job of uncovering his misdemeanours – so many defenceless families have been exposed. The list is endless... unfortunate young ladies who thought they'd got away with concealing bastard children; whole families whose reputations have been ruined by the selfish actions of a loved one who saw fit to illegally take his own life. The truth will always out. The investigators are asking for all the death certificates he signed in Reims in 1805. My apologies for any distress this may cause you.'

'Apart from that being the year that François died, I have nothing whatsoever to be distressed about.' She thought about the rat poison. She'd take that secret with her to the grave. Even she could never know the real truth of how he died.

'Think about poor little Clémentine. No one would ever marry her. Bad blood. This town talks more than you think. We both know Doctor Moreau covered up François' suicide.'

He couldn't possibly know, she told herself. *It's just the rumour mill that he's exploiting.*

'It was typhoid, everyone knows that. The rest is just malicious gossip.'

'Does truth matter? Gossip *is* truth in small towns and it will only be fuelled by Doctor Moreau's arrest – and his name is on that death certificate. I can protect you. All you have to do is give up your foolish vineyard venture and then you can live a life of luxury. You can't see it, but I really am acting in your own interests, if a little forcefully.'

'By blackening the Clicquot name? Don't dress this up as *help*.'

'You will be ruined without me.'

'I'm ruined anyway.'

'Consider it. I know you don't want to sell, but let me step in where Monsieur Clicquot has failed as a business partner. I will run the business and grow it. You could retain some part in it, add the Clicquot name to mine, and your dear husband's name will live on. As part of the deal, I will protect you, including using my position within the *mairie* to access and destroy Doctor Moreau's death certificate and finally put the rumours to rest.'

'Instead of fanning the flames if I refuse?'

'They say his body should have been staked at a crossroads to release his ghost, not buried in consecrated ground. They say his ghost haunts you and ruins all your associations with men. That is why your deal with Philippe Clicquot has expired and Louis has disappeared. Is your failing hobby worth it? You should do it for François and his poor father.'

She put her head in her hands. No wonder he owned this town.

'When are the investigators arriving?' she asked.

Monsieur Moët checked his pocket watch and tapped it. 'I'm afraid I can't give you much time. The notary came today to inform me that they're arriving tomorrow at two p.m. sharp.'

'Then you will have my answer tomorrow morning.'

'The papers will be ready.'

'I don't doubt you already have them prepared. Good afternoon.'

As soon as she was safely inside the press at Bouzy with Xavier, Nicole collapsed.

'What the fuck happened to you? I haven't seen you like this since François…'

'It's like he's died all over again. Xavier, can I be frank with you? You found us the day François died and you're the only one I can tell.'

She told him everything, about the typhoid and the rat poison, about Moët's threats. It was such a relief. He let her speak, didn't say a word, or show any emotion, and she was grateful for that, too. She needed a cool head when hers was exploding.

'The worst thing is that Moët knows he's right,' she continued. 'Doctor Moreau's name on François' death certificate will ruin the Ponsardin-Clicquot family name. Mentine's school friends will shun her, and everyone in Champagne who ever wanted to stop me has been handed the perfect gift.'

'You're running this place, I just follow orders. But if you want my advice, take your lead from the vines. Buy yourself some time and pray for a miracle.'

'If only it was that simple.'

'You've got it all wrong with a sore like Moët. He likes to swagger about like he's in charge. Underneath all that smarm, he's no different from a prize bull. All this time you've been saying no, but the only way to beat him is to say yes. Louis' name is on the contract with shares for this place, I think?'

She nodded.

'Get your lawyer to dredge up some legal bollocks saying Louis must be given a year to return. That gives you another harvest. If he doesn't come back, you go into partnership with Moët as agreed. That way, you've said yes, you've signed one of his bloody pieces of paper and he's off your case for over a year. Then you wait for a miracle.' He flicked his chin at the window. 'You've seen them happen year after year out there.'

At home, Nicole poured herself a glass of champagne to steady her nerves. These grapes had grown on the eastern slopes and she could taste the sharp frosts that had come late the year she bottled it, the year that François died. The harvest had been terrible and this batch was all they could salvage. No miracles that year, but she was decided. Xavier's advice was good. Delay the deal until harvest the following year, 1811. *Plant the seeds, nurture the vines, do everything in your power to make things grow, and pray.*

CHAPTER 16

March 1810

Needs Must

Did the smell of shit vary from town to town, like *terroir*? Nicole pressed a handkerchief to her nose to block plagues, but nothing could disguise the sickly-sweet stench of the open sewer.

Moët had agreed to her terms. If Louis didn't return by the 1811 harvest in over a year's time, they would become partners, an eighty–twenty split in his favour. The death certificate was safe until next year, and Xavier was right: Moët just needed a yes from her to keep him quiet for now. That didn't solve her immediate problems, though. In two weeks' time she would need to pay the wages, and the supplier invoices were piling up at an alarming rate.

She'd accepted Monsieur Moët's offer to pay her bottle supplier. He'd insisted, so that when their deal matured and he took over the business next year, he could be sure the bottles were good quality – another yes to reassure him, and one she couldn't really refuse in her straitened circumstances. It was one bill paid at least.

Nicole fingered her most precious possession in the velvet pouch in her pocket. The last thing of value she had, her gift from François, and the only thing she'd sworn not to sell for the sake of the business. But she had no intention of waiting for Xavier's miracle. She'd make her own while she still had time.

She focused on the three grubby balls of the pawnbroker sign down the street and pressed on, past the red-cheeked laundry women shaking out their washing and cackling at a private joke, past the men catcalling and playing cards together outside the café. Everyone except her *belonged* to someone.

The pawnbroker shrugged as she untied the velvet pouch and held up the yellow diamond that was the firefly's body. Even in the dim light, the sun sliced it into prisms. The last thing François had given her, and the most valuable.

The man picked it up and peered through his loupe, holding it up to the window. Dust swirled in the yellow light of the window. Worn jewellery, silverware and treasures were piled haphazardly in display cases.

He placed the diamond on his scales, counterbalancing it with weights.

Nicole narrowed her eyes. 'It's two carats. Those weights are wrong.'

'Nine hundred francs. Not a sou more, Madame.'

Nicole snatched it off the scale and wrapped it back in the velvet pouch. 'I do business on honest terms. Weigh it honestly and pay fairly.'

The man shrugged again. 'I have mouths to feed as, I suspect, do you. It's up to you.'

He was right, she had mouths to feed – he'd never imagine how many. Hundreds of employees and suppliers queued up in her head, hands outstretched. She unwrapped the necklace and admired it in the palm of her hand, the gold warming to her touch for one last time.

'Promise I won't be followed with the cash in my pocket and I'll take your price. I'd rather be robbed in here than on the streets.'

He didn't take his eyes off the velvet package. 'You have my protection, Madame. I guarantee it.'

Nicole counted the cash twice, folded the money into a leather wallet and pushed it deep into her pocket. Enough to buy another year, until Moët's deadline.

'Give me six months,' she said. 'I'll buy it back for more than anyone else can pay.'

'I'd be rich if I had a franc for everyone who says that. I don't expect we'll meet again.'

CHAPTER 17

March 1811

Luck from the Skies

Everyone knew that the first March full moon gave rise to a tide of bubbles and it sent all the vintners rushing to their cellars, including Nicole. Napoléon and his Austrian wife Marie-Louise had at last given birth to a boy, but that didn't stop his designs on the domination of Europe. His new son was to be crowned King of Rome and rumours of alliances to the advantage or detriment of the nation flew like forest fires around France. The war blighted all of their lives. In Reims, the wine sales that depended on European and Russian trade was still dead.

It was five months since her harvest was successfully brought in, laid down in Moët's paid-for bottles last October, the 1810 vintage. She had high hopes for that at least. The harvest had been perfect, and after four years, Madame Olivier and Mademoiselle Var had proved invaluable, her own women's tasting committee. When the men's tasting committee made sure year after year that the Clicquot blends would be last on their list, giving everyone in the region a competitive advantage over her, she just smiled and wished them well.

One of Nicole's favourite pastimes was to tell her fellow vintners of her women's tasting committee and see the barely supressed snorts of derision and hopeless shrugs on her behalf, whilst politely enquiring exactly who these *females* were. That their identity was top secret brought even more derision, but there was no way that Nicole could reveal Madame Olivier's involvement to her violent husband. Whatever they thought didn't matter. The indisputable fact was that her wines were far superior to any of her competitors'. Everyone knew that, and sometimes, at the markets, or at the feast of St Rémi, when Monsieur Moët and Monsieur Olivier were otherwise occupied, the kinder members of the committee would seek her out and tell her so, even ask her advice on the finer points of the blend or fermentation.

The dedication of the women's tasting committee to the craft was unstoppable, undertaking blind tastings and studying varietals in the privacy of their own homes so as not to arouse suspicion, then swapping tips and discoveries in Natasha's bakery on a daily basis. As a result, their instincts were honed and reliable. Nicole was still the 'super nose', but if she was unsure, they were ready with an informed verdict, taking pleasure in a colourful turn of phrase… *There's a north-slope dreariness to the top note… The tannins are as bitter as my granny's recycled coffee dregs… Bright and breezy as a walk by the sea.*

They also brought her invaluable insights from her competitors. Madame Olivier was married to a stalwart of the Reims vintners' cabal and Mademoiselle Var was so shy and retiring that no one thought for a moment to suspect espionage when she asked a pointed question about the latest goings-on with a simpering smile.

A glimmer of light. The winter had been harsh, but the black vines had fought off the frost bravely and now, in March, Nicole fretted about the fresh little shoots and how much time she had left before Moët's deal matured. Still no news of Louis. It was nearly five years since his arrest, and she had to believe that he was dead. She buried herself in work to stop the thought. If he was gone, he took what was left of her heart with him, and all her hopes of a legal split from Moët when the contract was due this autumn.

All she could do was keep going.

Nicole picked out a bottle from last year that she had marked. She had refined the blend with her committee and they agreed, all being well, this young champagne would taste of white flowers, crisp white bread and mint. She held it to a candle and smiled at the froth.

'The moon has done its job,' she whispered to it.

She imagined Monsieur Moët's response: '*The second fermentation is in process. Attention to detail, meticulous care. All this talk about the moon is superstitious nonsense amongst peasants.*'

By now, she and François would be waltzing through the cellars in celebration, with the workers laughing behind their hands. All the best wines were made with love.

Her sister was happily married and a rich housewife. Why could she not just be satisfied like her? Her parents worried about her constantly, but knew better than to try to persuade her off her course. Besides, they understood her responsibility to the business and her workers. And what about Mentine, studying hard at boarding school? Her daughter herself had asked to go to the top establishment in Paris and was showing a great appetite for learning and study. How could she just give up and teach her that a girl couldn't have the same dreams of success as men? She just had to keep going.

Putting the bottle back carefully, she trudged up the cellar steps, locked the door and went out into the evening to complete her lonely routine. She didn't sleep well nowadays, so she tramped the borders of her vineyards every night, to try to walk off the worry.

Through the vineyards, clods of clay and chalk weighed her boots and the dew wet her ankles as she hitched up her skirts to walk the familiar chalky paths. She paced until the lights of the press and cellar were no longer visible and she was surrounded by vines. When she reached the roofless shelter, she lay on the ground to watch the stars. The earth was cool on the back of her neck, gritty in her hair. She smoothed her hands over the sticky, pale soil and looked up at the velvet sky.

A shooting star crossed, just above the horizon, and she waited for it to shatter and die before she made a wish. The thing kept going. She stared at it, so long her limbs stiffened with cold. It stayed hovering, a bright sphere with a tail, fizzing away. She checked the constellations. All in the right place. Orion, her knight, reminded her of François, cold and brittle up there in the night sky, but undimmed. The tail was forked, and around the bright sphere was a cascade of shattered light, like a sparkling veil. The points of light rushed in a cordon of fine bubbles away from the central sphere. She imagined her ideal champagne, the first nose: orange peel, brioche, wheat, peach. The second nose: milky toffee, honey, walnut and vanilla.

A twitch of movement in the corner of her eye drew her attention away from the skies. She glanced around to see a sackcloth in the corner moving. She froze, then crouched, ready to run. It shifted, fell sideways and revealed a filthy man barely able to sit himself up.

'Wondering what the fuck that thing in the sky is?' he said. He had wild eyes, mud-caked skin covered in sores.

She'd know that voice anywhere. A slight German lilt, sewer mouth. Her heart soared.

'Louis! You're here, you came home. Oh, Jesus, you're alive.'

He was skin and bones, fragile as a chick in a nest. She wanted to hug him but she was afraid she'd hurt him.

'Any chance of getting a drink and something to eat around here?'

'My God, I thought I'd lost you! You'll have a feast and vintage champagne and everything you need. What happened to you?'

'I lost everything…'

'You have done everything I ever needed just by coming back. I don't care about anything else.'

'It's a comet, by the way.'

'What is?'

'That shooting star that won't go away. It's a comet. The field hands will be stroking their rabbits' feet and nailing their horseshoes the right way up. It brings omens of all kinds.' He looked at Nicole sideways. 'It's brought *me* good luck so far.'

'You can hardly even sit up; I'll need to get you a carriage. My darling, dearest Louis, it will take too long to explain now, but no one can know you're back, not yet, until we make a plan.'

'Well, that's no surprise. Nothing ever was straightforward with you.'

He was trembling with cold and his voice was barely louder than a whisper. She took off her cloak and wrapped it around him. He winced at the weight on his skin.

'Don't move a muscle and don't you dare leave my sight ever again. I'll be back with blankets and transport and you can stay with Antoine and Claudine and you'll get better. And listen, I want to know *everything*!'

She blew him a kiss and ran back to the house, not caring about the freezing night air on her bare arms.

She checked the horizon when she arrived at the stables. The *comète* was still there. So that must mean that Louis was *actually* back. Her champagne comet, Louis alive. She threw a saddle on Pinot and flew.

*

Antoine and Claudine were attentive carers to Louis. Nicole gave them what she could for his upkeep and he was bedridden, so keeping his homecoming quiet was easy for now. He spent the first few days drifting in and out of sleep, but as the days passed and the vine shoots toughened, Louis began to tell his story.

She visited every evening, bringing firewood so Antoine and Claudine could afford to lay a fire for him, and he talked as she lost herself in the flames and forgot her troubles for a while, lulled by Louis' stories of hoar frosts, frozen lakes, hardships and samovars of sweet tea. Unimaginable opulence of golden rooms, duck-egg silks and Fabergé eggs as Louis' fortunes rose and fell, until, finally, he was arrested as a spy when Russian relations with France declined.

It was a glittering evening, he told her. Lights filled the ball-room and chandeliers flickered with hundreds of candles. Louis was talking to the lovely Tanya Kurochkin when they came for him. Two soldiers marched up and whispered in Tanya's ear. She did nothing, just turned away from him, as did her friends and associates.

The men had flanked him each side, accusing him of spying for the French and escorted him out so roughly that he struggled to keep his feet on the ground. No one stopped them. He didn't even have time to stop for his new wolfskin coat – and it was the kind of weather that made icicles of your eyelashes. They roughed him into the back of a barred carriage, tapped the back with the blunt of their swords and waved goodbye.

It was only when his eyes became accustomed to the dark, and the stench of human waste stung his nostrils, that he began to shiver. The bare stone cell they'd thrown him in was crawling with cockroaches and the windowless room stole all sense of night and day. He came to look forward to the moment when the slot was opened in the great door and a thin bowl of grey gruel was passed through. He would try to elongate these moments of human contact in his mind, make up allegiances that didn't exist. He made the cockroaches into acquaintances, naming them for his friends. Louis described a tiny one, black and shiny, always busy, boldly leading the lines to the small spills of gruel he spared for them. That one was Babouchette. The clumsy brown one behind was Louis himself. The wayward one, always going in the opposite direction, François. Even Moët was represented, the biggest and shiniest of them, barging the others to get to the food first.

He wrote messages in Russian with the congealed gruel to communicate with the guards. *Thank you. Delicious. Hello.* Then, observations… *New hat? No moustache? In love? Is she beautiful?* The regular guard was young, a boy really. He was nervous at first, as if Louis might bite. Eventually he began to relax and smile. Louis lived for that smile. It was the sun on his face, his rain, his nourishment, his sunrise and sunset, the stars. He lost track of time. God knows how many months or years it was.

He had lost any sense of the years passing the day that Thérésa Tallien appeared with the guard, and he was afraid. She shone with health and the boy's eyes glowed at her attention. The slot slid open and there she was, steely eyes narrowed, holding a candle up to light the cell.

'Ah, there you are. Hiding from me in this miserable little place.'

She nodded at the boy and the door swung open, the boy proud of his part in Thérésa's plans.

Louis didn't move.

'We must leave immediately.' Thérésa held out her hand. 'Darling, take it. We will leave here together. Move quickly now.'

Louis turned to bid farewell to the cockroaches and Thérésa nodded in understanding.

'Your friends? Come. I have waited for death in one of these places. We will walk together.'

She took him to a hotel a night's ride away from St Petersburg, saw him installed with a bag of coins, and left. She had a ring on every finger, each one a precious gem.

'I cannot stay, darling. Take better care of the company you keep next time,' she said, then left.

Nicole closed her eyes to conceal her relief. Thérésa had left him to himself.

'You've suffered more than you tell me, Louis. You are brave.'

He looked at her, past her eyes and somewhere inside her.

'Just lucky,' he murmured.

She poured them both a brandy and stoked the fire. His cheeks were ruddier and fuller. She thanked her lucky comet. It might take time, but he'd make a full recovery.

'All those years in the jail, I thought of you, your shipment mostly ruined, business dead. For all we tried, Babouchette. Nothing but a cell full of cockroaches.'

Nicole nodded, hard times for all of them. Why had Thérésa not written to her to tell her about all this? Maybe she had and the letter was lost, or perhaps she didn't want to risk news of her using her contacts to release a French 'spy'. Thérésa lived and died by her ability to obfuscate and she always ensured she appeared to be on the winning side.

Louis recovered in the little hostel where Thérésa had left him. The winter was so severe that he had to wait for the spring melt before he could think of leaving. He got to know the family who ran the hostel. The father was German, like him. Thérésa had chosen well – he sympathised with his countryman more than most Russians would have. As he got stronger, he collected eggs and ran repairs, sitting by the range in the evenings, chatting to the bubble of the samovar, paying his way with his hands. He knew he didn't belong there, but he was afraid to strike out again into the unknown. The few visitors they had were hostile to the

French, the bag of coins Thérésa had left him was long gone and he had not a franc to his name.

'You should have sent for money, Louis. I would never have left you stranded...'

'How could I ask you for money when things were going so badly for you? I was no longer your salesman. Besides' – he sat up straighter – 'I had a lot of time to think in that jail. I wanted to return to you as an equal.'

He eventually left the hostel with the spring melt, gingerly striking out on a horse that he would pay his hosts for in better times.

When he saw the port at Königsberg and a Dutch frigate waiting to sail, he cried for the first time in his adult life. He secured a job as a cook to pay his passage, tasted his first champagne since his arrest at the party with the hundred candles at St Petersburg. He poured himself a thimbleful and sliced a sliver off the foie gras and it tasted like heaven as the ship cut the foam, salt spray on his fingers, speeding home. With the lights of Reims finally in sight, he didn't have an ounce of strength left in him, and he'd collapsed at the first shelter he could find, in the hut. That night two miracles had happened. The first was the comet, and the second was Nicole arriving at the hut and flinging herself on the ground to watch the stars. In his delirious state, he thought he was dreaming.

Louis was changed. Faint lines marked his smile, his eyes were flintier. He had lost the childlike way he had about him, lost some of his enthusiasm. He was more serious. She liked the change.

By April, the comet had disappeared and the time to disappoint Monsieur Moët with Louis' appearance loomed. He couldn't hide in Antoine and Claudine's spare room forever.

In the fields, the April sun was unusually strong and bud burst came early. She rode out every day to watch the leaves grow acid green once more, sending out curling tendrils to cling to the training ropes, supervised as the plants were trimmed and trained, ensuring all the energy from the thick stems could be transferred to the fruit when the time came.

Another month passed and the vines grew so fast that if Nicole stood for long enough, she could *see* them grow under the beating sun: warm but not too strong, caressing the plants and encouraging fruit. She could not remember a year where the conditions were so perfect you could have taken them from one of Chaptal's *Art of Wine Growing* pamphlets. She checked her roses, vigorous and free of blight or insects. By June, the comet had brought a good omen at least in this, and Louis was well enough for the dreaded meeting with Monsieur Moët.

She invited Moët to the press at Bouzy for one of his beloved 'inspections' of his future property. God only knew what he'd do when he saw Louis had returned and their contract was null and void, but at least it would be on her own territory, surrounded by her own workers.

She heard the carriage draw up on the gravel, the gruff orders to the stable boys to water the horses and the brisk march to the office door.

'You need to get that gate fixed, it gives the wrong impression,' he ordered as he stepped inside. When he saw Louis, he didn't miss a beat. 'Monsieur Louis Bohne!'

The men shook hands.

'The very same,' replied Louis as Moët slapped him on the back and drew him in for a manly embrace.

'You old rogue, you're back and looking hale and hearty. Collaborating with Russians has done you the power of good.'

'If you think collaborating with Russians involves lying half-starved, forgotten and filthy in a godforsaken hellhole, then yes, it's been a blast.'

'Madame Clicquot, no doubt you have invited me here to spring the return of your star salesman upon me with no prior warning to ensure it's as delightful a surprise as it has turned out to be. Wonderful.' He beamed, taking a seat at her desk. The man certainly had nerve.

'So, just to be straight, this means…' Nicole began.

Monsieur Moët held up his hand. 'Spare me the explanation. The situation is very clear. Our little agreement is rendered null and void with the miraculous return of the prodigal Monsieur Bohne. I'm very pleased for you.' He turned to Louis. 'You'll take over the reins alongside Madame Clicquot and I'm very happy she is in safe hands. I wanted to do everything I could to help and now there is no need, with a competent man at her side.'

'Since we're getting down to business so quickly, there is another aspect to your agreement with Madame Clicquot. Your threat of spreading rumours about my dearest friend and Nicole's late husband is just about as low as it gets. It saddens me to think a man of your standing would target his widow so cruelly. I hope this is an end to the matter and that you'll act honourably.'

Moët stood up to leave. 'My dear Monsieur Bohne, you insult me! I merely tried to do everything in my power to stop her getting further into debt and disrepute.'

'We appreciate your touching concern, but do I have your word?'

Louis held out his hand and Moët shook it.

'I will tell nothing but the honest truth, my dear friend,' he said, opening the door to leave. He turned to face them. 'By the way, whatever *did* happen to all that stock you left with? You damn nearly bankrupted her with your disappearance. Goodbye, Nicole.

I also noticed that the fence on the vineyard on the east slope is breached. I suggest you mend it before the wild animals get in.'

As soon as they heard the carriage wheels, they stared at each other in shock and Nicole could breathe.

'What the hell was all that about?'

'He took it far too well,' Louis replied.

'Look outside, it's just perfect. It's going to be the best harvest in a generation. Whatever he's got up his sleeve, he can't change that,' said Nicole.

The news of Louis' return was the talk of the town. At Natasha's *boulangerie*, Nicole delighted in the gossip. *Louis escaped from Siberia but his prick dropped off in the cold*, Xavier stage-whispered to Etienne whilst biting into a large chocolate éclair. *Thérésa seduced the Tsar to get him released from a filthy Moscow jail, disguised as a Sultana from India. India*, said the butcher's youngest daughter, in awe. *Louis bribed a hundred Cossack guards with Veuve Clicquot's best champagne to get himself released from the salt mines, then he walked all the way back to Reims*, was the story from a battalion of soldiers with a penchant for Natasha's *millefeuille*.

The summer flew past in a haze of sunshine; every day was spent tending her vines, checking the workers, planning the harvest with Louis. It was wonderful to have him at her side, helping with the running of things, a trusted sounding board for the multitude of decisions she needed to make on a daily basis. Nicole had been in the business for long enough now to know she had never seen a year like it, and she left nothing to chance. It would be a vintage year and her luck would change. It was just a matter of staying power. She was under no illusion that Moët had backed down quite so easily, but the only way she could think of fighting the unknown was to be as successful as possible.

It was months since she'd been into the centre of Reims. Mentine was spending most of the summer with her boarding-school pals, so she didn't need to be in the city to be near her daughter's friends. Josette had run all the errands in town and she couldn't bear to leave her vineyards, so she'd based herself at her little house in Bouzy for the whole summer to be close to the sweetening grapes. No need for all those big rooms filled with François' ghost, never mind the running costs of the grand house on the rue de la Vache.

Despite all that, she couldn't miss the church service in the cathedral where all the vintners and workers gathered together to pray to the harvest saint. By the calculations of the Réseau Matu, the harvest would be ready in about a week's time and she would be foolish if she missed the rites in advance of the harvest. Even if it was superstition, who was she to argue with hundreds of years of tradition and risk a last-minute disaster?

At the mews near the cathedral, she jumped down off Pinot, handed the reins to the stable boy, and pressed a coin in his hand. It was as though she'd burnt his hand as he winced away from her.

'No thanks, Madame,' said the stable boy, unable to look her in the eye. The coin chinked onto the floor.

'Don't be silly, take it. You work hard and I can spare it.'

'I can't, it's bad luck,' he said, ashamed. He grabbed Pinot's reins and busied himself with the tackle.

She left the coin and hurried down the rue du Marché to the cathedral square. A large notice caught her eye on Joan of Arc's plinth.

Births and deaths, 1805
Criminal activity: Doctor Aristide Moreau
Detained for Falsification of Cause-of-Death Certification
Convictions obtained for falsification:

And the first name on the list:

François Clicquot

The list went on, but she couldn't read.

A crowd of vintners and workers was gathered outside the cathedral, silently watching. The place was deathly quiet apart from one set of footsteps ringing around the square.

A pair of strong arms encircled her.

'Look at me, Babouchette, not them.'

She focused. Natasha.

'Ignore them, they don't matter,' she beseeched. 'I'll take you home. Where is Pinot?'

'The mews. The stable boy wouldn't take my money. Thank God Mentine can't see this.'

'They're peasants. They don't know any better. Come, Nicole. Hold your head up and get out of this square and let them go and pray their lies to their God. You don't need any of them.'

Natasha linked her arm, somehow got her up on Pinot, cursing the stable boy. Nicole spurred her old horse so fast he was rasping with exhaustion by the time they reached Bouzy. Natasha followed, but she was left far behind on the vineyard road.

Safe in her sunlit house in Bouzy, she allowed herself to think. *Don't break*, she told herself. *Don't give him anything he wants.*

The only way to beat this was to keep going. Her failure would only prove to the town that their superstitions were correct. 'Let the wine speak for you,' she whispered. It was something François had always said when he was teaching her at tastings. He told her it was like poetry and could tell the story of the land. That night, she dreamt of him in his good times. Moët's actions had brought her that at least. The next morning, she was resolved. To work.

Crossing the press yard, she held her head high, greeting workers, exchanging brisk pleasantries about their families and the day's work ahead as normal, whilst enduring sideways glances of sympathy or suspicion. *This will pass, just another little setback, like a hailstorm or a difficult harvest*, she told herself as she slammed the office door behind her.

Her hand shook with fury at Moët as she held her quill above the ledgers and buried herself in them. The figures were safe, neat, indisputable, unlike life or François or the chaotic vines, so vulnerable to disease, the weather, pests and whatever God chose to throw at them. And whatever regrets she might have had about the precious pawned necklace, it would protect her financially for a while longer.

That evening, after all the workers had left, she went alone into the cellars. The silence cocooned her and as her eyes became accustomed to the dark, the bottles gleamed reassuringly back at her. Every one of them was redemption. Every one the result of her management, her taste, her labours. Every one testament to François and her marriage and love for him and the vines. She wasn't sure how long she stayed there, just her and the bottles and silence, but when she emerged, the moon was high and bright. She trudged across the yard to sleep, and dreamt of the moment that François died a thousand times over.

CHAPTER 18

September 1811

Beginnings

When she heard the explosions, Nicole thought she was still having nightmares. But no, she was awake, and the light streaming through the drapes brought the relief of morning. Was it the boom of thunder, perhaps? She looked outside. Clear blue skies. Where the hell was it coming from? Underground? *Please God, no.*

'Josette!' she called. Her maid came running. 'Find Louis, wherever he is!'

Nicole flung a shawl around her aching shoulders and ran to the press. Workers scattered out of the cellars, holding handkerchiefs, rags, whatever they could, over their faces, coughing and spluttering. They couldn't have read the notices in town yet if they were still with her.

Xavier came running. 'It's the whole 1810 batch, a river of wasted champagne. Glass everywhere. It's all ruined.'

'*Those* bottles? The ones we ordered from Moët's supplier?'

He nodded. Nicole pushed through the workers staggering out of the cellars.

'Don't! It's lethal in there!' shouted Xavier.

She flew as far down the steps as she dared. Candles were too dangerous in this volatile place, so she waited for her eyes to adjust. Fumes choked her and the bottles were still blowing, spewing yellow liquid, glass knifing through the air.

All she could do was watch, stupefied, a scene straight from hell. At least ten thousand bottles ruined.

'Disaster after disaster. When will she learn?'

Nicole's eyes snapped open. Two women fussed around her. Blue sky, gravel, milkweed. She was laid out near the cellar door.

'Shh, she's come round.'

Nicole tried to sit up.

'Don't try to move, Babouchette.'

Thank God, Louis had come.

She closed her eyes to shut out the searing pain.

'Someone run for a doctor and get me something to staunch the blood,' he yelled.

He cradled her head and pressed on the wound, flung a blood-soaked cloth to the ground, and Josette handed him another. Her voice was a croak when she tried to speak and her fingers came away from her forehead smeared in blood.

'You fell, right to the bottom of the steps. What were you thinking? Were you going to be a heroine and single-handedly save every one of your bottles? You could have been killed in there,' he said gently, his anger subsiding. 'Now, let's get you inside.'

Xavier helped him lift her and, gingerly, they got her into her house.

'By the window,' she managed to croak. 'I want to see the press and the vines.'

She drifted in and out of consciousness, losing track of the days. Often when she woke, Louis was there, a bottle of burgundy by his side and *Don Quixote* on his lap. She had given him the book five years ago and he still hadn't finished it. He pretended to be reading when she opened her eyes.

'Bring me a mirror, will you, Louis?'

'What for?'

'I'd like to see. How long have I been here?'

Louis knelt by her bed. 'This is the first time you have spoken in three days. How do you feel?'

'The bottles that exploded were the ones from Moët's suppliers,' she whispered.

Louis darkened. 'Don't add that to your worries. It's happened to every vintner in Champagne at some point in their careers. Moët's a slippery, greedy bastard, but it would have been difficult for even him to arrange for an explosion. The mistake you made was to go into the cellars while they were still volatile. You need to rest.'

'Help me up. I need to see the damage to my cellars.'

She hauled herself up and the room swirled. It seemed she wasn't going anywhere.

'The doctor said at least a week. I'll run things until you're better. Mentine is being well cared for with her friends, so you have nothing to worry about. Just trust me.'

'With my life,' she said, sinking into her pillow.

'I'll sit here with you and tell you some stories if you promise to stay where you are.'

Smiling hurt. 'I'm listening.'

Day turned to night as the sun crossed the sky, beating down on the vineyards, turning the grapes sweet. Larks hovered just above the vines, amongst them poppies blazed and wilted and through the open window, birdsong punctuated Louis' stories. He told her about François before she knew him. The smallest incident was a tall tale, from a Norwegian innkeeper with a France-shaped wart on his nose, to a mouse who danced to François' violin at a customer's mansion in Schleswig-Holstein.

Josette fluttered in and out every now and then with fresh baked bread, Louis' favourite Neuchatel cheese and summer strawberries, which they shared as they talked.

Every morning when she woke, he was there watching her, hastily picking up *Don Quixote* as she opened her eyes.

By Friday she felt stronger and the doctor took the dressing off her forehead under Louis' watchful eye. Out of the window, Xavier was setting off to the vineyards. The sun was already up over the horizon, late to be going out into the fields, and the cellar door was wide open.

'Where are all the workers, what's happening out there? Who's overseeing it all?'

'I was there at sunrise, with Xavier. The sun and rain and soil are all doing their job without you. It's the best I've ever seen it. Perfect.'

'Why is no one here? The remaining bottles need riddling, I can't afford to lose even one more. I'm going back to work today, so you might as well tell me everything.'

Louis put down his book and sighed.

'There is nothing to salvage, Nicole, and it's impossible to even enter the cellar. One of the girls got halfway down the steps and fainted. Luckily, she wasn't hurt, but I've banned all cellar work. It's just too dangerous.'

'How long?'

'Impossible to say. Weeks, Babouchette. Maybe months.'

Josette came in with fresh croissants and coffee and a bowl of glossy blackberries.

'First of the year, Madame,' she said as she arranged the tray, plumping up her pillows.

Nicole breathed in the blackberries and her head whirled with jumbled memories. Stained fingers, musty sweet stuff, her sister's white dress smudged with purple fingerprints. The bloom of blood on a white sheet, the reproach of a sour berry.

'Babouchette?'

Louis' stare was sharp, so blue.

Josette fiddled with the fire. Her dress was torn. When was the last time she had paid her wages? Nicole couldn't remember.

'Josette, bring me my dress and my field overcoat, please. Don't look at Louis for orders, I'm much better, so just do as I say. I promise to go slowly, but I'm back to work today with immediate effect.'

'I was quite getting used to having you there, to myself, incapable of giving out orders,' said Louis.

Josette helped her dress and insisted on supporting her as far as the front door. Outside in the courtyard, she was vexed at how unsteady she was on her feet on the uneven cobbles, but when she arrived at the vineyard, the leaf she brushed was sun-warmed, the grapes sticky and pungent. Another week at the most and they would be ready. She could start anew. All the indications were that this crop was a once-in-a-lifetime best. Even better, the comet was back, fizzing above the horizon, watching over her and her vines. But she realised the yard was empty of people. The vineyards too.

'Emile!' She called her stable boy. He'd tell her what was happening, even if Louis wouldn't.

'He's at home, recovering, Babouchette. I didn't tell you until you were strong enough, but he was blinded. Glass in his eyes.'

She crossed herself. 'Jesus have mercy.'

Emile Jumel, the horse boy who ran errands to Paris and back for her. Rosy cheeks, a bum-fluff moustache, Marie's pride and joy. She tried to remember the colour of his eyes and couldn't.

'I'll visit them later. Would you send Xavier to withdraw five hundred francs from my personal account today?'

'Are you sure? It's a tragedy, but the losses you've already made…'

'Please, just do it.'

'Yes, Madame. I see you have made a complete recovery.'

Nicole smiled, but the despair nearly choked her. There would be nothing left.

'Enough soft-soap, Louis. I need to know everything, starting with why the press and fields are deserted at such a crucial time?'

'This may be 1811, and we've been through a revolution, but superstitions haven't changed. They say you're bad luck.'

'You mean Moët's poster campaign in the square?' she asked, sick to her stomach.

Louis nodded. 'I wish to God it was better news. That bastard was never going to go quietly.'

'I'll pay the workers more.' But she ran the figures in front of her eyes and she knew it was hopeless. She hadn't lost her ability to visualise her account books, at least. The red column expanded and hurt her head. The debts were mounting. It would be impossible to pay more and, anyway, there was plenty of work elsewhere in a harvest like this. Why would they work for a woman with a bad name and a string of disasters behind her? Moët had won. For now. 'At least I have you back,' she said.

'Absolutely.' He knelt and inspected the rose bush at the end of the row for infestations, unable to meet her eye. 'I'm out of savings and I need to earn a living again, with a baby on the way.'

He looked at her sheepishly. Nicole's mind was racing in confusion. Had she missed something when she was drifting in and out of consciousness?

'A *baby?*'

'You remember I told you about the family in the Russian hostel where Thérésa deposited me? The daughter was kind and she kept my bed warm at night. I was foolish, but I couldn't leave her like that. We married in the wooden church in the village. Her parents wept and I promised I'd cherish her. I'm all she has now. I'm collecting her from the inn at Rethel tonight to bring her home. She's learning French, trying her hardest.'

'You've hidden it from me all this time?'

'I hid it through selfishness, Babouchette. Forgive me.'

It was her turn to check the rose to hide her disappointment. She had got her Louis back, only to have him snatched away again. They had never *said* anything to each other, but the look in his eyes at her bedside, the little attentions to everything he knew she loved. She'd got used to having him to herself and it was only now that she knew she was losing something she didn't realise she had wanted. Foolish of her to imagine she would be lucky enough to ever love again. Her place was here, at the vineyard, with François' shadow beside her. She resolved never to show him her regret.

She stood up, brushed her hands off and said briskly, 'You did the right thing.'

'Not by you, though. I wanted to pretend. That week watching over you will have to last me a lifetime.'

'Don't even speak of it, Louis, it's impossible,' she said, blinking away a threatening tear and striding towards the press. 'If you have mouths to feed, you'd better get to work. Your first child will be born in the year of the best harvest we'll see in our lifetime. The year of the comet. We'll never forget it.'

She knew what she had to do next. There could be no wine without workers, and she had a business to run.

CHAPTER 19

September 1811

The Taste of the Terroir

Etienne's bar was always packed at harvest time, with men hunched over their pastis and beers after a day in the fields. Strangers wolf-whistled. Familiar faces avoided Nicole's eye, or sulked at the audacity of her entering their refuge.

Etienne came to the rescue, bustling out from behind the bar, wiping his face on his apron and kissing a welcome.

'I have a bottle of your Bouzy behind the counter. Will you join me?'

'Thank you, that would be nice.'

Her barouche was waiting outside, a safety precaution in case her plan went awry. It was never going to be easy walking into a bar full of men, and she wasn't quite sure how she was going to do this, but she *had* to act.

A hush descended as she pulled herself up onto the bar stool. Etienne passed the wine across the counter. She sipped and rolled it around her tongue: a red-brick vineyard wall and rainy summer.

'Villers-Allerand, north-facing slope, 1808. Pinot Noir. Hail in May, hot summer, then rain at harvest time. The harvest was small, but these were our best grapes.'

Etienne ran his thumb across the label and squinted. 'Very good, but it's your own,' he said. He reached beneath the counter and pulled out another, a white this time, and a clean glass. A couple of field hands next to her turned to look, elbows on the counter. Etienne showed them the label, concealing it from her.

Nicole breathed it in and swilled it around her mouth, spat into the bowl Etienne held out and wiped her mouth with the back of her hand.

'Almond, brioche, a touch of metal. Vintage Ruinart Côte des Blancs, his little vineyard right in the centre, the one he likes to patrol with the Mayor.' A few appreciative sniggers bubbled up. '1805...'

The year that wouldn't go away, the year François died. An easy harvest to remember.

Etienne discreetly studied the tasting ticket tied to the bottle. His eyes widened as he showed it to the small crowd that was gathering. 'Spot on, Madame Clicquot.'

'Bring out a sparkling next – your best. Half a glass for me, and the rest for the gentlemen at the bar. Open another if it doesn't go far enough.'

Most refused it and crossed themselves, but a few accepted and raised their glasses in a toast. The men solemnly tasted the champagne and whispered their tasting notes to one another. It was a serious business, tasting champagne. One glass was worth more than they earned in a week.

The comet was fizzing outside, like the cordons of bubbles in her glass. She swirled a mouthful.

'The Pinot is from the Aube. The Meunier from the Vallée gives quite a youthful exuberance and the Chardonnay provides the creamy backbone. The Chardonnay can only be from the Clos du Mesnil. Which means, *cher* Etienne, that I'm disappointed in you.'

'I've just served you my finest champagne,' he said.

'Exactly. I'm more than disappointed that you consider your finest champagne to be from that second-rate vintner Moët. However, I must admit that his 1802 vintage *was* very good.'

This turned a few more heads, and some grudgingly appreciative glances.

'Correct again, to the last grape,' declared Etienne.

She was a pariah, but who could resist the gossip? She had the attention of the entire bar room now.

'There is no taste, no grape, no wine that I couldn't pinpoint almost to the vine in this region. I grew up here, I taste and *feel* it. I hear things too. You think I'm a pitiable, widowed woman, playing at making wine in memory of my husband. Perhaps that's true, in part. But I *know* my vines, understand the press, the alchemy of the blend and I know you all understand that, too. You grew up here, like me, and it's in our blood.

'I make the best champagne and wines in Reims and I want to persuade you to come with me. You all know I have had setbacks. Who hasn't? I know it's the talk of the town. I can't pay you what Moët and the others are promising for this harvest, but every man and woman who harvests my vines this year will be rewarded, I guarantee it. See it as an investment in your future.'

'It's a set-up with Etienne!' shouted a man from the shadows at the back. 'She's desperate. What kind of brazen woman would come in here, trying to recruit for a failing business, especially with *her* background?'

Nicole couldn't make out who it was in the gloom of the bar.

'You are correct, Monsieur. I *am* desperate. This could be the best harvest any of us will see in our lifetime and I don't intend to let it pass me by. I am also offering everyone here an opportunity they won't regret. You have all seen the comet?'

Some murmured and nodded, some crossed themselves.

'Unusual things *do* happen. Take the comet as a sign that the world can turn upside down. A great, unbidden star with a tail can hang in our skies for months on end with no explanation, bringing with it the best harvest we have ever known. A widow with a nose for business and the best blend *can* help make you wealthy and provide for your families in return for loyalty.'

The man stepped out of the shadows. Moët's foreman. No doubt here to recruit too.

'Are you really going to turn down double wages on a promise from a woman with a failing business? Are you really going to go back to your wives and tell them what you're doing for a woman with a reputation, that they won't have a share in the rare bounty of this harvest? How do you know she didn't arrange this with Etienne in advance?'

This wouldn't be the first time she'd been doubted, or the last. She steeled herself to face him – she'd come up against his sort before. The only way to deal with him was to prove it directly to him.

'Go behind Etienne's bar and choose a wine for yourself and I will prove it to you. My only criterion is that it's from Champagne.'

'You want me to help you continue this charade? No. Men, I have my sign-up sheet here for tomorrow's harvest. Sign up and get back to your drinks. We came here to escape from the nags and dreamers.'

A few men shuffled over, embarrassed, to sign up with Fournier.

'Best night I've had in here in years,' one man shouted. 'Come on, if you're so sure, choose a wine. See what she comes up with. A night with the comet.'

'Put your money where your mouth is, Fournier. Choose a wine.'

Nicole scrutinised Fournier. Red face, cruel eyes. This man was not well-liked. Moët mistreated his workers, she heard, and Fournier was his enforcer.

'I'll make a bet with you,' said Nicole. 'Choose three wines. If I get them all, leave me to sign up whoever is willing tonight. Agree that you will not turn them away if they change their minds by tomorrow morning, or at least if their wives have changed their minds for them.'

'Come on, Fournier,' a man heckled. 'Too scared to take a woman's bet?'

Fournier stomped behind the bar, shooing Etienne away. After rummaging around, he placed a small glass of red on the counter.

Nicole tasted it. Her mind came up blank. The taste was full of sun, too full.

'This one's not from the region, Monsieur Fournier. It's from the south, somewhere hot.' She pushed the glass to him. 'I said it must be from Champagne.'

'That's where you're wrong, Madame.' Fournier triumphantly held up the bottle. 'Blondel. Vallée. No one wants to work for a swindler, Veuve Clicquot.'

'I know that wine. It's not the one I tasted,' said Nicole.

'Ah woman, thy name is vanity. I'll put it kindly. At best, you're mistaken. More likely, you're lying.'

'Who volunteers to taste from that bottle and this glass and tell me if it's the same wine? I'll need three people,' said Nicole.

Fournier was rattled. 'Will she ever stop and let us carry on with our drinks? This is a man's place. We've humoured you enough, *chérie*, now go home to your debts. They always said there was madness in the family. Takes one to marry one.'

Three men stepped forward and one spoke.

'We'll taste it. Fair's fair.' He was one of her own, a picker. 'Give her a chance. And no need for that kind of talk, if you don't mind me saying, Monsieur Fournier. François Clicquot was a good man and a fair employer, as is his wife.'

Men throughout the room crossed themselves, raised a glass to the sky and toasted him.

Thank you, François.

Etienne poured water for each man to clear their palates. Each one declared that the two wines were not the same. Etienne returned, studied the wine collection. He held his hands above the counter.

'I haven't touched a thing. Look.'

In a dark corner, tucked away, were several dusty wine bottles. One of them had fingerprints in the dust, newly made, with the cork halfway out. It had been opened and hastily stoppered.

The picker pulled it out.

'Bandol, Domain de L'Estagnol, Provence. Somewhere hot, like she says. Pretty low, Fournier, to cheat a woman.'

'It wouldn't be the first time.'

Whispers rippled around the room. The three wine tasters were the first to approach her.

'Where do I sign?'

Nicole picked up her ledger off the bar. 'Sign here. Six a.m. sharp tomorrow.'

They signed.

'You won't regret it, I promise.'

One by one, men came to sign. Not all, but enough for a good harvest if they were prepared to work long hours.

Outside, the evening was chilly. Nicole could taste the slick wet flagstones, grit and damp dust in the air. Mixed with the taste of Bandol, still lingering on her tongue, it tasted of relief. The comet was still there, tail fizzing. Good. This would be her best harvest. It had to be.

She stepped quickly into the waiting carriage, glad to be speedily whisked away. Fournier's words would not leave her.

Back to an empty house with only debts to greet her. Madness in the family. How dare he! She would be so successful that no one would ever question her, or Mentine's legitimacy as a good catch. And she would never need another man, not a husband, a business partner or a father. Her life was entirely her own.

CHAPTER 20

September 1811

A Widow's Genius

The world looked better through a bottle. Nicole held it up to the light, distorting the vines and turning everything bottle-green.

Emile sat next to her in her little courtyard office, adjacent to the presses and overlooking the vineyards. He still had gauze over his eyes, his fresh face scarred. She passed him the bottle. He weighed it in his hands and smiled.

'Heavy, much better, Madame.'

Nicole didn't smile back, not when he was still in pain. His mother had done him proud, against all the odds, and now this. She took the bottle back from him and remembered the yeasty smell of the explosions, the metallic taste of blood.

She patted his arm. 'Good, I'll agree to these ones. Thank you, Emile.'

'Is it a good harvest day, Madame?'

Nicole took his arm and led him outside. 'The workers are already out.'

'I can hear them!'

'It's perfect. You know how the early-morning mist can cling to the vines yet the sky above is blue and crystal clear? It's one of those mornings.'

'The grapes'll stay plump and juicy for the presses with the moisture.'

'You know more than I do and you're half my age!'

He puffed up the way he used to when he was delivering messages on horseback. 'I've grown up with it, Madame. At least until now.'

She squeezed his arm. 'And you'll do it for the rest of your life while you're working for me.'

Emile squeezed back.

The sun was so low that it was brick orange, bathing the fields in light. Her comet workers – as she now called them – had turned up at six o'clock sharp, as requested. They had all kept to their word and not one of them had reneged. What a glorious day! The comet was visible in the sky, even in the daytime, and the autumn morning was delicious, like blackberry jam and croissants.

Nicole helped Emile to the vines. His mother Marie was a familiar sight now, working at the land harder than ever, even though Nicole had paid them enough to support themselves without having to. She guided her son's hand to the donkey reins. His job was to lead the donkey under her instruction, to gather the grapes.

Antoine was there, still signing a queue of workers and Mademoiselle Var from the secret tasting committee was running a little crèche for the children of the women who needed work. In these hard times, even grandparents were out in the field.

Her parents rode by to offer solidarity, Papa nodding proudly to her at the sight of all this industry.

Nicole turned back, down the chalk path, towards her ledgers, which would not please her, she knew. Any other harvest, she would be out there, tasting grapes, imagining the blend.

Louis arrived for his shift, bouncing towards her, all energy and enthusiasm.

'Audacity, *sauvage*. How did you get so much of it?'

'Good morning, Louis.'

'You persuaded these men to work for half what Moët's offering. Everyone's talking about it.'

'They're country people, they're used to planting a seed and waiting for their reward.'

'I thought I was the one with the gift of the gab, but this eclipses anything I might have attempted.'

'I had to do it. I can't let Moët beat me after all he's done. It's a special year, I can feel it. I know you think I'm a superstitious peasant and you're right. This harvest will make us our fortune, the comet has brought a change in the air, and they feel it too. You know they're calling it Napoléon's comet? The war will end, we'll lay this down, and in time, it will bring us all the luck we need.'

'They know you're one of them at heart,' said Louis.

'How's Miss Rhinewald?'

'Mrs Bohne, you mean. She's well. Not long to go until the baby.'

'I'll still never forgive you for not inviting me to the wedding.'

'How could I let you outshine the bride?' He searched her eyes for her response.

'Don't talk to me like that, we both made our choices. I am married to my land and I'm happy.' It *could* be true, on the good days, she thought.

'You should have someone to share it all with.'

'I'm sharing it with you, in my own way.' If she didn't change the subject now, she wouldn't be able to account for her actions. She pressed on, 'I've been working on an idea I'd like you to see.'

'Haven't you had enough of those for one week?'

'Don't tease me, this is serious. It's a way of making Veuve Clicquot champagne the clearest, most effervescent on the market. Absolute clarity for every bottle and in record time.'

'If you've done that, it's a miracle. I'd be rich if I had a franc for every cellarman who says he can produce a flawless batch of fizz every time. They are always proved wrong. It hasn't been solved in thousands of years. It would certainly make my job easier if I didn't have to discount for cloudy bottles in every consignment. And it would nearly kill Moët if you succeeded! Do you ever stop?'

'You know the answer to that.'

He held her gaze, so she quickly turned and paced back to her office. Life was complicated – and lonely – enough. Her little Mentine would be home from her Paris boarding school at Christmas and the two of them were a family, however small. Eleven years old now, her little rosebud growing into a rose. In looks, Mentine was more like her aunt than Nicole – fair, tall, conventionally pretty, all milk, roses and almonds. But her *joie de vivre*, love of poetry and social justice were so like François at his best, and she was becoming a delightful companion.

Nicole opened her ledgers and her head was so deep in her books that she didn't hear the door open. At first, she thought she was seeing things. Standing there, cool and glamorous and beautiful as ever was Thérésa. Nicole collapsed into her friend's arms.

'You nearly scared me to death. How do you do that, sneak up anywhere you please?'

'Come here, no need for tears.' Thérésa dried her cheeks with her dress. 'I rescued your charming salesman and sent him back to you. Where is he? How could he leave you on your own like this?'

'He's at home with his pregnant wife.'

'How careless of you to let him slip through your fingers. Really, I don't understand why you don't make use of the opportunities widowhood offers at such a young age.'

Nicole laughed and shook her head.

'That's better, now stop being so *serious*. Well, more fool you, he was in love with you once. I suppose you feel you still have to *work* for your living?'

'You know it's what keeps me alive, Thérésa. You deal in men, I in bottles.'

'You are fooling yourself if you think that. You have every man here wrapped around your little finger. I heard about your "tasting" in the bar. You think they signed up for your talents? No. Men are the same everywhere, even in this backwater. Everyone here is a little in love with you, darling. No one can resist drawing near to a firefly and watching as it buzzes about.'

Her delight at seeing Thérésa clouded for a moment as she remembered her pawned firefly necklace. She banished the thought as soon as it appeared, a skill she had developed since François, essential for survival.

'If only that was true of Moët. I'm sure he'd actually kill me if he could find a way of doing it and stay respectable.'

'You've challenged the richest and most powerful man within a hundred miles. What do you expect?'

Nicole scrutinised Thérésa. She recognised the steel, the beguiling flattery like the finest vintage champagne – exciting and rare. A happy accident of white skin, perfect teeth, hair black as liquorice, a talent for flouting rules and being loved for it.

'You're looking at me in that way again. You won't find anything more than complete frivolity.'

'I see bravery, served up with sugar to try to fool me,' replied Nicole. Hurt skimmed Thérésa's face, chased by her dazzling smile. 'It seems business is not so good for you either. Where is *your* latest conquest?'

'I need a rest between the buffoons and a country retreat is just the thing. Marie Antoinette had the Petit Trianon, I have your little world full of grapes and field hands. You don't begrudge me a bit of fun?'

'I could never thank you enough for all you have done for me.'

Thérésa clapped her hands. 'I knew you had a soul under that tough exterior.'

'And *I* know you have a way of deflecting attention away from yourself when things are bad. Why are you here?'

'I need to lie low for a while. Things have got a little… awkward in Paris. You know how hot-headed men can be, especially when they're regarded as important and my current husband has a very high opinion of himself. I was hoping you could get your friend Monsieur Moët to have a whisper in Napoléon's ear, but you've completely ruined that for me now. It's been over a year since Joséphine was cast aside for that plate-of-whey Marie-Louise. These aristocrats really are inbred. She has the blood, but absolutely nothing else. God completely overlooked her for wit, looks or personality, poor thing. Joséphine's fall from grace has included me and while I'm financially secure – I haven't been foolish enough to give myself to several marriages without ensuring mine and my children's welfare – life is so dull without invitations and salons and being in the thick of things. Like you without your vineyards, I'm a flower without water.'

'What are you hiding from?' asked Nicole.

'What does any self-respecting grown-up ever hide from? Scandal, of course. My husband and his friends are such prudes.'

'You can stay as long as you like – I won't ask for details, and you are welcome, though you'll find my country life dull.'

'Oh, don't you worry about me, I can amuse myself. The men here may be a little gauche, but I'm a good teacher. I might even work on Moët myself.'

Nicole grasped Thérésa's hand – surprisingly cold – and squeezed it. 'The truth is, I will be glad of the company.'

'I refuse to stay without paying my way. What would it take to satisfactorily lay down your vintage comet champagne?'

'How do you even know about that?'

'You spend too much time with your head in your ledgers and mooning over grapes. The talk in this town is of nothing else. I have only been here for one day and I know all about it. A beautiful woman – don't shake your head, darling, it's a fact – a beautiful woman, alone in this godforsaken village, obsessing about wine, luring men out of bars to work for her, secret shipments, miraculous comets… from what I hear of François, he would have been proud – now you look like you want to cry again. Don't do that, it makes you blotchy.'

'I can't take a sou.'

'You most certainly will. It's purely business. I'll invest in you, show the whole of Paris and take all the credit. Don't you try to stop me. Napoléon wants to conquer the world, but he will never, ever conquer me. I want it for the same reason as you, darling. Freedom from men, respectability. To be above the rules, like you.'

As always, it was impossible to resist her beautiful friend. And why would she? They would both benefit, and she would have the added bonus of her company for as long as she cared to give it, which was all you could ever expect from a capricious goddess.

'Let's get you settled. Josette can make your room up and I'll ask Antoine and Xavier to stay here and keep an eye on the workers.'

'The faithful retainers? It seems I still have a lot to learn from you, my lady of Reims.'

'Loyalty is all I have left at the moment and yours is more valuable to me than anyone's.'

Of course country life wasn't dull for Thérésa. She employed Claudine to make her peasant dresses out of the best silk the dress shop could supply and wafted around, chattering to milkmaids, chewing on clover, picking autumn flowers from the hedgerows and threading them through her hair.

Her target was Moët. If anyone in the world could distract Moët from her destruction, it was Thérésa. Every day, she strolled the borders where the Clicquot and Moët vineyards met, pretending to inspect the vines on Nicole's behalf.

While Thérésa was out playing the country maid, Nicole hacked away at her makeshift invention in the cellar, with borrowed tools from Antoine, a feverish idea she'd had from her years of experimenting with the riddling bottles in the sand.

The kitchen table she had sacrificed for the purpose was old and solid, made of local oak and big enough for sixty bottles. As she made the holes with a bradawl, the wood released its scent of sap and sawdust.

Josette knocked on the door and Nicole tutted. She had given strict instructions – no one was allowed in the kitchen cellar.

'What is it?'

'Monsieur Bohne is here, Madame. I thought perhaps you might make an exception.'

Of course, for Louis.

'Send him in.'

Louis bowed. 'I am honoured to be admitted to your top-secret activities.'

'You should be.'

'What are you doing? Josette says you've been down here for days.'

Nicole held up the lamp to illuminate the old kitchen table with four neat rows of champagne bottles upturned, a total of sixty bottles. In her frenzy to make her invention real, she had scattered wood shavings everywhere and the tabletop was pocked with failed attempts, but the diagonal holes were exactly as she wanted them. The old table had taken a battering, but it *worked*. All the years of trying to make it work for François, trying to solve the problem that had eluded vintners down the ages. Just a few adjustments and efficiencies and *voilà*! All she'd really had to do was believe that she could do it.

'You're moving from viticulture to woodwork?' Louis asked, perplexed.

'It solves everything!'

'I know that look. You have a big scheme that will embarrass your father, give the village endless gossip and me more reason to worry about you than ever. What are you planning with that battered old thing?'

'It doesn't matter how it *looks*, Louis! It's the answer to all our problems!'

'We both have a lot more problems than a butchered kitchen table can solve,' said Louis softly.

'I mean the sediment problem! Times are hard, and it takes months for a skilled cellarman to reach your standards of clarity when it comes to champagne. How many times have you told me not to send you cloudy bottles?'

Louis counted on his fingers, and ran out of them very quickly. 'A lot more than I can show you this way,' he laughed.

'I've *solved* it, Louis! No more laying out in sand and hoping for the best with inexact positions and waiting for the sediment to travel to the cork instead of sticking to the bottom and sides. No more transferring from one bottle to another and losing all the fizz, and some of the precious wine, never mind taking up the time of my best cellarmen. And no more "clarifiers" from spurious sources.'

She took a bottle out, very gingerly so as not to disturb her work and held it up to the lantern.

'Look. The sediment is near the cork, ready to slip out without disturbing my bubbles.'

Nicole removed the staple, placed her thumb over the cork and felt the pressure, searched for the air bubble separating the sediment and wine. Just right, ready to go. A deft flick of the cap and the sediment shot out, leaving the champagne intact. She quickly replaced the cork and showed the champagne to Louis.

'Look! Clear as a diamond, and nothing lost. It takes less time for the sediment to travel to the cork, and reduces the labour time, too. The processing time for everything is halved!'

'Bloody genius!' Louis took the bottle and held it up to the light again. 'Clear as a sunbeam. My God, the weeks of labour for each bottle it'll save...' He inspected it upside down, then upright again.

'It's really simple. A few efficiencies and improvements to an age-old technique and I'll save thousands of labour hours. Look.'

Nicole dragged over the sandbox she'd hidden over six years ago, the day François had died, and demonstrated. She bent over, picked up two bottles, stood up to shake them a little, then knelt back down to place them in the sand. Then, at her riddling table, she showed Louis the same process with her new invention. Standing at her table with all the bottles in front of her at waist height, she shook and turned a whole row of fifteen in the time it had just taken her to do the same with the two in the sandbox.

Then, her *pièce de resistance*. She held up the neck of the bottle to Louis, ready to burst with excitement.

'Four chalk marks?' He was unimpressed.

'Yes! It's obvious! When I put the bottles back in the sand, it's never accurate and the sediment has to move again if I get the angle even half a centimetre wrong, which delays the process even further. With my riddling table, all the cellar workers need to do is to line the chalk mark back up and *voilà*. With this, I can turn thirty-five thousand bottles in a day, with practice. Each turn and the sediment travels a little further towards the cork. It's ridiculously simple, like all the best ideas, but it *works*. It's really just an exercise in time and motion, like I've seen in Papa's woollen mills.'

'Fifteen thousand bottles a day for mere mortals, and thirty-five thousand for you no doubt! Nevertheless, the advantage over all our competitors, thousands of flawless bottles turned in a fraction of the time, with half the labour. You've done it, Babouchette… all the sacrifices and gambles!'

She bowed and he applauded.

'Even with this, how will you manage to keep going? It will still be a long time before you can get the money in. The markets are still dead, even with thousands of bottles of flawless champagne laid down.'

'I don't know, but I'm doing this for *us*, Louis. For your family, for mine, for all the workers who belong here. I'm also doing it for *me*. I want to be first, the best.'

'You always have been.'

'I want to be the best in the *world's* eyes. Not just Reims, not even just France. This is our secret, Louis. Antoine knows about it too. We will pay the workers to keep quiet and only a select few will be allowed to work the champagne cellars. No one else must know about it. I'll lay down my comet champagne on my new racks and wait. The war will be over one day.'

'You can't afford to wait; Veuve Clicquot et Compagnie is on its knees.'

'My new lodger is making an investment,' said Nicole.

Louis held his head in his hands. 'Ah, the fairy godmother, La Tallien, with her ill-gotten gains.'

'The very one. And the more ill-gotten, the better, as far as I'm concerned.'

'She's a wonderful woman, but trouble is never far away when she's around. Please tread carefully.'

CHAPTER 21

September 1813

Rich Woman, Thief

Thérésa's house in Reims was the scandal of the town, but she was more than tolerated for her outrageous behaviour. These were austere times and she brought colour wherever she went. In Champagne, the shops were badly stocked. Napoléon had invaded Russia. His war ate up fresh young conscripts and spat them out maimed and broken. The returned were the lucky ones. Parents who had seen poverty take their loved ones as children before the revolution now saw their own children taken by war. Thérésa was a welcome distraction, their outrageous, glamourous local *célébrée*. She could dangle the great Napoléon from her little finger if she saw fit, bring mighty generals to their knees and, more practically, put in a good word for ambitious sons.

Nobody knew how she could afford such a lavish mansion on the rue de la Vache, but many suspected that Moët had a hand in it. Nicole never asked; she would rather not know. In the year of the comet, Thérésa's money had helped her lay down the Cuvée de la Comète and her presence had also helped her through the birth of Louis' first child, though she didn't know it. Thérésa was a distraction from watching Louis' eyes light up, first when he talked about his new little son, then at the sight of his increasingly confident new wife. She never met them together, but she saw them in town sometimes, or dropping Louis off at the press. They were quite the little family unit and Nicole hated herself for the bitterness she felt at their delight.

Louis was her business partner, they saw each other most days, and it would have been the most natural thing in the world to embrace the couple, to invite Louis and his wife to social occasions, or to give his son a tour of the vineyards in her pony and trap. But it was all she could manage to smile at Louis' happiness and wish them well. Anything else was too painful. Louis seemed to instinctively understand and never pressed the matter, or mentioned them too often to her, and she was silently grateful to her warm-hearted friend for his tact and care whilst being ashamed at her own feelings.

Her precious comet champagne stood in her new riddling tables, deep in the cellars, away from prying eyes, going nowhere thanks to the trade blockades and the war. Her business, her livelihood, everything she had, depended on this champagne making it to market.

After all the years of war, business was bad for everyone. The harvest would be difficult to bring in again this year with so many men away at war. Thérésa started to spend more and more time back in Paris. Parties and salons were the only thing that brought back her sparkle and she was easily bored by Reims and its little gatherings. Nicole missed her lively friend. Louis came to work, but left every day promptly at five to rush back to his family, so she was delighted when Josette handed her a note elaborately tied in pale pink silk ribbon. Only Thérésa would throw away such an expensive thing on a prosaic note.

Darling, how lovely to be back in the old town again. Paris stifles me. I am sure I was meant to be a country girl, with all the sweet air and champagne and visions of fireflies and starry nights. Please join me for tea and gossip this afternoon. I have so much to tell you.

Nicole folded the note. As a rule, she avoided town. She preferred to keep a close eye on her lands and bypass the gossip and pitiful looks she inevitably got on each visit, but seeing Thérésa would be worth it.

She stopped at Natasha's, feeling guilty as she grasped the polished brass handle of the *boulangerie*. It was a long time since she'd seen her. Natasha's bakery had always been the epicentre of the Reims gossip machine and Nicole just hadn't been able to face it, or, she had to admit, Natasha's penetrating questions. Easier just to get on with her work than face up to anything else.

'Babouchette. The prodigal returns.' Natasha shuffled stiffly out from behind the counter and kissed her. Natasha's cheeks were papery and her hair was more white than grey now. She pursed her lips. 'You are thinner than when I last saw you. What do you do out in Bouzy all alone with no one to talk to?'

'My vines are good company.'

'Well, I can see that. You neglect your friends for them.'

'Things are just so busy at the presses and out in the fields. My farming families are willing, but have their own land to keep up with so many lads away at war.'

Natasha put her hands on her hips and narrowed her eyes. 'Show me your hands.'

'Why?'

'Don't question your elders.'

Nicole reluctantly took off her gloves and held them out.

'Just as I thought. You've been out there yourself, haven't you? Digging and tying and pruning like a peasant.'

'No shame in that.'

'It's why I love you.' Natasha gestured to her counter, the shop, the ovens in the back. 'You are more beautiful than me, and considerably more successful, but we are the same, you and I.'

Nicole smiled. She hadn't realised how much she had holed herself away, reading Chaptal's theories on wine growing, obsessively checking her ledgers, roaming the vineyards inspecting every last detail, turning bottles in the cellar when labour was short, verifying the fermentation and praying to St Rémi for a good harvest and to whatever God was out there for an end to war.

'I got here early to get the best *religieuses*. Where is everything?'

Natasha stared at her darkly. 'You really haven't been anywhere, have you? There's a war on. The only thing I have are these *miches*.'

Nicole stared at the solid brown loaves on the bare counter, like clods of sodden earth.

'What are you living on? Nettles and blackberries?'

'I'm fine, really. Happy, in fact, with my grapes. I am not what you need to be worrying about. How are you coping with nothing to sell?'

Natasha sniffed. 'And vice versa. You deal with your business, I'll deal with mine. I don't need anyone fussing or worrying over me. At least I haven't sold the most precious thing my husband gave me.'

Nicole's heart lurched. Her firefly necklace. It was three years ago now that she had pawned it. 'Don't! He wouldn't have wanted me to give up on the business and I needed money.'

'I know,' said Natasha more gently. 'I just wanted you to know that I knew, and I am looking out for your interests, even when you stay away from me.'

'Is there nothing I can hide from you?'

Natasha folded her arms. 'Nothing. I have many more links in this city than you imagine for a poor old bakery widow. Monsieur Nadalié, the pawnbroker, has been a client for years.'

'A client?'

'The people who visit him are desperate. They need a little good news, and I give it to the people he refers to me. They believe that I can see into their future. I find whatever elements of comfort for them I can. There's always *something* good to come, even if there's bad, too. He told me about your transaction. Well, I suppose it has kept you in vineyards for another few years, but for shame.' Natasha tutted and muttered something under her breath.

Nicole was so choked remembering the moment François gave it to her, she couldn't respond. *This* was why she avoided company. Too painful. Better just to keep going with the business.

The door swung wide open and a child fell in through the door. Ginger curls, brown eyes, chubby cheeks like a choux bun. The boy ran towards her and hid behind her skirts, held on tight. With that hair, he could only be Louis' son. Nicole froze, avoiding Natasha's sharp eyes.

A girl of no more than nineteen or twenty came rushing after him, flustered. '*Pas si vite, Misha! Arrête!*' Her accent was similar to Natasha's. Black hair, pulled back, strands escaping to frame dark skin and large brown eyes, rosebud lips. *Big hands*, thought Nicole, as Louis had told her. He hadn't told her that she was so young and pretty. The girl panicked when she couldn't see her son. 'Misha?'

Natasha pointed behind Nicole. A nettle bite of envy pricked her neck.

The girl curtsied. 'So sorry.'

She prised Misha from behind her skirts as Louis stood in the doorway, with a look of – what? Panic, sympathy – in his warm eyes.

He scooped Misha into his arms, ruffled his curls. 'I have told you a million times, you are *not* to run off.'

The boy curled into him, giggling, and Louis was won over.

'Let me introduce you to my errant son.' He took Misha's pudgy hand and waved it to her and she smiled and waved back. 'And this is my wife, Marta.'

Marta looked at her proudly, and proprietorially linked Louis' arm.

Nicole kissed her on both cheeks, noting the cool reluctance on Marta's part.

'Well, Natasha. Have you managed to work your wonders?' said Louis, too brightly.

Natasha blushed. 'Of course, anything for my little Russian boy. *S dnem rozhdeniya.* Happy birthday.' Natasha pinched the boy's cheek and winked at Marta. From the kitchen, she brought out a *millefeuille* the size of a cauldron pot, topped with hedgerow fruits.

'How on earth did you come up with that when all you have to sell are those loaves?' asked Nicole.

Natasha tapped her nose. 'You are not the only resourceful woman around here.'

'It's a masterpiece!' said Louis. He kissed Natasha on both cheeks.

Marta said nothing, noted Nicole, a blushing, timid little thing. Natasha and Marta exchanged some words in Russian, and when Louis joined in with broken Russian, she felt sick with loneliness. She left with a feeble goodbye, berating herself for caring.

The florist only had a few straggly geraniums to sell, so she plumped for cherries from the *épicerie*. They would complement the blackberry of the Merlot she planned to share with Thérésa. Her outrageous friend always chased away her cares, if only momentarily. She put everything in her basket, and hurried to the mansion on rue de la Vache.

*

'*Ma belle*, you look like you've seen a ghost. Come and sit here.'

The maid showed her into Thérésa's orangery, steamy with exotic plants and orange trees. Thérésa lounged in a see-through dress, her skin dewy in the heat of the glass room.

Nicole kissed her and settled opposite her, dazzled.

'I've been waiting with bated breath for you all morning. I have had quite the hideous time in Paris. People can be *so* cruel.'

'Real trouble this time?' asked Nicole.

Thérésa blinked. 'Those grey eyes could bore holes in stone.'

They held hands and giggled.

'You're right, I'm sorry to say.' Thérésa stood. 'Don't move a muscle, I have something to show you.'

Thérésa glided over to a box so jewel-encrusted it was almost grotesque, the size of a large jewellery case. Nicole imagined the spice of the huge Indian rubies, the damp crevice where the inky blue sapphires once hid, the brown African river that had smoothed the emeralds.

'Promise not to be shocked?'

'I can never keep that promise with you,' said Nicole.

'At least, promise not to judge me?'

'That I *can* promise.'

Thérésa took out a necklace and put it on.

'Come,' Thérésa said. 'Take a closer look.'

It was a miniature portrait necklace, enamelled in Russian reds, greens and blues. The picture was clearly of the Russian tsar, Alexander I, side by side with a beautiful woman who was definitely not the empress, his wife. Nicole studied it closer. Whoever had painted it had got her ethereal white skin just right. The figure next to Alexander was unmistakably Thérésa. Underneath was an inscription: *in perpetuum.* Nicole searched the dusty corridors of her convent school education for the Latin: *forever*. The miniature portrait was surrounded by heart-shaped rubies, rich as claret, and underneath, scintillating on a delicate link below the image, was a diamond as big as an egg.

'He should know that affairs with you are never forever, Tsar of Russia or not,' giggled Nicole.

'I knew you'd understand.'

'Napoléon found out about this? Alexander I's army has killed thousands of French men. You could be hanged as a traitor!'

'He is being such an impossible prude about it, after all he's done, and he's threatening to tell my husband. Just a little flirtation, nothing more. And how do you think I secured Louis' release for you? It was impossible for me to give back such a lavish gift. I have six children, darling, and men are so unreliable these days. You're right, he's threatening to have me jailed as a traitor. I'm not sure even I can charm my way out of this one. You will help me, won't you?'

Nicole took the cherries and wine out of her bag. 'Tell me everything. Only crystal will do for this wine. It's ten years old.'

Thérésa rallied. 'Yes, everything you do is so *right*.'

'You would do better dealing in bottles like me. Life is so much simpler that way.' She offered her a cherry.

'Yes, but so *dull*.' Thérésa took a bite and smudged the juice from her lips. 'If this gets out, I will be frozen out of French society forever and my husband will be ruined, and that's if I can save my neck and keep myself out of jail. I'm a practical woman, whatever you might think. I'm not getting any younger and I can't lose another husband. If you help me, I can weather this storm, and when it's blown over, I promise I'll retire to a little mansion somewhere in Paris and even become respectable.'

'I will most certainly not help you to become respectable. But I will help in any other way I can.'

'No chance you'd sell a teensy bit of your land to Moët? Just to shut him up, he's being such a bore. He's very influential and I'm sure if I could tell him I've persuaded you…'

Nicole froze. 'Don't be ridiculous.'

'What would it matter to you? You could buy different land with the money, somewhere away from Reims, and be free of him. He's determined to stop you.'

'Put it out of your head right now. I don't even want to talk about it.'

'Darling, so stubborn to the end. All right, all right, it was worth a try. I'll never understand why you won't do the smallest thing to make your life easier.' Thérésa popped another cherry in her mouth, spat out the pip. 'Tinker, tailor, soldier, sailor, rich man, poor man, beggar man…' She picked up the final pip and looked Nicole straight in the eye. '… thief. What if I told your little trade secret? Moët would do anything for it, you know.'

'Unlike you, I have no secrets,' said Nicole, meeting her gaze with a growing sense of unease.

'Now *you're* not being honest with *me*,' said Thérésa. She ate another cherry and held up the pip. 'Rich woman?'

'What are you trying to do?'

Thérésa's eyes were granite. 'You're normally so perspicacious. I'll spell it out. Moët is friends with Napoléon. He could put in a good word for me, bring back my social capital, get me out of hot water. All you have to do is sell some of your precious land to him and invest the money elsewhere.'

'You're not actually serious, are you? It's more than just land, it's my life. And I'll never find such perfect, grand cru land on the open market. Families work centuries to own such prime spots and they never sell.'

Thérésa pushed the wine glass away. 'I'm deadly serious, Nicole. I'm rather busy this afternoon, so will have to cut this short. Your clever little invention, the riddling table, the one that means your champagne will be clearer than anyone else's in the world? Moët's dying to know all about it. Sell, or your little trade secret becomes public knowledge. The choice is yours, darling. Don't look so shocked. It's a tough world out there.'

'Who told you?'

'Men will tell you anything if you get them in the right way. Let me know your decision. So sorry, I must rush now. Can't keep Monsieur Moët waiting. I take it you'd rather not bump into him when he calls?'

Bundling herself out of Thérésa's grand mansion, Nicole hurried along to her cellars, reeling. There was not a minute to waste. How could she ever have thought that Thérésa could truly by anyone's ally, let alone hers? She had given herself to her so completely in the past that she thought that might count for something. She should have realised that their special bond was just another weapon that Thérésa used to get exactly what she wanted – complete devotion, and material gains. Nicole was just collateral damage. She felt sick with anger – and hurt, a foolish, naïve young girl again, despite everything that she had achieved. She should have been more watchful, and not let herself get blindsided by – what, love? Affection? Danger? She had worshipped all these things about Thérésa. What a bloody fool!

As soon as she reached the safety of the cellars, her heart slowed. The lamps lit her way like glow-worms on a spring night, bottles still and quiet and working their magic. She took a breath; it was her perennial place of safety. And there was a job to be done.

From her waist, Nicole took the heavy key, turned it, and quietly closed the door behind her. Four pairs of eyes stared out of the gloom, lit by a single lamp, gathered around the riddling table. Xavier looked more like an old bull every day. Antoine returned immediately to the task in hand of bottle-turning as soon as he was satisfied she wasn't a spy. Louis smiled a warm, concerned welcome. Emile felt his way around the table and along the walls to Nicole. He took her hands.

'What is wrong?'

She patted his young face. 'How did you know it was me?'

'From the moment you put the key in the lock, Madame, the way it turned, the sound of your footsteps.'

'There is nothing wrong, Emile, thank you for asking,' said Nicole.

'You are angry,' he said.

'Not at you. Now, how are things going?'

Emile went back to the table and picked up a bottle.

Antoine spoke quietly, without looking up from his task. 'The sediment that took us months to move to the neck and expel now takes weeks, and with no loss of liquid! Now that the 1811 year of the comet vintage have been through the full process of fermentation and riddling, we have a once-in-a-lifetime batch, ready to go. It's a remarkable invention, Nicole.'

'Shame there's no demand for the extra thousands of bottles,' said Nicole darkly.

'It gets one over on Moët and that's good enough for me and my men,' said Xavier. 'Wait 'til I tell the lads down at Etienne's bar. Moët's men will have to eat what they said about you. They'll have faces like smacked arses…'

'Do you not remember signing the document swearing you to secrecy before you entered this room? *No one* is to take this invention outside of here. Do you understand?' She looked each one in the eye, held it until they looked away, cowed. 'Perhaps the document means nothing to you, so I'll do it the old way. Each one of you is to swear. *Swear* to me that my secret is safe. You know what is at stake. A handshake will suffice.'

Antoine came forward first, carefully replacing the bottle in the riddling rack and shaking her hand. 'I swear,' he said simply.

Next, Louis. 'I solemnly swear on my mother's grave,' he said, bowing for extra effect.

Xavier approached, awkwardly pulling his cap down over his forehead. He couldn't look her in the eye. 'I swear, Madame Clicquot.' His massive hand gripped hers.

'Stay there,' said Nicole to Emile. 'I'll come to you.'

Emile held a champagne bottle to his ear. 'I swear,' he said, keeping the bottle at a diagonal angle. 'This one is ready.'

'How can you tell?' asked Nicole.

'I can hear it, feel the tension on the cap.' He ran his thumb over the top. 'Ripe as a plum. Ready to go.'

Antoine pulled his hooked knife out of his pocket, released the sediment onto the floor, then replaced the cap.

Nicole took the bottle and held it up to the lamp. Clear as a bell, the fine fizz still intact.

'Well done, lad,' said Antoine. 'It took me more than ten years to know when it was just right.'

Down here, as always, everything was just right. She didn't want to leave, but she knew what she had to do.

'There's only the four of you, so keep at it. From now on, all champagne is laid down in here on my tables and no one else is to know how it works, so it's down to you.'

The light blinded her when she opened the door from the *crayere*, the chalk cellar, to the street. Mellow sunshine. Perfect harvest weather.

Perhaps Josette could use one of Natasha's brown *miches*. She decided to go back to the square and the *boulangerie*. The walk and seeing her friend again might calm her.

The sound of marching drums assailed her ears before she reached it. There, in front of the cathedral, was Thérésa on a soapbox, still in her gauzy empire-line dress, looking radiant, with a crowd of young boys drinking in every word. She was a goddess, snake bangles on both arms. Moët stood next to her, proud. A platoon of soldiers stood in rank to one side and Thérésa addressed the crowd.

'There is no finer thing you can do for your country! You are resourceful in the fields, brave in battle, handsome in uniform. The cream of the countryside ready to fight for your great leader. You will return as heroes.'

The marching band struck up. The collection of farmhands, labourers, boys from the church choir, shopkeepers, husbands and sons followed them. Thérésa dabbed the corners of her black eyes with a handkerchief and waved. She was encouraging these men to certain death, cannon fodder for Napoléon's increasingly hopeless ambitions, to cover up her dalliance with the Tsar himself.

At the head of them was Xavier's son, Alain. He would be about the same age as Mentine, only just fourteen. Did his parents know? She searched the crowd of silent women, tight-lipped, watching their men file off. Amongst them Alain's mother, Xavier's wife. At that moment, it all made sense. A man like Xavier was easily flattered. He spent most nights at Etienne's drinking. She had seen him flirting with the young field workers, enjoyed being the big man. A perfect target for Thérésa. And there he was in the heart of her cellars, learning everything there was to know about her riddling tables. Now he was sending his son off to war to impress this glamorous goddess. She had found her mole.

CHAPTER 22

October 1813

Malevolent Madonna

It was a red sun at midday and a muddy grey haze plunged the countryside into eerie dusk. Nicole tasted the air and checked the clouds. It wasn't a storm, rather a dry mist. The sun reflected orange on the river, like a daytime sunset, and the air was thick with heat.

The world was on alert. The French were retreating. Change again. Young French lads were lying frozen solid on Russian soil, picked off by peasants with pitchforks and bludgeoned to death, and for what?

She hurried to the cellar to prepare, smoothing down her dress, the best one she had, far too big for her after all these years of hard work. Work that she was determined would not be lost to Moët under any circumstances. Thérésa had acted to the best of her abilities to gain whatever she needed at Nicole's expense, but two could play at her game and Nicole had the advantage of surprise.

She lined up the bottles and the cellar door creaked open.

'Monsieur Moët! You came!'

'As you see,' he said stiffly. 'You said you needed my help.'

'Thérésa persuaded me to be realistic.' She cleared her throat. 'I can't manage alone any more. If your offer still stands, I would like to join you in… a business deal. I don't like your methods, but I see now it's impossible without you.'

'Then Thérésa is a more remarkable woman than I thought, but we've been here many times before. Until you've signed…'

'Let me show you a secret.'

She knew he wouldn't resist. At the back of the cellar, she held up the light and Moët gasped. Ten neat bottles of champagne. Ten yellow labels, *Veuve Clicquot, Cuvée de la Comète*, the family's anchor symbol outlined beneath the script, with the addition of a comet burned onto the cork. She was proud of the new concept of a printed label, in addition to the distinguishing mark on the cork. Moët eyed them suspiciously. He hated any break with tradition and no doubt he would think her labels disgustingly commercial.

'Look, I have thousands more like this,' she said, handing him a bottle. 'Every one is the same. Not one of them will spoil. Each one uniformly free of sediment, with a mousse so lively I sourced a new bottle supplier for safety,' she said.

He didn't take his eye off the bottle. 'How did you do this?'

'This must be our secret, Jean-Rémy. I cannot realise the markets without you.'

He crossed his heart impatiently. 'Of course, our secret.'

She showed him a vine, wooden, but not dead. '*This* is my secret.'

He took it, felt for buds, held it up to the candle and scraped the bark to check for green underneath. 'What the hell is this dry stick?'

'It's a special grape varietal. The family has been developing it for centuries. It's from Rome originally and has been grafted to make the perfect grape for Reims soil. It guarantees no sediment, the clearest wine, the best fizz, every time.'

'Impossible!'

'You would think so, but here is the living proof, right in front of your eyes.'

He looked at the dead wood contemptuously.

'You know the Clicquot grand cru yard on the Grande Montagne, the one at Verzenay?'

'Middle, east slope, one of the best. Of course I know it,' said Moët enviously.

'That is where we planted the new Clicquot varietal.'

'I know those vineyards well, they're all Pinot Noir.'

'They *look* like Pinot grapes, but they're not. We call them the Clicquot-Ponsardin grapes. François' father Philippe gave us twenty to plant on our wedding day. All these years later, this is the result. It's a kind of miracle.'

Moët looked at her sideways. 'What does it have to do with me?'

'Between us, we own enough of the best land to revolutionise production. I can give you twenty of these roots. It will take time, but we'll leave a legacy for future generations.'

'How could I refuse an adventure – and profit – with a beautiful woman?'

'The east slope, your vineyard, next to mine. The soil there is perfect for them. It must be our secret.'

'There is no one else I would rather keep one with.'

Outside, the strange sky glowered as she waved goodbye to Jean-Rémy, clutching his sack of Pinot Noir vines, fully believing *this* was the great Veuve Clicquot trade secret Thérésa was dangling in front of him. Her riddling innovation was safe for now. The vines *were* her finest ones, she comforted herself, even if the mythical Clicquot-Ponsardin vines didn't exist. And if her exploding bottles were Monsieur Moët's doing – although Louis was right, she'd never prove it – he deserved this, and more.

That part was relatively easy. Next, she needed to manoeuvre with a more dangerous opponent, Thérésa Tallien, before her former friend could get to Moët with the real truth of the matter. She'd learnt a lot from observing Thérésa's intrigues over the years, seen how a mixture of desire, heartlessness and betrayal could get you everywhere. Nicole intended to play with Thérésa by her own rules from now on.

There couldn't be a more sumptuous Madonna than Thérésa, and the harvest feast of St Rémi was observed as usual. Revolution or no, Champagne couldn't risk any harm to their vines and everyone knew that St Rémi was watching for neglect; harvests had not been good after the revolution, apart from the glorious year of the comet. Thérésa sat next to Nicole in the Clicquot family pew, away from prying ears, but in full view of the congregation – and Thérésa never resisted an opportunity for drama.

Her solemnity was impressive, her hair demurely covered, silky strands carefully arranged to rebel beneath expensive lace. The cool cathedral air turned her skin to marble and a half-smile of adoration played around her lips as she joined the townspeople in prayer for their vines.

There was not a man in the congregation whose eyes didn't devour her, or a woman who didn't wish they could be her. She was their mother, their sister, their lover, their saviour, in one ethereal package. Nicole had no doubt that as they mouthed prayers to St Rémi for a good harvest in the soaring space, Thérésa was their idea of paradise.

There was only one man in the congregation who was not gazing adoringly at Thérésa. Every time Nicole looked up from prayer, Jean-Rémy was staring right at her, desperate to catch her eye. Nicole forced herself to smile back, and she had no doubt that Madame Olivier was observing closely, readying herself for the juicy gossip in the church hall afterwards.

Thérésa leant close. She smelt fresh as a meadow, musky as a cat.

'You are more wicked than I ever imagined you capable of. Poor Jean-Rémy is bursting with excitement! Careful he doesn't go spreading it all over town.'

Nicole watched dispassionately as the first grapes of the harvest were placed on the altar and whispered back. 'Has he written to Napoléon on your behalf?'

'Of course he has. I've delivered him the only thing he couldn't buy. You don't mind, do you?'

Nicole shook her head and lied. 'All forgotten.'

'Just business. I knew you would understand. Friends?'

'Friends.' She took Thérésa's hand and put it on her cheek. 'You *will* keep your side of the bargain and not tell him about my riddling tables?'

A line of vintners in red robes processed solemnly down the aisle. She would be richer than all of them.

'Of course not. I would never have done it anyway. You didn't actually believe I would, did you?'

'You can do anything you like to anyone and still make them love you for it.'

'Let's not talk about it any more.' Thérésa cupped her hands together to pray and lowered her eyes. 'I have never seen Jean-Rémy so happy. If you had any sense, you really would join forces with him, but I know how stubborn you are. Well, I can't advise you any more.'

At the press later that day, Louis slammed the door of the office behind him.

'What are you doing?'

'What do you mean?

'Flirting with that man in front of the whole town this morning at church.'

'It's none of your business. Go back to your wife.'

'I have your best interests at heart, Babouchette. I'm warning you. Natasha noticed it too.'

'You have no right to come in here, lecturing me. You make your choices, and I make mine.'

'Thérésa is involved, I know she is. You're playing with fire and you won't win.'

'I'm busy, the harvest is still coming in and there aren't enough men. Please concentrate on *that* rather than some imagined misdemeanour. The daylight's running out and the feast of St Rémi has at least motivated the workers that *are* here. We need to make the most of it.'

'Be careful, please.'

'Stop worrying about me.'

Louis left. Acid regret filled the space where he stood.

In the evening, she visited her parents at their grand mansion. She hurried past Etienne's bar, then past Thérésa's house, just a few doors away from where her parents lived. The big, welcoming windows of her childhood home lit up the evening with hundreds of candles burning on the chandeliers.

Her parents were worried Mentine would not be safe at boarding school in Paris. Rumours gripped the whole country that as the French troops retreated, the Russian army would follow. Everyone was afraid they would follow them right back into the French capital and attack the rest of the country from there, a terrifying thought in the quiet streets of Reims. Nicole listened, but she had other, more immediate things on her mind. She had only come to have an excuse to pass Etienne's bar.

She left early, to get back to Bouzy, she told her parents, but she had some business first. Gesturing for the coachman to wait, she hurried to the bar, still in full swing, celebrating the feast of St Rémi.

Etienne opened the back door, just at the time they had agreed.

'Did you give him the note?' asked Nicole.

'Don't worry, I did as you said. He didn't want to show anyone your letter of congratulations – best worker of the year, you say? He looked pretty happy about it, but he wouldn't show anyone what it said.'

'You know Xavier, he just likes to get on with it and he wouldn't want to tell the lads he was being praised by a woman.' *And he's totally out of his depth.* 'Thank you for your help though. My carriage is waiting, so I'd better go. Good night.'

The town-hall clock struck nine as she waited in the shadows. Xavier wasn't so drunk that he couldn't follow the instructions she had written. The pink ribbon she had saved from Thérésa's note was stuffed in his top pocket. She was pleased with that authentic touch. The evening was chilly now and he pulled his best tweed jacket tight around him, jerked down his cap over his eyes, headed for the side door of Thérésa's house and rapped on it.

When there was no answer, he rapped again, staggering slightly.

'It's me,' he whispered up at the window. 'Xavier!'

No reply.

'Thérésa!'

The timing was perfect: Thérésa was back in Paris, smoothing things over with Napoléon, thanks to Moët's help.

'Lovely evening, Xavier,' said Nicole, stepping out of the shadows.

His face fell when he saw her.

'I know everything. She's dangerous, you know, and using you.'

'She asked me to help with the garden.'

'At this time?'

He looked stricken.

'*I* wrote the note with the pink ribbon. You think she'd risk any proof in writing to you?'

She paused to let the information sink in, almost feeling sorry for her old friend.

'You told her about my riddling tables. What were you thinking? I thought we had an agreement.'

'I never…'

'What would your wife say about this?'

He hung his head. 'I'm a relief to her after all those fops and posers in Paris.'

'That's exactly who she's with now. We have known each other all our lives, haven't we?'

'I suppose so.'

'She's using you. It's impossible for a woman like her to really love any man.' *Or woman*, she thought ruefully. 'The great Thérésa Tallien would drop you like a stone if there was any whiff of scandal and she laughs at men foolish enough to fall for her. It was my trade secret she wanted from you, that's all. Have you seen her since you told her?'

He shook his head.

'Think about it. Your wife would be devastated.'

'You can't tell her. Not with our son away at war. It would break her.'

'Then stay away from Thérésa.'

He hunched over.

'We've been friends forever. You were my stalwart. I have paid your wages all your life, promised a share of the profits, but you would throw it all away for her?'

She could tell by the way he looked at her that he would do it all again if Thérésa gave him one ounce of encouragement.

'If you ever meet her again – and if you do, I'll find out – I'll tell your wife, you'll lose your job with me and you will never work in Champagne again.'

'You can't threaten me,' he hissed.

'I just have and you don't frighten me. Let's speak as equals. Give it time, Xavier, it will pass. The harvest is in. The vines are black and lifeless, but next year they'll spring to life again. Everything will seem different. Your wife and son need you. Make up for betraying your wife and putting my entire livelihood – and yours – at risk. I have a way you can make amends.'

'Spit it out, then.'

'Stay with me, Xavier. I understand, you are only human, and she is from another world. I will keep my promise to you about a share in the profits and I'll keep scandal away from you and your wife, but you have to promise me to forget her.'

She explained her plan. He agreed to carry it out to the letter. It was risky, but she was a vintner and everything she did carried risk.

He strode off into the darkness and she walked back to her carriage, exhausted. Even Xavier was prepared to betray her, after all they'd been through together. Moët was right about that much, this business was not for the faint-hearted. The more successful she became, the more enemies she seemed to make. And with so much at stake, she was forced to strategise like a general and double-cross people she'd counted as friends and allies until now. It was a lonely feeling, but she was actually quite good at it when it came to it and it gave her a satisfying sense of powerfulness.

The clock struck the quarter hour. Almost half past nine and she hoped that in another fifteen minutes her fortunes would change.

As she rode back past Thérésa's house, she told the coach driver to stop. She checked Thérésa's bedroom window and recognised the shape of Xavier's cap. He and his friends had always been adept at lock-picking. As a child, she herself had joined them plenty of times in locked barns to eat stolen apples and make dens in the hay.

It was true what they said, the old country ways were always the best – a simple bit of theft in the night.

CHAPTER 23

October 1813

The Spoils of War

The cathedral clock struck half past and Xavier emerged out of the gloom.

'Get in, quick!'

He jumped up, Nicole rapped on the window and the carriage lurched forward. He reached inside his jacket and dumped the sack on her lap. It was surprisingly heavy.

She peeped inside. The box was as breath-taking as she remembered and the glut of jewels glowed in the moonlight – more gems than most would see in a lifetime.

'Worth a bit, that,' said Xavier.

'Thank you. And I'm sorry.'

'Let me out here, *sauvage*. You're a braver woman than me, I'll give you that. I'd rather walk the rest of the way, if you don't mind. I'm a bloody idiot and I need to walk it off.'

Xavier hunched his jacket around him and disappeared into the shadows and she followed him with her eyes until he was out of sight. Poor Xavier. They had Thérésa's betrayal in common now, and a little less trust in the people they loved.

She held tight on the sack until she was safely in the bedroom at her house in Bouzy. The jewels shattered the candle flame as she opened the box. Nestled in the blood-red lining, there it was: the cameo given to Thérésa by Tsar Alexander, worth more than all her vineyards put together and enough to hold a powerful woman to ransom.

She admired it, ran her finger over the facets of the diamond, re-read the inscription: *in perpetuum*. There was a time when she had thought Thérésa's friendship would last forever, but no more, and a piece of her heart turned to ice. She put the necklace back in the box, hid it under her pillow and got the first full night's sleep she'd had since the day she gave Jean-Rémy the sack of Pinot vines.

The stagecoach to Paris was on time and she couldn't wait to be off and escape for a while. You could be anonymous in Paris, especially a widow like her from the countryside. She smiled to herself as the coach passed Moët's vineyard, the one that abutted her own Verzenay yard. The soil was freshly turned, the previous ancient and fertile Moët vines moved elsewhere and the new Pinot vines she'd given him proudly planted, carefully spaced, each with a pale compost circle of *fumure*. She held tighter onto the leather bag containing Thérésa's necklace and looked forward.

As soon as she arrived in Paris, she left her luggage with the bellboy at the hotel and rushed the short walk to the Musée Napoléon.

'The Greek and Russian icon room?' she asked the man at reception.

He gave her brief instructions and pointed. She knew from his face that Thérésa was already there. A man had a certain stricken look after she had dealt with them.

'Darling!'

Thérésa enveloped her in musky perfume and her lips brushed hers so briefly she wasn't sure it had happened.

'I'm so glad you could come!' said Nicole, ashamed at how overwhelmed she was by Thérésa's presence.

'How formal, don't be so silly. Why are you holding that bag like it's a new-born baby?'

'This? Oh, nothing. The stagecoach was late and I dashed straight from the hotel. I didn't have time to put everything in the room.'

'Why did you want to meet in this funny little place? It's completely deserted – we could die in here and they wouldn't find us for days, and to think that this used to be the Palais de Louvre. Now Napoléon's filled it with loot from his travels and lets the great unwashed finger the walls in pursuit of his revolutionary ideals to educate the masses through art.' Thérésa scrutinised her critically. 'You look haunted. What on earth has been happening in that quiet little place you invest all your energies in? Now, tell me what's in the bag.'

Nicole eyed the icon nearest to them. Russian, taken from a church. The scene was of hosts of angels, the holy trinity, and at the bottom a curious monster, sending out a black snake into the throng of saints.

'Napoléon's troops took that icon from a church in Russia.'

'What of it?' said Thérésa.

'Russia is our enemy now. Napoléon would take a dim view of any collaborators.'

'Yes he would, but he knows how devoted I am to the Republic.'

'I have evidence that suggests otherwise.'

Nicole took the box out of the leather bag. Thérésa didn't even flinch.

'That trinket? Don't be ridiculous. Are you trying to black-mail me?'

'You'll keep my secret, or your affair with the Tsar will ruin what status you have left.'

'You're angry about your little field hand. What's his name?'

'Xavier. He's a good man.'

'Very good. Surprisingly gentle, when it came to it.' Thérésa grabbed the box out of her hands and opened it. 'Where's the necklace?'

'I wasn't stupid enough to bring that, too.'

'I always knew there was steel behind those pale eyes.'

'They say the coalition army – Prussia, Austria and Russia – isn't far from Paris. If they invade and your love affair with the Tsar is made public, you're finished.'

'You think I don't know? The whole of Paris is talking about it. Everyone's burying their jewels in their back garden or hiding them in biscuit tins. It seems you have me exactly where you want me. How thrilling! In fact, I *had* rather hoped that I could escape to your little part of the world for a while to avoid all the chaos. I suppose that's impossible now?'

Nicole gave her a hollow laugh. 'You manipulated Xavier, my oldest friend and loyal employee, into revealing my trade secret so you could sell it to my enemies, persuaded him to send his son to the war, then dumped him, all to cover up your own misdemeanours, and you still ask for my protection? What twists of reality happen in your head?'

For the first time since she'd known her, Thérésa looked rattled and Nicole noticed faint lines that looked like worry. Good. Perhaps there was a heart in there somewhere.

'You think you see it all so clearly? Life isn't all neat ledgers and profit and loss and little country rivalries. It's cruel and promiscuous and indiscriminate as disease. Your noble field hand was more than happy to betray you and his family for a night with me. Life is a balance, my darling. I might have asked one favour in return for the many I have done you. I rescued your adorable salesman, gave you money and solace when you needed it and never asked for a thing in return. Your obsession with your business is equally selfish, you just can't see it.'

'You leave a trail of destruction while convincing yourself of your innocence, then blame it on a heartless world. But we all have choices. I will be very clear. Reveal my secret to Moët and I will use the necklace to expose you as a traitor. The consequences will be your own doing, no one else's.'

'Such alluring passion, but your family wealth affords you high ideals the rest of us can only dream of. Take this, it belongs with the necklace.' She handed back the box, stroked Nicole's cheek and left.

Nicole was left alone amongst the musty paintings. She thought about her riddling tables, now taking up a large part of her cellars, year of the comet champagne bottles lined up neatly, slowly turned a quarter each day until the moment of disgorgement. Reliable, her own to create and do with as she wanted. Her secret was safe, but her victory felt hollow. Thérésa was dangerously flawed, but she was life, excitement, magic. Even now, after all this, the thought of life without her was a little less bright.

She put the box back in the leather bag and hurried back to the hotel. It wasn't only for her, she comforted herself. Mentine was growing up and her future was secured.

CHAPTER 24

March 1814

Invasion or Liberation?

'Thank you.' Nicole kissed the nun on both cheeks.

Soeur Ayasse patted Mentine's luggage.

'Your trunk is here. Good luck, and take care, Clémentine. Pray the war is over soon and don't neglect your studies. Look after your mama, my dear!'

Nicole noticed that as Mentine hugged Soeur Ayasse there were tears in her eyes. Her little girl had friends she had nothing to do with any more and her face was more angular, new buds pressed at her dress, soft blonde hair, milky skin, a new sultriness to her green eyes. She was as tall as her now!

Nicole scanned the café for evidence of predatory men. Surely they would all be looking at her beautiful daughter? Everyone just carried on as normal, clinking cups, smoking, gossiping. No danger, but the urge to protect her newly grown-up daughter was overwhelming.

In the months since she'd last been here to confront Thérésa, Paris had become a different, more threatening, place. The camps of Cossacks, Russians, Prussians, British outside Paris threatened to break through the city gates. Everyone in this café would be weighing up the odds, telling their own stories of how Napoléon was out of support, out of control. Perhaps it would even be better if the allies beat Napoléon. At least the war would be over. One thing was for sure, she had to get Mentine home.

'Am I leaving Paris?'

'For now, yes. You mustn't worry, there's no danger yet, but just for a few months, it will be safer for you at home with me and your grandparents.'

'What about my friends? I'll miss them!'

'The main thing is to be safe. The moment the war is over, you'll come back.'

The coffee pot steamed and the gold-rimmed cups were so delicate you could see the liquid through the china. Mentine bubbled away and the room filled with a comforting din of voices. The starched white tablecloths, chandeliers sparkling on the high ceilings and spring sun pouring through the big windows made the war seem a million miles away. She hoped Xavier had bricked up her cellars, as she had instructed, to stop looting. Moët had already lost a quarter of his entire stock at Épernay, so Madame Olivier had written to inform her.

'And Thérésa said I was always to say no. A woman should use her power wisely and not give it away unthinkingly, don't you think, Maman?' said Mentine.

'Of course, sweetie,' said Nicole, not really listening.

'She gave me this dress. Have you noticed it's the exact colour of my eyes? My first empire-line dress. How lucky am I to be dressed by the most glamorous and fashionable woman in Paris?'

'*Thérésa* gave you that dress? When?'

'Just last week, when I told her you were coming to take me home. She was so sweet, she said I was growing up now and should have a dress to impress you with. Isn't that kind? Do you like it?'

Nicole made a mental inventory of clothes she had sent to Mentine in the last year. Little girl's cotton dresses, pinafores to wear over the top. The same clothes she'd been wearing all her life.

'It's beautiful. *You* are beautiful. I can't believe how much you've grown up.'

Her proud smile warmed her. Perfect, innocent, vulnerable.

'How often do you see Thérésa?'

'Every Saturday. She takes me to her house on the rue de Babylone. Her girls are my best friends. She says I can't live cooped up in a convent every day of the week. She gives me cakes and sweetmeats and clothes and takes me on carriage rides in the Tuileries with my friends. It's my favourite day of the week!'

Nicole thought of the pile of unopened letters from Thérésa she had thrown on the fire whilst she was in Paris and forced herself to remember the casual cruelty with which Thérésa had treated her. Could she have misjudged her friend?

'I must thank her for being so kind.'

'You must. She treats me like I'm her own daughter, Maman.'

All this for Mentine, despite the necklace?

'Can't I stay? Thérésa says there is no danger, that the Russians are gentlemen.'

'I'm sure she would.'

'A clever daughter,' interrupted a man on the next table. He was sitting alone, newspaper folded next to his lunch. 'Russian soldiers *are* gentlemen. But she has a wise mama, too. If you have somewhere to escape to from Paris, I would leave soon. I hope you don't mind my interrupting?'

His French was perfect, almost. Dark eyes, nearly black, and dark skin, even though it wasn't summer. Years of friendship with Natasha taught her to recognise the accent.

'You are Russian?'

'I am. And you too? There aren't many who recognise my accent any more. Russians accuse me of being French, but not many French accuse me of being Russian.'

'I'm from Reims, French through and through.'

'Where my favourite wines are from.'

'Mine too…' She smiled and turned back to her conversation with Mentine.

'I hope you don't mind my interrupting again, but I would get back to Reims as soon as you can. The Russians are peaceful invaders, liberators they say, but no war is without casualties. You should hire a coach and horses the minute you can. They're in short supply as so many are hoping to leave, so please don't waste any time. I couldn't overhear and keep silent, so I took the risk of being considered rude in full knowledge of my crime. I hope you can forgive me.'

'It's kind of you to take the time, thank you,' said Nicole. 'We're leaving tomorrow.'

'Today would be better.'

He took his newspaper and left.

Mentine giggled. 'He was funny.'

'You have a lot to learn! Finish your cake. We'll pack tonight. I'm not afraid to be in Paris, but I have to get back to protect my cellars.'

'The girls at the convent say the Russian officers are dashing. Do you think we'll pass some?'

'I hope not. It will be so lovely to have you home with me for a few months.'

'But what about *me?* Paris is so exciting compared to Reims and you'll be all distracted by your vineyards, like you always are, and I'll be thrown together with Josette and Grandma and Grandpa while you're out digging.'

'Mentine! The digging is for you, to secure your future.'
She rolled her eyes. 'Don't bother for me. I'm fine how I am.'

The Russian man was right. The next day, news spread like wildfire of the troops breaching the city gates, of scuffles in Montmartre, surrenders at Montreuil. The allies had taken the French troops by surprise. Napoléon was miles away, in Fontainebleau, and it would be days before he could reach Paris, by which time it would be too late. Besides, the rumours were that the French troops had lost faith in Napoléon. They were malnourished and war-weary. *We all are*, thought Nicole. Twenty-five years of constant war.

The Russian was right on another count too. Coaches and horses were in short supply. Every form of transport out of Paris was fully booked. Anyone with a bench on wheels was profiting, charging ten times the price. Nicole managed to find space for one person on a farm cart leaving tomorrow from Pont de Bercy on the road to Reims, leaving at midday. Mentine would have to squash in somehow. She took a deep breath. She would be escaping one war, but going back to her own, against Moët, against thousands of years of tradition where men did business and women stayed at home, with few exceptions.

The next morning, both their trunks were packed. Nicole put Thérésa's necklace in the leather bag and slung it over her shoulder. They would have to walk to the Pont de Bercy, with a boy pulling their trunks on a handcart. Even small boys in need of a franc or two were hard to come by and this one looked too skinny for his burden, but she was glad to give him the money.

The Avenue d'Alma was strangely deserted when they emerged from their hotel. Then she heard them. Tocsins ringing out all around Paris. Women rushing by with white rosettes pinned to their dresses, men with white armbands, dashing up the avenue towards the Champs-Élysées, the deafening sound of hundreds of horseshoes on cobbles.

'Please, what's happening?' Nicole shouted to a passer-by.

'The liberators. They're here, right on the Champs-Élysées!'

'Wait inside the hotel,' she instructed the boy with their trunks. 'Don't move. I'm going to see, but I'll be back in half an hour.'

The talk was of a Russian invasion, but a welcome one. After the bloody revolution, then decades of war and a man, Napoléon, who had declared himself effectively a hereditary aristocrat, what had it all been for? The Russians would help to depose the despot and restore peace, everyone agreed.

Today was a chance to witness history. As she and Mentine followed the crowds, there was the same charge in the air there had been twenty-five years ago on that hot July day of the revolution. At fourteen, Mentine was three years older than Nicole herself had been then. The expensive red woollen dress she'd worn at eleven years old attracted unwelcome attention for the little rich girl she was then, and today she was wearing conspicuous red again, this time a silk travelling robe, and a velvet cape to protect against the grime of the road. She held Mentine's hand tight, but just as on the day of the revolution, she couldn't resist the pull of the crowds.

She pushed through the crush, right to the front, just in time to see the incredible sight. Tsar Alexander on a white horse, surrounded by allied officers – the red of the Cossacks, the blue of the Russians, marching peacefully up the Champs-Élysées. Crowds cheered. The women's white rosettes signified their welcome, the men's white armbands happy surrender. There were even some whispers amongst the crowd about the restoration of the monarchy.

As she gazed at the spectacle, Nicole felt a strange flutter of recognition. The man to Alexander's left flank was the Russian from the café! He didn't see her as the battalions marched by in orderly ranks. Not far behind him was a gilt carriage, and inside a beautiful dark-haired woman, feathered headdress fluttering in the breeze. Of course, Thérésa wouldn't miss this victory parade for the world and there she was, not far behind the Tsar himself.

Mentine broke away from her and skipped through the ranks, screaming at Thérésa. 'It's me, it's me!'

Thérésa stopped the carriage, threw open the door and pulled her in. From inside, Mentine pointed and the carriage was manoeuvred to the edge. Nicole ran to it, desperate to get her daughter back.

Thérésa flung open the door once more for Nicole.

'How could you *think* of making poor little Mentine stand in this crush? And you're so tiny you'll get *trampled.* Jump up, there's plenty of room!'

Nicole shook her head. The days of allowing herself to be swept along in Thérésa's treacherous wake were over.

'I won't let you go back through that crowd. There's no telling when it might turn nasty. *Get in, now.*'

On the other hand, she was right, and why not take advantage of such a serendipitous encounter, as long as she went into it with her eyes open?

'*Please*, Maman.'

Nicole jumped up reluctantly.

'You quite stood out, this petite little figure with strawberry hair and a bright red dress. Very easy to spot and quite lovely! Where are you off to?'

'We're leaving Paris at midday from the Pont de Bercy. I have to get back to my cellars and I've booked a seat on the last cart out of here. In fact, we should get back to the hotel, I have a boy waiting with my luggage.'

'I'll take you to the Pont de Bercy for midday and send a soldier for your luggage. You can't drag poor Mentine back through that lot! You'll stay with me 'til then. I've missed you!'

Nicole glanced furtively at the bag in her lap.

'Just as I saw you last time, clutching that leather bag, my dear. Where are you off to with it now?'

Nicole gripped it tighter. This time, the jewelled box had the necklace in it. Since her last encounter with Thérésa, she never travelled without it, a slightly superstitious precaution.

'It's not much use to blackmail me with now. You *know* I'm always on the winning side. This one just took a little longer than expected. The Tsar is quite the celebrity in Paris now, and the only person worth being connected with.'

Mentine was entranced by the crowd, waving and delighted to be part of the show.

Nicole dropped her voice to a whisper. 'I have learned the hard way that none of your friendships are based on loyalty or love.'

'That luxury belongs to the rich; you would do well to understand that. Fortunes change, darling, we all know that. I hear yours are waning with the war. That necklace is worth a small fortune. Keep it and invest it in your little vineyards. I don't need Moët, or his friend Napoléon any more, they're both finished. Now – don't look at me like that. We are friends first, just a little business got in the way. All that's behind us now. Show me some warmth in those flinty eyes. I know they can melt from winter to spring in seconds.'

'Just business? I would struggle to treat my worst enemies the way you did me.'

'Take the moral high ground as much as you like, but *your* business is placed above everything, even your own child.'

Both women watched as Mentine blew kisses out of the window.

I hardly know this young woman any more, thought Nicole with a stab of regret.

Thérésa continued in a whisper, 'And as far as I can tell, poor Moët is your worst enemy and you have shown *him* very little mercy. Forgive me, please. I won't pretend I didn't know what I was doing, but I was desperate, and we're both fine now, aren't we?'

'As much as can be expected in these strange times. You twist my words, but too much has gone between us to ever feel the same about you again.'

'Oh stop sounding like a boring ex-lover! I will take whatever your big heart can give me and be satisfied with that. Tell me all the news since we last met, darling. I've missed all that charming country chat about vines and bottles and harvests and tasting the *terroir*.'

Despite everything, Nicole couldn't stop. As the victory parade slowly ascended the Champs-Élysées, she told Thérésa about her fears for her Cuvée de la Comète, her commitment to her workers, the sheer loneliness of being a woman running a business in Reims. They didn't discuss in front of Mentine quite why Moët was such a rival, or her bitterness at losing Louis to another woman, but she knew Thérésa understood and that was enough. How beautiful and beguiling this woman was in her victory. As strangely alluring as a cliff-edge.

When they got to the Arc de Triomphe, Thérésa gave instruction for their safe passage to meet their transport at the Pont de Bercy.

'I know you too well to ask you to stay in Paris for the victory party. You'll want to buzz around your vineyards, fighting off the Russians when they come trampling over everything in their big boots looking for the *veuve's vin mousseux* they adore so much.

Off you go and look after my little Mentine. She's like one of my own!'

'I know. Mentine told me how you've taken better care of her than I have and I'm grateful for it. In that sense, you *have* been more of a friend than I believed.'

'Oh stop. It was all for my own benefit. I missed you and she was the closest I could get. Now, fly away and do battle in Reims. Try not to be too serious, my little firefly, but do what makes you happy.'

And she was gone, back into the midst of the parade, the straight ranks of soldiers losing formation momentarily to make way for her carriage, a beautiful kink in the natural order of things.

CHAPTER 25

March 1814

Loot

The war had already reached as far as Champagne. As the cold, uncomfortable cart bounced over rutted roads, Mentine and Nicole clung to each other. A few miles outside of Reims, plumes of smoke rose amongst the trees and the army camps were visible from the road. It had been a squash at first with all the other passengers escaping the chaos of Paris, but now they were all gone and Nicole missed the comfort of the diverse crowd: a soldier returning home from Russia, two richly dressed silver merchants sitting on whatever they could stuff into a bag, and a pair of elderly sisters going to stay with family in the country. They'd all been dropped off one by one and now it was just the two of them and the driver.

'Look forward and don't catch anyone's eye if they pass us on the road. We don't know who's on which side any more,' Nicole whispered to Mentine.

The driver lashed the horses to speed up. She would use her own bare hands to kill anyone who even so much as *looked* at her daughter.

A small marching battalion of Prussians and Cossacks stopped to let them pass. Her heart stalled, but they saluted reluctantly under their sergeant's orders. Sullen, desperate, boots cracked and broken, uniforms tattered, cheekbones protruding hungrily through scabbed faces, some with grimy bandages encrusted in blood. She wouldn't like to meet them away from the command of their officer, and she feared for all her friends in Reims. Natasha's bakery would be irresistible, the everyday prosperity and bustle of her town extreme temptation to these hungry and war-weary men – and everything there for the taking with so many men still away and displaced, despite yesterday's surrender.

The lights at her parents' home, the grand Hôtel Ponsardin, blazed through the windows as if the allied troops weren't patrolling the streets outside at all. What was it about your childhood home, even when you were grown up, that always seemed safe?

Mentine was engulfed in her grandfather's arms and ushered into the warmth. Her mother fussed over the dark circles under Nicole's eyes.

'Take your coat off and relax for once, you look as if you're going somewhere,' said her mother.

'I am. I have to get to the cellars straight away to check them, Maman. Will you watch Mentine for me?'

'I don't *need* watching.' Mentine scowled. 'You promised you wouldn't leave me!'

'It's just for an hour or so. I'll come and say good night, I promise.'

'No, you won't, you'll be there for hours. There's always *something* going wrong and I've only just got home!'

Mentine clung to her, but she *had* to check on her stocks. Her father told her the Russian occupation was peaceful so far, but she knew there had been looting and everyone was on their guard. She prised Mentine's fingers off her guiltily. She'd been away too long.

When she got to her cellars at the Place des Droits de l'Homme, Xavier was standing guard outside, holding a hammer, a rake propped up against the wall next to him. Two skinny lads from the orphanage accompanied him, clutching a mattock and a spade.

The door to her cellars had been bricked up as instructed, but a big hole was smashed through.

'Xavier, I'm back! What happened?'

'About bloody time. While you've been poncing around in Paris with fops and low-lifes and God knows who, we've been fighting off thieves with *n'importe quoi*. I'll smash their heads in with a shovel if I have to.'

'I'm grateful, Xavier. But you shouldn't, it's dangerous. A spade's not much use against a musket.'

A half-scrubbed-off message was daubed in red paint by the cellar door. She squinted to make it out.

'*Wine... hel...*'

'Don't worry about it,' said Xavier.

'What did it say?'

He shrugged. The lads looked sheepish.

She gave them a coin each. 'You're relieved. Go and get something to eat. God knows you look like you need it.' She turned to Xavier when they'd left. 'What did it say? You might as well tell me what was there, Xavier. You know I won't give up.'

'*Wine whore. Help yourself.* We tried to get rid of it, I didn't want you to see...'

'Who did this?'

'The lads said they saw that dog-turd Fournier, Moët's foreman, with red paint on his hands. Fucking idiot.'

'Wait here.'

She squeezed through the bricked-up hole and ran down the cellar stairs, hundreds of them, kept going until she reached the cool *crayères*. Her heart stilled. The cellars were always her refuge, but even down here she couldn't get the word out of her mind. *Whore.*

It was completely dark, but she knew exactly where to find a lamp and she felt her way along the wall to the place, found the matches and lit it. The flame leapt. Her neat stacks were overturned, the racks plundered, her precious babies ravaged and looted. Vintage, young, white, red, rosé, it didn't matter. Never mind the financial ruin, the thought of her vintages lining the stomach of some unthinking drunkard…

She snaked further into the cellars in eerie silence, not a single cellar worker to be seen. Just let a soldier dare jump out on her; she'd cut him with a broken bottle if she had to – she knew the place like the back of her hand and she could outrun any bunch of ragged mercenaries.

Finally, she arrived at the place where the 1811 vintage was stored and her heart sank. Empty, only the outlines of the bottles left, voids in the dust. They'd taken her starry comet wines, her best. They couldn't have just happened upon them, not this deep in the cellars, and she suspected Moët's red-handed Fournier had his part in this, too. She felt on her belt for the keys to the secret door concealed behind the racks and hesitated. Light seeped out through the keyhole and around the edges of the door. Someone was in there. A chair scraped.

She picked up a magnum of burgundy and shrank against the wall, holding her breath. *Think.* If she turned the handle and it was locked, the person inside had a key and she probably knew them. She forced herself to grasp the handle, then turned. Locked. She used her own key to open it and came face to face with a gun. The bottle exploded as she dropped it, scattering wine and glass everywhere.

'Jesus, *sauvage!* Don't creep up on me like that!'

'Louis! What the hell are you doing here?'

'What the hell are *you* doing down here on your own? The place is infested!'

'There's no one here. And let them try. My comet wines, all gone!' He pulled her roughly to him. 'Christ, I could have shot you.'

'Did they get in here?'

'No, they're safe,' he said, gesturing to the riddling tables stretching off into the distance as far as the lamp could illuminate.

Honey-coloured Cuvée de la Comète champagnes, neat row upon neat row. A fortune in golden heaven, the entire stock she had laid down, all intact.

'Crystal-clear as a mountain stream.' Louis smiled. 'Your invention is still genius.'

'Thank God. If they want this, they can pay me what it's worth.'

'Then you're a better salesman than I. All I've been able to do is stop them from stealing it, so far.'

'I'll find a way. Have you and Xavier single-handedly saved what's left down here?'

'Every field hand and anyone who's ever worked for you has defended this place. Madame Olivier is running intelligence for us. It could have been a lot worse. Other cellars have suffered more than these and it's bad enough here. The men are coming back in the morning to brick the door back up. Xavier insisted on keeping guard and it was my intention to sleep with these beauties all night.'

'You love them as much as I do.'

'I was prepared to die for them in Russia. Go and get some sleep and leave this to me. You've just come from Paris with Mentine? You must have been travelling for hours.'

'Thank you, my faithful Louis. I'll be back first thing in the morning, with breakfast. I'll bring my mother's apricot jam. You try to get some rest, too.'

Back outside, the night had turned chilly and damp. Xavier was standing sentry, rigid in his post.

'I'll get some of the lads to replace you. You look exhausted.'

'No one's stepping foot inside on my watch. I'm staying put until every brick is replaced and they need a cannon to blast it open again.'

A man appeared out of the dark, bringing with him the stink of a soldier who'd been camping out for months.

'That's a promise you're not going to keep, peasant. Stand aside.'

Xavier and Nicole both blocked the entrance. More joined him. Cossacks, judging by the uniform, at least ten. But the uniform couldn't disguise the thugs that they were.

'We're not open,' said Nicole.

'There's a nice big hole behind you, *milochka*. Looks open to me.' He lifted the butt of his rifle. 'Stand aside if you don't want this in your face.'

A scar oozed on his forehead. Menace spread across the men's faces, one by one, as if someone had lit a fire.

'Fuck off, the lot of you!' roared Xavier, stepping in front of her.

The rifle butt smashed into Xavier's face. His nose exploded with blood and he fell, curled into a foetal shape, arms up to protect his head. They took turns to stamp on him.

'You're coming with me,' the scar-face growled as he dragged her to the cellar door. She bit him; he jumped back, clutching his hand. 'Bitch!'

'You will not take anything from me!'

He shoved her against the bricks and she smacked her head. The pain was sickening. His filthy hand fumbled under her dress. Her heel found his crotch and she kicked as hard as she could.

A gunshot cracked through the chaos and the men scattered like cockroaches. Xavier staggered to his feet.

'Bring me the woman. Help that man.' Two Russian soldiers caught Xavier before he could fall and gently sat him on the ground. 'And you! You're not soldiers, you're thieves! Get out of my sight before I court-martial you. This is a peaceful occupation. A liberation, not a backstreet brawl. If you want a drink, you *buy*. Go, now. I will bring liquor back to the camp for anyone who wasn't involved in this.'

A French accent, perfect, almost.

'Madame, I am so, so sorry for this. Are you all right?'

Her head hurt; no words came.

He gave instructions to two of his men to get Xavier home and stay with him until the doctor arrived, then carried a table and two chairs from the café opposite and set them up outside the cellar door. He took her arm and she flinched away, afraid.

'Please, you are hurt. Those men will be locked up; let me help. Sit.'

'I can't leave until it's bricked up,' she slurred.

'Understandable – of course not. Sit.'

She slumped onto the chair, cradled her head on the table and tried to gather her thoughts. Perfect French, almost. The man from the café in Paris, the Russian officer. The third time he had appeared.

'Don't you dare go a step further. Everything I've ever worked for is in there.'

'I have no intention of doing so. I'm just going to sit here with you until you're well enough to move. May I?'

He parted her hair and touched where it hurt; she winced. His fingers came away covered in blood.

'Let's get you home.'

'I can't. I have to stay.'

'Shh, you'll make it worse. Alright. We'll sit here for a while.'

He gave her his handkerchief.

'Press, hard.'

She sat up woozily and did as she was told. He put his jacket around her shoulders. It smelt of woodsmoke.

'I'll have my men stand guard. Try to trust us. It won't happen again.'

She blinked. He came into focus and she scrutinised his gaze for honesty.

'I have to stay. I can't leave it to anyone else, no one cares as much as I do, why should they? This is what happens when I'm not here.'

'I understand; please don't worry any more. We have a lot to prove before you can trust us. I'll wait here with you.'

A dog barked. Someone coughed. The cathedral clock struck the half-hour. Stars watched and her pulse slowed.

'So you're the famous *veuve*. I have toasted you, in a different life.'

She looked at him blankly.

'Veuve Clicquot. Of Veuve Clicquot et Compagnie. It's written over the door and I'm guessing you wouldn't be defending it alone with your head bleeding if it wasn't yours. It's the kind of commitment I imagine made you famous for your beautiful wines. Before this war made us enemies of the French, drinking your *vin mousseux* was a sign of immaculate taste. That was a million years ago.'

'My whole life is in those bottles.'

'Is it just you and them against the world?'

'That's how it feels sometimes.'

'Are you ready to go now? I promise my men will keep it safe…'

'I can't take that risk. I'll survive, really.'

'You need to survive beyond just tonight. Where is your beautiful daughter? Yes, Madame, of course I remember you from the café in Paris. Do you have someone who can look after you?'

'I want to stay. I need to think. You should go and get some sleep. And thank you for averting disaster.'

'I'll wait with you.'

'You don't need to.'

'I clearly do. I only left you for a day and look what happened!'

Laughing and crying at the same time hurt. In her delirium, she couldn't decide if she was happy or sad. Or, like she'd always told Mentine, both at the same time. She knew what would bring her back to herself.

'Do you want to taste some?'

'Wine? I thought it was only for French lips.'

'My comet wine will give me strength, remind me why I'm sitting out here in the cold with a Russian officer who's occupying my town while I try to defend what's mine.'

She reached inside the door, to the safe where Louis kept his sample wines for passing buyers, one of every vintage. She knew which bottle just by touch: the one on the right-hand side was always the best. She took two clean glasses off the shelf above. She put the lamp in the middle of the table, set out the glasses and poured. A starlit vineyard, hot summer, a fizzing tail mellowing the Pinot grapes, the south-east-facing yard at Avenay-Val-d'Or to absorb just the right number of golden rays. It was enough to forget the soldiers who'd been here just moments ago, the danger she and Xavier had been in.

He rolled it around the glass, studied the viscosity – the 'legs'– breathed it through his mouth and nose and raised it to his lips in a surprisingly delicate gesture for the size of his hands.

'Of all the grapes, a Pinot communicates the taste of the *terroir* the best. It is unmistakably from here,' he said.

Nicole chinked glasses with him.

'Cherry, raspberry, caramel.'

'Roses, plum, violets.'

He took another sip and smiled. 'Those too. What's your first name? You're not my idea of a wine widow. I was expecting a fierce matron, counting her francs on the surface of a barrel in grubby fingerless gloves.'

'If things carry on like this, you won't be far off the truth, and I won't be able to afford even the gloves. Nicole.'

'That sounds more like it.' He held out his hand. 'Alexei. Well, Nicole, I thank you for your delicious wine, but you really should let me take you home. I have a cart, with blankets…'

'I'm not good at taking orders from anyone. Even kind men who know about wine. I told you, I'm staying put 'til morning, and once I've made my mind up…'

'As you wish.' He took another sip. 'You have some well-placed south-east vineyards in your considerable collection, Veuve Clicquot?'

His eyes were dark and bitter, like her favourite chocolate.

'Right again. How do you know so much about wine?'

'Another life. Tell me about the comet. Was it 1811? It passed across our skies too.'

'The vintage of a lifetime. 1811 was a perfect year, for wine at least. I can taste the cool night sky when I first saw it in this wine. It was beautiful. Your men have guzzled at least half of it.'

She took in the braid on his coat, his straight teeth and glossy hair. There was a war-weary air to his demeanour, but he was clearly high-ranking, and she had seen him ride at the Tsar's side on the Champs-Élysées.

'If you want to prove to me how peaceful your invasion is and that you are in control of your thugs, the Russian army should pay me for it, fair and square.

'I would happily buy a case from my own pocket.'

'That would not do. I would like the Russians to acknowledge their actions against me, officially.'

He raised an eyebrow, amused but, she hoped, willing. 'I do have a certain amount of compensatory funds I can draw upon. But why should it be directed to you? Every cellar within twenty kilometres of here has been looted, and not just by Russians.'

'Because my wines are the most valuable and every vintner within twenty kilometres of here would like to see me fail. So far, I have refused to oblige.'

'You've made it very obvious you can fight! How much would you say is fair, Veuve Clicquot?'

'I doubt you can afford it. The war has made paupers of us all.'

'Try me.'

'Five francs a bottle.'

'You'll negotiate, of course.'

'I never negotiate. I have workers to pay and mouths to feed.'

'There will have to be some paperwork, but as a gesture of goodwill for Russian–French trade relations, I will see what I can do for at least some of the losses you have suffered, if you promise to go home now.'

'I'm staying with my bottles. But thank you.'

CHAPTER 26

APRIL 1814

Luck from the East

Natasha's face swam into focus. Nicole sat up; where the hell? Oh, in her town house in the rue de la Vache. The room she'd lain awake in the night after François died. Too many memories. She had to leave straight away.

'Where do you think you're going?' said Natasha gently.

'I can't stay here. It's haunted and I have to get back to the cellars.'

'The cellars are fine, guarded by your new Russian friend. He had to ask me where you lived. You refused to tell him, apparently,' she said, shaking her head proudly. 'You're not leaving; get back into bed. I'll cast a spell to scare off any ghosts.' Natasha sketched a figure of eight, turned around slowly three times and addressed the curtains. 'What's that, you won't leave until she's back in bed? You heard him, Nicole, get in and the ghost will leave you alone.'

Nicole stared at her.

'Seriously. I'm making light because I don't want to scare you, but he *means* it.'

Nicole got back in, just in case. Anyway, her legs had turned to jelly and her head was aching like it was clamped in a vice.

'That's better, my dear.'

'Did they get the bakery?'

'They wouldn't dare cross a *volshebnitsa*, a Russian enchantress. They're a superstitious lot, peasants, most of them.'

'I could have done with you there last night.'

'You have your own way of being enchanting, even when you don't realise it. Could you manage a *religieuse*? It's hard to come by the ingredients in these times, but I had a little chocolate hidden away for a special occasion and you coming back to Reims is it. I made them this morning.'

Natasha offered her the cake and Nicole broke a little off to be polite, though the pain turned it to ashes in her mouth.

'Mentine's growing up,' Natasha observed.

'Too quickly.'

'You are lucky. She's a beautiful girl, inside *and* out, a blonde version of François.'

He would have been a better father than she was a mother. She'd promised Mentine she would say good night and she'd failed her again. She'd failed the cellars too. She was spread so thin, she felt transparent.

Natasha opened the curtains, flung open the windows and the sun streamed in, the most beautiful spring day. A sudden gust of wind blew apple blossom into the room, which whirled around for a moment before it fluttered to the floor, like snow.

'East wind. Apple blossom,' said Natasha, narrowing her eyes. 'A good omen.' She scooped up the blossom and made confetti over Nicole's head. 'You could use some luck, and here it is from the east.'

'You always say you make your own luck.'

'Maybe.'

Mentine knocked and came in, hastily kissed Natasha, then threw herself on the bed. She waved an envelope at them. 'They are *so-o-o* handsome!'

'Who?'

'The Russian soldiers. A whole battalion was outside the house and one came to the door to deliver this. Look, it says Nicole Clicquot on the front! How did he know your name? Maman, the whole town is on fire with stories of how you stood up to looters, with only your boots to save you. A quick kick in the—'

'That's enough!' But she couldn't help smiling at her daughter's delight in her victory.

'Well, is it true?'

'Not entirely, though I did manage to escape from a sticky situation.'

'You hurt your head, Maman?'

'It's nothing. Just make sure you don't ever go out alone while they're here. Stay with me and *grand-mère* and *grand-père*.'

'But I'm so bored and there are all these new people in town and everything's happening outside and I'm stuck in here. Josette doesn't understand that I don't want to play tea parties and kids' games any more, but I don't want to hurt her feelings.' Mentine thrust the envelope at her. 'Aren't you going to open it?'

Inside was a cheque. Nicole double-checked. Six hundred francs. Enough to cover every last bottle that had disappeared from her cellars.

She opened the note.

I hope you will take this as proof that Russians can be trusted. The amount will also cover my own personal crate of Comet Pinot. Your cellars are safe now, so you can sleep inside for the next few days; it's cold out there at night.

When you are recovered, perhaps you could give your biggest buyer a tour of the vineyards?

Sincerely, Alexei

'What is it, Maman? A love letter?' Mentine teased.

'Don't be ridiculous. It's payment from the Russian army for everything they've looted from the cellars. Quite right too.'

'I told you, luck from the east,' smiled Natasha.

'Dull,' scowled Mentine.

Nicole endured three more nights in that room, but as soon as she was recovered from the blow to her head, she arranged to move to the press house at Bouzy. There was nowhere else she wanted to be. It was spring, the vines were sprouting acid green leaves, the field hands were out planting, and last year's blends were ready for bottling. Stocks needed building up again and there was no time to waste.

April was usually the time they'd ship the mature wines, packing off her precious babies ready for their next adventure, with Louis at the helm. Not this year. Nothing was going anywhere. Trade was eternally dead, shipping ports still closed to French exports. It was difficult to see how things could continue, but every time she looked out of the window and saw the vines growing afresh, hope sprang up again. Another year or two, and then perhaps things would be back to normal. Until then, hard work, and a little glimmer of hope with Alexei's promised tour. At least *he* was buying.

The press yard was covered in milkweed. The place ran without her, but it was looking neglected. She would stay here until she saw off hundreds of carts loaded with bottles again, if it took years. She bent down and tugged at the weeds. Might as well start somewhere.

'Haven't you got someone who can do that for you?'

A perfect French accent, almost.

'Ah, my biggest buyer. You're ready for your tour?'

'I've thought of nothing else since I tasted that Pinot.'

'Once you've tasted the *terroir*, you never forget it.'

'Is this where you sleep, out here?'

'Funny.'

'Which way for the tour?'

'Follow me. We'll start with the low-lying vineyards close by, then I'll show you the grand cru sites, and on to the slopes where we grow the Pinot. We'll walk, rather than take horses; you see much more that way.'

The air was charged, larks hovered and vine tendrils wound their fingers around the training poles, a firm foundation for the grapes to grow. Tight buds waited to bloom on the roses and ladybirds busied themselves, keeping them free of pests. There was something about being with Alexei that made sun shine brighter than she could remember in a long time.

As they walked together in easy silence, Nicole found herself drawn to studying him when he was distracted by a varietal or planting method. He was broad-shouldered, with thick black curls and his dark, pitted skin gave him a rugged air, at odds with his neat officer's uniform. He was authoritative and confident, but his glittering black eyes had a kind of hurt behind them which Nicole couldn't fathom.

'We have 390 hectares in total and we are lucky, the majority are grands crus or premier crus,' Nicole told him.

'And the best vineyards are on the east side, with shallow soil?'

'You still haven't told me how you know so much about wine.'

'I find the deeper the knowledge, the greater the pleasure. I enjoy learning about wine, and you.'

Something inside her leapt at his words.

'They're not really my vineyards, *they* own *me*. I'm completely dependent on their whim. There are bad years and good years and I have absolutely no control, I can only react with the knowledge

I've gained. It's a collective knowledge, gathered over centuries by thousands of people who've worked the land, and I intend to contribute as much as I can while I'm alive.'

She thought of her riddling tables, still her secret for now, to gain a competitive advantage. But if and when the secret was out, it would revolutionise the production of *vins mousseux* across the world.

By the time they reached Verzenay, the sun was high in the sky and it was unusually warm for this early in the year. As arranged, the table and chairs were set up under the old chestnut tree, a crisp white tablecloth and a bottle of her best Sauvignon, paired with *chèvre*, goat's cheese, the ideal partner.

'The least I could do for the first major buyer this spring. The war has killed trade, especially to Russia. I never imagined Russia would actually come to me.'

'I'm honoured.'

They took their seats, and Nicole was glad she'd left her hair loose and worn her favourite dress on this spring day. She liked how the pale blue-grey silk picked out her eyes and she hoped that Alexei would notice, too. It occurred to her that it was the first time she could remember that she, not Josette, had decided what she'd wear that day. She threw her riding habit on the back of the chair to feel the balmy air on her shoulders and smiled.

'Don't be. I'm totally mercenary. If you like this Sauvignon, you might be inclined to another crate. As things stand, you're my only market.'

Condensation on the bottle created hundreds of droplets of sunlight. Cut grass, lemon and gooseberries complemented the tang of the goat's cheese on her tongue. Candles of pink blossom weighed the branches and the birds celebrated the end of the war.

Alexei took a sip. 'And I intend to be a good market. Talk me through this one.' When he smiled, the look of hurt disappeared momentarily.

'It's a fine balance. These vines bud late but ripen early, so we plant them away from the other vines, right here in this vineyard. When they're ready, we pick them early in the morning to keep them fresh.'

She scooped up some chalky earth from around a vine, freshly composted with *fumure.*

'Smell this. Can't you taste it in the wine?'

'I can, it's fresh and mineral. Does everyone here taste of this earth?'

At this moment, it was exactly how she *felt* she'd taste.

'This one's from last year. Sauvignon doesn't benefit from ageing, it's best drunk young, but there's still finesse and perfume to be enjoyed. The name comes from *sauvage* and *blanc.* Wild and white.'

He looked at her through the bottle. 'Zest and flint, a perfect combination. I suppose your prices are astronomical and not even a comet to justify it?'

'Of course, but worth it.'

Alexei held up a little sketchbook and pencil. 'Do you mind? It's a beautiful view and not an army tent in sight. It's like there was never a time before this war.'

'Of course. I will leave you to it. Xavier, my foreman, is over there and I need to talk to him. I don't like the way they're wasting that precious *fumure,* spreading it too far from the roots; they won't get the benefit.'

'How can you see from here?'

'When it comes to my vineyards, I see everything.'

She felt him watching as she walked away, so she twirled a strand of her hair back into her bun.

'Who's the poser in the gold brocade? Is he here to requisition the vineyards?' Xavier asked, his face still painfully bruised and scabbed.

'Our biggest buyer.'

'You're getting them to *buy*? How do you do it? Only a few days ago, I was beating the ball-sacks off with sticks and now you've got them eating out of your hand. He can't take his filthy eyes off you.'

She grinned. 'He's just interested in viticulture and watching how things work.'

'Hmmm.'

'Stop it, Xavier, please. He's a genuine buyer and we need him. Now, the *fumure*…'

A new-minted sun, an appreciative buyer with money to spend, the workers out in the field again, gradually returning from war and desperate to bury their hands in the soil of their homeland. Perhaps Natasha was right. Luck from the east. Rumours were flying about the restoration of the Bourbon monarchy; two revolutions in one lifetime was enough for anyone, but Nicole would welcome her own revolution in fortune. Ironic that today, anyway, the Russian enemy was her friend, but her own town and the most powerful among them – Moët – was set against her success. They would prefer her to marry Moët than to sell to Alexei.

She finished with the workers and returned to Alexei. He tore a page out of his sketchbook and gave it to her. It was her, in profile, pointing to the vines and saying something. He'd noticed every detail, down to the teardrop earrings she'd forgotten she was wearing, and the loose hair she'd tucked into her bun as she walked away.

'It's very well-observed, you don't miss a thing,' said Nicole.

'It helps when dodging bullets,' he said bitterly.

'I'm sorry. Here am I worrying about compost and pests and you must have been through hell to get here.'

'We all have, I'm sure. You're a widow and I'm…' He stopped. 'I'm lucky to be here. There's no heroism in war – it's random, luck of the draw. I don't deserve to be alive and sometimes I wish I'd gone and others had lived in my place.'

'Don't say that! What happened?'

He shook his head.

The church clock struck a lazy four in the distance.

'I have to get back,' said Nicole. 'I promised my daughter and I seem to be forever letting her down.'

'Go on ahead, I'd like to stay here and draw. I can make my own way back – go on, don't be late. She won't be yours forever, you won't know how quickly it goes until she's gone.'

She didn't want to leave.

'All of this is for her. Let me know about the Sauvignon. I can get it delivered.'

'No need, I'll come and get it myself. That way, I get personal service.'

'I'll make sure I'm here for you.'

'Oh.'

He had a way of saying 'oh,' an eastern inflection shortening the vowel, that stuck in her head.

CHAPTER 27

Mid-April 1814

Reparation

Since Alexei had arrived, Nicole's world was more vivid. Funny she'd never noticed the tangle of forget-me-nots so blue against the cobbles, pushing up between the stones in the cathedral square, until this market-day morning. Swifts burst out of the sky from nowhere, whirling on pointed wings, and the planes were singing trees packed with fat little puffs of birds.

Mentine's warm arm linked hers as they passed the big cathedral and crossed the square, her own fresh spring flower. Her soft blonde hair was so like her aunt's, eyes the same blue-green as François', with lips full as orange segments. Her grandmother's demeanour, her grandfather's way of walking, Nicole's figure and perfectly duplicated fingernails – how does nature do that? Everything she loved, rearranged into Mentine, who was, again, her own person.

'Are you selling more wine, Maman?'

'Not really, *chérie*. You might not have noticed, but there's a war on.'

'You seem… sort of glowing.'

'It's a beautiful spring day.'

'And you've got a big fat cheque from that handsome Russian general. Everyone's talking about it.'

'Don't be silly, it's just the same old town gossip; I've told you a million times not to listen. Now, which colour are you going to choose for your new dress?'

Mentine cuddled into her and she kissed her head, breathed her in. She smelt clean and her hair was as warm and soft as it was when she was a baby.

Mentine nudged her. 'Look, it's him, your general!'

Alexei was right there, under one of the singing trees, sketchbook in hand, dark curls falling over his eyes as he concentrated on the task.

'Alexei, good morning.'

'Good morning, both.'

He knew there was two of them, even though he didn't look up from his sketchbook.

Nicole glanced at the drawing. A tangle of forget-me-nots growing out of the cobbles, flimsy smudges of blue, fragile against the stone.

'Your Sauvignon's ready for you,' she smiled. 'I even found some of the same *chèvre* we paired with it for you to take back to the camp.'

'I'm afraid I'll have to send someone else to collect it. This afternoon?'

His watchful hurt was unmistakable. She searched back through her words for what she might have said to upset him.

'If you come yourself, I'll open a bottle of my comet champagne. It will take your mind off things,' she dared to say.

'Is it that obvious? I won't be much company. Really, it's best if I send someone. Enjoy your outing with your lovely daughter.'

He returned to his drawing.

'Comet champagne? You never open that for anyone,' said Mentine as they walked on. 'He's old, maybe even as old as you, but handsome.'

'He's an important buyer,' she replied, hiding her disappointment at his words.

Mentine giggled.

'Don't forget that the Russians and their allies are occupying our country. Don't romanticise everything. Come on.'

Nicole ushered her into Claudine's dress shop. She'd promised her growing daughter a new robe to replace her wardrobe of childish pinafores.

Mentine tried on her new dress, a simple green satin that fitted her perfectly. François made a void beside her. He would have adored this child-woman, shy of her own beauty, but suddenly aware. There was no papa to get angry at the boys, or tell her she was beautiful when she was unsure, or hug her when she felt like a child again. Her own father had always made her feel adored, no matter what. Irises crammed in a vase in the shop window brought back the sharp memory of François filling the house with them after a bout of depression. The despairing lows only served to heighten the fragile highs.

Mentine pirouetted in front of her. 'I love it!'

'You actually don't look bad,' she teased. 'In fact, you're getting rather beautiful. Papa would have been proud of you.'

'Don't! I ache when I think of him.'

'Come on, let's get it wrapped and we'll go and show Mémé *et* Grand-père.'

Out in the sunlit square, the shops showed off the few wares the war allowed, horses clattered, children played and the world didn't care. Nicole looked for Alexei but he wasn't anywhere to be seen. She felt wrung out as she hurried back to her parents' house. A big delivery was waiting to leave the press at Bouzy, so she guiltily kissed Mentine goodbye and was glad to rush off. Work was the only thing that took her mind off François, and now Alexei.

When she got to the press yard, Xavier's broad outline was missing from the press office. After his bruised and battered appearance in the vineyard last week, she had sent him home to recover, and Louis wasn't due in until the afternoon. The whole place was dead. When Emile's friendly face emerged from the cellar door, she could have hugged him.

His eyes flickered. 'Madame Clicquot!'

He always knew it was her, just from her footsteps.

'Good morning, my lovely boy. Where is everyone?'

He scuffed up a few stones with his boot.

'What's happened now?'

'Monsieur Moët is offering double wages again. With the war, there's such a shortage of able-bodied men and workers are needed for bottling. Everyone's suffering and they need money…'

'Even the orphanage lads?'

Emile nodded. Times were hard. She'd had to put them on half wages and they'd already brought the harvest in and rejected Moët's offer once, so who could blame them?

'They do know about the delivery to be loaded today for Paris?'

'They said next week, when the Moët work is finished.'

No shipment meant no wages. The vicious circle spiralled downwards in front of her eyes.

'He didn't want me. But I wouldn't have gone if he had,' said Emile. 'That's better, you're smiling.'

She *was* smiling. What an extraordinary lad; she was lucky to have him on her side.

'I'm very glad you're here,' she said, patting his arm.

'You have a visitor. He asked me all about the press, so I showed him round, I hope you don't mind. He said he was a friend.'

'Who is it? Did he give you a name?'

She held his hand to guide him to the office.

'Yes, General Marin. He speaks good French, but he's Russian…
Is something wrong?'

'Not at all.'

Alexei was standing in the cellar doorway, head bent forward,
nearly touching the top, watching them.

'I decided those Prussian thugs can't be trusted with my precious Sauvignon, so I came myself after all. Emile here knows
every inch of this place and has been a great host. Moët's missing
out on your best man, but who can blame him for loyalty to such
a lovely boss?'

Her delighted smile felt foolish. He beamed back.

'So, will you lead me to it?'

'Is it the case from the Aÿ vineyard?' said Emile.

'Yes, but I don't want you carrying it up the cellar steps. If
you fall…'

'Just tell me where it is, and I can fetch it,' offered Alexei. 'And
I can also help with the loading of the shipment. You faced down
ten armed Cossacks and even *then* you didn't look as defeated as
when Emile told you about your men deserting you,' said Alexei.
'They'd be court-martialled for it on my watch.'

She shook her head. 'It's worse than a few drunks with rusty
muskets. It's five thousand bottles, hundreds of cellar stairs. A
day's hard labour for five experienced cellarmen, almost impossible
for one soldier, with the best will in the world. But thank you.'

'In that case, I'll get you ten men. It's the least they can do after
what happened at the Place des Droits de l'Homme. It's partly
because of them that your man Xavier isn't here, so we owe you.
Don't protest! Let someone help you for once. Even you need it
every now and then. Can I send Emile with a letter to the camp?'

Emile saluted. 'Yes, sir!'

'You'll find your way?' said Nicole.

'Of course, I live near there and I walk here every day. Easy.'

'Then I'll gladly accept. But please, after that, any debt to me is entirely settled.'

She hated owing anyone, even Alexei. However, she silently thanked Moët for his malice. Her order fulfilled and a whole day with Alexei at the press yard was irresistible.

Emile set off and Alexei helped get the carts into the yard, then she showed him down into the cellar. She would have to select the wine and load the crates with him. His men could do the rest.

'So, this is your dominion,' he said as they reached the bottles to be loaded. 'It's a bit dark and claustrophobic down here for someone who loves her freedom so much, isn't it?'

'It's where all the magic happens. Each bottle has its own life to lead.'

'Each one special, with its own personality?'

'Exactly! No two are ever the same, if you understand how to taste them.'

'Do you mind?' Alexei gestured to the cellars, stretching off into the darkness.

'Please,' said Nicole.

Alexei strolled around, surveying the stacks of bottles, the bottles in the sand ready for riddling, the reds, the whites, the champagne. While he did so, her mind was racing on the task ahead, picturing in her head the order of the loading, which batches should go, which still needed time, the despatch notes and instructions to the drivers.

When she looked up, he was there, scrutinising her, as if trying to work something out about her.

'Sorry, I was miles away. There's so much to get done,' she smiled.

'Of course, you never stop, I can see that. There's so much work in all this. I've never seen such an ordered cellar,' said Alexei. 'You put your heart and soul into it all. Do you know how much this town talks about you? You've defied them all with your obsession. Why do you spend all your time worrying about early frosts and workers' wages and pest control when you could be living an easy life? By all accounts, you come from a rich family, with everything provided, but you won't take a sou, insist on embarrassing your family and working your fingers to the bone on all of this. I'm impressed, Veuve Clicquot, but why?'

'At first, it was my husband's life, it's what brought us together. Now, it's my life. Nothing else, apart from Mentine, matters. I still miss him every day. He was like the vines, a cycle of nature. Sometimes he withered and sometimes he bloomed. In my heart of hearts, I knew he would leave me too soon.'

She hadn't meant to give so much away, but there was an honesty and directness about Alexei that made her want to tell him everything. It was a relief to let her guard down with this relative stranger.

He didn't let her down with the usual platitudes, but just blinked in sympathy. A lamp fizzed.

'I'll get started,' he said.

He shrugged off his jacket and pushed up his sleeves. A crude scar sliced the inside of his arm, the white vulnerable skin.

'How did you get that?'

He yanked his sleeve down.

'I deserve worse than this scratch. The blade that cut me killed someone very dear to me. I wish I had died instead.'

'Who?' she said gently.

His eyes clouded, but he didn't reply.

'Some scars just won't go away, will they?' she whispered. 'I'm sorry I pried.'

'Don't be.'

Hooves clattered on the press yard cobbles and they ran up the stairs to meet them. Ten strapping men jumped down from their mounts and stood to attention. Nicole scowled. The characters who'd tried to attack her cellars were standing there in her yard, sober and lined up in front of her as if nothing had happened, Emile riding with the soldier who had smacked her head against the wall. He helped Emile down from his horse solicitously.

'You brought *them* here?' was all she could say to Alexei.

'We owe you; it had to be them. They'll behave, don't you worry about that.'

'You can tie your horses over there in the stables,' Nicole instructed.

'Then report back here for duty,' said Alexei. 'You'll do exactly – *exactly* – as instructed by Madame Clicquot. For this afternoon, she is your general, in my place, and there is to be no subordination. You will address her as General and obey her as you would on the battlefield, without question.'

Even with her own workers, there was rarely such unqualified respect and willingness. Someone always knew better, or rolled their eyes, or had put their back out, or needed to leave early to help with the milking. It was like conducting an orchestra, running the press on a daily basis – a mixture of encouragement, instruction, cajoling, diplomacy and, above all, absolute knowledge of every single aspect of the operation to gain the respect of her workers and keep it all going in harmony.

Today all she had to do was say the word and it was done with unquestioning efficiency.

'I could get used to this,' laughed Nicole to Alexei.

'It's a match made in heaven. You're clearly used to giving orders, and they're trained to follow them.'

It was Alexei they were obeying though. He had a way with them, joining their ranks every now and then, then pulling back and overseeing the whole thing. Each man was rotated with scrupulous fairness, so that each took turns at the most back-breaking tasks, like heaving the crates up the hundreds of stairs and passing them up the ladders as the loads got taller on the carts.

As the sharp morning sun mellowed to afternoon, Nicole inspected the crates, calculating. She could count the bottles just by running her eye along them, she'd done it so many times. Two thousand five hundred and the same to go again. She called a break for lunch and Josette brought out the little they had and laid it out on the press table. Some cheese, a few stale baguettes and preserved fruit. They waited for the word from Alexei, then tore at it hungrily. Just men, desperate and hungry, somebody's son or husband or brother, land workers like most of the men who were on her books. Wouldn't they have done the same to the cellars if they were in Russia and the tables were turned? She prayed they all made it home to whoever was waiting for them. Did Alexei have someone waiting?

There weren't enough coffee cups to go around, so she took a sip and gave him hers. He took a sip and passed it back, the coffee warm and bitter, like him. They smiled to each other at the little moment of causal intimacy, until they realised men were exchanging lewd glances at the spectacle.

'Let's get back to work; we need to get this lot off. You have a business to coax back to life for your husband and his little family,' said Alexei, his gaze hardening.

Another few hours and the men were done. The carts clattered off towards her Paris buyers, driven by two of the soldiers.

She waved them off, wishing her bottles a happy future in ballrooms, at soirées, at, please God, celebrations of peace at last from the war.

'You know you move your lips when you talk to your bottles?'

'It doesn't count unless I do.'

He waved them goodbye, too, and she laughed happily, feeling carefree for the first time she could remember in a long while.

The men were dismissed after Emile had fed and watered the horses. It was the last of the hay, but at least she could afford to buy some more when the money was sent back from Paris. A few more months bought; no point in thinking any further.

Alexei picked up his jacket. 'Crisis averted, General. I really must get back to the garrison. Am I released?'

'Wait. I promised you something.'

She fetched a bottle of the Cuvée de la Comète and added it to the crate of Sauvignon.

'The first one to be opened since we laid it down.'

He picked it up, ran his thumb over the crude charred comet on the cork. The late afternoon was hot and still.

'Open it now,' he smiled.

'It won't be cold enough,' she protested.

'Well then. An idea. I have a little boat moored at Tours sur Marne. I've been escaping to it when I wish to draw. We can drink it there, cool it in the water and cool off ourselves, too. I think it's not too far to walk, *milaya?*'

Milaya. Natasha used to call her Daniel that.

The rowing boat was hidden in a little clump of trees in a quiet eddy of the river. He helped her in, held the boat so it wouldn't rock and tied the champagne to chill in the water.

The river was like glass, reeds flattened in the current. A sharp scent of water mint filled the air. Nicole lay back and trailed her hand in the water, looking up through the tree-filtered light to the sky.

Alexei took out his sketchpad and started to draw. She closed her eyes. The river meandered, silver and filled with promise, so different from the day François had shouted his grief at the raging water, not far from this place.

He opened the champagne and poured them both a glass. She took a sip.

'Draw it for me!' she laughed.

He gave her a comet, with a scintillating tail, as she'd seen it crossing the sky the year these grapes ripened.

She held the glass up to the light – as clear as the sparkling river thanks to her new invention – and chinked with him. Rich, toasty and nutty, notes of caramel and lemon. It was good, the best she'd ever made. She needed to get this to a market which could afford it, which hadn't been at war forever – Russia, England... A fish jumped and a fly was lost to the world in one quicksilver moment.

His next picture caught the moment the fish had snatched the fly in intricate detail, a ripple disturbing the glassy surface, the fish curved with the effort of jumping, iridescent patterns on its scales, like oil in the sun.

They finished the bottle and he kept drawing: a dragonfly, the light distilling through the trees, a mother duck followed by furiously paddling ducklings – she counted six, but he only drew five – and finally, the sun going down. She had forgotten the sun went down. She willed against the end of the golden evening, framed it like a picture in her head to look at later. The damp in the dusky air made her shiver.

'I've kept you out too long and I should get back to the camp. Come.'

He jumped out of the boat across the water and held his hand out for her. She reached for him, but the boat slid away and she screamed at the sudden cold as she hit the shallows.

He scooped her out, dress dripping, giggling with shock, and he hugged her, freezing, teeth chattering, dizzy. The moon shimmered a path on the river. He lifted her to drier ground, set her still, took off his jacket and put it on her. He turned up the collar against the chill, then slowly fastened each button. The jacket was heavy and warm and smelt of sweat and woodsmoke. The last birds swooped to roost and chattered with the setting sun and his bitter eyes fixed on hers and they didn't speak for a while.

'Better now, *milaya*? You're still shivering.'

'Better.'

Kiss me, she thought. He didn't move, but his eyes devoured her.

'I toasted you in another life and, in a different world, I would… You look too beautiful, dripping and cold in the starlight. I have to return, and so should you. It's not far back for you, I think?' He held out a folded piece of sketch paper at arm's length, cupped his hands around hers. 'Please, don't open it until you get back. My camp is in the opposite direction to Bouzy. Goodbye.'

She watched him disappear in confusion and studied the picture he had given her, tempted to open it. Instead she thrust it deep into her pocket and stumbled back, the moon lighting her way.

Back near the village, she took off his coat and folded it tight so that no one would see her in it – she didn't need to give the gossips anything else. Thinking back, he'd only sketched five ducklings instead of six. Why, when he noticed everything?

At her front door, Josette fussed over her wet dress, but she waved her away. The fire was made in the parlour and she drew up François' old chair and unfolded the picture, frozen despite the heat. It was a boy, about the same age as Mentine, in Russian uniform. Like Alexei, but not him.

She ran through the last moment she saw him, his arms clamped by his side. He had been stopping himself from putting them around her. He looked so alone, and angry.

CHAPTER 28

May 1814

A Glamorous Moon

The bakery kitchen smelt of yeast and cinnamon, the marble surfaces scrubbed until they gleamed, deliciously cool against the heat of the day. Natasha swirled the steaming water in the copper bowl and mouthed an oath. She beckoned to Nicole.

'Now, come, hold your face over the whirlpool and close your eyes.'

The steam formed warm beads on Nicole's face and she remembered Alexei wrapping his jacket around her, fastening the buttons against the cold.

'Stand back and let me see,' said Natasha. 'Here, take this.' She handed Nicole a starched tea towel, fresh with rose water and lemon, and turned back to study the shapes in the steam. 'A fish jumping, an artist, a wooden rowing boat…' whispered Natasha.

She swirled the great pot again, frowned and took the kettle off the hob, pouring in more water. A plume of steam misted upwards.

'Quick, breathe over the pot again.'

Nicole winced against the heat.

'Don't move yet,' instructed Natasha.

'What can you see now?' asked Nicole.

'Stand back,' said Natasha, making shapes in the steam and pushing it up, up until the whole kitchen was filled with it. 'More luck from the east.' Natasha bit her lip in concentration. 'A ship on the sea, very cold. Love, but not as you expect.' The steam swirled and curled back down from the ceiling. 'Luck and danger, in equal measure.' She took the bowl off the hob again and flung open the windows. The steam began to disperse. 'That's enough of that, it's nonsense anyway.'

'You always say that, but you still do it,' said Nicole suspiciously.

'It's the only way I can get you to see sense.'

'What do you mean?'

'How long have you been in love with General Marin?'

'Natasha, I'm not!'

'Be careful. Madame Olivier says she saw you in a boat with him at Tours, 'til late in the evening.'

'Is there nothing that woman doesn't see! I thought she was my friend.'

'She's also the biggest mouth in Champagne. A juicy piece of gossip like that is irresistible, friend or not. I told her to keep it to herself and I believe she will, this time, but don't give her anything else.'

'So you didn't see all those things in the steam?'

Natasha narrowed her eyes. 'You mean love?'

'No!'

'I don't need steam for that. I know you better than you think.'

'What does it matter? He won't do me wrong.'

'How do you know?'

'How do I know when my wine is ready? I just *know*.'

'But don't expect too much. That's what the steam tells me. Love doesn't always come to you how you would wish it. Just let it be what it is.' Natasha hugged her. 'I've got a good feeling about this and that's as much as anyone can predict, though people aren't always what they seem. Take care and be discreet, Babouchette, this town has more eyes and ears in its stones than you imagine.'

Along the lanes back to her Bouzy house, foxgloves, buttercups and cow parsley tangled together and the May blossom weighed the branches in white and pink sprays. She imagined the soldiers returning back from the front to this and thanked God for the end of the war for now, with Napoléon safely exiled to Elba.

In the fields, a few of her most loyal workers were back, out digging trenches, creating rows, according to the region's *planter à la route* methods, nice and ordered. Never mind the flowers, there weren't enough workers to get it all finished in time. She lashed Pinot to speed up and when she arrived at the press yard, Emile came running and took the horse's reins.

'There's a package for you.'

'Thank you, Emile. It's a hot day, so make sure he gets plenty of water.'

She patted Pinot and Emile led him to the stable, hugging his soft nuzzle.

The package on the desk had Alexei's handwriting on it. Nicole tore it open and folded out a cape in the same cloth as the jacket he had lent her, the one she still had in her room, next to her bed. She unpinned a note from the collar and took it to the window to read.

> *I gave you my jacket to keep you warm,* milaya, *but it's military issue and I must return it as soon as this war is finally over. I will be passing by your cellars in Reims this*

evening. Perhaps you could keep my cape and swap me
back my jacket. I can meet you there at 8 p.m. Send your
boy to the camp with a reply.

Alexei

A glamorous moon hung swollen in the translucent dusk as she
made her way to the cellars on the Place des Droits de l'Homme,
and Alexei was already waiting outside when she arrived. She
took the big key from her belt to open it – all the workers would
have left for the day.

He smiled. 'You're wearing it. Here.' He turned up the collar of
her cape against the cold and she lit a lamp to go inside, locking
the door behind them.

'I have your jacket, it's heavy!' Nicole handed it to him.

He shrugged it on. 'Heavier than you imagine, but it's all I've
known these past few years.' He nodded down the steep cellar
stairs. 'How many kilometres do you have down there?'

'The cellars go on forever, to nearly twenty-nine kilometres.
I know every inch.'

'Of course you do. Will you show me?'

'That would take all night!'

'Exactly.'

'Be careful on the steps, all the torches have been put out. Fuel
is scarce and everyone's gone home.'

In the cellars, the air was cool, a velvet-dark cocoon. She held
up the lamp.

'This is the first rack I ever saw, the day the revolution came
to Reims.'

'What happened?'

'I was a tomboy and foolishly picked a fight with the big boys. Xavier pushed me down here all those years ago to hide from them in the chaos. I thought it was like a fairy grotto.'

'Nothing much has changed, then. The world up there is changing, too fast,' said Alexei.

They walked on in silence, through the labyrinth of cellars. Kilometres of wine, carts, chimneys, she didn't want it to end. She stopped at the place, reached behind the rack of *vin de Sillery* and brushed off the dust.

FC♥BNP scratched into the wall.

He touched her arm. 'You have Mentine.'

'She is a joy. Amazing how you try so hard to impose yourself, but they go their own way whatever you do. Come down here.'

They walked and walked, each corridor with its own story. He listened, intently, asked endless questions. The hours passed until they were about halfway through, on the home trajectory. Impossible to tell if it was day or night down here, but morning couldn't be far off.

'You've heard so much about me. How about you? Tell me your story. I know nothing about you, apart from the fact that you're a general and you're Russian and you know everything there is to know about wine… and that you have a scar you don't want to talk about.'

'I prefer to be lost in your world for tonight. I will tell you one day, I promise, but for now this is your place and your story and you make me forget. I don't sleep, most of the time. It makes me a great soldier but a miserable human being. Can we just keep walking?'

They continued, just the two of them in the peace and dark. She didn't want it to be morning. Since the day François had died, she had felt so alone. Not tonight, with Alexei.

'Here. This was a highlight, the best harvest ever, 1811. My year of the comet wines. The racks have been rebuilt since I was last here. Your men guzzled some of it when they raided me.'

'I've done my best to make up for that, at least I hope I have... I'm intrigued about something. There were thousands of bottles of champagne in the shipment we helped load and not one of them was cloudy or spoiled as far as I could tell. How do you do that?'

She smiled again at his endless knowledge. Of course he had noticed her clear champagne; he missed nothing.

'Top-secret information, even from you.'

'Not even tonight, when it's just us?'

'Only four people in the world know.'

'Classified information is my speciality.' He saluted. 'All intelligence stops here.'

She studied him for a few moments, not sure she was ready to share her most precious advantage. He was nothing to do with the business, or Reims, or anyone she knew in this little town. He had done nothing but help her and, like her, he was endlessly fascinated by the charm of winemaking. He wasn't immoral, like Thérésa, or weak, like Xavier. And most of all, she was overwhelmed with a feeling she wanted to share *everything* with this man who had appeared in her life as mysteriously and portentously as the comet. Thérésa had given her a shard of ice in her heart, but this man was different. If he'd wanted to, he could have forced his way in weeks ago and she would have been powerless to stop him.

'Follow me,' she said, decided, fumbling for the key. She knew it by touch – the second largest on the key ring. She unclipped it and gave it to him, then led him to the riddling-room door. He put the key in the lock, but the door opened of its own accord.

'Louis! What are you doing here at this hour?'

'Early start,' he said, eyeing Alexei. They must have walked all night. 'And you are?'

Alexei held out his hand. 'General Marin. Good morning.'

'Of course, our biggest buyer. Madame Clicquot here is doing my job for me, it seems,' said Louis, closing the door behind him. 'Shall I use the key to lock up?'

'No need, I was just showing General Marin around.'

'But not in here, surely?'

'Yes, in here. He's interested, and don't worry, I trust him, though he might not look so trustworthy in that Russian coat.'

'Don't on my account. I was just curious,' Alexei murmured.

She frowned at Louis, who was simply staring at Alexei. Why was he being so rude?

'I think you're needed at the press yard for the bottle delivery?'

'Yes, Madame Clicquot. Of course, straight away.'

'Good,' she said.

He left, slamming the door behind him.

'I think I may be stepping on someone's toes,' said Alexei.

'I make the decisions,' she said.

'I'll remember not to cross you!' He opened the door. 'After you, Madame Clicquot.'

'Wait here, close your eyes.'

Nicole rushed around the room lighting all the lamps and turning them on to full blaze; the place always gave her a rush of excitement. The tables came into focus, row upon row of clear gold.

'You can open them now.'

He surveyed the tables, ran his hand over the upturned bottles. 'This is your secret? This is how you achieve consistent clarity in your champagnes?'

He walked up and down, admiring the ordered rows of the riddling tables as she explained how it worked.

'It's like all the best military campaigns. Unbelievably simple, gives you a massive advantage over the enemy, but no one's ever thought of it until now. This is going to make you a fortune, as long as you continue to fend off the Russian hordes.'

'At least one of the horde is welcome. If I could get it to Russia, it would be worth its weight in gold.'

'No one's buying because of the war?'

'It's impossible, French exports are totally banned. Louis, who you just met, was imprisoned as a French spy on his last trip there and I can't risk my staff, or the cargo being confiscated or dumped if it doesn't make it through.'

'Let me help you. I have some influence with the Tsar and when we eventually return, the whole country's going to be in the mood for celebrating.' He stroked her cheek. 'That's brought some colour to your face.'

She kissed him then, saw the glamorous moon in her mind's eye and the steam rise and curl in Natasha's kitchen and then she saw tears in his eyes. He pushed her away.

'I'm sorry, I shouldn't have...' she faltered.

'I am the one who should be sorry. Who *is* sorry...'

'You don't need to say another word. I'm so used to running things my own way, I thought...'

'Leave it there, so I keep my resolve for both our sakes.' He held her in front of him. 'Let me look at you, *really* look at you. Down here is another life. One where just you and I exist, and everything we dream of is possible. Outside, it's impossible.'

A moment passed and she saw the other life in his eyes.

'There's a penknife in the pocket of your jacket – give it to me,' she said.

She scratched something onto the wall.

AM + B-NC.

He took the knife from her and drew a comet underneath.

'Thank you for the night walk in your world. I'll never forget it,' he said.

'There's more to my world than this.'

They held hands until they emerged, blinking against the morning light.

Madame Olivier was on her way to the bakery, basket in hand.

'Ah, the Russian general and the French vintner at the cellar door! Good morning to you both, my dears, *bonne journée!*'

She hurried on by before Nicole could reply.

'I must go now, *milaya*. I'll create more problems for you if I stay. I'll write you a note and we'll meet again.'

The post was full of bills the next day, and the next, but she was busy as always, *à pied* early and collapsing into bed late, putting in a full day of work and spending her evenings with Mentine. No matter how busy she was, however, she couldn't stop herself hoping for the note he'd promised, or allowing herself to imagine a future together between Reims and St Petersburg, her wine empire stretching its tendrils across Russia like new vines.

No news came from him and after a week she heard rumours in the bakery that all Russian troops were heading back to the border. He couldn't just leave without saying goodbye, could he?

Pinot was happy to be saddled up and ridden fast to the camp. When she got there, it was deserted. Nothing but patches of campfire ashes and a hundred tent-shaped patches in the field where they'd been. A couple of soldiers were picking up litter and debris, trailing sacks for the purpose.

She spurred Pinot to the two men and they stopped and saluted.

'Madame,' said the one with the most medals on his jacket.

'*Bonjour, Capitaine*. Where is everyone?'

'Gone, Madame. We're going home at last. It's a long march back, but towards happiness and not a moment too soon. My son will be four years old now – he was a babe in arms when I left.'

'I have some final business with General Marin. When did he leave?'

'He hasn't been here all week, Madame, but he's not far, at Monsieur Moët's mansion in Épernay. Who can blame him; it's a bit grander than a tent in a field and they're old friends.'

Pinot stamped as she gripped his flanks.

'In fact, I'm desperate to get on the road after this and catch up with the lads.' The soldier fished in his pocket and pulled out a crumpled sealed note. 'If you're going back to Reims, could I trouble you…? He said I was to deliver this before I go, but it would save me a few hours.'

She blinked at the note. It had her name on it. She forced a smile.

'Happy coincidence. It's for me! He hadn't forgotten his business after all and I'm glad to save you some time. I wish you luck, my friend. Go home to your family and look after them well – you've earned peace for the rest of your life!'

He saluted her once more, tied his sack and kitbag to his horse and rode off, whistling with his fellow soldier.

As soon as he was out of sight, she opened the note. Two words: *I'm sorry.* And at the bottom of the envelope, something metal. She held it up to the light: a round cork-branding tool carved with a picture of a comet – exactly like the one he'd joined their names with on the cellar wall.

The realisation was a punch in the guts. She'd given him – and now Moët – the riddling tables.

CHAPTER 29

Mid-May 1814

Another Life

The doorway on rue des Murs was flaking and worn; the medieval walls bulged. Nicole had known Louis all these years and never been to his house. Washing hung across the road and slops piled up in the streets, landing wherever neighbours chucked it from the windows. She'd been so preoccupied with her own troubles, she'd never once stopped to think about the circumstances of her closest and most faithful business ally, and he'd never said a word to her about the pittance she paid him in these difficult times.

She rapped on the door and his wife Marta answered. She was thinner than she remembered, and her hands were red-raw. Marta stiffened.

'Madame Clicquot. What brings you here?'

'Is Louis… Monsieur Bohne at home?'

Marta beckoned her in with a jerk of her head and Nicole squeezed past her in the narrow corridor.

'I'm so sorry to disturb you in your home, but it's urgent.'

'Wait here.' Marta's Russian accent was much stronger than Alexei's.

Louis came running, buttoning his shirt collar and wiping his mouth with a napkin.

'What's wrong?' he said.

'Is there somewhere we can talk?'

His eyes narrowed. 'Of course, follow me.'

He took her to the parlour, overlooking the garden, and pulled out a chair for her. A threadbare rocking horse stood in the corner, the fire was dying in the hearth, home-made curtains hung at the window and the sun streamed in. A happy, cosy home. She felt like an intruder.

'What's happened?' said Louis.

'I've been a fool.'

'I doubt that. You take risks, but you're no fool. Just tell me.'

'I should have let you lock the door to the riddling room last week.'

His expression darkened. 'You mean the Russian buyer? What the hell has he done?'

'He saw everything, he knows everything, and now he's staying with Jean-Rémy at his house. I haven't heard from him since…'

'You were expecting to?'

'Desperately. I've been so stupid – and after all we've been through!'

He put his hand on hers. 'A woman capable of love and making mistakes, like everyone else. Here.'

She dried her eyes with his handkerchief and stared out of the window. The entire garden was a vegetable patch and Marta was hacking at the dry ground. Louis snatched his hands away when she looked up at them.

'I shouldn't have come.'

'I'm glad you did. This isn't the worst crisis we've ever faced. Your secret was bound to get out sooner or later, and you don't even know yet that it has.'

'I knew you'd understand, darling Louis. I can see that you are needed here, with your family, but if you are willing, I have a plan that might salvage something in this mess. I calculate that we still have *months* over everyone else and if we can be the first to ship to Russia, my champagne has already impressed enough buyers over there to stay in the lead. But it would mean asking you to go to Paris to call on any connections you can, and finding a way to get the year of the comet champagne shipped before anyone else has the same idea. It's a lot to ask, especially when Paris is in turmoil. I'd happily go myself, but a woman would be too conspicuous with all the curfews and…'

Louis held up his hand. 'You don't need to say another word. Of course I'll go. I would have had the idea even if you hadn't. We've survived drought, jail, revolution and near-bankruptcy. This is nothing compared to all that, a minor setback, that's all.'

'It's more than a setback, and my fault entirely. I've given away the only advantage we had.'

'I'll find a way. It's not just the winery, is it? You've fallen for that bastard. He doesn't deserve you, but that's not my business.' He frowned. 'Strange how we've both fallen for Russians and we are now trapped by our actions, but if things had been different…'

Marta appeared in the doorway, holding Misha's hand, a little carbon copy of his father, with his mother's eyes.

'Louis, *milaya*, Misha was asking for you.'

'Of course, I'm sorry, I must be going,' choked Nicole.

The rue des Murs blurred with her tears. Marta was absolutely right to fight for her little family. Louis was the best salesman in Reims and he could have found a job with any one of the merchants within a thirty-kilometre radius, yet he'd stuck with her, and Marta was working the land to put food on the table because of it. This plan *had* to work, for her, for Louis and his family, and for all the workers who depended on her.

*

When Nicole arrived back at the cellars, Madame Olivier was waiting for her in her office, a smear of powder barely concealing a swollen black eye.

'What happened?' asked Nicole.

'It looks worse than it feels. I must try not to be so clumsy with that barn door. He said he'd fix it, but the catch came off a week ago and he did nothing about it. Entirely my own fault, blundering around. It's much easier for me if you don't mention it again.'

Nicole bristled. 'Take my advice and leave all those unfixed catches, nails sticking up, and broken stairs your husband so regularly forgets, and never go back.'

'Some things are more important than a few bruises – I'd rather put up with them than invite scandal, like you, if you don't mind me saying.'

'What do you mean, like me?'

'I don't mean to pry, or gossip, but I couldn't help noticing your encounters with your latest buyer and the sparkle in your eye, which I see so rarely nowadays, when you're with him, which I must say is more frequent than decency allows.'

Dear Madame Olivier, she loved gossip and could never resist, but she always looked out for her.

'If this is your way of telling me to be careful, there's no need. There is absolutely nothing between me and that man. In fact, it can't have escaped you that the whole battalion have left town, along with him.'

'He hasn't quite left… I met him at Monsieur Moët's. Such a charming gentleman and he quite offended Monsieur Moët with his praise of you.'

'What do you mean?'

'He was at the tasting yesterday at Épernay. He *insisted* that none of Monsieur Moët's wines could hold a candle to yours and that he could never hope to beat the competition and Monsieur Moët was very ungallant and said—'

'I'd rather not know,' said Nicole. 'I'm sick of it all. But thank you for the information as always. You don't need to any more, you know. I worry that I am the cause of your black eye from all your... rushing around.'

'That's my business, thank you. Funny isn't it, that the town couldn't care less about this' – she touched her eye painfully – 'but they do about you and your comings and goings, which are nobody's concern and do no one any harm. Well, I must be going, but I thought you should know, that's all.'

'And I'm grateful, Madame Olivier, really. I just can't seem to pick myself up like I used to.'

Madame Olivier tutted, kissed her with a, 'No time for such talk, chin up,' and left.

Nicole slumped into her chair, opened the ledger, winced at all the red entries and closed it again immediately.

A slow week passed. The air was as stale as she felt and Nicole did nothing. The thought of the cellars, or the fields, or anything to do with the business was too depressing, considering the advantage she may have given her biggest rival. All there was to do was wait to hear from Louis.

She was sitting outside on the veranda looking idly at the rows of lavender and trying not to think, when Madame Olivier came bustling up the path, waving two letters.

'I promised Thomas at the *poste* I'd deliver them as I was coming this way. I wonder who they're from?'

Nicole grabbed them from her. 'Not who you're imagining, but thank you for coming out of your way, Madame Olivier.'

'Well, I'll leave you to it,' said Madame Olivier, straining to look at the contents. 'Unless you'd like me to wait for you to reply? I'm going back that way.'

'Very kind, but I can manage, thank you.'

Nicole hurried to her office to open the letters in private. One was from Louis, and the other's authorship presaged by the trademark expensive ribbon – Thérésa!

She opened Louis' first.

He was already in Paris, which apparently was packed, with barely a hotel room to be had. He was sleeping on a pallet at a friend's hotel, he said, though she suspected he didn't have the funds for anything else. The little she had been able to give him for the journey was pathetic. British and Russian troops were everywhere, mustering for their homeward journeys, but the whole place was rejoicing at the restoration of order. He was going to see tomorrow if he could secure an audience with the Russian ambassador, and to that end, he'd managed to find a place to hang his only remaining decent suit, slightly threadbare and out of fashion now, but respectable, nevertheless.

She thought of the first time she had met Louis – ruddy cheeks, shock of ginger locks, shaggy wolfskin coat and knee-high galoshes, exuding warmth and fellowship. Now his hair was thinning and all he had to his name was a threadbare suit and hope. Hope that rested on her shoulders alone. She prayed that his faith in her was not misplaced.

The ribbon on Thérésa's letter was slippery and smooth; it was a long time since she'd felt such fine material. She pooled it carefully on her desk – Mentine would be delighted – and opened the letter.

*I'm here in Reims, back in your little country backwater!
Paris is teeming with soldiers and so much boring politick-
ing, so I have escaped to tranquillity. Are we friends again
now? Come and see me straight away in the rue de la Vache.*
    As ever, etc.

Your Thérésa

It was an irresistible invitation.

Nicole hesitated by the mirror, tidied her hair, pinched her
cheeks and hurried to Thérésa's grand mansion in town. The last
time she was here was with Xavier, in the dead of night. Wherever
Thérésa was, the sickly-sweet whiff of scandal was never far away
and it would be a welcome distraction. What poor man had fallen
foul of her charms this time?

'You came! So we *are* friends again?' exclaimed Thérésa and
hugged her so tight her bun fell out. She fixed it back up.

'Of course. You know no one can resist you for very long.'

Nicole knew that she could never be as careless with Thérésa
again. But she was too much fun. When Thérésa was in town,
she brought colour and an edge of danger and she couldn't bear
to cut her out of her life completely.

'Oh, don't be silly. Come along.'

She hurried her through the house, arranged them both on
the sofas in the orangery and called for fashionable English tea.
Thérésa looked as fresh as the first day she'd met her nine years
ago. She couldn't even count how many husbands ago that was.

Thérésa took her hand. 'The last time we met, you and your
lovely Mentine were making a dramatic flight from Paris. You
say your life is dull in comparison to mine, but there's always
something gloriously portentous happening. You must tell me all
the latest gossip.'

'Oh, just the usual. My business is on its knees and the whole town is delighting in my demise. It's only what they think I deserve for having the temerity to work for a living.'

'Tsk, darling. Do I detect the spark has left my country firefly?'

'I've had my successes, but disaster is never far away.'

'You mean your friend General Marin?'

'Not you as well, listening to the town gossip?'

'I've heard all about how you single-handedly fought off ten Prussian ruffians, were rescued by their general and since then he's been buying your wine like it's water and following you around like a puppy dog.'

'You've got that *very* wrong.'

'I don't think so, *chérie*. I heard it all from the man himself.'

'Don't tell me he's another in your long line of victims?'

'Alexei! He's been a friend since I can remember. Don't look at me like that, not *that* kind of friend. Of course, one has to try, but he was too bloody honourable for any of that.'

Despite everything, Nicole was flooded with relief.

'Can we change the subject?

'So you *are* a little in love with him. And he with you, though he's done his best not to show it. Listen, I know him. He's married and, unlike most other men, he's loyal to the end, whatever the temptation. His wife needs him, and he won't have her taken from his home and put in an asylum, though God knows, it would be the best place for her. She's never been the same since their son died in Alexei's arms on the battlefield. He watched him bleed to death, helpless. I hear he cried like a baby and his wife collapsed when she heard and is like the walking dead, alive but lifeless.'

Everything fell into place. He'd tried to tell her in so many ways. The day in the square when he saw her with Mentine on the way to the dress shop, the drawing of the missing duckling, the constant look of pain in his eyes.

'He wanted to help you, but he didn't want you to know.'

'I don't understand. There's no one in France who wants me to fail more than Jean-Rémy, and Alexei has done everything he can to help him with *that* ambition.'

'Let me help things along a little,' said Thérésa.

Before Nicole could protest, she was whisked through the grand ballroom, into the next room.

'I'll leave you two to chat,' said Thérésa.

Sitting nervously by the fireplace was Alexei. He jumped to his feet.

'I'm leaving tomorrow for Paris, then back to the border and Russia. I wanted to explain.'

'You should have told me you had a family.' She surprised even herself in asking him that question before calling him out on his defection to Moët.

'I didn't want to break the spell.'

'I'm glad that's how you felt, too.'

'Thérésa gave me something,' he said.

It was then she saw the leather bag on the chair where Alexei had been sitting.

'Thérésa's necklace from the Tsar! Where did you get it? The last time I saw it, it was locked in my office drawer.'

'She said you stole it from her, so she got it back. Don't ask me how, she's got more of a head for manoeuvres than anyone I've known in my entire army career. Don't be angry, I was worried you wouldn't trust me, and she said this would help.'

He held it out to her. 'Proof that I am on your side. You know I could use it to buy myself a lot of favours, or sell it to Moët, but you should have it.

She took it, still not sure whether to trust him.

'What the hell were you doing at Jean-Rémy's?'

'He invited me and I accepted. I saw you struggling, the whole town against you, and one of the most powerful vintners in the country hell-bent on bringing you down and I wanted to do something about it. He thinks I'm brokering a deal for him to get his comet champagne to Russia before you've even thought about it. All the time he's trusting me to get him through the trade blockades to St Petersburg buys you more time. The truth is, I don't have as much influence as he thinks when it comes to trade matters.'

Nicole looked at the necklace and smiled. This could be her biggest coup yet.

'*This* gives you all the influence you need.'

She leapt to her feet so she could think straight and look at the plan she was forming from all angles.

'I understand you're one of the Tsar's most trusted generals? You can at least get a message to him where others couldn't?'

'There are lines of communication open to me, yes.'

She *could* trust her heart, after all. Her judgement in the cellar, when Alexei and she had walked throughout the night and she'd shown him the riddling tables, had been sound. Nicole put the necklace on and pirouetted at this delightful development.

'Tell me and I'll do anything you ask to see you so carefree,' he laughed.

'The Tsar is not going to want such a lavish gift to another woman to fall into the wrong hands. And of course as one of his most faithful servants, you can make sure it doesn't... at a price.'

'What price would that be?'

'Louis is in Paris trying to get an audience with the Russian ambassador. Perhaps, with the help of this necklace, Louis will discover that the ambassador will miraculously allow as many shipments as we can get to Russia in the next six months while the trade ban is still in place. Veuve Clicquot will be the only French wine allowed into the country, six months ahead of all our competitors, including my old friend Jean-Rémy.'

'I know the ambassador well, and he's well-versed in cover-ups for the Tsar's misdemeanours. I'm travelling to Paris tomorrow, then mustering for Russia. It's perfect timing for me to deliver the message along the chain of command. Thérésa had an idea that the necklace would serve you somehow. That's the easy part, my beautiful vintner. But how do I bear leaving you and your magic empire of charm and commerce?'

'Then don't. Stay, get yourself another tour of duty in France.' She could lose herself in his black eyes, which were warm as coals.

'If I was selfish, I would stay. But too much has passed that I could ever make anyone else happy and I couldn't do that to you, my beautiful, determined alchemist. I am married to grief and you to your wines. But in another life…' He broke off to stoke the fire. 'I should take the necklace and be on my way. I couldn't leave without telling you I was on your side, and how achingly difficult it is to go.'

'Not yet!' said Nicole. 'You know everything about me. Stay a while. Tell me something of you, so I can think of you when you're gone.'

He told her about Russia, the way the mist clung to the lake in the early mornings, about the French tutor who had helped raise him, taught him to draw, to observe colour and detail. He also taught him the language and all about French wines. He told her the name of his son. He was Nikolai and he had loved fishing and riding horses. He told Alexei he loved him as high as the tallest tree and wide as the lake, the one where you couldn't see to the other side. Alexei promised that nothing bad would ever happen to him while he was with him.

He stoked the fire again and turned to face her.

'I was enchanted by you the moment you walked into that café in Paris. The way you moved through the tables with such quick steps, your delicate, elfin features and that fire in your eyes. When I saw you fighting my men outside your cellars, it was the first time I'd felt anything since Nikolai. I was furious at my men. And you looked so determined and frightened, I just wanted to scoop you up and hold you tight forever.'

'You know that other life you talked about which has me in it and no one else?'

He smiled. 'Did you know that in Russia, we must pay a ransom for our brides?'

'I think the gifting of the entire Russian champagne market is sufficient in this case.'

'I thought you'd refuse to speak to me again.'

'Impossible. But you're leaving tomorrow. Will we ever meet again?'

He shook his head.

'Can you live a life in a night?' asked Nicole.

He picked up a pink cushion.

'After the ransom, a rose-coloured cloth is held over the newly-weds' heads.'

He led her into Thérésa's new ballroom, the opulent confection of gilt and mirrors just an illusion, she knew. Alexei took two candles from the sconces, lit them and gave one to her.

'Hold this in front of you.'

He held the cushion over their heads and linked her arm.

'Now, walk very slowly.'

In the mirrors, they were reflected a hundred times, and as many different lives were possible.

'Now we stand on the cloth. That means we're married and, traditionally, this is where I would kiss you.'

'We French are revolutionaries, but we don't mind sticking to tradition on special occasions.'

He held her close, paused to smile at the sheer luck of this moment, bitter eyes filled with desire, and kissed her. Outside, the sky turned indigo and the mirrors reflected it back, shrouding them in the whispering dark.

'I have a country *dasha*,' Nicole murmured as she pulled away. 'A little place amongst the vines in Bouzy. It's perfect for a honeymoon.'

'Tomorrow I leave for the border.'

'Then we have at least twelve hours and we can make each hour a year.'

'You know I don't sleep?'

'Who sleeps on their wedding night?'

'You are sure? I can only give you tonight.'

'Very occasionally fate puts something your way that will make you happy, even if it's wrong, and you know you just have to grab it and think about the rest later.'

They walked to Bouzy across the fields, the secret ways where Nicole knew she was unlikely to encounter anyone. Glow-worms lit their way in the overgrown places, making their own constellations in the undergrowth.

They talked, about their hopes and fears, their lives and loves and how it would have been for them if they had met in a different world. They dreamed of the impossible world they would create, filled with marvels and magic and love.

At the house in Bouzy, he carried her across the threshold and up the stairs. In the dark, he made her feel like melted sugar. When she woke in the morning, he was there, looking at her.

'I was watching you breathe.'

The sun created a thread of crimson on the horizon, and they lay there without speaking, listened to the dawn chorus, watched the sun climb above the mist. A swarm of mayflies billowed up in front of the window, the light turning their transparent wings to flimsy lace. These creatures lived for years in the riverbank mud and they had one dazzling day in the sun, felt its heat, saw the green fields, the sway of wheat, the irises on the verges, the puffs of cow parsley, the thorny branches weighed down with May blossom and found their love in the swarm. Nicole understood one day was enough.

CHAPTER 30

July 1814

Klikoskaya

Ten thousand bottles of comet wine despatched to Russia! In her dreams, Nicole followed them, whispered to each of them in the night. They were safe with Louis. He had staked his whole life on this moment and she was ashamed he had to be hidden like a criminal on a Dutch ship, using his coat as a blanket, and sustaining himself on meagre rations, bought with Alexei's money.

News was intermittent and slow. She imagined shipwrecks, bottle explosions, robberies. Even with Russian protection, so much could still go wrong.

For now, the trade routes were hers alone, no one in Reims was any the wiser and she seized the chance to take the market.

When Xavier came heaving down the press yard waving a letter, she ran out to greet him. He thrust it in her hand.

'From Louis. But forget that for now. The old bird's laid out, they reckon she's on her last legs.'

'Who? You're scaring me!'

'Natasha. I'll take you now in the barouche and I'm driving – just for once, don't bloody well argue with me!'

Natasha looked tiny in the big bed, her long grey hair thick on the pillow, eyes still bright, but her face different, lopsided. A line of salt circled the bed and hundreds of candles burned in the stifling room.

Nicole hugged her. 'Natasha, what happened?'

'Don't! The salt line mustn't break!'

She stroked Natasha's cheek. 'Don't worry, I didn't touch it.'

'They're here, but they can't cross the line,' she muttered.

'Who, *chérie*?'

'The aristos who killed my Daniel. The Restoration, my arse. They're after me now, but they can't pass the salt line.'

'Of course they can't get you. No one ever could.'

Natasha smiled with half her mouth and Nicole's heart beat in fear. She gripped her hand.

'Don't be afraid, I'm ready. Maman is here,' Natasha murmured.

'But *I'm* not ready. I know you, you can *will* yourself back. Let me blow out some of these candles, and open some windows. You can't breathe in here.'

'Don't touch a thing. Everything is as it should be.' She closed her eyes. 'Just let me be. I'm happy. I saved every sou, baked a hundred thousand loaves to afford this many candles. And stop those tears. I want to hear everything before I go. *Everything*. Send me off with the good news you have in your pocket.'

Louis' letter. She'd forgotten all about it.

'He's reached Russia. But please, Natasha, not now...'

'I knew he would... luck from the east. Keep going.'

'The first bottles off the ship sold for twelve roubles each! He sold hundreds of crates right there and then on the harbour for fistfuls of money and fights broke out to be the first. He's staying in a hotel at the port, he's not going a step further. They're desperate, queuing outside his hotel day and night and he's making them grovel for my champagne.'

'No more than you deserve. And General Marin?'

'He was right in the middle of it all, directing the whole thing like a military campaign. Will I ever see him again?'

'I only see Daniel. He's waiting for me. Make sure they make me pretty for him when they lay me out.' She turned away.

'Don't go, Natasha. Please stay.'

'I go when I go. You will be happy, that much I know for sure, but first, two more things. See the box on my dressing table? Open it... Don't break the salt! Take out the folded document.'

Nicole scanned it. Natasha was bequeathing the bakery to Emile and Marie.

'Marie's too old to work in the fields and Emile loves this place. Marie fought for the revolution and she deserves it. Come back to me and sit next to me.'

Nicole laid her cheek next to hers.

'Be kind to Jean-Rémy, Babouchette,' Natasha wheezed. 'Forgive him. He just loved you too much, in his own arrogant way. This town is too small for feuds and he can't fight you any more.'

Nicole nodded to please her. *Never*, she thought.

Natasha held her face. 'You're lying. Promise! Jean-Rémy has confided in me over the years. That will surprise you, I know. At some point in their lives, everyone in this town has hoped I could tell their future – rich, powerful, or poor. He loves you in his twisted way, and when he learns that you have truly beaten him, you must be kind. Be better than him.' Natasha fumbled under her pillow. 'One last thing.'

'Don't say last,' Nicole whispered.

'Hush, let me finish, it's important.' Natasha took her hand, dropped a velvet bag into her palm and closed her fingers around it. 'Don't open it until you know the time is right.'

Nicole squeezed her hand. 'I can promise that.'

A candle guttered and fizzled out.

'I'll light it again for you.'

'No! Leave it out, it's meant to do that. You know by now not to argue and that I'm always right.' Natasha managed a smile, but her breathing shallowed. 'It's time,' she whispered.

The light dimmed and Nicole held her tight.

She left as she said she would, fell quiet and limp with her eyes wide open. As in life, she saw everything.

Xavier found Nicole curled up next to her. It was dark outside. She'd lost track of time, but the silence was lit with spirits. He crossed himself.

'I thought she would always be here. Come on, let me take you home.'

Nicole waved him away. She stayed all night, relit the candles when they sputtered, tended the salt line, brushed Natasha's hair, wrapped her in her red Russian shawl to make her beautiful for Daniel.

'Give Daniel my love,' she whispered.

Was Natasha really inside the rigid dark coffin, so final? The priest looked away discreetly as Nicole held up the salt bag Natasha had left her for this moment. She made a figure of eight on the coffin and the salt skittered and bounced and blurred.

Mademoiselle Var and Madame Olivier from the secret tasting committee leaned on each other and threw a cork to land on the salt.

'*Courage*,' they shouted, echoing the word they used for the first sip at their tasting sessions.

Madame Olivier's husband shot her a malevolent glance. She would no doubt pay later with a bruise.

Louis' Marta threw a chamomile sprig on top of the salt and cork, Natasha's favourite, and mouthed a Russian prayer, adjusting the veil on her expensive new hat. Their fortunes were rising thanks to Veuve Clicquot et Compagnie. They exchanged watery smiles. Nicole silently thanked Natasha for this new *entente cordiale*. Even in death, she still fixed everything.

Say hello to St Petersburg for me, she mouthed and closed her eyes to catch the tears. A hand on her shoulder startled her.

'I'm sorry for your loss. If there's anything I can do…'

She shook her head and recoiled.

'She was a good friend,' he pressed on. 'Not just to you, but to all the lost and disaffected in this town. She made the ultimate sacrifice for the revolution. I'll never forget the image of her in the square that day, cradling her dying husband.'

Be better than him, reminded Natasha.

'I thought she'd be able to defy death with all her spells and amulets,' said Nicole.

Jean-Rémy studied his shoes. 'She asked me to tell you something.'

'Oh?' Natasha would never send messages through him.

'I went to her for weather forecasts; she had incredible foresight in these things. It was me that sent Xavier for you when I saw she was so ill. She made me promise to do something for you in return for her protection from the afterworld.' He cleared his throat. 'Of course, I don't believe in all that hocus-pocus, but the words of a dying woman cannot fail to have resonance. I have been arrogant…'

'Yes, you have.'

'I only wanted to protect you, but it seems *I* needed protecting from *you*. The war is over. This town needs all the success it can get and Reims is yours now as well as mine.' He held out his hand. 'Peace?'

She glanced back at the grave. The mourners were starting to drift away, back to their lives.

'Peace.' She took his hand. 'To the future and new friendships.'

He smiled. 'I can stop tending those Pinot vines you gave me now. Worst grapes I've ever tasted.'

'Desperate measures… I'm sorry.'

'I have something for you,' he said, handing her a worn document.

François' death certificate, Natasha's final act of magic. And nothing like success to win you friends in unexpected places, at least while things are going well.

'Ah, my two favourite vintners, in perfect harmony, so nice to see you reconciled. Just as it should be. I wish Natasha were here to witness the happy moment. Come now, darling. Frowning like that will give you wrinkles.'

'Thérésa! I never thought you'd come!'

'You're surprised, *ma belle*? Let's blame Natasha. Don't ask me if any of her spells ever worked, but here I am.'

Jean-Rémy bowed and left. Thérésa was a glamorous raven in her black feather dress, cut lower than appropriate. A sickly man in a frilly shirt escorted her.

'I almost forgot. Meet my new companion, Xavier de Bourbon.'

'Bourbon? A word alone?' said Nicole as she pulled Thérésa aside. 'Is he related to the old king?'

Thérésa scoffed. 'I never thought anyone as fat and corrupt as old Louis XVIII would have a place back in France, but there you are. Of course he's connected. You don't think I'd waste my time with such a fop if he wasn't going to lead me straight to the new king.'

'You know Natasha hated aristocrats. Perhaps it's time to get back to Paris where you belong.'

'Natasha would understand. I don't need the money – thanks to my investment in your wonderful business – but life is so *dull* if one isn't at the centre of power.' Thérésa leant close, lips brushing her neck. 'I'd stay if you asked me,' she whispered.

'You would tire of me and this little town,' smiled Nicole.

Thérésa caressed her cheek, crossed herself at the graveside, then swept away with grief-stricken poise, leaning heavily on her Bourbon.

The priest led a procession back through the cemetery. Nicole blew a final kiss to Natasha and joined the line. Everyone but her had a loved one with them, but Mentine was waiting for her at home and Natasha wouldn't want her to be sad. She lifted her chin and broke away, unhooked the latch on the cemetery gates and walked out towards the vineyards.

By September, when every last drinkable bottle was safely in Russia and the workers had left for the night, Nicole polkaed through the empty cellars. Incandescent at their turn of fortunes, Louis' letters were a delight: *the abscess of the last twelve years has finally been lanced… I can't tell you how sweet it is to bring you such good news, my heart is bursting with joy to bring you the balm to heal the wounds you so little deserved…*

The Champagne region became wildly fashionable with the return of the troops. Casks of Pippin apples and Rouselette pears piled up at the borders, and Emile and Marie supplied a thriving black market in Rémois *nonette* cakes until their tills overflowed.

Nicole studied her ledger. All black now, her loyal workers paid the double wages she had promised. In the press yard, carts buckled under the weight of deliveries, smuggled out under the cover of night.

The vine leaves were turning. It would be harvest time soon, and she was newly appointed to the tasting committee alongside Jean-Rémy and the others. The only woman ever to be accepted into the inner circle. In the barrels, new wine was fermenting just as it should and outside a ripe orange moon hung above the vineyards, a good augur for the crops and for Reims.

Across the sea, Veuve Clicquot champagne was changing hands for more than a month's wages a bottle and in St Petersburg they called her Klikoskaya. General Marin came up with the name and it stuck, according to Louis, regaling prospective buyers with tales of her spark and elegance in winemaking.

She picked out a bottle from the crate of comet champagne she'd kept for herself, for a special occasion, and ran her thumb over Alexei's comet brand on the cork. '*I'm saving you for him,*' she whispered, wondering if he was reunited with his wife, whether the familiar fields and buildings of his homeland sharpened his loss. She slid the bottle back. '*Don't forget me.*'

It dawned on her then, and the loneliness was crippling, that it was unlikely she would ever open the bottle to share it with Alexei. Evening was falling, the autumn air was damp and chilly and here she was, with only her bottles and ledgers for company. All this, for what? She lit a candle against the dark and it fizzed like champagne as the flame jumped and brightened. Natasha always said you could see the world in a flame. She stared. Nothing but a translucent blue arc steady on the wick, the flare of light above it devouring the air. It guttered and extinguished, though not the slightest breeze had touched it. Of course!

She grabbed the little key to the secret compartment of her bureau and felt for the velvet bag that Natasha had given her. With the candle relit, she untied the strings and looked inside.

Her firefly necklace, and a note.

*I kept this safe for you, guaranteed against my bakery. Fulfil
the promise I made to my good friend the pawnbroker, and
pay him back. You can afford it now.*

The yellow diamond threw prisms as she held it up to the
light. François' last gift before he died!

If I go first, remember me by it, and he had laid it on her skin,
fixed the clasp at her nape. *François always makes the darkest days
into the loveliest*, she had thought as he smiled at her reflection
in mirror.

She slipped it on, the jewel warming to her touch, and stepped
outside. A big harvest moon was presiding above the vineyards and
the sweet, plump grapes were ripe for picking. Across the yard,
the press and cellars that would work their magic stood ready.

You're right, Natasha. This is what it's all for. For François. For us.

His dream, and hers, and she had made it reality. It would be
a good vintage, at least this year. After that, who could know?

A LETTER FROM HELEN

Dear reader,

I want to say a huge thank you for choosing to read *The French House*. If you did enjoy it, and want to keep up to date with all my latest releases, just sign up at the following link. Your email address will never be shared and you can unsubscribe at any time.

www.bookouture.com/helen-fripp

I hope you loved *The French House* as much as I enjoyed writing it. Nicole's determination and drive struck everyone she met, and I've loved breathing life into her once more, along with her (real and imagined) band of allies, renegades, misfits and rebels. As I wrote and researched, I was enchanted by the alchemy of wine-making and the vineyards, fascinated by the French Revolution and intrigued by the year of the comet champagne.

Nicole Clicquot was a remarkable woman. She came from a wealthy family and had absolutely no financial need to keep the vineyards and business going, but we know from historical records that she was obsessed with it, often staying up to the early hours, poring over ledgers and thinking about ways in which she could improve production.

She was deeply in love with her husband, François, and there are historical accounts of them riding out side by side to oversee the vineyards together. Nicole was also a highly respected 'nose' and could take her place alongside the very best in this profession, discerning which blends would make the best wines.

What motivated her in her endeavour? It would not have been easy for a woman to go it alone in a man's world of business and wine. Why did she not just re-marry and settle into a life of ease with her family in Reims? It was these questions that set my imagination alight as I delved into the company archives, courtesy of Veuve Clicquot Krug Ruinart in Reims. Here, I found original correspondence between Nicole and her ebullient and faithful star salesman Louis Bohne. There were the neat accounts ledgers she kept, written in her own hand, with her notes in the margin, noting all the highs and lows of the business. There was even a letter written to her granddaughter, advising her how important it was to always be 'bold and audacious' in everything she did.

Armed with this first-hand material, I walked the chalky paths amongst the vines, visited her rustic house and press in Bouzy and the grand family mansion in Reims, strolled along the banks of the river Vesle rendered a pale green by the chalk soil, and imagined her story.

I have worked hard to ensure the accuracy of historical events and place, but I have also played with chronology and facts in places, and of course this is a work of fiction, inspired by her story. And what an inspiration! Over two hundred years later, Veuve Clicquot is an international luxury brand with a reputation for producing some of the finest champagnes in the business.

If you enjoyed the book, I'd love it if you would write a review. It makes such a difference helping new readers to discover my books for the first time.

I'd be delighted to hear from you, too – you can get in touch on my Facebook page, through Twitter, Goodreads or my website.

Thanks,
Helen Fripp

hfrippauthor

@helenfripp

www.helenfrippauthor.co.uk

BIBLIOGRAPHY

Biggs, Charlotte, *A Residence in France During the Years 1792, 1793, 1794 and 1795, Described in a Series of Letters from an English Lady: with General and Incidental Remarks on the French Character and Manners*, T. N. Longman, 1797

de Brissac, Elvire, *Imaginary Journey around Barbe Nicole Ponsardin Veuve Clicquot 1777–1866*, Éditions Grasset & Fasquelle, 2010

Busby, James, Esq, *Journal of a Recent Visit to the Principal Vineyards of Spain and France*, Smith, Elder and Co., 1834

Conner, Susan P., *Public Virtue and Public Women: Prostitution in Revolutionary Paris, 193-1794*, The John Hopkins University Press, 1994

Cronin, Vincent, *Napoleon*, HarperCollins, 1971

Doyle, William, *The French Revolution: A Very Short Introduction*, Oxford University Press, 2001

Ducamp, Emmanuel and Walter, Marc, *The Summer Palaces of the Romanovs*, Thames and Hudson, 2012

Epstein, Becky Sue, *Champagne*, Reaktion Books, 2011

Faith, Nicholas, *The Story of Champagne*, Hamish Hamilton Ltd, 1988

Gastine, L., *Madame Tallien, Notre Dame de Thermidor. From the last days of the French Revolution Until her Death as Princess de Chimay in 1835*, Translated from the French by J. Lewis May, John Lane, The Bodley Head, 1923

Guy, Kolleen M., *Drowning Her Sorrows: Widowhood and Entre-preneurship in the Champagne Industry*, University of Texas at San Antonio, 1997

Guy, Kolleen M., *'Oiling the Wheels of Social Life', Myths and Marketing in Champagne in the Belle Epoque*, Duke University Press and Society for French Historical Studies, 1999

Le Baron Ponsardin, Société des Amis du Vieux Reims, 1952

Levy, Darline Gay; Applewhite, Harriet Branson; Durham Johnson, Mary, *Women in Revolutionary Paris, 1789–1795*, University of Illinois Press, 1979

Mazzeo, Tilar J., *The Widow Clicquot: The Story of a Champagne Empire and the Woman Who Ruled It*, Harper Perennial, 2008

Troyat, Henri, *Alexander of Russia: Napoleon's Conqueror*, Translated from the French by Joan Pinkham, Grove Press, 1982

Uzane, Octave, *Fashion in Paris: The Various Phases of Taste and Aesthetics in Paris from 1797 to 1897*, William Heinemann, 1898

Texts from Veuve Clicquot Krug Ruinart

The Roots of a Historic Vineyard, The House of Veuve Clicquot Ponsardin, 2012

Une Promenade dans le Petit Marais Rémois, 2005

The 1811 Comet, Veuve Clicquot Heritage, 2014

A Voyage to a Triumphant Return in Russia Summer 1814, Veuve Clicquot Heritage, 2014

ACKNOWLEDGEMENTS

With warmest thanks to Nick for being there; Katja Willemsen for being a brilliant collaborator and all-round pixie; my editor, Ellen Gleeson, for her insights; my agent, Kiran Kataria, for believing in me; Isabelle Pierre from Veuve Clicquot Krug Ruinart for her invaluable help and access to the archives; Paul MacKenzie-Cummins for my other career, without which this would not have been possible; Christine, Beth, Andrew, Sam and Grace for endless encouragement; Jemima for just being lovely; and to Rosalie and Michael, where it all began.

Made in the USA
Las Vegas, NV
13 December 2021